HEAVENLY MOVES

AMY BRIANT

Bella
BOOKS
2013

Bella Books, Inc.
P.O. Box 10543
Tallahassee, FL 32302

Printed in the United States of America on acid-free paper.

First Bella Books Edition 2013

Edited by Nene Adams
Cover designed by: Judith Fellows
ISBN: 978-1-59493-334-9

About the Author

Amy Briant is a native Californian and the author of two other novels - *Shadow Point* and *Romeo Fails*.

PROLOGUE

I remember the summer of 1982. That was when the Fabulous Murdock Sisters were still fabulous and the worst thing that ever happened to me from opening somebody else's mail was a paper cut. That was when I first heard the name Jackson Miller.

The Murdock sisters were living that year in a charmless older building next to the bowling alley. Margo, the younger sister, worked at the bowling alley as assistant night manager. Afterward, we could never remember if the lank red hair, the grim stare and the unlit cigarette had always been part of Margo's look or if they came with the Bowl-O-Rama job.

Mona Murdock and I were best friends from way back. Her family moved next door when we were both seven. Six-year-old Margo did not, of course, go around with an unlit cigarette dangling from the corner of her mouth. But I contend she already had the grim stare down. I found Margo an unnerving child, as did most everyone.

In June 1982, I had finally moved into my first apartment without roommates. It was a tiny, sunny place near the beach with a lumpy paint job and reluctant plumbing. I was so happy to be living solo, I wouldn't have cared if the pipes sang "Hello! Ma Baby."

My life in that brief, hot as hinges summer, is sharply defined in my memory. It had boundaries: the North of work, the South of late nights and cold beers at the bowling alley, the West of my new apartment and the aimless East of a stalled love life.

CHAPTER ONE

My name is Heavenly Wilcox, "Hev" to my friends. And yes, my parents were flower children. Don't even ask what my brother J. D.'s initials stand for. It could have been worse, I guess—Heavenly isn't near as bad as Moon Flower or something. We actually started life as Jennifer and Carl, but somewhere in the sixties, Mom and Dad had our names legally changed in an outburst of peace, love and understanding. Oddly enough, they kept their own.

In the summer of 1982, I was twenty-two and had dropped out of college for the last time. Mona barely lasted a year before bailing to put all her efforts into her musical career. We both elected to stay in San Tomas rather than return to the small town outside of Sacramento where my parents, my brother and the Murdocks' grandmother still lived. In addition to the university, San Tomas was a beach town about an hour south of San Francisco. Our hot and dusty hometown did not beckon.

Margo, the younger Murdock sister, had one more year to go on her bachelor's degree. Degrees, I should say, as she had undertaken a double major in business administration and political science. She had recently begun muttering about law school under her breath after particularly long nights at the Bowl-O-Rama. She'd turned twenty-one a few weeks prior and was already sick of her newfound bartending duties. Suffice it to say, the bowling alley lounge did not attract the cream of San Tomas's drinkers.

Unlike me or her sister, Margo had to beat guys off with a stick. From a strange little strawberry-blond girl, she'd grown into a beauty. She was a little taller than me, and while I was more or less average in most respects, Margo had the drop-dead, killer body. Plus that red hair (often chemically enhanced) and the unlit Marlboro. She rarely had much to say to people she didn't know, but that didn't seem to deter the opposite sex. If I were male, I would have been scared to death of her and that grim stare, but most guys (and girls) thought she was hot.

Her older sister's musical career would have been helped by some of that heat, but Mona apparently took after another branch of the family. She was just as pale-skinned as Margo, and with the same piercing blue eyes, but with dark brown hair instead of red. She hated being called "petite" and "elfin," but the girl was just small. People always expected Mona to be demure, like it was a rule that short people were more polite. Mona was definitely not polite or demure. Try rude, brash, extroverted, usually loud and always opinionated. Mona's world was black-and-white and she had no patience for anyone dumb enough to think there might be a gray area.

Between these two opposites, I was normal, average and boring. Five foot seven, one hundred twenty-five pounds, average build, medium length light brown hair. Not that I was gross or anything, but I didn't have Margo's bone structure or Mona's attitude. I guess my green eyes weren't so average, but who cared. Of the three of us, I was usually noticed last, if at all.

I did have a cool car, though. J. D., my brother the mechanic, had fixed up a '73 Camaro for me in his spare time. My parents bought the car at his suggestion and it was a gift from the family when I went away to college. J. D.'s skills didn't extend to paint, so the Camaro was primer gray, perennially awaiting the day when I'd have enough money to get it painted. I actually kind of liked the primer gray. J. D. had souped up the engine and would lavish attention on the car whenever he came to visit me. Sometimes I think he really came to visit the Camaro.

Since quitting school, I had waited tables for a while and then went to work for a temporary agency. The one skill I did possess was being able to type seventy-two words per minute, most of them in English. My mother had assured me this skill would serve me well at UC San Tomas—it probably would have if I'd gone to class on a regular basis. After doing fine in public school for twelve years, I arrived at college with no burning ambition or great talent. I couldn't stand most of my fellow students and the teachers were all either condescending or encouraging me to get in touch with my inner self. I hate that crap. I couldn't seem to settle on a major, and I was lying awake nights thinking about all that tuition money just flowing down the drain. Finally, I quit. If school was making me that unhappy, I decided, I should get a job and try to make some money instead of just spending it.

Turned out—of course—I hated working as a temp too. I had to get up every morning as if I would be going to work, put on makeup and pantyhose and the whole nine yards. Ugh. Then I'd call the agency just to be told they didn't have anything for me today, dear. Try back tomorrow…Three months before, however, I'd landed a long-term assignment at the county Public Defender's office doing clerical work. It was almost like a real job and paid well enough to enable me to move to my new apartment.

CHAPTER TWO

Saturday

After a week in my new place, I was almost one-third unpacked. A bright Saturday afternoon did not inspire me to finish the job. I kept getting sidetracked to something just a little bit more interesting. I was seriously considering leaving the rest of the boxes at the curb on trash day. After all, if I hadn't needed them all week, who's to say I needed them at all?

All traces of the previous tenant had been erased by the time I moved in. When I went to see the apartment for the first time, though, his stuff was still in it. Good stuff too—expensive-looking furniture, a beautiful rug on the living room floor, framed prints on the walls, lots of pricey booze in the kitchen. A little more high class than my Modern Milk Crate decor. I asked the landlord's agent, an efficient woman in her late thirties, when the guy was moving out as the ad had said the apartment was available immediately. She told me he had diligently paid his rent up until three months prior, but then apparently just took off. She herself had made the call to the police department at the landlord's direction when it became apparent the tenant had abandoned the apartment.

"What happened to him?" I asked her.

"Nobody knows. The cops said it happens all the time, young guys just take off after some girl or drug deal or whatever. We'll put his things in storage once we've rented the apartment."

My job at the Public Defender's office had taught me to see the criminal possibilities in almost any situation. "They don't suspect, uh, foul play, do they?

She laughed. "Oh, Lord, no! I'm sure they would have told us if that were the case. I know they checked the hospital, the morgue and the jail at the time his disappearance was reported, but that's just a routine part of the process. And he wasn't in any of those places. He just decided to split. I guess we'll never know why. But don't you worry, this is a safe neighborhood and a safe building. In fact, the man who lives next door is a retired policeman."

I was not actually that thrilled at the prospect of living next door to a cop, but I didn't share that with her. My personal experience with the San Tomas Police Department included two (so far) speeding tickets, which did not endear them to me. Mona's band endured regular interface with the police—parties where the band was hired to play but the neighbors complained about the noise, a drunken brawl at one of the clubs downtown and once when her drummer's truck got broken into during a recording session. To be fair, the cops were probably pretty sick of college kids, but they always seemed to treat us with borderline rudeness at best. I didn't really have anything against them, but living next door to one wasn't a selling point for me.

Eyeing the upscale furnishings, I asked the woman if any of the stuff would remain. No, she said, they were going to store it all for a while in case Mr. Miller came back.

"I don't think he will, though," she added. "He didn't have a wife or a job or anything to tie him down. I think he sailed his boat off to Mexico or somewhere and he's never coming back. Some days that sounds like a pretty good idea, don't you think?"

She laughed again. She certainly was jovial about the whole thing, I thought. I dislike inordinately cheerful people like that— they bring out in me an urge to poke them with a stick.

"So his boat's gone too?" I asked her.

"You know, I don't really know," she said with a slight frown. "I guess I assumed that since he left his Porsche in the garage. We're putting it in storage too."

"How'd he pay rent if he didn't have a job?" I inquired curiously. I seemed to be asking more questions about the tenant than the apartment.

"He told us he'd recently come into an inheritance. Said he was going to take some time off, maybe write a book about sailing, shop for a house…His credit report was solid, so that's all we cared about. And he was a good tenant for the six months or so he lived here. So, Heavenly, what do you think? Would you like to fill out an application?"

I took another look around the place. It looked pretty darn perfect to me. Tiny and eccentric, maybe, but the rent was in my range and it was only two blocks from the beach and marina. I fished in the back pocket of my jeans for a pen.

"Sure," I told her. "I'd love to fill out an application."

Shows you what I know.

* * *

A few weeks later, I moved in with the help of the Murdock sisters. We discovered the place had a few quirks. For example, once the bathroom door was closed, it required considerable effort to reopen it. Unfortunately, it was Mona, the claustrophobe, who discovered that particular quirk. As we struggled to free her, her sister Margo coolly remarked that if you had to go, it was certainly better to be trapped inside the bathroom rather than outside. This did not calm her sister, who emerged flushed (no pun intended) and wild-eyed a few moments later.

Another funny thing was the trapdoors. I expected perhaps one trapdoor in the ceiling that would access the crawl space above. There was one like that in the living room. There was also a second trapdoor in the ceiling of the kitchen, not far from the wall that joined my apartment to the neighbor's. In addition, there was a third trapdoor in the floor of the bedroom. Mona and I tried pulling that one up and almost gave ourselves hernias. Since Mona pictured somebody coming up from the apartment below through that trapdoor into my bedroom, I put the dresser right on top of it. Actually, Mona not only pictured it, but had to vividly act it out for me, including my gory death at the hands of the bloodthirsty monster. Thank you, Mona.

Toward the end of the afternoon, I grabbed the last box (foolishly marked "Misc.") out of the trunk of the Camaro while Mona supervised and Margo loitered near the mailboxes just off the driveway. These were a motley trio of rusty, different colored, regular house-sized mailboxes nailed to the supports for the staircase. No orderly bank of shiny, little, locked, metal doors like you'd find at a big apartment complex. Things tended to be a little more idiosyncratic down at the beach.

"Hey, Mars," the supervisor called to her younger sister, "Check out Hev's mailbox."

Margo glanced about as if such a pedestrian task were beneath her, but then shrugged and opened the mailbox marked with my apartment's number. She pulled out a fistful of mail and took it upstairs.

"Last box, Hev?" Mona asked, peering into the Camaro's trunk.

"Yeah, thank God," I said, handing it to her. She headed upstairs while I locked the car.

A neighbor's vehicle was in the driveway next to mine, a spotless Mercedes coupe that looked brand new. I wondered who drove that. Probably the retired cop, based on the layout of the apartments, but it seemed like an awfully expensive vehicle for a cop. And it didn't really go with the neighborhood either. You live in a cheap apartment in a crummy building, but you drive a brand-new Mercedes? That seemed like a disconnect. On the other hand, maybe that's how one affords a brand-new Mercedes.

I hadn't met any of the neighbors yet. We must have been on different schedules. There were only the three apartments in the building. Me, the retired cop next door and the people in the sole ground-floor apartment, which was directly below mine. The space below the cop's apartment was devoted to the two single-car garages assigned to the Mercedes and my Camaro. There was no garage for the third apartment, just a brick parking pad on the Highland Avenue side of the building. I'd seen a little blue Datsun B210 parked there, covered with typical San Tomas bumper stickers exhorting us to visualize world peace, visualize whirled peas, practice random acts of kindness and visit the Mystery Spot, among other things. Under the veranda and behind the stairs was the front door to the Datsun owner's apartment. A shiny black Vespa scooter was often parked there in the shadows, suggesting the possibility of a second occupant.

Back upstairs, I took the mail from Margo as she lounged on the couch. It was a love seat, actually, and a sleeper to boot—it would pull out into a narrow single bed that was as uncomfortable as it was convenient. Mona sat next to her sister, the two of them a study in contrasts as always. Mona slumped on the love seat in a position meant to express maximum exhaustion and weariness, her feet propped up on the footlocker which served as my coffee table. Damp wisps of hair framed her face. I used my T-shirt to mop the sweat from my own brow. Margo, however, was cool as a cucumber. How did she do that?

Since I had just moved in, I seriously doubted any of the mail was for me. I chucked a supermarket flyer and other junk mail. Looking through the six remaining items, they were all indeed addressed to the previous tenant—Jackson Miller. For a missing person, he had pretty cool mail. Two envelopes were from the San Tomas Yacht Club, one stamped "Final Notice—Slip Fees Overdue." I assumed the proximity to the marina was the reason Jackson had rented the apartment. A rich guy like him could certainly afford better, but I didn't think there were any apartments closer to the marina than our building. Or maybe he just loved a deal. What looked like another bill was from Pembroke's, a local hoity-toity men's clothing store catering to the preppy set. An investment newsletter, an elegant embossed envelope from an art gallery in San Francisco and a postcard from a Napa winery inviting him to a tasting session rounded out the pile.

"Hey, check out the fancy mail for the guy who used to live here," I said to the Murdocks, fanning it out on the footlocker. They leaned forward to view it while I told them about him disappearing and all the cool furnishings that had been in there before. They were mildly interested at best, but I still found the whole scenario intriguing. Based on the mail, it looked like my predecessor had been living the good life.

No personal letters, I noticed, but maybe he'd arranged to have the correspondence he cared about forwarded and bailed on the rest. Just because the guy seemed to have plenty of dough didn't mean he hadn't skipped out on his creditors. We saw stuff like that every week at the Public Defender's office.

"Hev? Are we done here?"

Two identical pairs of blue Murdock eyes were staring at me from the love seat. I set my musings aside and took them out for cheap Mexican food and margaritas, the agreed upon payment for their help with moving.

* * *

So one week later, I was supposed to be finishing the unpacking. I sat in the tiny living room still surrounded by boxes, piles, odds and ends. It was a beautiful Saturday afternoon outside, with the beach just two blocks away, so my motivation for the chore was low. A gentle sea breeze wafted in the open window along with the sounds of the traffic on Highland. With a prod from my conscience and a sigh, I was about to open one of the boxes when I heard a truck pulling up to the curb below. The mailman? Yay—another distraction. He was already back in his vehicle by the time I got downstairs to the mailboxes. One of my new neighbors was getting his mail too—a mean-looking man in his fifties with a potbelly the size and shape of a bowling ball. The cop, I presumed. His graying brown hair was slicked back with some form of petroleum product and his wardrobe seemed focused on polyester. He didn't look up as I approached. Of course, my mailbox was right next to his. I decided on the positive approach.

"Hi, my name's Heavenly, I just moved in. You're in apartment two, right? I'm your next-door neighbor."

He looked down at my outstretched hand and then back at my face, squinting a bit in the sunlight. "Werner. Keep the noise down or you'll be sorry we ever met."

I was already sorry, but bit back that easy reply. "No problem, Mr. Werner, and I'm sure you'll do the same," I responded evenly.

He was already walking away, evidently not expecting any reply. "And stay away from my car," he called over his shoulder, gesturing toward the Mercedes. "I better not find any dings or dents, missy."

I considered telling him just where he could find his ding *and* his dent, but he was already up the stairs and at his front door, thirty feet down from mine. As he opened the door, I could hear a dog whining and barking and the scraping of nails on the hardwood floor. Sounded like a big one too, for such a small apartment. The dog evidently wanted out in a bad way, but after a moment's scuffle, the door slammed shut on Werner's "Goddamn it, get back!"

Turning back to the mailbox, I said out loud, "Okay! Nice to meetcha!"

Shaking off the unpleasant encounter, I checked out my mail. Three envelopes. The first one was for "Occupant" and full of coupons for local businesses I would never patronize. The second was a stupid card from my brother J. D., congratulating me on my new place. Smiling as I went up the stairs, I opened the third envelope without thinking. A one-page typewritten letter on plain bond paper was inside. Shaking it open, I read: "Miller—You can run, but you can't hide. I found you before and this half-assed disappearing act won't keep me from finding you again. Somebody might even get hurt this time."

Startled to say the least, I noted the letter was unsigned and undated. There was no return address on the envelope, which was postmarked a day before in San Tomas. It was addressed to Jackson Miller at my address. I had stopped halfway up the stairs, but now continued. As I turned right at the top of the stairs toward my door, there was a flick of the curtains in number two. Oh great, an asshole and nosy.

I went into my apartment and closed the door behind me. I read the brief letter again. I felt like I should call 911 or something, but then realized that was ridiculous. I didn't even know Jackson Miller and the letter, while threatening in tone, didn't really say anything overtly criminal. The single sheet of typing paper and the envelope were generic as could be. Nothing suspicious or unusual there. I put the letter back in the envelope and tried seeing if I could stick the flap back shut with a little spit. That worked for about one second. I unearthed some tape from a previously unopened box and resealed the envelope. With a black felt-tip pen from the same box, I wrote on the envelope "Not at this address—opened in error," hoping the Postal Service wouldn't track me down and shoot me.

I put the unsettling letter aside to place back in the mailbox on Monday morning and looked with exasperation at all my boxes and piles. Where could it all possibly go? How could I have acquired so much shit at such a young age? I wondered if I could store any of it in the crawl space. I hadn't looked up there yet, but maybe at least some empty boxes could go there.

I found the flashlight, then improvised a ladder with a milk crate on top of a chair in the kitchen. That got me just high enough for my hair to brush the ceiling. I eased the trapdoor thingy back. It wasn't literally a trapdoor since there were no hinges, just a wood-framed opening in the ceiling about two and a half feet square. A white-painted piece of plywood sat on top of that and covered the opening.

I pushed the panel to the side, hoping that a cornucopia of spiders and dust bunnies wasn't about to rain down upon my upturned face. Standing up on my tiptoes on my wobbly, makeshift ladder, I raised the flashlight and shone it into the crawl space. It definitely didn't qualify as an attic. It didn't even extend over the entire area of the room. Instead, what I saw was a shadowy tunnel, maybe three feet in height and width, which stretched behind me to the trapdoor in my living room and ahead of me into the darkness past the flashlight's beam. It wasn't an air-conditioning duct, because the apartment didn't have air conditioning. There was rarely a need for A/C in northern California by the beach. If you wanted air, you opened a window.

The floor of the passage I was looking down was the bare bones of the apartment, wooden rafters spaced about a yard apart with the dry wall of the ceiling below. No good for storage—oh, well. In the weak beam from my flashlight, I could see some kind of wiring and some PVC tubing. Something electrical? Plumbing? I had no idea.

As glad as I was to be living there, I can't say I was that impressed with the actual construction of the place. The outside staircase to the second floor, for example, always made me feel like a foot could go through one of the rotting wooden steps at any time. If the metal railing didn't fall off first. And I'd already found out that a fuse would blow if you even just thought hard about electricity. Clearly, the place was a tax write-off for the owner. Fine by me—I was thrilled with the cheap rent and hoped they wouldn't be demolishing the place any time soon to build condos.

I shone the flashlight again down to the far wall. And realized there was no wall there. The crawl space went right on over my kitchen and into the neighbor's. Great design, somebody! In any event, having met my neighbor, I wasn't too worried about it since there was no way he'd be crawling around in that tight space. Not with his gut.

I put the cover back in place and climbed down. Kind of a strange apartment, no doubt, but for that rent and the close proximity to the beach, I could tolerate a lot of strange.

I checked my watch. Yay! I had screwed around long enough so that I could abandon unpacking without guilt. It was time to get ready to join the Murdock sisters for a little Saturday night entertainment.

* * *

Mona picked me up around seven o'clock in her car. Originally purchased by her grandmother in 1963, it was a very large, American vehicle of unknown pedigree. The nameplates identifying the make and model had long ago fallen off. We called it the Monamobile. The original, bright lemon-colored paint job had faded to the palest of yellows, almost white, with patches of rust throughout except for one replaced side panel in a dark and disturbing shade of green found nowhere in nature. As always, the backseat was a mess, littered with fast-food debris, candy wrappers, soda cans, miscellaneous papers, broken bass strings, picks, a few random articles of clothing, bottles of motor oil, a naked plastic baby doll without the head (don't ask) and who knows what else. Mona tended to throw trash over her shoulder into the back and only clean it up about once a month or so. With the trash, the duct-taped seats, a big crack in the windshield and the mismatched, rusted exterior, it was a vehicle only an owner could love. Someone had once told Mona it looked like the car of a serial killer. She loved it.

The car's chief virtue was its size, because in a pinch, all four members of Mona's band and their equipment could squeeze in. The trunk alone was big enough for a rhino. Its size was also its chief vice, however, as the gas mileage was outrageously bad and it was a real bitch to park. I remember the alignment was shot that summer too, so even though we'd be driving in a straight line down a straight road, Mona's hands would be at nine o'clock and one o'clock, instead of ten and two like the driver's ed teacher instructed us. You could always hear that car coming, though.

In a rare demonstration of charity, Grandmother Murdock had given Mona the car in our senior year of high school when the old lady finally bought herself a new one. It was somewhat of a mixed blessing for Mona as the frequent repairs it required cost a lot of money she didn't have. But it was better than nothing, I guess.

Younger sister Margo didn't have a car, preferring to save her hard-earned cash for grad school. There was a bus stop a block from their apartment and the bus ran straight up the hill to the university, so that worked out well, as did the fact that her job at the Bowl-O-Rama was right next door. When absolutely necessary, she got a ride from her sister or me, or borrowed the Monamobile. Not to mention there was usually some guy around to drive her wherever she wanted.

Mona didn't even try to park in the driveway. She merely stopped at the corner of Highland and Third and honked. I was waiting for her and ran down the stairs to the car. It only backfired twice during that brief interval. Her band had played a gig that afternoon—a private party at a house for some kid who was off to join the navy—but she was alone in the Monamobile when she picked me up, which meant she had already dropped off her equipment and fellow bandmates. The other members of Bertha's Attic (Mona was an English literature major for that one year of college—she'd read *Jane Eyre* at least three times) all lived up by the school or in the dorms. The band practiced in a rented garage near the campus as well.

"Margo's stuck at work, so we're meeting her there," she informed me, "there" meaning the Bowl-O-Rama.

"How was the party?" I asked tentatively.

She was always in a foul mood after playing gigs that required lots of cover tunes and limited or no originals. Mona hated cover tunes, except truly obscure ones that might as well have been her own originals. Gigs with lots of cover tunes were the ones that paid the bills, though. Mona was an artist, but she was a realist too—not always an easy combination.

"It was grim," she said with a scowl. "We had to play 'Freebird' twice."

"Yikes," I said.

"Yeah."

We drove in silence for a little while. She shifted in her seat, squirming a bit in the confines of a pink satin dress. It had once been someone's prom dress, but Mona had made the skirt mini and otherwise butchered it into a rock-and-roll statement. Black leather go-go boots and fingerless sequined gloves completed the look, along with several pounds of accessories. Just looking at her made me feel ten degrees warmer. As usual, I was dressed for comfort, not style, in khaki shorts and a lime green tank top. The sun had not quite set, but the temperature remained near eighty degrees. We both had our windows down, enjoying the breeze.

Miraculously, a parking space was open in front of her apartment building. Even better, it was the first space on the block, so she would not have to attempt parallel parking in a car nearly twenty feet long. Mona's mood instantly improved.

"Fuckin' A—right in front!" she exclaimed as she pulled the Monamobile into the slot.

As we went in the front door of the building, the car continued to buck and shudder on its own. I heard it give a final rattle and cough as I shut the door behind us. Mona was already halfway up the stairs on her way to the third floor. The first floor of the building was inhabited by a Chinese restaurant and a shoe repair shop. An inconspicuous door between the two businesses accessed the apartments above. The two apartments on the second floor housed the manager and a gaggle of Nigerian exchange students from UCST. The Murdock sisters' two-bedroom apartment was on the third floor.

It felt hotter inside Chez Murdock than the eighty degrees outside. There was no beer, so I grabbed two wine coolers from the fridge while Mona changed. I put one on the counter which separated the galley kitchen from the small living room and took mine to the dilapidated fake leather couch. By sitting in the far left corner, I avoided the duct-taped spots. We called it the Benny Hill couch because of the very rude noises it made when you got up.

The only window in the living room took up much of the west wall from about knee height to almost the ceiling. It overlooked the grimy street below and the equally unattractive apartment building across the way. There was an orangey glow in the western sky, but the sun was hidden behind buildings.

Sitting on the couch, the kitchen was to my right. A short hallway extended beyond it to the bathroom and then to younger sister Margo's bedroom. In front of me was Mona's piano, with her three-quarter size stand-up bass propped in the corner next to it. The piano was another "gift" from Grandmother Murdock. Mona had inherited her musical talent from her mother. No one else had ever touched the piano. Her grandmother was more than happy to see it go with Mona to San Tomas. I think it was almost as bitter a reminder of her dead daughter as the two girls themselves.

Emerging barefoot in black running shorts and a tour shirt from a Journey concert, Mona took her usual seat on the battered piano bench, snagging her cooler along the way. She slugged down about half of her "Tropical Passionfruit," then set the bottle carefully on the coaster on the piano. No one else—certainly not me or Margo—was allowed to put anything on the piano. With her back to me, Mona began to play one of her own compositions, an eerie and remorseful tune she was still working on. I was already sticking to the couch, but was too hot to move. It was close to sundown, but we hadn't bothered with the lights. As Mona pounded her way into a chorus that always filled me with dread, a thin trickle of sweat ran down my left temple. I thought of the strange letter I had opened a few hours before: "You can run, but you can't hide… Somebody might even get hurt this time…" Sipping, I made a face at the overly sweet taste of the wine cooler and wondered if Jackson Miller had taken off because of threats from the author of the letter. Despite its vague wording, I wondered again if maybe I should tell somebody about the letter, like the landlord or even the cops? Certainly not that jerk next door…

The room, too hot before, suddenly seemed stifling. In the dimming light, Mona was wailing something about a choice between the water or the flame. I was not looking forward to the moment I'd have to get up and peel my tender flesh from the leatherette. Knowing Mona, she might have been planning to play just the one song, or she might have been ready to jam for an hour to get all the Lynyrd Skynyrd toxins out of her system. But having been cooped up in my own apartment all day, I was ready to go out. I pulled off a shoe and aimed carefully. My right sneaker hit a low F just as she paused for breath. She stopped playing. With the last chord still ringing in the air, she turned to face me, slowly and ominously, then fixed me with an imperious stare.

"Do you have *any* concept of the creative process?"

"Oh, come on, Mona, we're sweating like pigs up here. Let's go get some free air-conditioning next door."

"It's probably stupid league night," she sniffed huffily. She finished her drink in two gulps, held up her hand, palm out, then treated me to a sonorous burp. She knew we were going to the Bowl sooner or later, but wasn't about to miss an opportunity to argue the point.

I played along. "It's not league night, it's Saturday. Besides, you don't bowl anyhow and you're out of beer," I said persuasively. "You know I hate these froo-froo bevvies. Gimme my shoe and let's go."

She lined me up in her sights and hurled the shoe at me, but it bounced harmlessly off the fake leather. I didn't even flinch—she never could throw worth spit.

Mrs. Romanoff, the manager, was lurking on the second-floor landing. It was even hotter there than in the apartment. I wanted nothing less than to pause in that airless space, but she greeted Mona grumpily, then bullied her about her "late" rent payment. It was the third of the month and rent was not technically late until after the fifth, but the apartment manager was of the Bird in the Hand school. Mona assured her she would have it on time. Impatient, I shifted from one foot to the other, which drew the Romanoff's attention. She glared at me suspiciously.

"You," she said. "You have pets?"

After a moment in which I played back her question in my head to make sure I'd heard it correctly, I answered "No…" in a careful tone which usually went over well with the Public Defender's many mentally ill clients.

"Sure," she said with a sudden, nasty smile that revealed a gold tooth. "Sure, sure." She turned toward her apartment, pausing with her hand on the doorknob to look at me again, still muttering, "Sure, sure, sure," under her breath.

"What a wacko," I said to Mona when we finally stepped outside.

A slender young Hispanic guy with a snake tattooed on his neck—that had to hurt—slunk into the building as we left.

"Who was *that*?" I asked. "The concierge?"

"Shhh," Mona whispered fiercely, pulling my arm and dragging me in the direction of the Bowl-O-Rama. "You're not supposed to notice him. That's the Romanoff's boyfriend."

"Her boyfriend!"

That Mrs. Romanoff, fiftyish, as of yet undetermined ethnicity, though undeniably statuesque, would have a Latin lover half her age had definitely never crossed my mind. Although Mona was never one to let the truth hurt a good story.

"Yes, shhh!" She had my arm halfway out its socket. "His name is Flaco and he's an illegal alien, so don't notice him."

"Illeg—"

"*Shhh!*"

Luckily for me, orthopedically speaking, we were now crossing the threshold of the bowling alley. At not quite eight o'clock on a Saturday night, the 'Rama was hopping. The sound system trembled and rumbled with Rush's "Tom Sawyer." In the lounge, Margo was tending bar with reptilian grace. The ever-present, unlit Marlboro dangled from the left side that night. A tight, black, French-cut T-shirt accentuated her flawless pale skin and lank red hair. Plus, it showed off her boobs and no doubt at least doubled her tips.

"Mon. Hev," she greeted us economically.

"The Romanoff's bitching about the rent," replied her sister testily.

Margo stoically took this in, drawing us two draft beers without asking. Her slender arms were taking on some definition with the constant lifting and reaching of her new job.

"Did you get paid?" she asked her sister, referring to that afternoon's gig.

"Yep," Mona said, sampling her beer.

"In cash?" Margo pursued the point.

"Duh," Mona rolled her eyes in an exaggerated fashion.

Margo nodded and drifted down the bar to tend to a customer. I grabbed two maraschino cherries and a red plastic beverage stirrer from the bar tray. Now I could say I'd done the fruit part of the food pyramid that day.

"So, what's the deal?" I said to Mona, trying to get a better handle on our plans for the evening. "Is Margo going to hang with us tonight or does she have a date?"

All three of us were unattached at that particular moment. Margo, *la belle dame sans merci*, tended to flit from guy to guy and usually had two or three of them on a string. But as soon as it looked like a guy was getting serious, she would dump him. I privately thought she should focus more on quality and less on quantity.

Her sister Mona, on the other hand, was sort of the opposite. Her strong opinions and wildly independent spirit (perhaps that's just a nice way of saying grumpy and strange) were not that much of a turn-on for most guys, to tell the truth. She'd dated a few musicians here and there, but nothing much ever came of it. She usually had a crush on some unattainable guy, enjoying her tortured, unrequited love from afar in some masochistic way. Must be an artist thing.

The only way the two sisters were alike in the romance department was that neither one could seem to find the right guy. I wasn't having too much luck in that department myself. Everything seemed so confusing lately. When I was a kid, I'd had this picture in my head of what my life would be like when I grew up and went off to college. Exactly none of that had come true so far.

I'd had a boyfriend for a while in my first year in San Tomas, when Mona and I lived in the dorms. I shuddered now to think of that relationship—what the hell had I been thinking? I guess I'd been thinking college girls are supposed to have boyfriends. Right? Right. And I liked guys. There was nothing wrong with guys. I just couldn't seem to meet any who were even halfway interested in me. Mona said I was too quiet around guys. Well, she was way too loud around everyone, so I discounted that opinion. There was certainly no way I could ever be a man-eater like the flame-haired Margo—I couldn't begin to compete with that kind of woman. I didn't even want to. So where exactly did I fall in the whole spectrum of guys and girls and relationships? I couldn't even explain to myself how I felt about that. It was all very complicated.

"A fucking date—I'm so fucking sure," Mona muttered.

I should have known better than to bring up the subject. Any mention of her little (and more attractive) sister's love life always made Mona grumpy. Shrugging neutrally, I washed the cherries down with a swig of beer, then started chewing on the stirrer. Mona's latest inappropriate crush appeared to be the new drummer in her band. I had no hope for her finding true love this time around either, because Pete was way out of her league, tall and handsome, with hazel eyes, cropped brown hair and a fledgling moustache. He was working on his degree in biochemistry at UCST. He was a pretty good drummer and he and Mona got along well as musicians. As people, though, he seemed to tolerate Mona's many affectations more than enjoy them. Gorgeous, tall and slender older women (like twenty-four) would show up at gigs from time to time and carry cymbals until they broke a fingernail. I personally thought Mona had no shot with him, but forbore to share this with her. Since he was the band's third drummer in twelve months, I didn't want anything to break the spell.

He was not to be mistaken with the other band member named Pete—or rather, Petey, as everyone called him. Petey Houlihan, the guitarist, was red-haired, freckle-faced and looked like he was about sixteen. At age nineteen, he considered this a serious defect. He had recently dyed his hair jet-black after cutting it very short except for one lock falling over his right eye. Which looked ridiculous, but Petey was such a nice boy that nobody wanted to hurt his feelings. To verbally differentiate between the two (visual differentiation was not an issue), we'd taken to referring to the drummer as Handsome Pete behind Petey's back.

Even though Petey looked more like Huck Finn than Eric Clapton, he was a rock star when he played guitar. Even Mona said he was the best musician in Bertha's Attic—after her. He had told us all to call him Peter, not Petey, but who could look at that face and not say Petey? He was a little taller than me (meaning he towered over Mona), skinny, but in excellent shape thanks to not having a car, which really sucked for a musician. He rode his bike all over campus, where he was a music major and down the hill into town, where he sold pizza by the slice at Rocco's. Arguably the worst pizza place in a fifty-mile radius, Rocco's was at least conveniently located across from the Moonglow, the biggest nightclub in San Tomas. Due to ongoing problems with its neon sign, the Moonglow was known as the Mongol to its slightly dyslexic faithful.

Rounding out Bertha's Attic was LeClaire, the keyboard player. She was the oldest of the bunch at twenty-five and not a student. She described her heritage as half-Jamaican, half-French and half-Irish. That was about as much sense as I ever got out of the girl. She and I never could seem to communicate. Which was one reason I never had her cut my hair, her chosen occupation. I had noticed her patois accent seemed to dissipate under stress and when drinking, so I suspected she had invented her island upbringing. That hardly mattered, of course, as she was an inventive keyboardist with excellent equipment and strong backing vocals to Mona's lead. Her appearance was striking too. She was tall enough so the audience could see her behind her keyboards with her mirrored sunglasses and beaded braids a-swinging. She, Handsome-Pete-the-drummer and baby-faced-Petey-the-guitarist formed an interesting backdrop to Mona's fervent intensity on lead vocals and bass.

The rest of the band often showed up at the Bowl-O-Rama, the Mongol or Rocco's, our three main hangout spots. Although I knew each of them as individuals, it often seemed to me that "The Band" was a single entity with one brain in some Star Trekian way. I, of course, was excluded from the mind meld as a mere friend of Mona's, part-time roadie and second-class citizen. The band, or some subset thereof, would also turn up unannounced any time, day or night, at the Murdock sisters' apartment.

Thus, I was not surprised to see Petey Houlihan wander through the doors of the Bowl-O-Rama lounge. His unnaturally black hair was damp and his pink cheeks looked freshly scrubbed. He wore motorcycle boots, raggedy black jeans and a Rocco's T-shirt with the sleeves cut off. Up close, I could see he hadn't shaved (probably in weeks) and sported nearly invisible stubble.

Pulling up a stool next to mine, he said, "Hey, Hev, hey, Mona."

"Hi, Petey," we answered in unison, then laughed at our synchronicity.

"Pete-errr," he said, essentially to himself.

Mona called to her sister, "Yo, Margo, how about a Shirley Temple for Petey here?"

As Margo brought him a foaming-over soda, I turned to Mona. "Hey, I forgot to tell you something weird happened this afternoon."

"What, did you actually unpack a box?"

Ignoring that, I said, "No, I accidentally opened a letter for the guy who used to live in my apartment. And it was like a blackmail letter!"

Mona widened her eyes, but canted her head at a skeptical angle. The other two were listening as well.

"What did it say?" Petey asked curiously.

"You can run, but you can't hide and somebody's gonna get hurt and basically, I'll get you, Jackson Miller and your little dog too!" I finished with a theatrical flourish of my well-gnawed drink stirrer.

"Holy shit, Hev," Mona exclaimed, but before she could go on, her sister interrupted her.

"Okay, you guys, you know young Pete-errr can't sit at the bar here, so go find a table inside, all right?"

"All right, all right."

The three of us grabbed our drinks and headed into the main area, hoping to snag a table by the snack bar. All the lanes were occupied, but that was no problem since our plans had more to do with drinking than bowling. The deafening noise of balls hitting pins was augmented by Roxy Music's "More Than This" at top volume. The snack bar had a few tables made of white wrought iron that looked like outdoor patio furniture. They were a bit out of place inside, but had the virtue of being difficult for the customers to damage. One small, unsteady, circular table was unoccupied, so we left Petey there putting sugar packets under the pedestal in an attempt to balance it. When I got back to the table with my onion rings, he was watching Mona, who was still in line, with an expression I couldn't quite decipher.

My chair faced the front counter of the bowling alley, about fifty feet away, and I noticed Flaco and Mrs. Romanoff were in line to reserve a lane. Could he really be Mrs. Romanoff's illegal alien lover? I couldn't wrap my mind around that one. I pointed them out to Petey, just to make conversation. He nodded. He'd seen them both before at the Murdocks', he said.

As Mona rejoined us, the inimitable opening bars of Ozzy Osbourne's "Crazy Train" could be heard over the sound system. Petey, of course, had to play air guitar along with Randy Rhoads while tipped back precariously in his wrought-iron chair. Mona couldn't help but start to rock out herself, singing along with Ozzy into her french fry microphone. I contented myself with head bobbing.

"That is one fuckin' A great guitar part," Mona said.

Nodding vigorously, Petey brought his chair's front legs back onto the ground with a thud and said, "Fuckin' egg! We ought to—" He stammered and stopped when he noticed Mona and I had ceased our movements and were looking at him oddly. He blushed. "What? What is it?"

"What did you say, Peter?" Mona asked.

He knew for sure he'd screwed up when Mona called him Peter. "Nothing. What? I just—"

"You said 'fuckin' egg,' didn't you?" Mona grilled him.

"No." Pause. "Maybe." Pause. "No."

Her cackling interspersed with snorts, Mona grabbed my forearm with one hand and beat on the table with the other. "He…" Snort. "…said…" Snort. "…EGG!" Peals of laughter.

I disengaged her claw-like grip and leaned toward Petey to tell him I thought it was "A" for amazing and not "egg." His look said, "Oh." We both rolled our eyes at Mona's continuing hysteria which abruptly ended as Ozzy gave way to Asia. She hated them. She refocused on her food and swapped some of her fries for some of my onion rings without asking, which she'd been doing since we were eight years old.

Searching for safer conversational ground, Petey asked me again about the mysterious blackmail letter. Not letting me answer, Mona jumped in with, "Well, what do you expect, living in a criminal's apartment?"

"We don't know he's a criminal," I retorted.

"Oh, yeah, well, where'd he get all that money? How come he didn't pay his bills? Why is somebody blackmailing him? And where is he now?"

Petey's head swiveled back and forth between the two of us as he struggled to catch up.

"I don't know!" I said to Mona. "Like I told you before, the property manager said he got some family inheritance or something. Maybe he sailed his boat off to Tahiti and bailed on the bills."

Darkly, Mona said, "Or maybe you're right about the blackmail and his body's under that trapdoor in your bedroom."

"Shit…" I said disparagingly.

Petey offered earnestly, "You probably would have smelled a dead body by now, Hev."

"Shit!" I said more strongly. "Can we just talk about something else, please? Don't you guys have band business to discuss or something?"

Of course they did, so we passed the rest of the evening without further speculation regarding Mr. Jackson Miller. The band business currently occupying their every waking moment was an exciting development—Bertha's Attic had recently been asked to play the Mongol for the first time. Since it was the biggest nightclub in San Tomas and had been the launching pad for many popular bands over the years, this was a huge opportunity for them. The gig was the result of months of relentless pestering of the club's booking agent by Mona. Bertha's Attic was to be the second of three bands on a Thursday night later in the month. Thursday nights were "Dollar Nights" at the Moonglow, one dollar being the price of admission as well as the special reduced price for a pint glass of draft beer. It was a great way to see live bands—both the up-and-coming and the established local stars—plus get drunk for only five bucks or so. Depending on one's capacity.

Assistant manager Margo didn't have to close for a change, so around midnight, the four of us headed downtown to Rocco's. Petey's bicycle didn't come close to filling up the trunk of the Monamobile, and I could hear it sliding around back there on the corners. No doubt we all would have preferred to go across the street to the Mongol, but since it was a Saturday, a big-name band from San Francisco was playing and the ticket prices were too rich for our blood. Too bad, because we adored Bonnie Hayes and the Wild Combo. Mona had practically worn out their album, both the tape and vinyl versions.

Rocco's had no live music, but it also had no cover and we could count on Petey to score us free pizza if we wanted any. (Really crappy pizza, but free.) Plus, if the owner wasn't there, the bartender would serve Petey. We left there just after two, returning Petey to his dormitory only slightly hammered. Margo was at the wheel, having had little to drink. I'd noticed she hardly drank at all on the nights she tended bar. Cruising back down the hill to the beach, Mona filled Margo in on our speculation regarding the Jackson Miller saga, such as it was. Margo cocked an eyebrow, but offered no comment, preferring to focus on her driving.

As she pulled up in front of my building, Mona was regaling us again with her delightful suggestion that Jackson's dead body was stashed under my trapdoor. Margo stopped at the corner to let me out. A light was on in the downstairs apartment, but the top floor was dark. Half joking, Mona said, "Smell anything, Hev?"

We all inhaled. All I smelled was the salt sea air underscored by the poisonous emissions of her grandmother's car. "Later," I told them, climbing out of the car.

"Later," intoned the Murdocks.

They waited, though, until I opened my door, turned on the light and waved before they took off. The Murdock sisters and I had been watching out for each other for fifteen years. As Margo pulled out and gunned it down the empty street, I saw Mona's bony white arm "flying" out the passenger window, rhythmically waving up and down to simulate a wing. After a second, Margo's left arm appeared out the driver's side to make the second wing. Shaking my head, I laughed and started to shut the door. The street had returned to near total silence with their departure.

Before I could close the door, however, I heard the whine of a scooter approaching. Stepping back out onto the veranda, I saw a single headlight coming down Highland toward me. Sure enough, it was the black Vespa, its driver wearing a black leather jacket and black helmet. The driver glanced up at me as the scooter neared the curb and I realized I was framed in the light from my open door. I instinctively took a step backward, then listened as I heard the scooter steer a course up onto the parking pad and then stop in its spot underneath the staircase. Sounds of the downstairs apartment's door being opened followed. I was curious to meet my downstairs neighbor, but hesitated, wondering if this late hour was the right moment. If he or she was anything like Werner, I thought, the encounter could definitely wait. I was about to turn and go back inside my own apartment when a voice called softly from below.

"Hello?"

I stepped to the edge of the veranda and looked down. In the light now spilling out from the downstairs apartment, there stood a slender girl, her face upturned to mine. Pretty, in a tomboyish way. Her leather jacket was unzipped, showing a white T-shirt underneath. Her honey brown hair was cut short and curled slightly. She ran a hand through it. Her helmet was in her other hand.

"Hey," she said with a smile. "I think we keep missing each other. I'm Jules."

"Hi," I said. "I'm Hev. Short for Heavenly."

"Excuse me?" she said. I was used to that.

"Heavenly, you know, like the heavens above." I pointed skyward.

"Oh."

"My parents are weird," I explained for the one millionth time in my life.

She smiled again, charmingly, still looking up at me. "So are mine," she said. "My name's Julian, actually."

We were speaking quite softly in deference to the hour. And in fear of waking Werner up, at least on my part. Another voice spoke then, indistinctly from the first-floor apartment.

"It's the new neighbor," said Jules in response to the voice.

The owner of the voice emerged to stand by Jules and look up at me. Jules looked like she was about the same height as I was (although it was hard to tell from my veranda perspective), but the girl standing next to her was clearly much taller and bulkier. Her black hair was short too, shaved on the sides and the back, longer on the top. It was a style popular at the time. If you were a guy. She was barefoot in fatigue pants and a blank tank top. Multiple tattoos were visible, as were many earrings in both ears, glittering in the moonlight. Looked like she had at least six holes per side, filled with an assortment of studs and small hoops. I'd seen other girls like her in San Tomas and on our occasional forays into San Francisco. I was afraid of them.

"This is Ashley, my roommate," Jules advised me. "Ashley, this is Hev."

Ashley and I exchanged heys. She didn't look all that pleased to meet me. I felt nothing but alarm upon making her acquaintance.

She turned to Jules and peevishly mumbled, "You're late."

Uh-oh. I didn't want to get in the middle of that, especially at two thirty in the morning. I sketched a wave to Jules, who nodded and gave me one last smile as Ashley stalked back into their apartment. As I backed away from the railing, I saw Jules's shoulders go up and down as she sighed, then heard her walk into her own place and shut the door.

I took in one more breath of night air, then went inside, closing and locking the door behind me. I wondered what all that drama was about. I trod lightly on my floorboards as I quietly got myself to bed, not wanting to inflame the delicate sensibilities of either Werner or Ashley. What a pair.

CHAPTER THREE

Sunday

Sunday morning. I didn't want to get up at all, but the alarm began peeping insistently at ten forty-seven. It was the Fourth of July. Yippee. I groggily remembered being awakened earlier by the sounds of Werner washing his silver Mercedes coupe at eight o'clock sharp, his car stereo tuned to National Public Radio. I'd always wondered who listened to NPR. God, I hoped this wasn't a Sunday morning ritual with him, but I had a bad feeling it was.

I dragged myself into the bathroom. Glancing out the north-facing window toward the west, I saw that it was an absolutely gorgeous morning. Mona, Margo and I had decided earlier in the week to hit the beach that day and it looked like we had made the right choice. They were due at my place at eleven and showed up semipromptly at twenty-six past the hour. By then, I had showered, shaved various body parts and absorbed enough aspirin and Coca-Cola to be ready for public viewing. I had a new one-piece swimsuit, royal blue with antifreeze green zigzags. I was admiring myself in the full-length mirror on the door between my bedroom and the bathroom when I heard the Monamobile pull into the driveway. I hastily donned shorts, Keds and my shades. From my doorway, I saw both Mona and Margo exit via the passenger side door, as the mere foot and a half between Mona's car and Werner's gleaming Mercedes was not nearly enough room to permit egress from the Monamobile. As they extracted a cooler and other items from the car, I grabbed my little folding beach chair and a beach towel. My contribution to the festivities was to be the twelve-pack of beer I had purchased for the occasion, so I grabbed that out of the fridge too.

"Hola!" I greeted them as the three of us converged at the foot of the stairs.

Margo the Gorgeous was resplendent in a broad-brimmed black straw hat with a white band, big white sunglasses, a white terrycloth beach wrap and black sandals. Mona was significantly less glamorous, but still making a statement of sorts in her purple knockoff Dolfin shorts, an Adam and the Ants tour shirt and rubber flip-flops she'd bought for forty-nine cents at the drugstore. Fake Ray-Bans framed her visage. She always required a great deal more equipment than other people for a simple trip to the beach, so we took a minute to redistribute the load amongst us. Cooler, boom box, beach chairs, towels, bags—clanking slightly, we negotiated the two blocks downhill, and then slogged across the sand to a good spot.

Mona and I set up our chairs facing the surf, with Margo on her towel on the other side of her sister. Team Leader Mona distributed food and drinks, then set up her boom box on the flat top of the cooler. I ripped open a bag of potato chips and watched as she carefully sorted through the twenty-some tapes she'd brought. After much deliberation and pursing of lips, she started us off with AC/DC. Food and music thus dealt with, she shucked off her shorts and shirt to reveal her same old ratty, red, one-piece bathing suit from high school. I felt a renewed surge of pride and contentment in my new suit.

Well, at least until I glanced over at Margo, who had shed her cover-up and was reposing on her towel on one elbow. Black bikini, black straw hat and white sunglasses. Killer bod. Red hair. She was a total knockout. Feeling deflated, I glanced down at my green zigzags on a royal blue background. Several of the zigzags now had pieces of potato chip on them. Mortified, I dropped the bag and brushed myself off.

"Hey, watch the chips, ya bonehead!" Mona said, retrieving the bag from the sand.

The beach was pretty packed, of course, for the Fourth. The temperature was in the low eighties, which made the chilly water look more tempting than it was. Some idiot girls were playing paddle ball at the water's edge. Why do people only play that at the beach? It always looked like about as much fun as playing fetch with a dog that won't.

We weren't actually on the ocean. There were beaches north of town that were directly on the Pacific, but San Tomas itself was within the confines of Monterey Bay. Since those ocean beaches involved parking on the shoulder of Highway 1 and lengthy hikes through fields of brussels sprouts, the bay beach by my apartment was a lot easier to get to. The marina too was just a couple of blocks away. From where we sat, I could see sailboats leaving the shelter of the breakwater and heading out into the bay for a Sunday voyage. Surfers were also part of our panorama, although the bay beach waves were usually two to three feet max. Scenic, though.

There was plenty of scenery on the beach too. Mona and Margo played their favorite game of rating male bodies on a scale of one to ten, which always involved a lot of arguing. I piped in an occasional opinion, but since they'd been known to suddenly join forces and turn on me without warning, I mostly kept my scores to myself. I carefully avoided scoping out the female bodies because (a) I was quite certain I would suffer by comparison and (b) I didn't want anyone to think I was...well, scoping out the female bodies. When not engaged in conversation with the Murdocks or eating, I kept my gaze fixed on the horizon, unless it was obvious to any and all that I was looking at a guy, a dog or a baby. As if anyone was watching. As if anyone could see what I was looking at with my sunglasses on. It was very tiresome to be so insecure, but I hadn't found a way to quit. I didn't know if Mona or Margo was suffering through the same silent struggle. I certainly never brought up the topic.

And I certainly didn't comment on any of the female bodies so lushly displayed on the beach that afternoon. Although, it was weird—both Mona and Margo occasionally would, as in, "That girl has such pretty hair" or, "Man, I wish my butt looked that good." How come they could, but I wasn't allowed to? Where did my brain get these rules? I had no idea. Margo, in fact, would not only comment on other females, but since we'd moved to San Tomas, I had even seen her flirt with women to get something she wanted. I knew she had no intention of doing anything other than flirting with them, but it nonetheless made me very uncomfortable. Queasy, almost.

My never-ending internal struggles notwithstanding, we passed the afternoon in the usual way: prisoners of Mona's musical tastes, enjoying the sun and wrapping our beer cans in paper towels to avoid censure from the lifeguard. Mona popped in a new tape. The dulcet strains of Ozzy Osbourne's "Crazy Train" filled the summer air. A brilliant idea struck me.

"Hey, Mona," I said.

"What?"

"You guys should do 'Crazy Train' as your encore!"

There was a trend that summer among the local bands in regard to encores. A group called Plan B had started it. Their encores were always Rolling Stones songs. Another band followed suit and would only do Allman Brothers songs for their encores. Pretty soon, everyone had staked out their claims to their "encore bands." Everyone except Bertha's Attic. Mona revered Bruce Springsteen as a higher power, so one might think he would be the obvious choice, but that, to her, would be sacrilege. Besides, she bucked trends as a matter of course. And sometimes they didn't even get an encore, anyhow. When they did, lately they'd been playing the WKRP closing theme—mostly, I suspected, because Mona enjoyed shouting the incomprehensible lyrics into the microphone. Her face squinched in concentration, she appeared to be pondering my suggestion. As far as I knew, no one else had picked Ozzy for their encores. I watched her wheels turning.

Abruptly, though, she reached over and stopped "Crazy Train" mid-song with a scowl and put the Go-Go's on instead. I guess she didn't appreciate my input. Well, la-di-da. I didn't really care. It was just a thought.

"Hey, Hev!"

I turned to find my new neighbors Jules and Ashley walking up the beach toward us. Jules had a multicolored, striped beach towel wrapped around her waist like a sarong. A Hawaiian print bikini top in vibrant yellow and orange completed her outfit. She had an excellent tan, as befitted one who had lived near the beach longer than I had. Ashley was solid and imposing in mirrored shades, cut-offs and a frumpy, black one-piece with broad straps and a nonscoop neck. A beach towel matching Jules's was cast over her shoulder. In the daylight, she looked to be about five foot ten. Her tattoos and piercings garnered some sidelong looks from the tourists on the beach, but she seemed unconcerned. I envied her lack of self-consciousness. I said hello and introduced them to the Murdocks.

"Your name is Jules?" Mona asked.

Jules flashed me a smile and I caught the unspoken reference to our brief discussion of weird parental naming practices the night before. I couldn't help but smile back.

"It's short for Julian," she explained, "which is a little town in the mountains east of San Diego. My parents honeymooned there and they fell in love with the town and the name. In fact, I was probably conceived there, but they won't admit to that part of the story."

She and I laughed and even Mona gave a grudging smile. Margo, as usual, had gone silent around strangers and I had yet to hear Ashley put together more than two words in a row. Mona tended to view new acquaintances as potential fans for the band and/or business contacts (until fate proved them otherwise, at which point she would drop them like a hot potato), so I could count on her to be sociable for the moment. She was, in fact, chatting with Jules about Southern California—the Murdocks had some relatives down there—just like a normal person. She asked Jules if she was from the south. No, Jules replied, both she and Ashley were San Tomas locals. Mona then took off her sunglasses and peered at Ashley.

"Do I know you?" she said.

Ashley looked startled at being directly addressed. She shook her head no and nudged at a shell in the sand with her toe.

"No, really, you're a horn player, right?" Mona continued her interrogation.

I was amazed to see Ashley blush slightly. She mumbled something under her breath and was busily avoiding eye contact. Who would have thought the woman would be shy with all that body art and the fierce hair? Mona, with all the sensitivity of a bulldozer, was hot on the trail now, though. She snapped her fingers, trying to summon her memory. I knew she would obsess until she remembered, so I hoped it would be soon. It was. She stopped snapping and pointed dramatically at Ashley's generous chest.

"I got it!" she proclaimed with satisfaction. "You play trombone with that all girl ska band, right? The FemTones. Yeah, I saw you guys at Chi Chi's once."

Ashley mumbled a yes, her voice gruff (probably from lack of use, I thought). Chi Chi's was a small club on the south side of town in a commercial district. It was known as a gay bar for both men and women, but featured a lot of live music which made it a popular spot for just about everyone. Bertha's Attic had played there in the spring. I remembered they had made a total of sixteen dollars that night.

During all this chitchat, I'd had a chance to covertly take a closer look at Jules. Why is it that a girl in a bikini top and a towel around her waist looks more naked than a girl in a bikini? Is it because the mind imagines there might not be anything under that towel? Or is that just my mind? Maybe a better question was, why must I constantly mortify myself with all these off-the-wall thoughts?

Up close and in the daylight, Jules looked just as pretty as the previous night's encounter had suggested. She and Ashley were a study in opposites—Beauty and the Beast, I thought rather unkindly. A light dusting of freckles played across the bridge of Jules's nose. My height, but quite slender. Tiny, short, golden hairs on her forearms gleamed in the sun. A freckle just to the left of her navel was the only distinguishing mark on a perfectly tanned and flat stomach. Her hair was damp, the curl returning as it dried. Her nails were short and unpolished, like mine. I hate fussing with longer nails—always breaking or chipping or needing a touch-up. Totally not worth it, in my opinion.

I offered a beer to Ashley, who took it with a nod. She was really warming up to me, I could tell. Jules took one too, with a more ebullient expression of gratitude.

"Thanks," she said, her hand touching mine briefly as I gave her the can. Obviously seasoned campaigners, they both made sure their backs were to the lifeguard station before they popped the lids. A hint of triceps definition played beneath the surface of Jules's slender upper arm as she opened the can. Ashley's upper arms were more like hams. Mona handed them a couple of paper towels to better conceal the contraband.

"Cool suit," Jules said to me.

My dented self-esteem rose a notch or two. I thought it was awfully nice of her to compliment my new suit, especially since hers looked so much better than mine.

"Did you get it at Stan's?" she asked, referring to the sporting goods store on the mall.

"I did, as a matter of fact," I told her.

"I saw it on the rack there last week when I was shopping for a bikini," she said. "I was hoping they would have that design in a two-piece, but they didn't."

Out of the corner of my eye, I noticed Margo sit up. She and Mona exchanged a glance.

Ashley had already drained her beer. That's one advantage of being the Strong But Silent type—you can drink a lot more when you don't have to waste time on nonessentials like speech. She looked around for somewhere to throw her can, spotted a garbage barrel twenty feet away and trudged off toward it without a word.

Jules, Mona and I chatted for another minute. A minute in which Mona managed to mention her band would be playing Dollar Night at the Mongol in eleven days and Jules and Ashley should definitely come and bring *all* their friends. Mona never missed a chance to promote the band, because—obviously—the more people who showed up for the gig, the more likely they were to get another gig. Jules told her they would try to make it, touched my arm briefly as she thanked me again for the beer, gave me another one of her warm smiles and then set off with Ashley when the taller girl returned.

Margo muttered something to her sister that I didn't catch. Mona nodded her assent.

"What?" I said.

"Total lesbos," Mona repeated for my benefit. Margo nodded.

"What?" I said, half laughing. "I don't think so."

"Come on, Hev," Margo felt roused to declare, "you're always such a dunce about these things." She flapped a hand at me dismissively as she took off her sunglasses.

"Oh, I'm a dunce?" I responded combatively. I felt the heat rise in my face.

Mona said, "Well, you've got to admit, the big one is clearly a lez."

She had me there. "Yeah, I guess so," I admitted. "But that doesn't mean Jules is. I think they're just roommates, you know?"

"How big is their apartment?" Margo asked with a sly smile.

From the layout of the building, we all knew it couldn't have been any bigger than mine. Which was not big at all. Tiny, in fact.

"Well, maybe they're just trying to save on rent," I said.

Mona looked skeptical. Margo rolled her eyeballs at me, then sank back down on her towel, face down. She reached back with one hand and undid the strap of her bikini top so she wouldn't get a tan line.

Mona said, "Well, as long as they show up for my Dollar Night gig, I don't care who they fuck."

Which broad-minded philosophical statement seemed to close the topic. She grabbed another beer from the cooler and put a new tape in the machine. Billy Squier.

We closed up shop at quarter to three, as Margo was due at the Bowl and Mona had band practice. The climb up the hill was easier with the cooler almost empty. My apartment seemed cool and dim after the brightness of the beach. I made plans to rendezvous with Mona later to watch the municipal fireworks from her rooftop.

After the Murdocks departed, I returned to the full length mirror to examine my flesh for signs of tanning. Nothing. It had to be an optical illusion that I looked even paler than I had that morning. I'd probably wake up all burnt on the morrow, but, in the meantime, at least I smelled pleasingly of Coppertone and outdoors.

Domestic chores and a regrettably small amount of unpacking filled the rest of my afternoon and evening. I drove to Mona's around sunset. Made it in four minutes flat—not the record, but close. The meters on her street didn't operate on Sundays, which was good since I was saving my precious quarters for laundry day. The Chinese restaurant that took up most of the first floor of the Murdocks' apartment building was still optimistically open for business at eight o'clock on Fourth of July night. Glancing in the window as I passed, I recognized the two customers as some of the Nigerian exchange students who lived upstairs. Freddy, the middle-aged owner of the restaurant, lounged in the open doorway, fanning himself with a menu.

"How about some dinner, Miss Heavenly?" he tried with a smile.

He knew I never ate Chinese food, though I often had a beer there while watching Mona shovel down broccoli beef and spring rolls. He'd at least convinced me to check out some pretty decent Chinese brew.

"No, thanks, Freddy, but happy Fourth of July!"

Shaking his head at my stubbornness, he waved me by. The next doorway was the locked entrance to the apartments. I pushed the button for Mona and Margo's place on the plastic intercom box. The intercom buzzed and clicked, but there was no answer from above.

Stepping back, I yelled at the top of my lungs up at the apartment, "Mona! Mona, it's me! Open the door!"

I thought I heard her faintly yell something back, but was saved from further discourse by the Nigerians, who had finished their meal and were nice enough to let me in with them. Up on the third floor, I opened Mona's door without knocking and startled her, as she was standing right there, still futzing with the intercom.

"Oh. You're in."

"The Nigerians let me in," I told her.

"Well, let's go on up," she said.

The fireworks were due to start at nine o'clock, but the tenants of her building always gathered on the roof to party before, during and after the show. The roof was easily attained via the fire escape and used by all the tenants to barbecue and hang out laundry. Mrs. Romanoff indulged her green thumb with a little rooftop garden in one corner. Mona was dying to have the be-all-and-end-all party up there and have her band play, but the Romanoff had not yet been convinced. I thought twenty bucks and a pint of sloe gin would do the trick, but Mona was still exploring the more economical possibilities of sucking up.

"How was practice?" I asked her casually as we climbed the metal stairs. I knew the band was working on some new material that Mona was keeping secret from me and Margo. Petey had let something slip about new songs for their upcoming Mongol gig.

I was hoping Mona might reveal something by accident as she was usually relatively mellow and relaxed (for her) after a practice session.

"Fine," she said suspiciously, knowing I was fishing.

There was still some light in the sky way out to the west, but darkness had descended on the town spread out around us. Lights twinkled pleasantly on the ground, as did a few stars above us. As Mona reached the top of the fire escape, a gust of barbecue smoke engulfed her. Coughing, she quickly moved from sight. I followed her up and found the party had started without us.

Somebody had set up a stereo and the college radio station was playing at medium volume. Jimmy Cliff was jamming. The school tried to promote the station as K-UCST, but of course, the call letters were limited to KUCS. Thus, the dorms and many a bumper were littered with butchered stickers extolling the virtues of SUCK.

All the Nigerians and their buddies were clustered in the corner over the grill. I couldn't tell what they were trying to barbecue, but it involved a great deal of heated discussion and hand gestures. I wondered if it was some exotic African dish. Once in a while, they would share a steaming pot of something with Mona and Margo. If I happened to be there, I never ate anything, but everybody knew I was hell of picky and hopefully no one took offense. Since we had started college, I had never known Mona to turn down free food of any description. Some folks (including, unfortunately, her grandmother) thought Mona was lazy because she didn't have a real job. Since I was a witness to her daily struggle to make ends meet, I thought she was one of the hardest-working people I knew. The band barely made expenses, let alone a profit. What money they made was turned back into rent on the practice space, repairs and enhancements to the communally owned sound system, photographs and flyers and, from time to time, recording sessions. Mona was always hustling, finding gigs for the band to play, playing solo gigs, giving piano and bass lessons, sitting in when some other band's bass player was sick and even working as a copyist for the UCST orchestra. She and Petey would sometimes play with little Pignose amps or acoustic instruments on the pier or on the outdoor mall the city had created downtown on several blocks of Pacific

Avenue. The meager amounts she collected in her instrument case often ended up being her food budget for the week.

Speaking of struggle and food, I wandered over to the grill to see what the Nigerians were up to. Good old American chicken and hot dogs—yay. I greeted Winston, the oldest of the bunch at twenty-eight and their de facto leader, as he oversaw the cooking efforts.

"Good evening, Heavenly," he replied solemnly in his Oxford accent.

Winston was a nice guy and a good neighbor too. After a couple of drinks, we could get him to say words in his native tongue with clicks in the middle. That always slayed Mona. She was over by the pony keg talking to the Romanoff, in the corner of the roof nearest to the Bowl-O-Rama. The bowl's large neon sign was maybe ten feet away, zzz-ing away loudly. Its close proximity was alarming to me, but at least it kept the area free of bugs. The Romanoff was finishing a declarative statement as I joined them.

"And that's how I met my third husband, my darling Dmitri…" Her attention was diverted by the quivering of the fire escape rail. Someone was coming up. "Oh, I hope that's Flaco," she said to Mona, then looked back toward the fire escape.

Mona gave me a smirk at the mention of the Latin lover.

The Romanoff continued, "He was going to bring a watermelon if he got off work in time. I tell you, it's a joy having my nephews and nieces in my life. He reminds me so much of my second husband, Jaime, who was his uncle. So industrious, that boy…" Further revelations were suspended by the arrival of Freddy with his cook and dishwasher. Sloshing her drink, the Romanoff rushed over to welcome the three men like she was Zsa Zsa or somebody. I guess she was a little loaded.

"Oh, my God, he's her *nephew!*" Mona said to me in an undertone, meaning Flaco.

Well, that certainly did make a lot more sense than the whole secret boy toy scenario, I thought.

"Where's the fucking food at this party?" Mona asked crankily.

"Winston's working on it," I told her as I helped myself to a beer from the keg. "Oh, look, Freddy brought something."

Turned out to be a big industrial-sized bag of fortune cookies, so everybody had fun reading their fortunes out loud and swapping them for a better one.

Mona's read: "If you seek a monsoon, the raindrop will find you."

Mrs. Romanoff beat Mona to it by a split second. "What the hell does that mean, Freddy?"

Everybody cracked up. When he replied that he wasn't responsible for the fortunes as he bought the cookies from a firm in Holmesville, a largely Hispanic town about twenty miles south, everybody laughed again to Freddy's bewilderment.

My fortune said, "Beware the smiling stranger at your door." Not sure I liked the sound of that one, so I traded with Winston for his "The path to a new beginning is beneath your feet."

The city fireworks show started promptly at nine o'clock. Everybody gathered at the street edge of the roof to ooh and ah. We had a grand view from up there. Some kids down the block were lighting firecrackers in the middle of the street. The Nigerians on either side of me laughed over my head at a joke I didn't hear. Back home, we always had a neighborhood Fourth of July party with tons of food, games for the kids and firecrackers after dark. I wished we at least had some watermelon on the roof that night. Didn't seem like the Fourth without it. My folks and the Murdocks' grandmother were probably downing some right about now in some neighbor's backyard.

I suppose I could have succumbed to a little homesickness at that point, but staring off toward the west with fireworks shimmering overhead, alone in the midst of the crowd, with a cold beer in my hand, I felt pretty content. I hoped life would get better, but at that moment, I had no worries.

That was about to change.

CHAPTER FOUR

Monday

On Monday morning, I put Jackson Miller's letter in the mailbox for the postman to deal with.

Work was a six-minute drive away. Many of the city and county municipal offices were located in a large, ugly, concrete building fronted by a large, ugly, concrete plaza. A large, ugly, concrete fountain was waterless due to the continuing drought. Splotches of gray and white paint masked the graffiti on its sides. No one, not even the city and county employees, ever hung out in the municipal plaza. A few spindly trees would probably provide some shade to the concrete benches in the twenty-first century. Even on calm days, some architectural anomaly ensured that the wind would be blowing trash through the plaza. Occasionally, a stray dog would lope through. In the meantime, the security guard was kept busy rousting skateboarders from the dried-up fountain.

The county courthouse, however, was a lovely brick building erected in the 1920s. It was thankfully not in the municipal plaza, but one block over on Pacific Avenue. Also to be found in the courthouse were the offices of the district attorney, the clerk of the court and the county clerk. A small cafeteria in the basement provided sustenance to both the innocent and the guilty. Well, at least those out on bail.

For reasons that were never clear to me, the Public Defender's office was neither in the courthouse nor in the city/county office building. Instead, it was located on the second floor of a two-story building on the far side of the plaza. The first floor was occupied by a podiatrist, who owned the building. I secretly wondered if the municipal planners had just flat-out forgotten about the Public Defender when it came time to divvy up the offices. In any event, we were still just a block from the courthouse, so it was no big deal. Except when it rained. The attorneys hated that. The criminals probably did too.

I parked in the employee lot, scuttled through the deserted plaza, ran up the one flight of stairs and whisked through the door of the Public Defender's office at exactly one minute past eight. The office manager, a dour Asian-American woman in her forties, gave me a darkling look, but made no comment on my sixty seconds of tardiness. Divorced, a smoker, with no hope of advancement, Stephanie had gone to work for the county one week after graduating high school. I figured she was entitled to her depression.

The two other clerical workers in the office were Ethel, a chubby, grandmotherly sort who typed all the attorneys' briefs and motions, and Tasha, a thirty-four-year-old African-American woman who was the receptionist. Her husband was in graduate school at UCST and could stay home with their three-year-old during many of Tasha's working hours. Tasha not only worked the front desk and answered the phones, but was responsible for updating the records for juvenile court cases. Ethel covered the misdemeanors and Stephanie took care of the felonies. As low girl on the totem pole, I took care of filing, photocopying, assembling the next day's schedule for the attorneys based on a printout from the clerk of the court's office, covering the front desk when needed, helping out with the phones and any other miscellaneous errands that needed to be done.

I wished them all a good morning and settled down at my desk, cramming my backpack into the bottom drawer. My desk was strategically positioned at the end of the long hallway that bisected the office. My little cubbyhole had probably originally been intended for brooms and mops, but it gave me the illusion of having my own space. Stephanie had a small office to herself on my left. Tasha and Ethel had desks in the area behind the reception counter. The counter itself faced the entrance across a small lobby with eight scarred chairs and a dusty fake ficus. Stephanie's office had a glass partition through which she could see Tasha, Ethel and the front counter, but thankfully not me. If she stuck her head out her office door, however, I was only about three feet away. She was light on her feet too, so I tended to be fairly alert while at work.

She had left me a note saying I would cover the front desk that afternoon in Tasha's absence. That meant I had until noon to get out the next day's schedule, known as the calendar. The information regarding which case would be heard in what courtroom at what time was generated each day by a computer in the clerk of the court's office. One of my jobs was to go pick it up every day, plus drop off any outgoing interoffice mail for the courthouse offices.

It was a typically busy Monday. After my mail run to the courthouse, I had the calendar finished by ten thirty and passed out copies to all the attorneys. I then worked on the never-ending filing until lunch. A steady flow of alleged miscreants kept me occupied at the front desk during the afternoon. They all looked guilty to me.

I didn't even think about Jackson Miller again until I got home and opened the mailbox. The mailman had taken away the letter I'd left that morning. A single buff-colored envelope now lay on top of a glossy magazine. I didn't subscribe to any magazines, so that obviously wasn't for me. I pulled it out first—a sailing magazine with "spinnaker knockdowns" as the lead article, addressed to Jackson. The buff envelope was also addressed to Mr. Jackson Miller and came from the parole office of an East Coast state.

Hmmm. Maybe Mona was right and the guy was a criminal. I'd met several people on parole since I went to work for the Public Defender's office and they all fit that description. Or maybe he used to work for the parole office? That could be a possibility. Or maybe he had a dopey friend like me who worked there and would send his friends mail in official envelopes just to scare them. Okay, I admit it, I did that to Mona once. Worked too.

I was so deep in thought contemplating the possibilities, I didn't notice Werner coming up to the mailboxes. His sudden appearance in my peripheral vision scared the bejesus out of me. I involuntarily gave a small shriek and jumped, clutching the mail to my chest. "God *damn!*" I said with feeling, regaining some composure.

"Sorry, uh, Miss, uh…" he said with an obsequious smirk.

"Heavenly," I answered in a regrettably hostile tone. Don't ever startle me. I get real mean. I flipped shut my mailbox's door. Werner was either eyeing my chest or the mail I still held there. "Can I help you with something, Mr. Werner?"

That brought back the eye contact. He smiled. He certainly hadn't been this friendly before. "I was just wondering if you'd gotten any mail for the man who used to live in your apartment," he continued. "I promised him I'd keep an eye out for his mail."

His eyes had strayed again to the letter and magazine, both of which I now held at hip level. (Fine, it was the mail, not my bosom. That department rarely held men entranced.) I wasn't warming to this guy and scaring the crap out of me definitely hadn't helped our relationship. And something seemed off about this conversation. Why was he all smiley today? Lying to him seemed like the most appropriate response.

"Nope, all for me," I replied breezily and turned to go up the stairs.

I could feel him watching me the entire way. Creepy! Inside my apartment, I locked the door and leaned my back against it, exhaling. After a second, I heard his car door slam and the Mercedes pull out of the driveway. Whew.

I dropped the mail on the love seat with my backpack and went into the bedroom to change out of my work clothes. The office dress code was pretty casual, thank goodness, though Stephanie was wont to look askance at some of my bolder flights of fashion. I put on shorts and a tour shirt, opened a few windows and returned to the mail. I sat down and held the buff envelope up to the light. Couldn't see a thing—darn those eastern taxpayers and their high standards. The phone was on the footlocker in front of me. I dialed Mona's number.

"Yo!" she barked into the receiver.

"It's me."

"Hey."

"Hey. What are you doing?"

"I gotta get ready for my solo gig at the coffeehouse tomorrow." Mona always had a gig coming up somewhere, with or without the band.

"Oh, yeah, in the marina! Are you psyched?" I asked her.

"I guess," she said somewhat diffidently. "I'm used to playing for drunk people, you know? People on caffeine might actually pay attention. You're coming, right?"

"Absolutely. Hey, check it out, I got more mail for Jackson Miller, the Mystery Man."

I told her about the letter and the magazine and my two encounters with Werner at the mailbox, mentioning that he was a retired policeman. She hadn't even met him, but she was as suspicious of him as I was.

"Fuckin' cops, man…" she said.

"He's retired, though—"

"Once a cop, always a cop," Mona intoned. "But forget Werner, Hev—you should check out this Jackson Miller guy at your work. What's the good of all that technology if you're not willing to bend it to your own purposes?"

I could hardly argue, since that very thought had been tiptoeing around the back of my mind.

"You should go to the library too," Mona said, always happy to provide me with direction in my life.

"And check out a Nancy Drew?"

"Yeah, well, you might pick up some tips, George. But really, maybe there's something in the newspaper from when the guy disappeared?"

"That's a good idea," I admitted. "I guess I could do it tomorrow on my lunch break."

"And check him out on the PD computer?" she said again.

"I'm not supposed to…"

"Oh, come on, Hev! You're such a goody-goody."

"All right, all right, I'll do it," I said, caving. I knew I wanted to anyhow. If I could ever get a good look at the devil on my left shoulder, I wondered if she would look exactly like a tiny Mona Murdock.

"Killer," she said, the final word on the subject. "Now, should I wear my leather pants tomorrow for this gig at the coffeehouse?"

"I thought we were walking down to the marina from my place. Isn't that going to chafe?"

"Yeah. Probably. Shit."

I knew she would wear what she wanted no matter what I said. It was fun to talk about it though. We ran through her wardrobe options for pants, tops, accessories and shoes. "Go-go boots again?" I ventured.

"Nah, this is a piano gig, so no heels. I can't handle the pedals in heels. I guess my gray suede boots."

Soft suede boots with quarter-inch heels, composition soles and tops that folded down were very big that year. I coveted Mona's pair, but of course, her shoe size was too small for me. "Bitchen. And you get free dinner too, right?"

"Big wup, probably a cup of coffee and a danish. Okay, look, I gotta go, I gotta work out the set list."

She always agonized over the perfect selection of songs to play at each gig. Not that it seemed to make a huge difference, but Mona was a big believer in "you get out of it what you put into it." For this gig, she was getting fifty dollars and dinner for four forty-minute sets. Paying her dues, she called it. Maybe someday it would actually pay off for real. Sometimes it seemed to me that luck played a much larger role in life than most people were willing to confess. The relationship between money and brains, or money and talent, continued to elude me. Maybe the secret to making money was to not give a crap about other people. Well, that was getting easier every day, so maybe I'd be a millionaire by thirty.

I told Mona I'd see her at my place the next day after work. She told me not to forget to go to the library on my lunch break.

"And don't forget your freaking library card, either!" was her parting shot.

I decided on a chicken pot pie for dinner, a staple of my diet in those days. While my entrée transformed from a frozen hockey puck into a delicious repast, I turned on the stereo and took another look at Jackson's mail. I flipped through the sailing magazine, but learned nothing beyond the fact that it was a sport dominated by blond white people with good teeth. I was itching to open up the letter from the parole folks, but couldn't quite square it with my conscience or the federal statutes. Instead, I got a pen and wrote "Moved—Return To Sender" on both the envelope and the mailing label on the magazine. I wondered how much more of his correspondence I'd be getting.

Could Werner have been telling the truth about Jackson asking him to take care of his mail? I noticed I had moved to a first-name basis with him in my mind. For some reason, I felt like I was on his side, whatever side that was. Maybe it was just living in the same rooms where he had so recently lived. Somehow, I had come to identify with him and even felt oddly protective of him. Surely, the man couldn't be a criminal. I couldn't be sleeping in the same room where a criminal used to sleep, making ice cubes in the same fridge and hanging my clothes in the same closet. It just didn't seem possible.

And Werner. There was definitely something weird about that guy. As if on cue, his dog starting barking next door. I wouldn't have heard it over the music except the song was just ending. I glanced out the peephole in the front door. Yep, I caught a glimpse of the Mercedes below, sliding into the garage. How did a retired cop afford a Mercedes? As a quasi fellow city/county employee, I couldn't believe they got paid that well. The barking crescendoed as Werner opened his front door, then died away as he slammed it shut.

I went to check on my pot pie, prodding it with a fork. Looked ready to me. I grabbed my one and only potholder to pull it out. I then nearly dropped it when Werner pounded on our common wall. Somehow, I managed to keep my dinner from flying across the room and set it carefully on the kitchen counter. He kept pounding on the wall. I thought I could hear him yelling something, but I couldn't make out the words. I trotted into the living room and turned the stereo down, then returned to the common wall in the kitchen.

Oh. He was yelling, "Turn it down!"

Good gosh, it wasn't even seven o'clock yet and the music wasn't that loud. Man, what a jerk. I considered pounding on the wall myself and yelling something unladylike, but controlled my inner child. After all, I *had* just moved in, maybe it *was* a little loud and I didn't *really* expect him to be a Marshall Crenshaw fan, now did I?

Geez. I hate always having to be the better person. I went back to the stereo and turned it off before he had an embolism or something. I was planning to watch TV while I ate dinner anyhow. As I sat down with my pot pie, it occurred to me that my research need not be limited to Jackson Miller. I could do a little fact-finding about Werner tomorrow too. Between the computer and my buddies at the Public Defender's office, I bet I could find out all sorts of info about Mr. Asshole Ex-Policeman. And you never know when that kind of stuff can come in handy.

CHAPTER FIVE

Tuesday

Thanks to a benign confluence of green lights, I actually made it to work five minutes early on Tuesday morning. Of course, I found out that Stephanie had called to say she'd be in around ten o'clock, so my virtue went unnoticed. Again. At least her absence meant I could screw around with the computer without fear of getting busted. As long as I had a file in front of me and concentration apparently furrowing my brow, none of my co-workers or the attorneys would suspect a thing.

But first, I quickly made my rounds across the street in the courthouse. Back at my desk, I whipped out the calendar in record time. I made copies, then dropped one off on each of the attorneys' desks, earning a variety of grunts, nods and one actual "thanks" in the process.

Okay. I had a little more than one hour before Stephanie would descend upon the office like a black cloud of administrative efficiency. Before I could start my top secret investigation, though, two of the attorneys approached. Carmen, newly promoted to felonies, was enmeshed in an assault with a deadly weapon case. She beat out Leo—misdemeanors and a foot taller—by a footstep.

"Hev, can you help me out with my exhibits? I've got the drawings of the scene roughed out here, but I need something larger for the jury."

She handed me three sketches on notebook paper. Six years older than I, Carmen was short, brunette, intense, elegantly attractive, focused, ambitious, well-dressed, well-groomed and blessed with gorgeous light brown skin. In other words, my complete opposite. I admired her, I liked her and I wished her a safe trip back to Krypton. "Sure, Carmen, I'll take care of that today."

"Thanks." She was already off and running to her next agenda item.

Leo was lost in contemplation of a stain on his tie. Six foot three, prematurely gray hair, sparse beard and perpetually rumpled. His shirt was wrinkled, his pants were baggy and one of his shoelaces was frayed and missing the little plastic end thingy. He somehow managed to be both skinny and flabby at the same time. He needed a haircut and was forever losing stuff. In his late thirties, twice divorced and rumored to be a heavy drinker, he maintained a happy-go-lucky attitude that frankly baffled me. Actually, the twice divorced part baffled me more than the attitude—who would marry this guy?

"Do you need something, Leo?"

"Oh, yeah, uh, I can't find the Simonson file. Can you find it for me, please? I got a one o'clock hearing."

"Geez, Leo, I found it for you twice last week!"

"I know, I know, sorry. You're just so good at finding stuff, Hev. And I can't look, I've got a client in my office waiting for me."

He tried the hangdog puppy eyes on me. Gawd. I stifled the urge to roll my own eyes. Glancing at the clock, I saw the precious minutes were ticking away. Sixty-three minutes now before Stephanie's arrival. If she didn't show up early.

"Okay, okay, I'll have it on your desk by quarter to one."

I shooed him away and logged into the county judicial database. The computer beeped. A moment later, HELLO HEAVENLY appeared across the top of the screen. A brief menu followed, inviting me to select information by name, docket number or court date. I chose name and input MILLER, JACKSON at the cursor. Several seconds passed, accompanied by clicking and whirring. Green letters on the black screen then spelled out NO MATCH FOUND.

Damn. I tried again, in case I had misspelled something. NO MATCH FOUND. So, Jackson Miller had never been charged with a crime in San Tomas County. I guessed that was good news, actually. The computer wouldn't search with the last name alone, so there was no point in inputting Werner, not that I really thought I'd find anything on him anyway.

Mona's library idea was still on my list for lunchtime. I was disappointed, though, that the computer was already a dead end. I exited to the menu screen and tried to think what to do next. Of course—get a Coke.

My desk was at the end of a very long hallway that passed through the lobby and then through a doorway into the area where the attorneys' offices were. At the other end was a kitchenette and the restrooms. In between were many small offices on both sides of the hall, each occupied by at least one attorney. Eight-foot-tall shelves lined the walls of the hallway, each full to capacity with client files. It was my never-ending and probably impossible task to ensure that the files were in correct order by docket number. Some days I thought Stephanie had created the task just to torment me, but in truth, the files were in substantially better shape than when I first started working there. To the point where I was becoming protective of them and tended to nervously watch whenever I saw an attorney returning a file to a shelf. And then dart over there to make sure it was in the proper order once he or she had left. Especially if it was Leo.

The kitchenette wasn't a room, but just a sink, some cabinets and a fridge at the end of the hall by the restrooms. I got a Coke— my own—out of the fridge, then leaned my back against the door as I opened the can. My work day was looking pretty full: exhibits for Carmen, finding the lost file for Leo, lunch trip to the library for more research…

A sudden flash of inspiration struck. What if I were six foot three and a bonehead? I moved somebody's cereal bowl into the sink, then crawled up on the counter. Yep, there on top of the fridge was the missing Simonson file. Maybe I was cut out to be a detective after all.

Leo's office was just around the corner, the last one at the end of the hall. I knocked softly on the closed door, then entered without waiting for a response. Leo was in conference with a large

African-American woman who was loudly cataloging her problems with someone named Darnell. She had a crying baby on her lap and two other children under five and was paying no attention to any of them as she reeled off her litany of grievances. The older kid was trying to insert himself under the desk and the toddler was solemnly chewing on Leo's stapler. Leo gave me a frantic look as if I could somehow be of help. Yeah, right. My back was to the client. I dropped the Simonson file into his inbox from a height of six inches and gave him a bland look before leaving him to his woes. Maybe I was just a temp, but sometimes that was a good thing.

As I headed back to my desk, I could see that Stephanie had arrived and was giving Ethel the third degree about something. I took Carmen's sketches, some poster board, colored markers, a ruler and my Coke into the unoccupied conference room off the waiting area. San Tomas County had no budget for graphic artists—hell, we were lucky to get the markers. Though no Da Vinci, my minimalist efforts were hailed by the attorneys who were overwhelmed by their caseloads. Leo, always quick to (a) spot a sucker and (b) find someone else to do his work, had first employed my limited talents in this area. After he won three verdicts in a row—to everyone's surprise, including his own—the other lawyers took note of my ability to draw straight lines, Xs and print in block letters. In addition to the calendar, filing, the front desk, phones and whatever else Stephanie could dream up, I now was regularly asked to create Exhibits A, B and C. No increase in pay, but I did get to whiff markers on county time.

Slightly woozy, but artistically fulfilled, I delivered Carmen's poster boards just shy of noon. Since our guy was the defendant, I used a green X instead of a red one to show his position when the alleged (yeah, right) crime took place. I hoped she appreciated that subliminal nudge for the jury. She was on the phone annoying a judge while eating her power lunch of carrot sticks and yogurt. She glanced up and mouthed "thanks" to me as I propped the poster boards by her file cabinet.

The office was closed every day from noon to one. Ethel locked the door behind me as I lurched out into the bright sunlight for my own power lunch. The fresh air cleared my head quickly. Another beautiful day—my favorite kind, with big, fat, puffy white clouds in a brilliant blue sky. I picked up an orange soda and two hot dogs with mustard, pickle, tomato and onion from a cart on the mall. Like so many other things in San Tomas, "the mall" was completely different than what you'd expect. In San Tomas, the mall was actually a several block stretch of Pacific Avenue lined with shops, restaurants and other businesses. The city had narrowed the street to a picturesque, one-way, winding thoroughfare, broadened the sidewalks and added lots of pretty, tourist-attracting touches like palm trees, benches and flower boxes. The courthouse anchored the south end of the mall. At the north end, Pacific Avenue dead-ended at Bay Street, another major artery. At that end, the Mongol was the anchor, with Rocco's right across the street.

One thing about working downtown and by the mall: just about everything my heart could desire was within walking distance on my hour lunch break. I'd been known to hit the bank, get my hair cut, buy concert tickets at Tower Records and eat lunch all within my allotted sixty minutes.

My goal that day, however, was more modest. The public library was just one block away on Front Street, so I cut back up there while I scarfed down my wieners and pop. Licking my fingers as I entered, I headed for Periodicals. The clunky microfiche machines might have put me in a low-tech panic, but fortunately I had wrestled with them many a night at the UCST library during my fling with academia. Now I just needed to figure out what time frame I was looking for.

It was June when the landlord's agent told me Jackson Miller had paid rent until three months prior. Counting backward, I calculated that meant he had last paid his rent in…March? And disappeared sometime in April? Or maybe she meant he had last paid his rent for the month of February and took off in March? Or April? Okay, what the hell did I know. If I stopped paying my rent, I pictured being evicted within minutes, not months, but that probably wasn't how it worked.

Well, I had to start somewhere. I asked the Periodicals librarian for issues of the *San Tomas Bay Reporter* from mid-March through mid-April. He came back a few minutes later with a deceptively small and slippery stack of microfiche. I selected a machine and placed the first film in the slot, following the instructions taped to the table. It didn't take long to figure out that I could not go through every issue word by word. The *Reporter* wasn't that big a paper because San Tomas wasn't that big a town, but even so, there were a lot of closely printed columns to wade through. Okay, Hev, use your brain, I told myself. You can skip sports, the classifieds, the comics...Except for *Broom-Hilda*, of course. Only a fool would skip *Broom-Hilda*.

I looked at my watch and saw it was twelve thirty-three already. Damn. I quickly decided to just scan pages one through three of each issue. In this town, Jackson's disappearing act surely would have been worthy of pages one through three. I normally never read the newspaper and I remembered why as I scanned page after page of bullcrap. Did anyone really care about the garden club's twentieth anniversary, the new lights for the high school football field, the number of tourists expected for spring break?

Twelve fifty-three. Orange pop and onions were repeating on me in a disturbing fashion. I was zooming through the first April edition when I saw it:

MAN DISAPPEARS

SAN TOMAS—Police are asking for the community's help in locating Jackson Miller, 29, a recent arrival in San Tomas from the East Coast. Miller was unemployed and had been renting an apartment in the Marina District. He has not been seen since early March. His next-door neighbor reported him missing after Miller failed to show for a fishing trip the two men had planned. Anyone with information on the missing man's whereabouts is asked to contact the San Tomas Police Department immediately.

Werner reported him missing? But Jackson had "asked" him to watch for his mail? That was perplexing...The small photo which accompanied the article appeared to be a driver's license shot. It showed an average-looking, thirtyish guy, clean-shaven, dark hair, thin in the face.

I hit the print button to get a copy of that page. The machine spit out two copies although I'd only asked for one. Oh, well. I grabbed both and fumbled with the machine to eject the microfiche. I'd have to come back tomorrow and see if there were any follow-up stories. It was almost one o'clock and I was going to have to run to make it back on time. I slapped two dimes and the stack of microfiche down on the startled librarian's countertop as I bolted for the door, prints in hand.

Good thing I was wearing flats that day—and every other day—because I did run all the way back. Winded, I charged up the stairs and swooped through the front door just seconds after Ethel unlocked it. As usual, a crowd of clients had been waiting to get in. They were milling about the front desk, so my entrance was camouflaged by their activity. I eased past them and slid into my chair on the very stroke of one o'clock. I grabbed a pen and was studiously examining a file when Stephanie poked her head around the corner to see if I was there. I felt her suspicious gaze on the back of my neck, but didn't look up seeing as how I was so hard at work. When she withdrew, I let out a breath I didn't know I'd been holding. I pulled my microfiche prints out from underneath the file and reread the article about Jackson's disappearance. Still didn't make much sense. I folded both pages and stuck them in my pants pocket.

It was back to the Sisyphean filing in the afternoon. I would dream of docket numbers that night, I knew. When five o'clock rolled around, I bade my co-workers farewell and headed for home, looking forward to Mona's gig. Just for kicks, I took a different route home than my usual, one that would take me maybe eight minutes instead of the usual six. Traffic was temporarily stopped a block up Bay due to a freight train rumbling through, but I was going the other way. The railroad tracks had once served a long-abandoned ice factory on that corner of Bay, but the business had been shut down for years. Plans circulated from time to time to renovate the dilapidated old wooden structure into a theater or shops, but never seemed to get anywhere.

Mona was standing in my driveway when I got home, staring toward the ocean. Album cover shot, I thought and wished I had a camera. She looked like a total rock star dressed in black leather pants, a red tank top, boots and enormous dangly earrings with her black bag and mike stand at her side, the backdrop of the garages behind her. The big, fat clouds from earlier in the day were moving out to sea to cluster at the western horizon. It was going to be a gorgeous sunset, although the winds were picking up as the day waned.

The Monamobile was nowhere in sight. "Where's your car?" I asked through my open window as I pulled up in the driveway. I hoped it hadn't broken down again. She couldn't afford that.

"LeClaire dropped me off," she told me, mentioning the keyboard player from Bertha's Attic. "It seemed easier than parking over here. You'll give me a ride home, right?"

"Sure, if you'll open the garage for me."

She moved her bag and mike stand over to the side of the garage door, out of the way. A gust of sea breeze came through the passenger window and blew my hair in my face, but Mona's gel-laden spikes were immune to such petty natural forces. She heaved the heavy wooden door up, then turned to me and struck a brief muscle man pose as a comment on her door opening abilities. But another strong gust of wind caught the door and shook it hard enough to start it back downward. Mona realized the door was coming down on her head just as I opened my mouth to yell. She lunged forward, hit the ground and rolled toward the car, the edge of the door missing her by scant inches. It hit the ground with a shuddering jolt as Mona got back on her feet, laughing and dusting herself off.

"Dang," she said, "that was a close one!"

"Jesus, Mona, you almost got yourself decapitated there!" My heart was in my throat, while she was laughing it off. Typical. She grabbed her mike stand and used it to hold up the door while I eased the car inside.

As we carefully shut the door together, she said, "You better watch this door, Hev, since you don't have my catlike reflexes. Does it always do that?"

"No," I replied, "but it's pretty windy today. You better believe I *will* be watching it, though, after that little demonstration. And catlike, my butt."

She started doing her Bruce Lee moves, but was hampered by the bag and mike stand. Ignoring her, I headed over to the mailbox to see what that day's yield was. The yield was nothing. Nothing at all. Not even a supermarket flyer. Hmmm. I frowned at the empty mailbox.

Mona hi-yahhed herself up to my side. "What'd you get? Anything for—" she lowered her voice dramatically, "The Man Of Mystery?"

"I got nothing. I got a rock."

"Yeah, well, I gotta rock too and in about forty minutes at the marina, so can we please haul on down there now?"

"Yeah, let me just stash my pack. I'll be right back." I ran up the stairs and threw my backpack on the love seat. In record time, I used the facilities, grabbed my ID and five bucks, then ran back down the stairs, where Mona was pointedly examining her watch.

"Punctuality, Heavenly, is a virtue," she said in her grandmother's voice.

"Okay, okay, let's go already then," I said, taking the mike stand from her and pretending to follow it like a quivering divining rod toward the marina. It was only four blocks away—two blocks over, two blocks down. It was unlikely we'd find a better (or freer) parking space closer than my own garage, so it made sense for us to just walk down there, especially since there was minimal equipment to carry. Lots of other people, both tourists and locals, were out for a walk too, enjoying the breezy, warm evening. We paused for the stoplight along with several others headed in that direction.

I wanted to tell Mona about my library trip, but knew from past experience that right before a gig was not the time to discuss anything of substance. I'd tell her later when she wasn't distracted. In the meantime, I asked if Margo was coming. The answer was no, she had to work. Margo worked a lot that summer. In fact, the only reason she wasn't holding down two jobs was that the Bowl was able to give her so many extra hours. The Murdock sisters were equally ambitious, although in different ways. Unlike me, the pathetic sloth without even a five-year plan. My mind tended to go ominously blank when I thought of my future, especially now that I had dropped out of college. I tried to focus on the positive, though. For example, having a job that didn't involve the phrase, "Would you like fries with that?"

"Well, how about LeClaire and the rest of the band?" I said to Mona. "Are they coming?"

"No, they're all working or had a night class or something," she sighed. "So I'm really glad you made it. At least there'll be one friendly face out there."

She was twitching with impatience at the red light, but after making our way down the steep hill to the esplanade—the fancy word for the sidewalk at the water's edge—we strolled through the doors of Cap'n Cino's coffeehouse with time to spare. A chalkboard sign outside the door announced, "Live Music Tuesday 6:00—Mona Murdock!" The rock star immediately ditched me to go in search of the manager, grabbing her mike stand from me on the way.

You might think it would be hard to merge the nautical and coffee themes, but Cap'n Cino's had really outdone themselves. A stuffed swordfish high on one wall had an old blue speckled coffeepot speared by its sword. Another wall had a fishnet with mugs tangled in it. A blue and green mural on the ceiling showed a bevy of saucy mermaids—their long, golden tresses discreetly covering the naughty bits—enjoying espressos in tiny cups with King Neptune looking on approvingly. Each of the dozen or so small round tables had a hand-drawn map of Java laminated on its top, with tall ships sailing the seas. *Here Be Monsters*.

The coffeehouse was a fairly recent addition to the marina scene, but already a popular spot. The location, the fancy coffee drinks and the live music formed a winning combination. I hadn't been there before myself, not being a coffee drinker, but had heard of it. And I had to admit the large, open, sunny room with a great view of the boats in the marina and the water beyond was very inviting.

All the tables were occupied by one or more people, so I took the last seat at the espresso bar and ordered a Coke from a college kid in a sailor hat and a blue and white striped T-shirt. A dollar fifty for a can of Coke and glass of ice! I'm so sure. Oh, well, at least my job didn't require me to wear a stupid costume. I now had three and a half bucks left for dinner, including the tip.

Mona had finished her brief confab with the manager and was busy setting up at the upright piano on the small stage. Since this was a solo gig with Mona playing the piano and singing, set up was minimal. I could see she'd already taped her set list to the music rack with her ever-handy duct tape, since a stray gust from an opened door or the ventilation system could send loose papers flying—not good mid-performance. If you don't know any rock musicians, you might think their favorite thing is groupies or drugs or non-brown M&M'S. Wrong—rock 'n' rollers love duct tape! Trust me.

Mona, the Control Queen, always preferred to use her own mike stand, boom and microphone. Extracting the latter two items from her capacious bag, she was ready to plug into the house PA system a few moments later. After a quick sound check which consisted of her striking a few chords on the piano and saying "check one" into the mike, she gave the manager a thumbs-up. He was now behind the espresso bar and saying over the PA, "Good evening, ladies and gentlemen, and welcome to Cap'n Cino's! Tonight, we are proud to present the musical stylings of Miss Mona Murdock! Please give her a hand…"

I saw Mona wince first at the "musical stylings" and second at the "Miss," but she brightened a little at the small burst of applause that greeted his announcement.

"Thanks" was all she said before launching into her first song, a driving, rhythmic tune of her own about invisible and murderous people in an alternate universe. (Hey, she wrote it, I'm just describing it.) Even if you didn't catch all the words, the implacable building to the climax would get your blood boiling. It was a good, energetic way to kick off her set, I thought approvingly. The crowd already seemed interested, with some heads bobbing and toes tapping.

It was a pretty decent crowd for early on a Tuesday. There must have been close to forty people in there and everybody seemed to be enjoying their iced coffees and biscotti. A large ceiling fan moved the air around without cooling it much. Besides the tables and the espresso bar, a high counter ran around two of the walls where you could stand and enjoy your drink. A few people were reading newspapers or giving their orders to wait staff, but most were attentive to Mona's performance. That was good, because it pissed her off when people had the nerve to converse while she was singing. This gig might have the potential to become a regular thing, so I didn't want her to blow it by getting mad at the audience.

She acknowledged the scattered applause for her first song with just a nod and immediately started the next one. This one was sort of a medium speed gospel hymn. The melody was uplifting, though if you listened to the lyrics, you'd realize she was singing about the interpersonal dynamics of women in public restrooms. You'll just have to trust me (again) that this juxtaposition worked. Something about ugly ducklings and swans…

"They're all homecoming queens in the john…" Mona belted her little heart out on the chorus and the crowd seemed to like it. More people drifted in from outside when they heard the music. The waitresses hustled to keep up with the orders.

The sailor boy who'd sold me my Coke braved the stage between the second and third songs to take Mona a glass of ice water.

Her "Thanks, Ahab" got a laugh and suddenly everybody was in a good mood and having some fun. Mona's lyrics ranged from disconsolate to blistering to impenetrably obtuse, but who listens to lyrics? People dug the music and her singing. Anyone could see she was totally putting herself out there. Her full, throaty, pitch-perfect voice beautifully complemented the funky, not-too-badly-out-of-tune coffeehouse piano. I felt a burst of pride in my chest—hey, everybody, that's my best friend!

She kept going with more songs of her own and her usual in-between-songs sarcastic banter, which the audience fortunately found amusing, then finished the first set with an impassioned cover of "Walk Away Renee" that wowed the crowd and left them wanting more. The applause was definitely more than polite, even downright hearty with a few hoots and hollers thrown in for good measure (okay, that was me). With a big grin, she thanked them and said she'd be right back after a short break. The Tubes came up over the PA as she joined me at the bar.

"Killer set, Mon," I enthused. "It's going great, don't you think?"

"Yeah, pretty good," she replied with a smile, her face aglow with conquest.

There were no seats at the bar and I didn't offer her mine, knowing she was way too hepped up to sit between sets anyhow. Sailor Boy appeared and asked her if she wanted anything. She requested a tall water, no ice, with a lemon wedge, which he promptly assembled for her. She drank deeply after squeezing the lemon into it. Good for the throat.

The guitar player from another local band was there with his girlfriend and they came up to say hello. His band was headlining the Mongol that Thursday and Mona promised she'd come. An easy promise, since we were there every Thursday for Dollar Night anyhow. His band, Plan B, was one of the most popular rock groups in San Tomas that year. They were probably the closest thing to professionals in town, as in making a living at it. All five of the members were survivors of other local bands, including one guy who had played with the Doobie Brothers for an album. They played about half covers and half originals, successfully carving out a niche for themselves between the Mongol and various top forty bars in the area.

Some yahoo in a tie who'd been sitting at a table near the stage with his office buddies was waiting to talk to Mona next. I had never seen her not get hit on at a gig. Not to sound surprised—it's not like she was bad-looking. She wasn't. It's just that, (a) we all suffered by comparison to Margo the Beauteous and (b) having known her basically all my life, I couldn't really look at Mona objectively in that regard. She was like a sister to me. Looks aside, it was her attitude and onstage swagger that attracted them. When I tried to act confident like that, it came across totally fake. Which it basically was. Unfortunately, ninety percent of the guys who could work up the nerve to approach a Real Live Woman Musician turned out to be total losers. Also, since the gay community was both prominent and active in San Tomas, the occasional woman would also make a move. Mona loved the star treatment, regardless of its source.

I tuned out of Mona's conversation with the yahoo. As I glanced at the mirror behind the bar, I was startled to see the reflection of a man just behind my right shoulder who hadn't been there a half second before. I turned and looked at him, shifting in my seat to regain a few inches of personal space. He was just some scraggly guy trying to order drinks. All the caffeine in the air must be making me jumpy, I thought. I took a sip of my beverage and watched the crowd in the mirror.

The place continued to fill up and the volume of conversations and laughter was more than equal to The Tubes' "Talk To Ya Later." The temperature as well as the noise level had been steadily rising with the influx of customers. Three guys straight from the cover of my newly acquired yachting magazine came in the front door and caught the waitress just as she passed. Their Top-Siders and tans reminded me of Jackson's overdue slip fees. I wondered if his boat was still here at the marina. Maybe Mona and I could check it out after the gig.

She was ready to start her second set. The manager re-introduced her and the applause was loud and boisterous this time. She said "thank you" and gave them a moment to settle down. There was a wolf whistle from the back of the room. She flashed a smile, then took a deep breath, evidently gathering her forces. She began to play a song I'd never heard her play in public before. Simple, clear chords rang out in the now respectful silence. The beauty and sadness of the music were matched by the words—a story of love lost to betrayal and a heart that would never be quite right again. The song rose and fell like the tide, building to a tumultuous peak, then dying to the quietest of endings. The hush that greeted the last chord belied the fact that there were now close to seventy people in that packed, humid room. Then they went crazy, clapping and stomping and yelling their praise. Mona loved it. I could tell from the fierce smile on her lips that she was in her heaven. I let out a primordial "Woo!" to celebrate her triumph. Yay, Mona.

She rewarded their good behavior with an Elvis Costello cover and even let them sing along on the chorus. She cruised through the rest of her sets in happy fashion. From the look on the manager's beaming face, a return engagement was a lock. He was still smiling when she played her encore—a happy, rollicking ditty called "Montana" that Mona had told me was about sexual incompatibility:

If you were the US of A
I'd live in your heartland
With occasional trips down Mexico way
But I'd never go to Montana
No I'd never go to Montana
Never go 'less you said it's okay

If you were ten pounds of kitty litter
I'd buy a poodle
But I'd probably end up giving it away
And I'd lock you in the closet
Yeah I'd lock you in the closet
Spend my time chasing off strays…

Even I didn't get that one. But the manager, mopping his profusely sweating forehead, seemed thrilled with the large quantity of overpriced food and drink he had sold. He booked her for another solo gig on a Wednesday in three weeks and was coy about the possibility of Bertha's Attic opening for a bigger name on a Saturday night in August.

Best of all, he paid her the fifty dollars in cash without any hassle and Sailor Boy brought her free dinner soon afterward. Chicken salad in pita bread, but she was so high on her victory she would have eaten anything and thought it was great. Having paid for my sandwich (three bucks plus tax—whew, under budget), I was a little more attuned to the taste. Not bad. I liked the water chestnuts the cook had included in the chicken salad. Crunchy.

It was half past nine and dark when we left. Mona was always way fired up after a gig, so it was easy to convince her to walk down toward the slips. She had the mike stand and I had the bag this time. Stars twinkled above as the clouds had receded entirely. It was a lovely night, but I soon realized I was in possession of very little actual information. I could see lots of boats in the marina, but I had no idea which one was Jackson's. I didn't even know the name of the boat. In fact, I didn't know for sure his boat was at this marina. It could be in Monterey or the South Pacific, for all I knew.

Further investigation was halted when we came to a locked gate that denied us entry to the slips themselves. Mona asked me what the fuck we were doing down there anyway. It was quiet at the marina. Faint reggae from somebody's stereo and the water lapping at the boats were the only sounds.

"I don't know—looking for clues, I guess," I told her.

"Yeah, well, I don't see any, so can we go now?"

We stood on the slightly undulating, floating pier which provided access to the boats. The last light on this stretch of pier illuminated the chain-link gate blocking our way. I hooked my fingers in the gate and rested my forehead on the cool metal. It felt kind of relaxing to stand there and undulate, but I heard Mona popping her gum and knew she was growing restless. Turning, I noticed a light in the windows of a tiny shack to our left that I had assumed was bait related. On closer inspection, however, the sign on the door read "Marina Manager—For Slip Rental, Inquire Within."

"Aha!" I said to Mona.

"What?"

"I said 'aha' as in a clue, ya bonehead." Stepping over to the shack and sweeping my arm dramatically, I intoned, "I give you: the Marina Manager!"

Mona eyeballed me with a Mona look, then walked to the door of the shack and knocked on it with the base of her mike stand. Actually, since the base of the stand was quite heavy, she perhaps unintentionally pounded on the door in a fair imitation of the police department. I immediately heard from within the sound of a chair overturning, coughing, a muffled curse and then choking noises. There was a pause, then the door opened to reveal a furtive-looking, thirty-ish male who appeared to be struggling to comprehend our appearance on his doorstep. He looked around to see if anyone besides us was lurking in the shadows. Nope, just us. He coughed again, into his fist. I glanced at Mona—if that was marijuana in the air, it certainly wasn't our beeswax, right?

"Hey, man." Mona took the bull by the horns.

"Hey," he replied cautiously, looking like he might decide at any moment to fly up into the streetlight like the moths fluttering above us.

"Are you the marina manager?"

"Assistant manager," he reluctantly shared, coughing once more. His dark beady eyes darted back and forth warily from Mona to me.

"We're looking for our friend's boat—you know Jackson, Jackson Miller?" she said conversationally.

The guy abruptly went from medium paranoid to completely paranoid. "No visitors without boat owners," he said with narrowed eyes.

"Well, yeah," I said, "that's what we're trying to do, find the owner. We were hoping you could help."

"Nope," was all he said as he stepped back and shut the door in our faces. The lights went out a second later. Should have brought Margo, I thought.

Mona looked like she was ready to break the door down, but I grabbed the mike stand from her and started back up the pier.

"Come on, let's go," I told her.

She followed after sticking her gum on the guy's door. That'd fix him. We were almost back to my place when I realized I'd seen the assistant marina manager before. He was at the gig—the scraggly guy standing behind me trying to order drinks. I told Mona that.

"Well, so what?" she said, ever supportive.

"So…nothing. I just remembered, that's all."

Back at my building, Werner's Mercedes was not in the driveway and his apartment was dark. Jules's little black scooter was gone too, I noticed as we went up the stairs. Ashley was in, though. Lights were on in her apartment and I could hear her playing the trombone. She was good. I don't know why I was surprised. The mellifluous tones caught Mona's attention too, of course. Ashley was playing some old song from the thirties or forties. Catchy. As we went in my front door, Mona started humming along, then sang the next line out loud. As far as I could tell, she knew all the words to every song that had ever been written. When she wanted to, she could sing without artifice, without any rock 'n' roll rasp, making her voice pure and sweet. I liked it best that way.

"Do you think she can sing?" Mona asked. She seemed to be pondering something.

"Who? My neighbor?" I asked, somewhat startled. Sing? The woman barely spoke.

"Yeah, that big dyke. What's her name again?" Mona turned to me with interest.

"Ashley," I supplied.

Skepticism must have been writ large upon my countenance because Mona said, "What?"

"You need a trombone player?" I asked, my surprise no doubt evident.

"Not for the band," she said. "But LeClaire and I have been talking about a side project, doing old standards at restaurants and hotel bars. You know, old people music like Cole Porter and Gershwin tunes. Old people tip big, man. She'd play keyboards and I'd be on my standup bass. But it would be way better as a three piece—if we add a horn player who can sing, we could do three-part harmonies. That would be killer…"

Her voice drifted off as she imagined the killerness of it all. From a business standpoint, it did sound like a good idea. San Tomas was full of retirees and other old people. The trio she described could play lots of places the band could not, like jazz clubs and the hotel and restaurant circuit, like she'd said. Although the visual of the three of them on stage together was a bit alarming. It made good business sense, though. But…Ashley?

"Really?" I had to confirm. "You're not…scared of her?"

"Scared of her?" Mona laughed at me a little. "Why would I be scared of her?"

"But…" I tried again. "Well, what about the gay part?"

Mona scoffed at me. "Look, I know what I want and she knows what she wants and never the twain shall meet, so what's the problem? It'd be just like playing with a guy I wasn't interested in. Shit, if I had to rule out all those guys, I'd be playing a hell of a lot of solo gigs."

She cackled at her own wit. I should have known she'd be chock-full of sexual self-assurance. Insecurity was simply not in her nature. Then she looked at me searchingly.

"What, are *you* scared of her?" she demanded, her tone incredulous.

"A little," I had to admit.

Mona chewed on that for a moment. "If you're going to be scared of one of them, I would think you'd be scared of Jules," she finally said.

Now I had to laugh. "Why would I be scared of Jules?" I asked her in disbelief.

"Because she's the one hitting on you," Mona said with certainty.

I stared at her for a long moment. And finally shook my head. "You're wrong," I said. Not even to my own ears did I sound entirely convinced.

She shrugged. "Hey, as long as it doesn't bother you, no problem," she said.

Ashley had moved on to another old song downstairs. This one sounded mournful.

"What's she playing now?" I asked, just to change the subject to something, anything else.

"'I Got It Bad And That Ain't Good,'" Mona replied, her voice carefully neutral. "Duke Ellington."

"Yeah, well," I struggled for some witty comeback. And gave up. "Look, are you ready to go or not?"

"Just let me pee first."

A few minutes later, we headed downstairs. Werner's dog apparently didn't like the scales Ashley was now playing. I heard him start to howl as we hopped into the Camaro. The streets were empty of pedestrians at that hour, although I thought I saw a shadowy (and scraggly?) figure melt back into an alley as I made the turn onto Highland Avenue.

"Did you see that?" I asked Mona.

"What?" she said.

I shrugged it off. Could have been someone walking his dog. Or a homeless person. Or nothing. Why would the assistant marina manager have followed us anyhow?

At ten o'clock straight up, we turned onto her one-way street. The bowling alley was closed, its neon sign turned off, so the street looked even more desolate than usual. There was trash in the gutters and skittering down the sidewalks in the night breeze. The streetlights always seemed dim to me on this block, as if they weren't too enthusiastic to be there either.

There was a parking spot right in front of Mona's building, but a white van with its flashers on was double-parked there, blocking my access to the space. The rear doors of the van were open, with large cardboard boxes visible within. I pulled up alongside to see if the driver was inside, but no dice. I decided to wait for a moment to see if the driver would appear. If he was about to leave, I could park there. Otherwise, I'd have to circle the block since there were no other spaces open. As Mona started cursing under her breath at the delay, I saw the front door of her building open and Flaco hurried out toward the van. Visiting his aunt again? At ten o'clock on a Tuesday night? He certainly was a devoted nephew.

"It's Flaco," I said to Mona.

She nodded, then leaned over and honked the horn briefly to get his attention, as if he could overlook the V8 rumbling ten feet away from him. I hated it when she honked my horn, especially when I was driving. My only consolation was that she did that to everybody. Except LeClaire, her keyboard player—the one time she tried it on her, the Irish/French/Jamaican keyboard player got so incensed she threatened to put a voodoo curse on Mona and almost ran her Karmann Ghia off the side of Highway 1.

Flaco held up one finger in the universal gesture meaning "just a second, please." Reaching into the van, he picked up one box, then stacked another on top of it and carefully walked back into the building while balancing his load. Looked heavy.

Mona was restive. "Look, Hev, I really want to get out of these leather pants!"

"Well, go ahead then," I told her.

As she dashed into the building, Flaco came back out, flattening himself against the doorway when he saw the look on her face. Grinning, he jogged to the van and closed the rear doors. He glanced over and gave me a little wave as if he recognized me. I automatically waved back. I supposed he might have seen me around, much as I'd seen him. Hopping into the driver's seat, he put the van in gear and motored off down the street.

It only took me three tries to parallel park my car so that it was not an embarrassing distance from the curb. By the time I finally got out of the vehicle, Flaco was coming back up the street on foot. He must have found a parking space nearby. It was nice of him to give me the parking spot, I thought. Gentlemanly.

As he came abreast of me, he smiled and said, "Cool Camaro. Is it a V8?"

For some (completely stupid) reason, I hadn't expected him to speak English and was momentarily taken aback, finally stuttering out, "Uh, yeah."

He seemed not to notice my stupidity. He opened the door to the building and politely gestured me in ahead of him. Hmmph. Laying it on a bit thick, I thought, but I merely muttered "thanks" and self-consciously went through the doorway and up the stairs, keenly aware he was a few steps behind me and probably scrutinizing my butt. At the second-floor landing, he peeled off to go in the Romanoff's apartment. I turned and said "good night." He gave me another big smile and wished me a good night in turn, then went in the manager's unit without knocking.

He had really nice teeth, I thought while I climbed the stairs to the Murdock sisters' apartment. Nice cheekbones too. I had also managed to notice he was wearing old jeans and a light blue, V-necked T-shirt. Although he was slender, he sure had lugged those heavy-looking boxes around without much problem. Glimpsed in the T-shirt, his arms and chest looked strong and tan, although he certainly wasn't muscle bound. He looked a little older than me and the Murdocks—mid-to-late twenties, maybe.

When I reached the top of the stairs, Mona was standing in the open doorway of her apartment waiting for me. Barefoot, she was now attired in cut-offs and a faded, black Led Zeppelin T-shirt with the sleeves rolled up a turn or two. I saw that her toenails were painted with black nail polish.

As I passed her, I looked down and said, "That's attractive," in a wholly insincere voice.

She pushed me as hard as someone who is five foot one and ninety-seven pounds can push. I staggered into the apartment and bounced off the kitchen counter, while she went into her ninja moves, punctuated with shrill yelps. I countered with a few moves of my own.

Margo appeared in the still open doorway, keys in hand. Mona and I froze. As usual, our antics were not worthy of Margo's commentary. She may have slightly flared one nostril. She stepped past her much shorter sister and grabbed the phone off the counter which separated the tiny kitchen from the living room. Paying out the extra long cord, she went back into her bedroom, closing the door behind her.

As Mona shut the front door, I told her of my encounter with Flaco.

"No way! He speaks English?" She looked as floored as I had felt.

"Sí, señor. He's actually kind of attractive, don't you think? Nice smile, at least."

"I guess so," she said musingly. "I just never thought of him that way. And why is he always hanging out with the Romanoff?"

I shrugged, not knowing the answer. I had aunts, but I sure didn't hang out with them on any regular basis. I thought of a different question, though. "What's Margo's deal?" I said, pointing toward the back bedroom where she was still ensconced with the phone.

"Some new guy," Mona told me. "Somebody in Sacramento, I think—the phone bill keeps going up. She must have met him when she went home for the weekend last month."

Margo's relationship with her grandmother was less contentious than Mona's. This was partially due to the younger Murdock sister possessing qualities her grandmother valued like being a good student, staying in school, working a "real" job and being tall, slender and pretty. But it was mostly (I thought) due to the fact that strong-willed Mona and her grandmother were more alike than either cared to admit. They'd been butting heads for years. And if Margo had multitasked by picking up a new man on one of her occasional visits back home, that wasn't too surprising—she'd find a date at a seminary.

But the ever-changing sperm donor in Margo's life was not worthy of our commentary. We passed the remainder of the evening in our usual fashion, talking back to the television in a regrettably rude fashion. When Margo eventually joined us, we filled her in on the gig and our marina adventures during the commercials. I showed them the print of the newspaper article about Jackson's disappearance, which was rather crumpled from having spent the afternoon and evening in my back pocket.

"So what's the big mystery again?" Margo asked with an eyebrow elegantly arched. "The guy just took off, right? That's no crime." She shrugged dismissively and handed the print back to me.

Maybe she was right, I thought. But where was the fun in that? I wasn't sure what the next step in my investigation would be, but I was stubbornly resolved to continue. There were things I wanted to figure out that summer—and one of them was the whereabouts of Mr. Jackson Miller.

CHAPTER SIX

Wednesday

I forgot to set the alarm and woke up at seven twenty-eight a.m. I hate starting the day when "shit" is the first word formed in my brain. I brushed my teeth in the shower, didn't wash my hair, skipped the makeup which I hardly ever wore anyhow now that I was "in" at the Public Defender and was on the road a mere twenty-two minutes later. I compensated for my lack of awakeness by listening to Boston at about a hundred decibels on the short drive to work with the window wide open. I walked through the door at one minute before eight, feeling like my hair was standing up straight on end and my eyeballs had been rolled in grit, but nobody seemed to notice anything amiss.

Thank God, it was Wednesday. The Public Defender saw no new clients on Wednesdays, which was a blessing. Wednesdays were quiet and peaceful and not edged with the borderline hysteria and threat of violence that colored the rest of the week when the lobby was packed and a line of people was out the door. I made my mail run and did the calendar. It was noon before I knew it.

There was a small cafeteria in the old courthouse across the street which was popular with the attorneys. I'm not a big fan of cafeterias, so I rarely ate there except when I had a hankering for a BLT. My aversion to cafeterias stemmed from my elementary school years. It mostly had to do with peas and the frequency with which they appeared on the grade school menu. God, I hated peas as both vegetables and weapons. And talk about your borderline hysteria and threat of violence—public school cafeterias are the original breeding grounds of that ambience. Once I grew up and realized I was never required to eat peas again, my tolerance for cafeterias marginally increased. It was cheap, at least. A banner swaying above the entrance to the cafeteria proclaimed it to be Burrito Day!

I got my BLT and Coke, then realized too late I should have got them to go. The place was full of city and county employees enjoying their burritos! I could hardly see an empty chair in the small dining room, let alone an empty table. I was about to ditch my tray, wrap my sandwich up in a bunch of paper napkins and find somewhere to dine al fresco when I heard my name.

"Heavenly! Hey, Hev—over here!" It was Leo, the misdemeanors attorney, waving at me from a table for four he shared with one of the Public Defender's investigators.

They weren't my first choice for luncheon companions, but beggars can't be choosers. I slid into a hideous orange plastic chair next to Leo, who beamed at me with a mouth full of tortilla. He already had salsa on his tie. The orange plastic chair went perfectly with the mottled linoleum and the flesh-colored modular tables. "Fuck You" was artlessly carved into the tabletop on my side. Bon appétit.

"Hey, Leo. Hey, Terry," I said to the other guy, the investigator, whom I'd met on a few occasions but never really talked to.

The two investigators for the Public Defender's office were more often in the field than the office. They weren't cops—the cops were on the district attorney's side. They were more like private detectives, except they were county employees, working solely for the Public Defender, helping to find witnesses, verify alibis and otherwise assist the defense attorneys in building their cases.

Terry was an ex-cop in his fifties, a balding, bullish blond guy with a straggly moustache and a morose demeanor. The other investigator, whom I'd seen even less of than Terry, was a fortyish woman named Barb, a big-boned, genial, chain-smoking brunette with a lot of dark ringlets piled high on her head and, it was rumored, a gun in an ankle holster.

Terry poked gloomily at his salad and said to me, "How's it going, kid?"

Leo, after glancing around to make sure there was no judge or officer of the state bar association in view, poured something from a small flask into his Styrofoam coffee cup. "Irish," he said to me with a twinkle when I caught his eye. "Top of the morning to ye."

Why am I having lunch with two middle-aged men? I asked myself. I took a bite of BLT on wheat and hoped they were leaving soon. At least my sandwich was good.

"So, better than when you were on the cops, right?" Leo said to Terry, apparently continuing a conversation they had started before I sat down.

"I guess," Terry answered, glum as always, pushing a cherry tomato around his plate.

My brain finally noticed I was sitting at a table with an ex-cop, who no doubt knew Werner, the retired cop! They were even about the same age. Terry knew all the cops in town. And all the crooks too. No wonder he was morose. Knowing all the dirt on everybody would certainly give me an ulcer. From wishing they would leave, I was suddenly filled with anxiety that they would leave. In fact, Terry was pushing his plate away and preparing to rise.

"Uh, say, Terry," I said, très casually, "do you know a cop named Werner?"

He looked surprised that I had addressed him, but sat back down and considered my question. "Paul Werner?" he asked. "Patrolman on the west side? Good-looking young fella?" That last bit came with a grin for me and a wink for Leo, who leered back immediately. God, men are so tiresome.

Hoping I hadn't said that sentence out loud, I said, "No. An older guy, retired, bowling ball gut, kind of a jerk?" And then hoped Terry wasn't best friends with him. But I needn't have worried.

"Oh, *that* Werner!" he said with distaste. "Yeah, I know that sack of—" He caught himself just in time. He turned to Leo. "Remember that guy? He was working vice in seventy-nine when all that stuff went down?"

"Oh, yeah," Leo said darkly. He turned to me. "Why are you asking about him, Hev?"

I didn't have a lie ready and I more or less trusted their discretion. Well, Terry's. "He's my new neighbor," I told them.

"Yeah, well, your new neighbor's a fuckin' creep," Terry said, abandoning his attempt to not curse in the cafeteria. "Gimme some of that, would ya?"

Leo accommodatingly poured him a slug of "Irish" in his cup. He waggled the flask at me, but I shook my head in horror, which made him laugh. He wouldn't be laughing if Stephanie caught him, I thought.

Terry was normally a man of few words, but I hoped the liquor might loosen his tongue. "So why is he a creep?" I asked.

"Well, for starters, he won a bunch of money off that big 49ers' loss last season. That's when he bought that fancy Mercedes he's driving."

"He bet against the Niners?" I was aghast.

Terry nodded as he took a sip of his whiskey. "See, I told you. Guy's a creep. He was bragging about it too, which pissed a lot of people off. Actually, nobody much liked him before."

"Against the 49ers?" I said a second time. I couldn't get past that heresy. After a terrific season, the 49ers had won the Super Bowl in January and my chest still swelled with pride when I thought of it. Go, Niners!

"Yeah, can you believe it?" Leo chimed in. It was beyond his ability to sit quietly and listen when he could be talking.

"Is he a big gambler then?" I asked the both of them.

"No, and that was the weird thing," Terry responded. "The other guys were always betting on sports and Werner never did, so it was kind of strange when he came in one day and said he'd won all that money on the Niners game."

"He's from back east someplace, right?" Leo asked. When Terry shrugged, Leo added, "I mean, I guess he's no fan of San Francisco."

We all sat for a moment in silence and considered that. Leo topped off his cup again and offered the flask to the other man, who declined. Terry glanced around to make sure we weren't being overheard, then leaned forward to continue with his report. Leo and I simultaneously leaned in as well.

"People don't like to talk about this, but there were rumors Werner was on the take when he worked for vice. A whole bunch of vice cops got investigated about three years ago. Some of them got fired too, but Werner just got reassigned. Some people thought he snitched on the other guys to save his own skin. That didn't help his popularity much either, so nobody was too sad when he decided to retire the first of this year."

I mulled all this over, but it merely seemed to confirm that Werner was a jerk. No news flash there. I said to Terry, "How about Jackson Miller—does that name ring any bells?"

He thought for a moment, then shook his head. "Nope, never heard of him. Must be clean."

An image of my mailbox popped into my head. Was Jackson clean? What about that envelope from the parole office back east?

"Hey?" Leo peered at me quizzically.

I was still wondering about parole. Was Jackson on parole? That would mean he had been in prison. Did parole transfer from state to state? I didn't know. And I wasn't about to ask Leo or Terry, although they no doubt knew the answer. I could figure it out for myself. Plus, I felt like I had already way overshared with the two of them. Both men were now looking at me curiously. I hadn't really meant to get into my personal business with them—it had sort of slipped out. I usually kept a pretty firm line between my work life and my private life. I was more than halfway regretting I had initiated this little chat with them already. What had I really learned from it? Not much.

"Who is Jackson Miller?" Leo asked me. "Another neighbor?"

"No, no, just some guy. It's nothing, Leo."

"Are you mixed up in something, Heavenly?" Terry inquired, sounding a bit paternal, which was the last thing I needed or wanted. "I could make a few calls, if you like."

"No, no," I reassured both of them. "I was just wondering about my new neighbor. There's no problem, guys. Thanks for the info." I was on my feet, collecting my trash and theirs on my orange plastic tray like a good little clerk. "See you back at the office," I told them.

Terry was still looking at me speculatively, but Leo was finishing off his flask. I was glad my fate wasn't being decided in a courtroom that afternoon.

Back at my desk, I decided the next thing to do was find out the number for the local parole office. That turned out to be an easy one. I asked Tasha and she pointed to the photocopied pink sheet of frequently used numbers we all had at our desks. Hers hung on the wall above her phone. Sure enough, in a box at the bottom I hadn't noticed before, there were numbers for parole, probation, social services, drug counseling, a halfway house and a bunch of other stuff I hoped I would never need.

Now that I had the number, though, I wasn't sure I had the nerve to call. I was beginning to wonder what I was trying to accomplish anyhow. Jackson Miller was gone and I didn't know him from Adam. What did I care where he was or why he'd left? Why couldn't I get him out of my brain? Because your own life is so damn boring and empty, the little voice in my head said. Sad, but true. I spent the afternoon filing and tried to clear my mind with the numbing routine.

Yet after work, I found myself back at the public library. I asked the librarian for more back issues of the local newspaper. I was there until they closed at six, but there was no further mention of Jackson's disappearance. He really had dropped off the face of the earth. With no family or employer in the area, I guess nobody had raised much of a fuss.

Heading home, I thought again about my curiosity. Maybe it was just that Jackson Miller was the most interesting man I had(n't) met in a long time. Girls on TV met interesting guys all the time. Me—not so much. Let's see: back in high school, I'd had a few horrifying dates with geeky boys whose shyness and awkwardness were matched by mine. The only long-term boyfriend I'd ever had was in my first year at UCST and even that had only lasted a few months. I'd gone out with a few guys since then, but hadn't felt any connection.

For the last several months, I hadn't even met anybody with potential. Mona knew tons of guys, but they were all musicians, an unreliable and temperamental breed as far as I was concerned. The last three good-looking men I had actually met, not just seen on TV or on the street, were Public Defender clients. They were good looking, but seriously lacking in other areas. One was a biker with a meth lab in his garage, another was a gang member who'd broken his pregnant girlfriend's jaw when she came home ten minutes later than expected and the third was a Russian immigrant who was a schizophrenic, shoplifting crack addict. I was in a dry spell, no doubt about it.

My dorm boyfriend—I still grimaced when I thought about that time. When Mona and I were freshmen, we'd had a room together in the coed dorms. It was an unspoken assumption that Mona and Margo would share digs once the younger sister came to UCST, but for that first year, Mona and I were roommates. Kyle, my boyfriend, was a junior who had a single room down the hall from us. Later, of course, I wondered what kind of a loser junior still lived in the dorms. At the time, though, I was convinced this was going to be the beginning of my new, exciting life—living away from home on my own (sort of), going to college and meeting all sorts of interesting people.

Kyle was older and he seemed to know everything about the school and the town. I thought he was an intellectual (who were in short supply back home) and so smart. He was a philosophy major and had cool glasses and longish hair. Mona didn't like him, but that didn't bother me much since Mona had never liked any of the guys I'd gone out with. To make a long story short, Kyle and I were together for about six months, but I finally broke it off when he started playing the Grateful Dead constantly and burning incense night and day. That shit was why I'd left home.

At least he had relieved me of my burdensome virginity. Not that the sex was any good, although perhaps fairly representative of its kind—awkward, bony, all elbows and knees, a little painful, jerky. About the best thing you could say was that it was over quickly. He certainly was not open to my shy suggestion or two—how dare I imply he might be doing something wrong? He knew what he was doing—he was a junior, by God! He'd immediately turn over and fall asleep, while I was left to stare at the patterns on the ceiling of his third-floor dorm room cast by a light on the quad below that filtered through the trees. One night it occurred to me I could simply break up with him. What a relief! I dumped him the next day.

Kyle wasn't a bad person, but looking back, I had no idea what I had seen in him. That new, exciting life had kind of crapped out on me too. Here I was, twenty-two, a college dropout, working for the county and no plans to speak of. Jesus, no wonder Jackson Miller was filling my head. He was having way more fun than me and he was probably dead.

I tried to shake off these dreary thoughts as I pulled into my driveway and put the Camaro in the garage. Upstairs in my apartment, I felt at loose ends. Wednesday was band practice night, so Mona was busy. I was free for the evening. Free to be bored. I was at least looking forward to Thursday night, Dollar Night at the Mongol, a ritual we never missed. Sometimes I'd go to band practice and hang out at the rehearsal space with Bertha's Attic. Not tonight, though, for three reasons: a) it was too hot to be in a small room with one door, no windows and no air-conditioning, b) I didn't feel like being temporarily deafened and c) Mona had actually told me I couldn't come since they were working on their new secret songs. She wanted me to hear them for the first time at next week's Dollar Night, aka The Big Gig! As a result, I was on my own, feeling dull and restless.

I should have been unpacking boxes, of course, but I just couldn't summon the necessary energy. I had finally shoved them under my bed, just to get them out of the way. At least then I could rest assured that no one was hiding under there. Us single girls have to be security conscious, you know. I thought of calling my folks, but Wednesday was their community garden night. God, that meant more Mason jars of canned vegetables this Christmas. Vegetables I had been putting down the disposal since tenth grade biology and the chapter on salmonella and botulism.

Sometimes I wished for normal parents, not that I actually knew anyone with a pair of those. The Murdocks had been raised by their grandmother, a formidable and capricious woman who had chased me off her property with a broom in 1968. Admittedly, Mona, Margo and I had been plotting to throw berries at the side of her house, but we had not actually got beyond the point of stockpiling a few dozen of the fruit. I had more sympathy for Grandmother Murdock now from the vantage of adulthood. Lord knew she'd had her hands full with Mona and Margo, the ill-planned offspring of a deceased daughter whose problems preexisted her embrace of barbiturates. Mona only vaguely remembered her mother. She had one memory of riding in a car and having candy handed to her over the front seat. Another was of a shadowy figure in a frightening confrontation with her grandmother. Margo, the younger sister, had no memory of her mother at all. The name of the father of the girls, if indeed it was the same man, went to the grave with the wasted body of Eliza Murdock. Grandmother Murdock still lived next door to my parents and continued to terrorize the neighborhood by all accounts.

I decided to walk down to the little market on the corner and pick up a few essentials—two potatoes, Coke, beer and toilet paper, to be precise. It wasn't a long walk back, but the bag was heavy and the evening air was still quite warm. The continuing heat wave was very un-San Tomas-like. Back at my apartment building, I set the bag down for a second on the bottom stair to wipe my brow with my shirtsleeve.

The door to the downstairs apartment opened and Jules emerged, barefoot. She was fighting the heat in a pair of gray gym shorts and a red tank top. Apparently, it was too hot for a bra. "Hi there," she said to me with a smile. Something about her manner made me think she had been watching the street, waiting for me to return.

"Hey," I responded, trying not to think of Mona's remarks about Jules hitting on me. Because they weren't true. Surely not... She leaned on the railing of the staircase, her bare arms making my brain go down a checklist: tan, toned, slender, smooth... "Do you by chance have a Phillips head screwdriver?" she asked. I don't know what I'd been expecting her to say, but it certainly wasn't that.

"I do." I had a whole set of them, in fact, thanks to my brother J. D.'s birthday present to me the past year—a pink toolbox with far more tools than I ever planned to use. "What size?" I asked, hefting my grocery bag back to my hip.

"Ummm..." She hesitated.

"Why don't you come up and see what I've got?"

She followed me up the stairs and into my kitchen. The toolbox was in one of the cabinets, for lack of a better place to stow it. I put my groceries away while she rummaged through the pink box.

"Wow, you've got quite a selection here," she said, her back to me as I put the beverages in the fridge.

I explained about J. D. as I covertly peeked at her long brown legs. Now why couldn't I tan like that?

"This one looks about right, I think," she said, turning around and holding up a screwdriver for my inspection. "I'll bring it back ASAP, I promise."

"No rush," I replied. "Keep it as long as you need it."

As I walked her to the front door, she cast a few discreet glances around the living room and through the open door into my bedroom, checking out what I'd done with the place. Which was not much. Catching my eye, she laughed at herself. "Sorry. Busted. I didn't mean to stare. You've just got so much more space than we have."

"Really? I thought our apartments were the same size."

"Well, yeah, they are," she responded. "You're right. It just feels like you've got a lot more space than we do, because we've got so much stuff crammed in there. Makes a big difference when there's only one person living here, I guess."

No matter what the Murdocks had said, I still could not picture this very attractive girl being the significant other of that trombone-playing behemoth downstairs. No way. But it was only a one-bedroom apartment.

As if picking up on that thought, Jules said, "Of course, it's mostly Ashley's stuff. That's why she got the bedroom and I got the couch."

"Oh, so your 'room' is the living room?" I said, making the little quote marks with my fingers. If there was relief in my tone, I hoped she didn't hear it.

"Yep, it's a mess down there. Don't ever try to make a one-bedroom apartment into a two bedroom. It really doesn't work," she laughed. "But we couldn't find a two bedroom in the neighborhood that we could afford and Ash always wanted to live by the beach... so here we are."

"Have you known each other long?"

"Yeah, we went to high school together at good old San Tomas High. Class of '79."

That made her (and Ashley) a year younger than me. Twenty-one. Same as Margo.

Jules had her hand on the doorknob. She paused for a moment, as if she expected me to say something. I couldn't think of a single thing to say. Jesus, I suck at small talk.

"Well, thanks again for the screwdriver, Hev," she finally said. "I'll return it soon."

"No problem," I told her again. "Take your time."

After she left, it occurred to me I could have asked her what she needed the screwdriver for. But I really didn't give a shit. That's why I suck at small talk—I'm just not that interested in stuff I'm not interested in. Other people seem to get all sorts of warm and fuzzy feelings and signals out of their boring conversations. I'm just bored. There's some code the rest of the world is exchanging that I've never been privy to.

Oh, well. When in doubt, bake a potato. And then eat it while rereading a favorite Robert B. Parker mystery. Do not think about your downstairs neighbor's bare legs.

CHAPTER SEVEN

Thursday

For a change, I awoke early on Thursday morning and debated the consequences of calling in sick for a mental health day. In the pro column was, of course, not going to work. Always high on my list.

The con column, unfortunately, was longer. Like not getting paid. Also, I felt confident that Stephanie's reaction would not be positive. I knew I was scheduled to cover the front desk that morning because Tasha had to take her little girl to the pediatrician. If I didn't show up, they'd be seriously short-handed. And having slept on it, I had decided I really did want to call the parole people about Jackson and the phone number was at the office.

Aw, damn it. The angel on my right shoulder won out again. I got up and got ready for work.

At three minutes before eight, there were already a dozen sorry souls in line on the landing and stairs outside the still locked office door. Muttering, "'Scuse me, pardon me," I made my way through the crowd. Junkies, hookers and petty thieves reluctantly stood aside. An emaciated woman in a stained and torn fatigue jacket three sizes too big for her accused me of cutting in line. Nobody likes a cutter. Her eyes were sunk deep in their sockets and her hair looked dead. She was probably about my age, but she looked twenty years older. And none the wiser. Before I could defend myself, a deep voice from the back of the line boomed out, "Don't you be botherin' Miz Hev'ly now, you crackhead honky ho!"

The group turned as one to view the source of this chivalry. It turned out to be Mr. Thibodeaux, one of the Public Defender's best (?) customers. He knew all the staff by name due to his frequent visits to our office. Homeless and mentally ill, he wasn't too bad a guy for all his scuffles with the law. Crazy as a loon, of course, but not a bad guy. I smiled my thanks to him and received a snaggle-toothed grin in return. As I opened the door with my key, the junkie he'd berated said something to him and I heard him tell her, "You best stop yo' ignorance 'fo' I snatch you bald, Jolene…"

I went on in and was at the front desk ready for action by the time Ethel let the mob in at eight o'clock precisely. Stephanie looked on approvingly from behind her glass partition.

By quarter after ten, I was ready for a break. Jolene, Mr. Thibodeaux and all the rest had been processed, interviewed by the paralegal and assigned attorneys. Mr. T. must have got his meds refilled. He was pretty organized that day for a man convinced the television was sending him secret messages. I thanked him again as he waited for Leo. He cheerfully assured me his latest fracas was all a frame-up and he'd be declared innocent once the Director of the CIA stepped in. I glanced at his paperwork—he was accused of shoplifting six cans of Beauty-Glo hair spray from the supermarket. And a jar of pearl onions.

My first meeting with him in my first week on the job, had not been so cheery. He'd been in a foul mood that day and I hadn't helped by completely mangling his name when I called him up to the front counter.

"Mister…uh…Thib…Thib-o…ducks…"

He stormed up, slammed his paperwork down and thundered, "Thibodeaux! The 'H' is silent! The 'X' is silent! Now where is Miss Tasha? She knows my name."

I had apologized and told him Tasha was out that day. I was trying to be professional, but in truth, cowering a bit in the face of his fury, his crazy gray hair sticking out every which way and his maroon checked, polyester sport coat, which looked like it had spent a good part of its existence at the bottom of an alligator-infested swamp.

Fortunately for me, Leo had appeared at that point and took him off to his office. I could hear them going down the hall, Mr. T. still sputtering and griping about me— "The 'H' is *silent!* The 'X' is *silent!*"

I'd had a few run-ins with other "clients" (as the attorneys called them) before I'd perfected my unflappable work poker face and steely composure. And I learned to make sure the countertop was always free of sharp objects. Blunt ones too.

Good times at the Public Defender.

Back in the present, Ethel agreed to cover the front desk for me while I went on break. Since I was covering for Tasha, Ethel had already made the morning mail run while Stephanie herself prepared the calendar. I went down the hall and used the facilities. I started to grab a Coke from the refrigerator, but stopped when I caught a glimpse of Leo's dark and empty office, the last one at the end of the hall. He always kept his blinds drawn, probably in deference to his hangovers. I knew he was still in court handling arraignments that morning. I also knew he wouldn't mind if I borrowed his phone for a personal call.

Now good old Stephanie might mind, but that was why I wasn't using my own phone at my own desk. She was nowhere in sight, so I grabbed the Coke, then stepped into Leo's office and shut the door behind me. The pink frequently called numbers sheet was taped to Leo's desk. I found the number, then carefully examined the receiver before putting it to my ear. Last time I'd used it, it was all gummy from God knows what. I gave it a quick spit shine on the thigh of my pants to be on the safe side before I dialed.

"Parole office," said a woman's voice. I could hear typing and another phone ringing in the background.

I gave her my best impersonation of an honest, dependable, professional Public Defender employee. "Hello, this is Heavenly calling from the San Tomas County Public Defender's Office. We need some information on a gentleman who may be a mutual client of our offices." Even as I gave her my name, I wondered why the hell I was doing that. What a stupe. It just naturally came out when I opened my mouth, though. Stupe.

The woman responded, "Well, I doubt we can give you anything over the phone, but do you know the name of his parole officer?"

"Uh, no," I answered.

"What is the name of the parolee?" I heard her typing and bringing up the computer screen on her end.

"Last name Miller, first name Jackson."

Computer keys clacked and then stopped. There was a long pause on the other end. A very long pause. Finally, she asked, "And what was your name again?"

I suddenly panicked. I had no legitimate reason to call on behalf of the Public Defender's office. I really didn't want to jeopardize my job. Hell, I didn't even know the right questions to ask.

I realized I had now created just as long of a pause as the one to which I'd been subjected. I said, "Well, um, I'll have his attorney call you back later, okay? Thanks, 'bye."

I hung up abruptly. The door opened and Leo walked in. He looked befuddled, then pleased to see me sitting behind his desk. Before he could dump any work on me, I got up and out of there in a hurry. "Thanks for letting me use your phone, Leo. Gotta go now, break's over."

His plaintive "But—" followed me down the hall.

Ethel still stood placidly where I'd left her, vigilantly overseeing an empty lobby. I thanked her and resumed my station. A steady trickle of indigent lawbreakers kept me occupied the rest of the morning.

I called Mona from a pay phone on the mall during my lunch hour, just to check in. I told her about my botched attempt to call the parole office. I could practically hear her rolling her eyes at my feeblemindedness, but she surprisingly admitted she probably wouldn't have done any better. "Why do you even care about this shit?" she asked.

"Forget about it. Let's talk about Dollar Night. Who's playing tonight?"

"Plan B is the headliner, Spawn of the Torment is the second band and I forget who's opening. Just think, though—only one more week 'til we'll be up there!"

Having her band play at the Moonglow was the pinnacle of her rock 'n' roll career so far. With more glory to come, fingers crossed. "I can't wait," I told her honestly. I was almost as excited as she was. My friend, the rock star!

My lunchtime was just about over, so I told Mona I'd meet her at her apartment around eight thirty. At the office, Tasha had arrived, so it was back to the filing for me. I got so caught up in the mindless routine of it, I unintentionally stayed two minutes extra. Cripes, workaholic alert!

At home, Werner drove up just as I was putting the Camaro in the garage. Oh, joy. Hoping to avoid him, I hurriedly closed my garage door and headed toward the stairs, skipping my mailbox. I'd get the mail later. Just as I reached the bottom of the stairs, though, he got out of his car and called to me.

"Miss Wilcox—Miss Wilcox!"

Unwillingly, I paused with my hand on the rail and my foot on the first step. What the hell did he want, anyway? And how did he know my last name? I didn't remember giving it to him. It wasn't on my mailbox, either. It was on my *mail*, though—my mail that I never got the day before. Hmmph. I'd gotten mail—junk mail, at least—every day I'd lived there so far until yesterday. But why would Werner take my mail? I was getting paranoid, I thought. I slowly took a couple of steps up the staircase as he approached. He stopped at the foot, looking cranky and peering up at me.

"Did you get any more mail for Mr. Miller?" he said.

Ha—a ploy known to every cop and mother. I could have told him the truth, I suppose, but I didn't trust him any more than I liked him. And I didn't like him at all. "No, Mr. Werner, I haven't received *any* mail for him, so I couldn't have received any *more* mail for him. Is that it?"

"No, I also wanted to tell you to keep the music down."

"Well, pounding on the wall pretty effectively communicated that to me the other night."

He squinched up his eyes a little, apparently not liking my tone. Can't say I cared for his either. Something perverse inside me then made me say, "I'll bet Jackson played his music a little too loud too. Am I right?"

He took a step toward me and I felt a cold chill at the malice on his face, though his words were mild. "No, he was quiet. Very quiet."

"The kind of guy who wouldn't scare the fish on a fishing trip?"

Now why did I have to say that? I should have turned and run to my apartment about four sentences prior. Sometimes I really feel like someone else is controlling my vocal cords. Stuff just comes out of my mouth and I can't stop it. I sounded argumentative and pissy, even to me. All I can say is I was sick of that guy trying to mess with me. Sometimes I just got so tired of people looking at me and then instantly dismissing me as someone of no consequence—I could practically see them ticking off the categories in their minds: female, young, plain, average, worthless, stupid...

Werner got very still after my fishing trip comment. If I had disliked the malice on his face before, the look I saw now was truly frightening. "What did you say? About a fishing trip?" His voice was low and menacing.

"Nothing," I said defensively, trying to be cool. "I just heard you two were planning a fishing trip before he took off. Common knowledge."

Common knowledge if you went to the library and looked up the paper from three months ago. I was sorely regretting this entire conversation and wanted only to retreat to my apartment. Or better yet, the Murdocks' apartment, across town from this psycho.

Werner was digesting my bald-faced lie and it looked like it was tough going. He took a step back and squinted up at me. I took the opportunity to move up the stairs a step.

"Yeah, well, you tell your friends at the Public Defender's office to stay out of police business, young lady. Keep your snotty nose out of it," he snarled.

I moved up another step, then turned and frankly ran up the rest of the stairs. My hand was shaking, but I got the key in the door and my butt in the apartment. I slammed the door shut and watched through the peephole. He never did come up the stairs, but I heard his car start and drive away a minute or so later.

My heart was pounding. What the hell was that all about? How did he know about my Public Defender connection? Had Terry gone ahead and made some calls to his contacts on the police force, even though I'd asked him not to? Why all this hostility and threats from Werner, and why now? Breathe, Heavenly, breathe. My instinct was to get out of there before he returned. I'd planned on heading over to Mona's anyhow since we were going to Dollar Night. She wouldn't mind if I showed up three hours early.

I was trying to be calm and rational, but the encounter with Werner had unnerved me. I still had my backpack over my shoulder and my keys in my hands. I checked out the peephole to make sure the Mercedes was still gone, then headed back downstairs to my car, stopping briefly at the mailbox to get my mail. I left the junk mail in there, but grabbed the sole piece of real mail, which was a Department of Motor Vehicles registration notice forwarded from my old apartment. Oh, yeah, probably should have told the DMV I moved. The yellow postal service sticker showed my new address. I shoved the envelope in the back pocket of my jeans.

I felt much better once I was in the Camaro and driving away. The guy was just a jerk, that was all. Maybe Terry had made a call and that somehow tipped Werner off. Another possibility also occurred to me—one of my occasional work duties was delivering subpoenas to the police department to call them as witnesses in Public Defender cases, which meant I wasn't entirely unknown there. God knows I saw plenty of cops at the courthouse every weekday and any one of them could have noticed me and Terry talking at lunch. Terry was supposedly super discreet, though.

In any event, I thought it wise to head over to Mona's and hang out there for the evening. I stopped on the way to get some dinner at a fast-food place. Dollar Night on an empty stomach was a bad idea.

I parked by the bowling alley. The soothing cacophony of balls striking pins wafted out the open double doors as I walked past to the apartment building. I noticed Freddy had set out a couple of white plastic patio furniture tables and matching chairs in front of his restaurant. That was new. Both tables sported brightly colored umbrellas from the beer distributor. Three guys speaking Spanish were drinking beer at a table about six feet from the Murdocks' front door. As I got closer, I realized one of them was Flaco.

He, like the other two, was clad in a paint-splattered white T-shirt and off-white overalls. Flaco laughed at something one of the other guys said and saw me when he tipped his head back for a sip of beer. He gave me one of those quick head jerks that means "hey" and I responded in kind.

As I pushed the intercom button for Chez Murdock, I was peripherally aware of them talking in Spanish just a few feet away. The intercom squawked at me. "Mona?" I said.

A blast of white noise was the only answer.

I tried pushing the button again and the damn thing went dead. Curses were upon my lips, but Flaco came to the rescue. "Can I let you in?" he said, appearing at my side in the doorway with keys in his hand.

"Thanks," I said gratefully.

He had just the slightest accent that made the most commonplace statement sound kind of sexy somehow. He smiled and gestured me in. As I crossed the threshold into the dim interior, I was very aware of the mere inches that separated us.

"You are friends with the girls upstairs, right?" he asked. "I'm Flaco Gutierrez. My aunt is the manager here."

"Heavenly Wilcox," I told him.

We shook hands briefly, me on the inside, him on the out. His grip was strong and warm. And dry, which was good, because nobody likes the jellyfish.

"Are you coming in?" I asked.

He still stood in the open doorway, the evening sun making a halo around his shadowy form. He shook his head wordlessly. I heard his buddies hooting and laughing in the background. One of them made obnoxious kissing noises. I felt a flash of hostility at all the male buddies in the world since time began. Jerks. My gratitude had turned to embarrassment. For no good reason, perhaps, except that painful self-consciousness was my habitual state in those days.

"Yeah, well, thanks," I said rather tersely, then shut the door on him.

As I climbed the stairs to the Murdocks', I felt the bass thumping from someone's stereo. Theirs, as it turned out. Of course. The door was locked, so I pounded on it with both fists, venting some of my irritation from the encounter with Flaco with a little sound and fury of my own. "Mona! Margo! It's me, Hev—let me in!"

The door flew inward and Journey flew outward at about ninety decibels. I stepped inside and saw Margo's back disappearing down the hall to my left toward the bathroom. Mona and Petey the guitar player were in the living room, singing along with Steve Perry, who was exhorting us to not stop believing. Mona had her hairbrush for a microphone, Petey a wooden spoon. That Journey album was one of our absolute favorites that year. As Petey broke into falsetto harmony, I joined them for the final chorus, grabbing a whisk from the kitchen for my mike. Way better than a wooden spoon.

The song was ending as Margo returned. As she turned the volume down on the stereo, she asked her older sister, "Does it bother you that Steve Perry can sing higher than you can and you're a girl?"

Belligerently, Mona instantly fired right back, "Does it bother you that your butt is bigger than your brain?"

We all paused to ponder this anatomical certainty. I cracked up first, then Petey, then Mona and finally Margo caved too, until we all had tears in our eyes. I took a seat at the counter and ate my burger and fries while the rest of them decided what to do for dinner. They, meaning Mona and Margo, decided on Chinese food at Freddy's before we headed off to the Mongol. Good thing I'd stopped for a burger, I thought. Petey's culinary thoughts and opinions were, of course, ignored on general principles. He always cleaned his plate no matter what was on it anyhow.

After the Murdocks had finished changing for the evening, the four of us trooped downstairs to the restaurant. I was wearing what I'd worn to work that day—black jeans, black flats and a short-sleeved, rayon blouse with a paisley print in turquoise and fuchsia on a white background. As usual, I would win no fashion award, but it was good enough for Dollar Night at the Moonglow.

There certainly wasn't a dress code—I think the San Tomas city charter prohibited such things. Everything from raggedy shorts and T-shirts to the baddest black leather was acceptable on Thursday nights. Now Friday and Saturday, you'd better look sharp if you wanted to be cool, but it seemed to be generally understood that Thursday nights were merely a tune-up for the weekend ahead. Some people were always looking to get laid any day of the week, but Dollar Nights had a more casual, hanging-with-your-friends kind of atmosphere.

Petey wore carefully ripped blue jeans, his biker boots and a bright blue muscle shirt which said "Peavey" on the front. He actually did have some muscles for a skinny guy— "guitar player body," Mona called it. He'd done his fingernails in black polish since the last time I'd seen him.

Mona herself was attired in a short, black, denim skirt with a gray pinstripe running through it and a red, boat-necked, three-quarter-sleeved cotton top with a big black question mark on the front. From her ears dangled different, but equally obnoxious earrings—one was a silver skull the size of a maraschino cherry and the other one...Upon closer inspection, the other one resembled nothing so much as a trout lure, but I kept that thought to myself. A gold stud resided in the third hole, which was a recent addition to her left ear. I never could remember what, if anything, left ear versus right ear meant, but Mona wouldn't have given a shit anyhow. From the age of seven, I had always admired how she did what she wanted and damned the consequences. I just didn't have it in me to live my life that way, not at seven or twenty-two. Constantly worrying about what other people thought totally sucked, though.

Fishnet stockings and red high-tops completed Mona's look that night. Her hair was spiked to perfection and pointing off in several different directions. Her makeup was heavy on the eyeliner. She'd told me once that her goal was to dress so that no matter where she was, people would think "that girl must be in a band." Mission accomplished.

Her sister Margo looked stunning as always, but she had the body to make a potato sack look good. She was in Princess Grace mode that summer, as I recall. Or was it Audrey Hepburn? I don't know. Somebody gorgeous from the sixties. Margo's light yellow sundress clung in all the right places and hung in all the right places. How the hell did she do that? No panty line either. (An obvious answer to that question presented itself, but nothing untoward was revealed through the lightweight woven fabric.) A simple strand of pearls and pearl earrings were her only adornment. Fake pearls, but so what? White leather sandals with narrow straps and three-inch heels shod her shapely feet.

Freddy was ecstatic to see us come in since the place was now devoid of customers. Was I relieved that Flaco had gone? I guess, maybe in the back of my mind, I'd thought he'd still be down there…Anyhow, Freddy rushed over with menus and greetings.

"Miss Margo *and* Miss Mona! And Miss Heavenly! I am honored to have you here."

His eyes flicked over Petey, but he either didn't know who he was or didn't care. Poor Petey—he seemed to have that kind of underwhelming effect on people. Fortunately, he rarely seemed aware of this.

Freddy seated us at our choice of table and presented the menus with a flourish. His wife appeared from the kitchen and greeted us with a torrent of friendly Chinese. She didn't speak much English, but we got the drift. Freddy waved her off to go get water and tea,

then took our orders, which was just a beer for me. Mrs. Freddy
returned with the non-alcoholic beverages before he'd finished.

I was next to Mona in the small, horseshoe-shaped, red
leatherette booth. Matched her high-tops nicely. Petey was
crammed in between her and Margo on the other side, but he
seemed to be enjoying that. Margo examined the mysterious bottle
of sauce found on each of Freddy's tables. The label was all in
Chinese, except for the cryptic sentence, "Let the meat." We still
hadn't figured that one out.

I told Mona of my latest encounter with Werner. She dipped a
fingernail painted in black nail polish into her ice water and sucked
on it thoughtfully as I finished the story.

"What a dickhead," was her only comment.

Petey, on her other side, reclaimed her attention with a band-
related question. Margo and I exchanged wan smiles in mutual
recognition of our never-ending exclusion from such weighty
matters. Margo and I didn't talk that much and never had, but (a)
Margo didn't talk that much to anyone, period and (b) since Mona
and I told each other everything, and Mona and Margo told each
other everything, it was kind of a moot point. We had all the same
information. We just didn't feel the need to discuss it much.

With no other customers to tend to, Freddy brought the food
quickly and the three of them dived in with gusto. Freddy handed
me a beer with a smile and a wagging forefinger, letting me know
he still hadn't given up on converting me to Chinese food one of
these days. For his sake, I hoped he'd find some other customers
sooner than that.

His restaurant was attractively decorated in red and black.
Chinese artwork on the walls added a classy touch. The food was
good too, per the Murdocks. I worried he'd chosen a bad location,
though. Two doors down from the bowling alley wasn't exactly
prime real estate.

The fortune cookie with my second beer was another dud—
"Open your eyes and follow your heart." Sappy drivel, I thought.

By prearrangement, Mona was going to spend the night at
my place since Margo had some kind of late night tryst planned.
Whether she was meeting her "date"—I have to use quotation
marks since the word meant something very different to Margo
than it did to me—at the Mongol was unclear, but there was no

point asking for details. Margo always played her cards close to her chest.

The other three elected me driver for the night, which was fine with me. When we finished dinner, Mona carefully stashed her backpack and her bass in the trunk of the Camaro since she couldn't stand to be parted from a musical instrument for twelve whole hours. It was a tight fit in the backseat for Petey and Margo, but the drive to the Mongol only took a few minutes.

The small parking lot behind the club always filled up quickly. We parked for free in a municipal lot just a block away and ambled over just after eight thirty. We would often not get to Dollar Night before ten o'clock, but apparently none of us had anything better to do that particular Thursday. I asked Petey who was opening. A speed metal trio from the university called Jalapeño Douche, he informed me.

"Catchy name, eh," I muttered to Margo as we followed Mona and Petey under the marquee toward the box office. Glancing upward, she caught the name on the sign and gave a small frisson of distaste. The other bands listed were Spawn of the Torment and Plan B.

We each paid our dollar and made it past the bouncer, though he lingered uncomfortably long over Petey's fake ID. Fortunately, as he glanced up to say something to Petey, he saw Margo there in her pale yellow dress and immediately forgot what he was about to say. He shoved the ID into Petey's chest without looking at him and motioned Margo forward eagerly. He was still looking after her as he gave my ID a cursory glance and waved me in without a word. Excuse the fuck out of me for not being Princess Grace, pal.

Ah, well, it was no use being mad at Margo—she couldn't help it anymore than any of the rest of us can help being what we are. Whatever that is.

The crowd was pretty thin that early on a Thursday night. The Mongol was rumored to have been a Quonset hut and a roller rink in previous incarnations. It was certainly big enough. As we entered, on the right was a room with several pool tables. On the left was the large front bar, done up in a Casablanca-ish motif. One could enter these areas without a ticket for the show.

The hallway narrowed to a second doorway, where a second bouncer was stationed at the entrance to the inner sanctum. You didn't need to show him ID, just your ticket. Having safely passed that final gatekeeper, our little group tromped on by the inner bar on the left, restrooms and coat check on the right, past the staircase that led to tables and the soundman's aerie on an upper level and finally down a few steps to the big dance floor.

Little tables adorned with the obligatory candles-in-the-red-thingy-with-string-on-it lined the walls. The big stage was at the end of this long rectangle, a good ten feet or so higher than the dance floor. The soundman was playing the English Beat at a moderate volume, echoing off the high ceiling.

Since we were there so early, we scored a table down by stage right and got to sit down for a while before the first band started at nine fifteen. Mona had been calm (for her) throughout dinner, but I could tell that now she was actually inside the club and in sight of the stage where her band would be playing in one short week, she was starting to freak. From similar past episodes, I knew she'd shortly start cycling between anticipatory exhilaration and anticipatory agony.

"Are any of these bands good tonight?" her non musical sister asked, coolly surveying the scattered crowd for anything worthy of her attention. Finding nothing, Margo glanced back at the three of us. "Well?" she demanded.

Mona ignored her—she was scanning for the waitress, so Petey jumped in. "The first band is Jalapeño Douche. They're speed metal with sort of a Latin edge. The drummer has a lot of killer percussion stuff. They're pretty cool. I heard 'em up at school a couple times."

Having flagged down the waitress and ordered the first pitcher of beer, Mona was now ready to interrupt this tale told by an idiot. "What? They suck, man! You must've been wasted if you thought they were good."

Petey mumbled something about one song being okay.

"Yeah, well, one song doesn't cut it, buddy. I can't believe those assholes get to play here before we do."

Yep, here went the agony part.

"Okay, fine, what about the second band?" asked Margo.

Petey and I glanced at Mona nervously. She hated the second band for at least three reasons, none of which were particularly compelling, but if Mona hated something, she really hated it. She was a great hater.

The first reason was their name, Spawn of the Torment—what the hell was that supposed to mean? (like "Bertha's Attic" was so intelligible to the illiterate masses) Second, they always sprinkled their sets with cheesy, popular, cover tunes to pander to the crowd. Which Bertha's Attic did, too, but not nearly as much as Spawn. Mona hated having to play songs written by other people, but considered it a necessary evil. It was a strategy that was certainly working well for Spawn of the Torment—we'd seen them at several gigs that year. Third and most heinously in Mona's opinion, the local newspaper's pop music critic had once described Spawn as a "richer, fuller, fleshed-out Bertha's Attic." (They had a top forty-type female singer who didn't play any instrument, plus a horn section.) The flames of Mona's ire, always easily stoked, burned white-hot when she'd read that review. She hated being compared to anyone else, favorably or unfavorably.

Since Margo had just seen their name on the marquee and certainly knew of her sister's feelings on the subject, I wondered if she'd brought it up just to mess with Mona. She was certainly capable of such behavior. They were both pretty mean to each other on a regular basis. A sister thing, I supposed.

For example, there was the there's-your-boyfriend "joke." Not that I thought it funny, but thankfully I was usually not the butt of it. It had started back in junior high school. Mona or Margo, upon espying a particularly inappropriate male would say to her sister, "Hey, Margo, (or Mona as the case might be), there's your boyfriend!" Particularly inappropriate males included winos, middle-aged men wearing black socks with Bermuda shorts and those tie-dyed, poorly groomed deadheads with whom San Tomas was so richly populated. Also known as "granolas" to the three of us. None of us even laughed at the "Hey, Mona, there's your boyfriend" line anymore, but perhaps it provided the two of them with a necessary outlet for their sibling rivalry.

I knew they loved each other, but family members sometimes reserve their coldest hostilities for each other. I was glad my brother J. D. and I didn't have that kind of a relationship—maybe because of our different genders, maybe because of the bigger gap in our ages. Or maybe because we weren't Murdocks.

Fortunately, it appeared Mona was continuing to ignore her sister for the moment. Petey and I followed suit. At least Mona liked the headlining band. Everybody loved Plan B that summer. They were starting to play some gigs up in the city, plus Monterey, San Jose and Sacramento, so they'd probably get too big for their britches pretty soon and desert San Tomas forever. Wasn't that everyone's goal? Except for those of us with no place else to go.

The club started to fill up a little. Jalapeño Douche's guitarist was on stage fiddling with his amp. The drummer took a seat behind his monster kit and the bass player appeared as well. With no fanfare, the English Beat suddenly cut off, the lights dimmed and a baritone voice said, "Ladies and gentlemen, please welcome Jalapeño Douche!"

They immediately launched into their first song. No one was dancing, but a handful of people stood widely scattered in ones and twos on the large dance floor, gazing up at the band. Petey was right, it was definitely speed metal with a Latin edge. Which meant it was very loud and furious, but the drummer was great. I kind of liked their first song, which must have been the good one Petey was talking about. The rest of the set was unfortunately marred by shrieking feedback the sound guy was unable to overcome. This was apparently the same house sound guy Bertha's Attic would be forced to use the following week, so that didn't bode well.

Mona and Petey went upstairs at some point to stand behind the soundman's area and see what he was up to. The waitress appeared midway through the set with four glasses and the pitcher, so I ended up buying. The band didn't pause much between their songs, so there was little opportunity to converse with Margo in the din, which I'm sure was fine with both of us. Despite the unrelenting barrage of sound and the murky shadows all around, I felt myself relax a little bit and unclench a few muscles I hadn't realized were still clenched. The encounter with Werner had been disturbing, no doubt. And I wasn't sure if I was more concerned by Jackson's disappearance or my growing obsession with the matter. Didn't I have anything better to do? Well, no. Not really. I sat back and sipped my beer in the thunderous, shrieking darkness.

The lights came back up with the conclusion of Jalapeño Douche's set. Halfhearted applause might have been in support of their musical talents, but was more likely for the cessation of the feedback. The English Beat came back on the PA (a welcome return to actual music) as Petey and Mona rejoined us.

"...and then I'll rip his fucking spleen out," finished Mona, apparently already plotting her revenge on the soundman in case he didn't shape up in the next week.

Petey nodded, amused, then looked past my shoulder at some new arrivals. "Hey, isn't that that guy?" he said to the three of us, rather undescriptively.

We all turned to see the ubiquitous Flaco, still in his paint-stained overalls and still with his buddies, come down the three stairs to the dance floor. They were walking right toward us, pint glasses in hand. Flaco appeared to laugh out loud when he saw us at our table. I instantly felt like a fool and realized I was sitting straight up and practically gawking at him. Good Lord, sometimes I wondered why they let me out in public. Hoping my blushing was at least partially concealed by the semidarkness, I quickly turned around and focused my attention on my beer glass. I felt the urge to squinch my eyes closed, but resisted. He would simply walk by with his friends and that would be that. No need to get all het up.

"Heavenly?"

There was a hand on my shoulder. There was a *hand* on my *shoulder*! Be cool, be cool, be cool. Jesus, what a moron I am. Look up, for God's sake. Smile. Say something. "Oh, hey, Flaco." I felt a thrill of dread in my stomach as I realized I had sounded exactly like Jan Brady. Except she never said, "Flaco." As I recall.

Flaco smiled at me, however, as if I were not a complete idiot. His friends had passed us by and taken up station at the foot of the stage. Flaco greeted the Murdocks and Petey. He took his hand off my shoulder when he reached forward to shake Petey's hand.

Turning back to me, he said, "Maybe we can dance later."

I nodded, smiled and said something intelligent like "uh-huh." He looked at me for one more long moment, smiled at the entire table and then moved on toward his friends. I watched him go. Nice butt, even in the overalls.

I glanced back at my companions. Oh, God. Here we go. Actually, Petey was guzzling his beer and completely oblivious. Mona and Margo, though, gazed at me piercingly with some most unnecessary astonishment.

"What?" I said indignantly. "Can't I talk to the guy?"

But Margo just nodded at me appraisingly and all Mona had to say was, "Hey, go for it, Hev."

The lights were already dimming again as Spawn of the Torment took the stage. They kicked off with Joan Jett's "I Love Rock 'n' Roll." Uninspired, I know, but a crowd-pleaser. And adding the horn section worked well, believe it or not. The dance floor started to fill up nicely. I glanced over where Flaco and his buddies had been, but didn't see any of them. Oh, well. The night was young. I could certainly wait for a cooler song to be our first song to dance to, right? If I even wanted to dance with him...

Spawn's lead singer wore a leather miniskirt, fishnet stockings and black Chuck Taylor high-tops. Which, unfortunately, was rather similar to Mona's outfit. I hoped she wouldn't notice. The singer had also dyed the tips of her hair hot pink, which the spotlights accented. Her top was sort of stretchy and rippy and glow-in-the-darky. Obviously something she had constructed herself. Well, anyhow, it showed enough cleavage to accomplish what she'd set out to accomplish. If she wasn't careful, bopping around like that, she'd pop one right on out.

The band shifted into one of their originals, a medium-tempo R&B song I liked (although I would never admit that to Mona). Something about "felt so good when I stopped." Cool horns too.

As more people came into the club, the dance floor was getting crowded. There were people dancing about two feet away from us. We all scooted our chairs closer around our rather tiny table to claim our territory as Spawn of the Torment segued into Joe Jackson's "I'm The Man." Which was a bit odd with a chick singing lead, but whatever. This was San Tomas, after all.

Two guys dressed like Mods descended on the table and took the Murdocks off to dance. Where the hell was Flaco anyway? You say you want to dance, then you just go off and disappear like an asshole...

Petey tried to say something to me over the din, but I couldn't hear a word. He stolidly chugged his brewski, looking a bit grim. I yelled, "What?" back at him, but read his lips just yelling, "What?" right back at me.

I waved him off and stood up to catch a glimpse of the band, ten feet above the crowd on the large stage. The horn section was boogie-ing along with the singer in a simple dance routine as the guitarist blazed through his solo. (They were taking a few liberties with Joe that night.)

I stood on my chair for a better look as they brought it home, the guitar player rocking till the very end when the drummer closed it with a single snare shot. The people up on the side balconies were all on their feet too. The dance floor erupted in applause, but the band had already started a slow one, not wanting to lose them.

I glanced back to my right toward the stairs and the bar, preparatory to stepping back down to the floor. Without meaning to, I looked right into the face of a man at the bar who was staring at me. He was thin, with a moustache, wearing glasses and a baseball cap. An average-looking guy. What was not average was the intense way he was surveying me.

A hand touched my elbow and I started. Oh. Finally! It was Flaco, helping me down from my perch. I forgot all about the guy at the bar staring at me. Some part of my brain realized the band was now playing "Magnet And Steel" by Walter Egan. A few years old, but still a goodie. I guessed Flaco had been waiting for a slow song. Just like a guy.

He leaned in as I stepped down and said, "Shall we dance?"

He still had his hand on my elbow. Some guys always have to have a hand on you like you wouldn't know to go without their direction. Ugh. Without a word, I slid my arm up until I could take his hand, then led him onto the dance floor, threading our way amongst couples in varying stages of clinch.

I spotted Margo with the taller Mod, but didn't see Mona anywhere. I let go of Flaco's hand and he immediately put it on the small of my back, guiding me toward an open spot. It felt okay to have his hand there, I guess, but it felt kind of weird too, like there was a camera on us or something. In reality, nobody was paying us any attention at all. Just my usual excessive level of self-awareness that I could never seem to turn off.

Reaching the open spot, I stopped and turned to him—he was closer than I had anticipated. His body was very warm. I hoped the paint was dry on the overalls, because it was going to be all over me. I took a big breath, which went in and out a little ragged. I slipped my hands around his shoulders, while his found my waist. We moved slowly in the near darkness. My face was near the juncture of his neck and right shoulder—fortunately, the snake tattoo was on the other side. He smelled like sun and wind and outdoors and a wee bit of turpentine. Not an unpleasant combination, although somewhat flammable. He felt bony and sweaty. Unfamiliar. Guys never felt the way I expected them to feel. I was glad our clinch wasn't any tighter than it was.

The song was ending. I tilted my head back to look into his eyes. His hands slid up my back, then returned to my waist. His eyes gleamed, half-seen in the dim light. He hadn't spoken while we were dancing, but that didn't bother me. I hadn't said anything either, but I was going with my strength.

He reached up and gently pulled my hands from around his neck, then gathered them in his. Was that a tingle I felt? Other girls always talked about tingling. I felt...something, but I wasn't sure it qualified as official tingling. Flaco leaned in to say something in my ear.

"I have to go," were his words.

He raised my left hand to his lips and kissed my palm. That sounds better than it felt, actually. As in it sounds romantic until you have to wipe your hand on your pants to get rid of the spit. He leaned in and kissed me on the cheek. And then he left!

The son of a bitch just turned and walked out like fucking Zorro or somebody without another word. I couldn't believe it! There I was, having a total romantic moment *by myself*! He didn't even ask me for my number or anything. I was shocked and amazed, looking where he'd gone through the crowd like Moses through the Red Sea. The girl in the nearest couple on the dance floor gave me a sympathetic look, which almost earned her a smack upside the head. I felt like Prince Charming without Cinderella at a minute past midnight, except I don't remember him being so pissed. And I was supposed to be Cinderella, not the prince, right?

Fuck. And now I had to go back to the table with all my friends. Shit. People were starting to bump into me as they milled about on the dance floor awaiting the next song. The lead singer was saying something to the crowd as the guitarist quickly retuned his Les Paul. I finally gathered my wits and made my way back to the table, now seriously overcrowded by the arrival of the rest of the band. I didn't even have a chair to return to. Great. Just fucking great.

I think I must have mouthed those last three words as I approached the table, because Handsome Pete the drummer stood up and gave me his chair with a questioning look. I started to thank him as I sat down, but his attention had already been diverted by the passage of some hot chicks in full meat market mode. He happily wandered off after them without a backward glance.

LeClaire was laughing with Petey over something. Margo hadn't returned to the table yet. Which left Mona, Mod-free, staring directly at me. Kind of like that weird guy at the bar had been. I glanced over at the bar, but couldn't see anything through all the people. Turning back to the table, I saw Mona had picked up her chair and was coming around to sit next to me.

The band on stage kicked into another original, announced by the singer as "Dance Like You Mean It." The crowd gladly complied. The room temperature had risen noticeably since we'd arrived.

I'd left a beer behind, but I had no clue as to which half-empty glass on the table was mine and I really didn't want anybody else's backwash. The pitcher was empty too. Shit. I'd have to wait for the waitress to swoop by again or brave the bar.

Mona sidled up to me with her chair, then parked her skinny patoot in it. Petey must have told her about Flaco asking me to dance. "So?" Her imperative demanded information from me.

To tell the truth, I didn't know whether I should be fuming or exhilarated. I told her what had happened, from him helping me off my chair to him walking out.

"Damn, Hev," she said in a commiserating shout, as normal conversational tones were precluded by the volume of the band. "He didn't even ask for your number?" she asked.

I shook my head.

"He didn't even kiss you?"

"Well, shit, you don't have to scream it to the world!" I hollered back at her. "And he kissed my cheek!" I added defensively.

Mona gave a wordless "eh" shrug. The band was wrapping up a lengthy jam sequence and she turned her attention to the singer who was returning to the mike for the final chorus:

You better dance like you mean it
I already seen it
Your feet better be sincere.

Margo finally came back with her smirking Mod in tow, but ditched him as she sat down rather unsteadily on her sister's lap in the absence of an unoccupied chair. She checked out the assorted beer glasses much as I had. She picked one up, but eyed it uncertainly.

"Is that yours, Mars?" her sister asked in the relative quiet between the end of the last song and the start of the next, which was going to be Spawn of the Torment's final number according to the lead singer's banter.

"I do not believe so," Margo replied.

Mona and I exchanged a look—Margo's elocution always got precise when she smoked pot. No doubt she'd been in the parking lot with some guy sharing a joint. Margo had tried just about every drug that came our way in San Tomas: marijuana, magic mushrooms, hashish, acid on special occasions, sometimes a little coke if somebody offered her some. No heroin, thank goodness. And this was before crack. I don't think she ever did any crank. God knows both Murdock sisters had enough natural energy that amphetamines didn't beckon.

Margo did drugs the way she did sex, never giving it a thought beyond the passing moment of pleasure, but her sister Mona had taken the opposite route and did no drugs at all. Being the older sister, perhaps her vague memories of her mother, who had died from drugs, steered her in this matter.

For some reason I could never adequately explain to myself or anyone else, I just never felt like it was right for me to do drugs either. I didn't care if others did them, but a voice in my head always said "Nope" when it was my turn. It wasn't even a "No!"—just a laconic "Nope." I'm not sure where that came from since I drank like a fish in those days. Maybe it was one of those "child of hippies" things—it's hard to find things to rebel against when your parents are flower children.

Anyhow (and speaking of fish), since I definitely needed a beer right then, I got up to go to the bar. Mona pushed Margo off her lap into my empty chair and came with me, snagging a twenty dollar bill from Petey on the way.

"What was up with your Mod?" I asked Mona as we shouldered our way through the crowd.

"Psssh," was her disparaging response. "Couldn't even dance."

Just between you and me, I'd wondered if the guy who'd asked Margo to dance had cajoled his buddy into asking Mona so he wouldn't have to approach the table (and Margo) alone. She had that kind of effect on guys. Sometimes, one brave guy would come up alone and ask Margo to dance. If she turned him down, he'd turn to me and Mona and say something like, "Well, does one of you want to dance?" Note to guys everywhere: not an effective technique!

Margo the Beauteous, of course, always seemed to find guys at Dollar Night to dance with, to buy her drinks, to get her stoned, to take home and sleep with if she was in the mood. Mona and I, although ostensibly there to find guys as well, had little to no success in that area. Oh, well, I thought. Between Flaco and Jackson and Werner, I had too many man-related emotions swirling around my head, so I determined to just enjoy the rest of the evening as best I could on a limited budget.

At the bar, I glanced curiously up and down the row of stools to see if the guy who'd been staring at me was still there, but didn't see him. Mona was right behind me, in fact I could feel her pointy little chin pressed into my right shoulder blade in the crush of the crowd. Ow. Only the barstool in front of me kept me from pitching headfirst into the bar. The bartender saw me and I pantomimed "two pitchers" to him.

Back at the table, a good-looking guy was taking Margo off to dance. Handsome Pete was nowhere to be seen, but Petey got Mona to dance with him as soon as she set down her pitcher. That left me and LeClaire, but some guy she knew appeared and whisked her away too. Man, my self-esteem was taking a beating that night. Fine, I'd just hang here with my two brand-new pitchers of beer. Except I still didn't know which glass was mine. Oh, well, we were all friends and hopefully no one had anything too communicable.

I selected one that could have been mine, dumped what was left in it into another glass that had a wadded up napkin jammed in it and poured myself a fresh beer. That was, of course, when I realized I had to pee, but I couldn't desert the table or the pitchers since I was the only one there. Damn it.

Spawn of the Torment was giving it all they had. The dance floor was packed. Some girls were dancing together near our table at the perimeter of the crowd, but that was a common sight at the Mongol. Sometimes the Murdocks and I got out there and danced with each other if we liked the song and there were no guys to dance with. Not a big deal in San Tomas, although I wouldn't have done it with anyone other than my lifelong friends. I wouldn't want anyone to get the wrong idea.

A really gross-looking guy popped into my field of vision and asked me to dance. I gave him a small smile, but shook my head no. The song was obviously almost over anyhow, plus I couldn't leave the table, plus he was really gross. Poor thing. On the other hand, everywhere I went, I saw really gross-looking people in couples, so maybe I should spend my sympathy on someone more deserving. Like me. Darn that Flaco, getting my hopes up and dashing them. What the hell was that all about?

Thank God the song was over and everybody was coming back to the table. The lights came back up. The sound guy put on David Lindley's *El Rayo-X* album—excellent choice. The guys started pouring everybody a new beer and the gals all set out for the restroom. About time, but now we had to face the interminable wait in line that was a certainty between bands. Argh.

Mona, Margo, LeClaire and I added ourselves to the queue. LeClaire and Mona were dissecting Spawn of the Torment's performance, song selection, wardrobe and every other detail. Margo still looked stoned and appeared to be mesmerized by the rhinestone hairpiece on the back of the head of the girl in front of her. The air was thick with the conversations of the women around us, many of them heavily made up and dressed to kill. Some, though, were as casual as I was and there were a few looking downright ragtag in jeans and T-shirts. There was, of course, no line at the adjoining men's room and guys were going in and out of there as quick as could be. Someday, female architects and plumbers will rule the world and there will actually be the right proportion of women's toilets to men's in public places.

We finally breached the entrance. Much floofing of hair and touching up of cosmetics was in progress within. As usual, in the presence of many other women, most of whom seemed to know exactly what they were doing, I felt anxious and out of place. It was a major, if temporary, relief to shut the door on the stall and have a moment of privacy. If you can call peeing in a room jammed with about fifty other people privacy. Outside, I found only Mona waiting for me. Margo and LeClaire would need floof time.

We were at the foot of the stairs that led to the balcony where the soundman was. All kinds of people were passing by us, heading for the bar, the bathrooms, the dance floor. Margo eventually emerged from the little girls' room, looking radiant in her pale yellow dress and red hair. Mona asked her where LeClaire was.

Margo, laughing, said, "She's cutting some girl's hair in there for five bucks. She's got a whole clinic going on."

Mona nodded approvingly at this show of entrepreneurship. I glanced up the stairs again as a surge of people started down. Uh-oh. The Staring Man. His eyes flicked past me, though and he walked right on by without making further eye contact. Maybe he hadn't been staring at me at all, maybe he'd been looking at someone behind me. Whatever. Sometimes I wondered what it would be like to be invisible. Sometimes I thought I already was.

Even though the headlining band wasn't playing yet, there were quite a few people on the floor, either dancing to the music on the PA system or making sure they had a good spot for when the band came on. We sat back down at our table, borrowing some unused chairs from adjacent tables so everybody had a seat.

Cocktail waitresses hurried to fill their orders before Plan B took the stage. Mona had her bandmates in a huddle off to the side, discussing strategy for next week. As "Your Old Lady" ended, the crowd on the dance floor stilled for a moment and I saw a sturdy figure forging her way through the dancers toward our table. It was Ashley, my downstairs neighbor. Her version of Dollar Night fashion was her favorite fatigue pants, black and white checked Vans and a Siouxsie & the Banshees T-shirt with the sleeves rolled up to more prominently display her tattoos. Her hair was spiked and her earlobes glittered with a diverse array of studs, hoops and dangly earrings. She was pulling along a much smaller and giggling girl by the hand. They seemed to be headed for the door. They passed within three feet of the table, but thankfully didn't notice us. In their wake, however, sauntered Jules, checking out the crowd between sips of her beer.

She looked a hell of lot cuter than her roommate in her white jeans, white Keds and a peach Ocean Pacific tank top with some kind of surf design silk-screened on it. Her gaze fell on Margo first, who was lighting a cigarette from the candle thingy on the table. As if feeling my eyes upon her, Jules turned her glance on me next. The small smile playing about her lips grew wider as her eyes met mine. She held up a hand in greeting, which I returned. She slipped into Mona's empty chair between me and Margo as the soundman changed gears again, switching Mr. Lindley for a Stevie Nicks/Don Henley duet I particularly enjoyed. Her thigh brushed mine when she sat down and I eased back a little to give her room. She leaned in to speak.

"Hey," she said with a quizzical grin. "I thought I might see you here."

"Why is that?" I asked, although it was a safe bet to find anyone in their twenties in San Tomas on a Thursday night at the Mongol.

"Ash says your friend Mona is quite the musician. She said she's seen her band up at school."

"What's she studying?" I asked, just to say something.

"Oh, she's not in school. She just hangs with me up there sometimes. She's a cashier at Shopper's Bend," she said, mentioning a popular local grocery store named for its location in the "bend" of a major street as it ran alongside the river. In another town, Ashley's appearance might have precluded her from being hired for a job in the public eye, but this was San Tomas. The other cashiers probably had Mohawks. Or were nudists.

"Oh," I said astutely. Her perfume was subtle and nothing exotic. Which was good—I hated getting a noseful of someone's heavy musk or cloyingly sweet scent. Hers was more natural, almost like a hint of peach. Or maybe I imagined that because of the color of her shirt.

"I go to UCST, though," Jules said. "Computer science major, believe it or not."

She laughed, glancing at me through her lashes as she tilted her head back to take a sip of beer. Her eyes were an interesting shade of blue, only a bit darker than the aquamarine earrings she wore. I didn't know why I'd gone so tongue-tied. For some reason, I couldn't think of anything to say to her. I smiled and tried to mask my confusion by drinking deeply of my beer. In the background, Don Henley was singing something about knowing he'd never want to leave.

"So do you want to dance?" she said.

I thought I must have heard her wrong. "Excuse me?"

"You look like you're enjoying the song—I thought you might want to dance," she said, that smile playing on her lips again.

"Yeah, right," I laughed. I mean, sure, there were girls dancing together, but I didn't want to be one of them. I certainly wasn't going to slow dance with Jules at the Mongol in front of God and everybody. She had to be making a joke.

Mona sat down across from me and grabbed her beer. Jules leaned back. Mona noticed her as she wiped her mouth with the back of her hand. "Hey, Jules," she said. "Say, is Ashley here?" She looked around for her new favorite trombone player.

"No," Jules said. "She just left. I've got to be going too." She stood.

Mona said, "You're gonna miss Plan B?"

She was shocked. Missing the headliner on Dollar Night was unthinkable to Mona. But Jules said she had an early class. She said, "See ya," to both of us rather abruptly and walked out quickly toward the exit.

"That was weird," Mona said to me.

"What?" I said sharply. I hoped she hadn't heard Jules ask me to dance—I would never hear the end of that.

"Them leaving before the headliner," she said, looking at me strangely. "What are you so jumpy about?"

"Nothing," I said.

She shrugged and turned away, talking to LeClaire about their side project idea. I had to shrug too. Maybe Jules was just fooling around—people say strange things when they're drinking.

The lights dropped and the announcer told us to welcome Plan B, which the crowd did enthusiastically. The rest of the night passed like any other Thursday at the Mongol. Although I fought it, I felt myself slipping into a bit of a Flaco-induced funk. I felt foolish, like he'd played a trick on me somehow. I kept trying to shake it off, only to return to it in my mind again and again. Was I just doomed to be a loser?

And that weirdness with Jules hadn't helped any either. At least I didn't literally cry in my beer. I danced with Petey a couple of times, once with Handsome Pete, plus with a couple other anonymous guys who asked. The band was hot and the night was hot. If nothing else, I must have lost at least two pounds from sweating. By one forty-five, the last of the encores was done and the Mongol staff was shooing everybody out. The night air felt incredibly clean and crisp after the fug of the club, even though it was still unnaturally humid and warm outside.

It was two a.m. when we finally left the Moonglow. The others had parked in the same lot I had, so we walked over there as a group, the band engaged in a heated discussion of the soundman's many moral and mental defects. Finally, we said our good nights. LeClaire drove off erratically in her noisy rattletrap of an orange Karmann Ghia and the two Petes headed back to campus in Pete-the-drummer's pickup.

There was no traffic and every light was green or blinking yellow as Mona, Margo and I quickly crossed the sleeping town in my Camaro. We dropped Margo off first, then headed for my place. With the usual post-Moonglow ringing in my ears and the rush of sticky air through my window, I almost felt as if I'd gone temporarily deaf. Mona slumped in the passenger seat, silent for a moment, then began her usual routine of ransacking my glove compartment for a tape worthy of her attention. I hoped I hadn't left Christopher Cross in there. I would suffer horribly for that violation. She settled on Eric Clapton's *Slowhand* album and turned it on low. All seemed quiet at the beach, but about two blocks from my apartment I saw ominous blue lights flashing. I glanced over at Mona. Eyebrows raised, she looked back at me.

"Hope it's not..." she started, but then faltered as we pulled up to see no less than six cop cars parked around my building.

Mona reached out and turned the music off, her eyes wide. None of the cop cars were actually in my driveway, but it was blocked by a large white van with the county seal on its door. Several uniformed and plainclothes officers stood around in various attitudes of interest. Two were crouched down near Werner's closed garage door, shining flashlights on something. I could see several of the neighbors out on their porches or balconies soaking up the free drama. Nothing like a little tragedy to bring out that community spirit. A cop was talking to Jules and Ashley, who were standing outside the open door to their lighted apartment. As I watched, the two girls went back into their apartment, closing the door behind them.

I hesitated in the intersection. I obviously couldn't park in my garage or driveway. Third Street was essentially blocked by all the official vehicles. Ashley's car was in her parking spot, not that I would dare to park there anyhow. Two of the men who'd been standing near the cops on the driveway went around to the back of the van and pulled out a stretcher. A uniformed police officer strode up to my car and managed to shine his very large flashlight directly into my retinas.

"Arrrrrggghhh," I said, throwing up my hands in front of my eyes.

"Move along, people," he said in a tone that brooked no discussion.

Except to Mona, who was always ready to discuss anything. "Hey, man, she lives here! What's going on?" she said pugnaciously.

"You live here?" he said to me, still blinding me with eight D batteries. "Let's see some ID."

I squirmed around in my seat and withdrew my driver's license from the back right pocket of my jeans. Averting my gaze, I gave it to him while I awaited the return of my vision. While he examined my ID, I realized (duh) it still showed my old address. I squirmed around the other way and pulled the unopened DMV notice from my back left pocket. He was still studying my driver's license like he'd never seen one before in his life.

"I just moved here," I explained, handing him the envelope. "Here's some mail showing the new address."

He was a big muscle-bound guy with bulging biceps and a crew cut. His body language underwent a shift as an older guy in a suit came over. "What's up, Pacheco?" the older guy said.

"Oh, Lieutenant Stokes, she says she lives here. Here's her ID and stuff." He shoveled my license and mail into Stokes's hands, who examined them in the light from Pacheco's flashlight. He bent down into my window.

"Why don't you ladies pull over and park right there?" He pointed to the small, scruffy lawn in front of the building.

"That's my driveway and garage right there, sir," I offered. As if they'd let me park in a crime scene. I'm always saying totally stupid things to authority figures.

Stokes shook his head and pointed again, emphatically. "Park over there," he said.

As I complied, I said to Mona, who was all agog, "Landlord's gonna love me parking on the grass."

She looked like she was having the time of her life. Sometimes she really bugged me. I felt like I was going to throw up—a knot of anxiety and dread had formed in the pit of my stomach. I hadn't clearly seen what was beside Werner's garage door, but it was bigger than a breadbox. About the same size as Werner, actually. I guess it could have been the dog, but I didn't think they'd send six police cars for that.

I parked the Camaro and killed the engine and lights. Stokes and a buddy were right there to let us out of the car. Speaking of the dog, I could hear his muffled barking coming from Werner's apartment. He sounded frantic to get out.

"Kinda late, ain't it?" the buddy asked. His badge identified him as Detective Grausteiner.

It was still pretty warm, but I shivered as I stepped out of the Camaro. I could smell the ocean.

"We were at a club," piped up Mona.

Stokes turned to her. "Let's see your ID, miss."

Mona wasn't carrying any purse or bag. Her clothes had no pockets. Turning away from the three of us for a moment, she appeared to suffer a minor convulsion. Turning back with a smirk on her face, she produced her driver's license.

"Mona M. Murdock," read Stokes. "You gir—uh, women go to UCST?"

"No, sir," I said nervously. Why did I always have to sound totally guilty when I talked to cops? I hadn't done anything. "I work at the Public Defender's office and Mona's a musician. I just moved in here last week. Was somebody...hurt?" My voice trailed off with the last sentence.

Grausteiner snorted. "Yeah, somebody was hurt, you might say."

Stokes made a small hand gesture which had the effect of stopping Grausteiner from whatever he was going to say next. "How well do you know your neighbor, Miss Wilcox?"

"Mr. Werner, you mean?"

"Right, Mr. Werner."

Swallowing, I stole another glance toward the garage door where the two guys from the white van were now taking flash pictures. In the bursts of light, I could make out a black hump...a still figure lying facedown in a puddle...But it hadn't rained...

"Miss Wilcox?"

"Oh. Well. I just moved in. I mean, I met the guy, but I didn't really know him or anything. He just, you know, lived next door. You know?"

After a pause, both men nodded and exchanged a glance. Grausteiner popped his gum.

Stokes said, "Well, I'm sorry to tell you this, ladies, but Mr. Werner's dead. Looks like the garage door came down on his skull."

Mona jumped a little bit, no doubt remembering just how close my garage door had recently come to her skull. I felt like my entire body was starting to go numb.

Stokes went on, "Appears to be an accident. Did you know he used to be on the force?"

Mona said, "I know he was a—"

I had a sudden sense the next word to come out was going to be "a-hole" so I spoke up quickly, cutting her off. "Yeah, somebody mentioned to me that he was an ex-policeman. Did anybody see what happened?"

Grausteiner, not answering my question, said, "A late night jogger phoned it in about an hour ago. But you ladies weren't here then, were you?"

"God, how awful," I said, as Mona shook her head "no" in response to Grausteiner's query. I hugged my arms around myself. I was feeling colder and sicker with each passing moment. First the threatening mail, now a dead body. Great new apartment, Hev. Way to pick 'em.

Stokes reached into a pocket and withdrew two business cards. Handing one to me and one to Mona, he said, "We might want to talk with you again. Just routine. Officer Pacheco will take down your home and work numbers, if you don't mind. Thanks for your cooperation, ladies." He turned and walked back to the driveway, conferring there with one of the white van guys.

Grausteiner gave us a nasty grin, popped his gum again, then followed his partner. The headlights of the van came on. The stretcher was being loaded into it. I did not want to see what was going on, so I turned away toward the ocean and took a few deep, cleansing breaths.

Mona grabbed my arm. "Holy shit, Hev! Can you believe this?"

For a moment, I couldn't speak and amazingly, I felt the sting of tears. I didn't even like the old bastard, yet here I was feeling sorry he was dead. The suddenness of it was scary—a few hours ago he was here bitching at me, now he was erased. Shaking off my emotions and Mona's grasp, I took a step and leaned against the side of the Camaro. I realized my left hand really hurt and slowly unclenched it from my keys. I rubbed the palm of that hand against my thigh.

Pacheco came up with a little notebook. There were enough headlights on now so he didn't have to use Satan's Flashlight. He handed back our IDs and my DMV mail, evidently having copied down some of the information after Stokes returned them to him. He asked both of us a few more questions, got our phone numbers, then said we were free to go. I turned toward the stairs, but Mona had one more question of her own.

"What about the guy's dog?" I heard her say as I trudged wearily upstairs.

Pacheco told her some of the cops were going to look after it. Maybe one of them would adopt it, he said.

Mona ran and got her bass and our backpacks out of the car and locked the doors. I opened the apartment door and turned on the light. As Mona came in, the clock on top of the TV said it was just shy of three a.m. I felt incredibly tired. I told Mona I'd see her in the morning. She asked me if I was okay. I told her I was. I heard her singing quietly to herself and getting settled in the living room as I lay down on the bed, fully clothed.

CHAPTER EIGHT

Friday

I awoke in the exact same position four hours later. I felt like crap. Through the closed door connecting the bedroom to the living room, I could hear Mona playing her electric bass acoustically. Either she had just written the worst song ever or she was doing fingering exercises. The slapping, rhythmic sound was sort of soothing. What was not soothing was the fact that I now had to get up and go to work.

I took a long shower and brushed my teeth. It felt like I was moving in slow motion, but I couldn't summon up any energy. I found myself standing in front of my open closet, dully staring at my clothes, unable to make a decision. Finally, I dressed all in black, apropos to my mood, and went out to the living room. Mona had apparently never gone to sleep. She was often fired up after a gig (hers or someone else's) and would stay up all night playing and composing. By the crumpled pieces of paper at her feet, I knew she'd been trying to write.

"Hey," I said.

"Hey," she replied without looking up, fingers continuing to move. "Time for work?"

"Yeah, you want a ride?"

She looked up at me then, still playing. She looked tired, with dark circles under her eyes, but somehow still fresher than the reflection I'd just seen in the bathroom mirror. Sometimes four hours of sleep is worse than none.

"I think I'll just hang here for a while, okay? I'm in the middle of something and I don't want to lose the flow. I'll catch a ride with Margo or whatever later."

Her sister had a spare key to the Monamobile.

"Okay, just lock the door when you leave, all right?"

She nodded while rolling her eyes in a nonverbal "duh," still mostly focused on her bass. She knew I was neither a breakfast nor a morning person, so my total lack of hospitality was the norm. I grabbed a cold Coke, my keys and my backpack and left without another word. Both my stomach and my people skills would awaken around nine thirty—until then, it was best not to engage me in conversation. Too bad work started so damn early. Fortunately, graciousness and a sunny attitude were completely lost on many of the Public Defender's clients. Turned out lots of crack addicts and hookers weren't morning people, either.

The Camaro's tires spun a bit coming off the sandy "lawn," but I pulled out without too much trouble. I avoided looking over at the driveway. I tried to focus on the road and drive carefully. But my mind kept returning with little jolts to the events of the night before. Werner was dead. I didn't really know what to do with that information. The cops said it was an accident, so it wasn't like I needed to fear random acts of violence in my new neighborhood. I hardly knew the man and hadn't liked him anyhow, so no grieving seemed required. It was just weird. I had never known anyone who had died. I couldn't get my brain around it, so I decided to push it to the back and try not to think about it. Let my subconscious work on it instead.

I was eleven minutes late to work, which earned me a reproachful glare from Stephanie, who was (of course) standing at the front desk staring directly at the front door as I walked in. "Sorry, I'll make it up," I said to her as I headed for my little corner of solitude.

I did the calendar and made the morning mail run, then worked on the filing in a desultory and uninspired fashion. Sometimes I could get into the Zen of it and sometimes not. I ate lunch alone in the courthouse cafeteria. Morbid parallels between eating by myself in a room filled with strangers and the fact that we all die alone—sometimes in the dark of night on a cold cement driveway—hovered at the back of my mind, but I drowned them out by crunching on my standard BLT and some Fritos extra noisily.

I covered the phones that afternoon which I hated since it always entailed getting yelled at by some irate person. The Public Defender's customer base was a cranky bunch as a rule. I explained to several callers in a row that, yes, it was likely a bench warrant would be issued if they failed to appear in court as scheduled.

"But I have a cold," insisted one astonished and self-righteous client, who could not believe his personal time was being so infringed upon. Could the judge really be so monstrously unfair as to expect him to show when he was wracked with sniffles?

I brought his information up on the computer screen—a wife-beater. The monumental self-importance and irresponsibility of criminals never failed to amaze me. Such vanity—and so little reason for it. The one common characteristic they all shared, from speeders to murderers, was an overweening belief that they were more important than anybody else on the face of the earth and the rules should not apply to them. I knew I would make a terrible crook, as I was constantly plagued by the nagging feeling that there were many people more important than I. It's not that I was so unworthy, just that I didn't seem to be making much of a dent in the world so far. Ah, well, crime—another career option shot.

The wife-beater wanted to leave a message for his attorney—Carmen, as it turned out. She'd probably get him off and he could go back to his normal routine of collecting unemployment, scratching himself and kicking the shit out of his spouse. If I ever went to law school (not that I ever would), I would definitely have to be a prosecutor, not a defense attorney. I don't know how the Public Defender's lawyers did it. In theory, it was nice to think everyone deserved a vigorous defense, but in practice, I thought the world would be a better place if most of our clients were lined up and shot.

In this sour mood, I limped through the long afternoon. I got a paper cut from my message pad which didn't help. Plus, as much as I was trying not to think about it, I couldn't help but revisit the events of the past night. Unbelievable. First, the guy who lived in my apartment disappears, then the next door neighbor gets killed by the garage door. Maybe I should just move in with the Murdocks, I thought, before the bad luck spread to me. It all just seemed like too damn big of a coincidence.

Maybe it's not a coincidence, the little voice in my brain said.

"...venly—Heavenly," Stephanie was saying from her doorway peevishly.

"Oh, sorry, Stephanie, what?"

"I was just saying I need to leave early today, so can you and Tasha handle it on your own after Ethel goes home at four?"

It was already quarter of four. In my peripheral vision, I saw Tasha pause in the main office area. I glanced over at her and we exchanged a split-second, deadpan, deeply meaningful look. Smoothly glancing back to Stephanie, I assured her we'd be just fine and wished her a good weekend. I even pasted on a big goofy smile at the end just to assure her of my pure intentions. I don't know if she bought it, but she packed up her purse and gave some last-minute instructions to Ethel about some motion due in superior court Monday morning. She signed my timecard for the temp agency as she left. Shortly thereafter, it was time for Ethel to depart. As the door swung closed behind her considerable backside, I got up from my desk and joined Tasha at the front.

The phones had mostly stopped ringing, as they sometimes did on Friday afternoons. I guess the crooks were all getting ready for the weekend too. There were no customers in our little lobby either, so it was dead quiet. At four o'clock on a Friday, many of the attorneys had already split as well. On the rare occasions when Stephanie left us mice in charge, Tasha and I liked to play a little game. A little game called Who's Going Home Next?

She said, "So, what's it gonna be, Hev? Rock, Scissors, Paper? Arm wrestling? Obscure State Capitals?"

The hell of it was, Tasha always won. I'm such a bonehead. Why did I even play when I always lost? I guess there was always that slim chance that this would be the time. Rock, Scissors, Paper had never been my game, however. Arm wrestling was out too. Although slim, Tasha was built—she could kick my butt up and down the stairs any day of the week. Obscure State Capitals was enticing, but I always fucked up the Dakotas. And Tasha knew it. (Pierre? Bismarck? Pierre? Bismarck?)

"How about we just flip a coin?" I said.

"How about I just leave now," she disdainfully replied, "seeing as how you always be losing?" She threw in a little head jerk too, with "always." Not the most gracious of competitors, our Tasha.

"Okay, okay, okay," I said, "just give me a second to think…"

Her response was cut off by the appearance of Leo, who had lumbered down the hall unnoticed while we bantered.

"Fridge Wars?" she said to me under her breath, then turned around quickly to Leo and said, "Why, Leo, honey, did you get that call for you on line two?"

The line two light was not blinking or even glowing, but Leo would never figure that out. "Who is it?" he asked cautiously. God forbid it might be a client asking him to do some work on a Friday afternoon.

"I believe it was a lady, isn't that what you said, Heavenly?"

She caught me off guard. I was still weighing the advantages and disadvantages of Fridge Wars. This game consisted of having to eat a spoonful of the grossest thing we could find in the fridge at the end of the hall. Whoever could eat the most spoonfuls won. As the attorneys were responsible for cleaning the fridge, it never got cleaned except when it was Carmen's week. Thus, month-old yogurt, moldy pasta and cottage cheese that used to be milk were the norm. Tasha, damn her, had a cast-iron stomach to go along with her rocklike muscles and pathological liar tendencies. I'm telling you, the girl was practically invincible.

First, we had to get rid of Leo, though. I said to him, "Oh, uh, yeah, Leo, I think it's that court reporter from Judge Mendelssohn's courtroom? What's her name, uh…"

"Yvonne?" he asked with a slight intake of air.

I actually felt kind of bad seeing that little uprush of hope in his bloodshot eyes. The whole office knew he had the hots for her. I thought she was a hard-faced babe who looked like she could match him olive-for-olive on vodka martinis, but maybe that's love. He was already tottering back down the hall to take the (phantom) call in private. Tasha and I knew we had at least two and a half minutes before he'd resurface, complaining about the vagaries of our impenetrable phone system.

"Hurry up, Hev—make up your mind!" Tasha told me.

It was already four minutes past the hour. The sweep hand steadily ticked away the waning seconds of Friday afternoon. "Okay, okay...uh...fuck."

I tried to think quickly. I always got rattled too easily during Who's Going Home Next? All right. What could I best Tasha at? A dare to lick the dust off one of the fake ficus leaves in the lobby? No, no, I had sworn to myself no more licking after that last time. Crack open a window, climb up to the roof via the outside fire escape and remove a major article of clothing? Nope, that might get at least one of us fired. Tasha tapped her pencil impatiently on the front counter.

Leo must have been having a really good day, because he was already walking back up the hall. "Hey, there was no call on line two," he said aggrievedly.

"I'm sorry, baby, she must have hung up," Tasha told him with the utmost sympathy and sincerity.

"Yeah, well..." he mumbled grumpily. "Anyhow, what I was going to say to you girls before was, why don't you take off? I can cover the phones."

Tasha and I exchanged amazed/grateful looks before hastily thanking him and bolting for the door as quickly as we could turn off our typewriters and computers and grab our bags. The outside world seemed especially beautiful and benevolent prior to five p.m. on a Friday. God bless all occasional purveyors of good deeds, regardless of their drinking habits, tie stains and other shortcomings.

It was great to be home so early, especially after a particularly trying week. As I tossed my keys on top of my bedroom dresser, I saw Stokes's card there, where I'd put it the night before. I gave a little shudder as the image of the garage door coming down on Werner's head surged through my brain again. I shook myself mentally and tried to put it out of my mind. It was Friday, for gosh sakes. I couldn't imagine myself needing to call Lieutenant Stokes, but I put his card in my backpack anyhow. At least that way I wouldn't keep seeing it and be reminded of things I wanted to forget.

Thank God it was Friday. I was looking forward to (a) no work, (b) fun with my friends and (c) my brother was supposed to stop by for a visit that weekend as well. Speaking of fun, it would have to be cheap fun. Having frittered away most of our limited funds at the Moonglow the night before, Mona and I had planned a sufficiently low-budget evening of entertainment to kick off the weekend— laundry night.

I showed up at the Murdocks' around seven that evening with my four bags of laundry. (We hadn't done laundry in a month. It was such a hassle hauling it to the laundromat, we tended to put it off until absolutely necessary.) Mona added five more bags of her own, plus her boom box and backpack, as we loaded up the Monamobile.

"Margo coming or does she have to work?" I asked.

"Nah. She's got the night off, but I think she's got an M-A-N lined up."

"Same one as last night?" I asked, only slightly curious.

I didn't really care. Mona shrugged. Both she and I had stopped trying to keep track of the luscious redhead's hyperactive love life long ago.

But the redhead surprised us at that point by showing up just as we were ready to leave. You never knew with that girl. Sometimes she was happy to hang out with us. Sometimes she played the princess, treating our plebeian plans with great disdain. But I guess everybody has to do laundry, sooner or later.

"Well, hurry up if you're coming with," Mona grumbled at her, ever the bossy older sister, as she got in the car. As if we were in such a hurry.

"Okay, okay," Margo said, the unlit Marlboro dangling from the right side that night. She quickly ran upstairs and came back down with two bags to add to the mountainous pile in the backseat. She was in a severely pissy mood, so I slid over with no argument and gave her the window so she could smoke. I still had plenty of space between her and Mona in the broad front seat of the Monamobile.

Just to mix it up, we had selected a laundromat in a part of town called Treasure Cove, strategically located between a 7-Eleven and a crappy country-western bar with a dimly lit dirt parking lot. I forget exactly why that one was supposed to be a "good" laundromat, except for the fact that on previous occasions, we'd had it to ourselves on Friday nights. It certainly wasn't the closest one, but nothing was ever that far away in San Tomas.

In honor of the weekend's start, Mona plugged *Born To Run* into the tape player. Although she worshipped at the altar of Bruce, it was tacitly understood that even mere mortals such as Margo and myself were allowed to sing along with Mona and Mr. Springsteen on "Thunder Road" and "Tenth Avenue Freeze Out." Mona's deep alto was perfect for a duet on "Backstreets." Not wanting to risk having to walk home, neither her sister nor I would dream of joining in on that one.

Treasure Cove was known for some of the best surfing in the area. There were a few houses irregularly set amongst the swampy ground near the cove and not a whole lot of anything else. The laundromat/bar/convenience store conglomeration was an oddity on the main avenue, but it apparently served the residents' basic needs for clean clothes, booze, potato chips and diapers.

The combination of a window seat and good music seemed to have perked up Margo's spirits by the time we reached the laundromat. I was feeling pretty good myself. I shrugged off lingering thoughts of the night before which, try as I might, kept popping up in my head like apples bobbing in a barrel. No point in worrying about things you can't control, I told myself.

We were in luck as the laundromat was empty again. The country bar next door was doing a good business based on the loud music and chatter emanating from its open doors. We brought our many bags into the laundromat, then went into the 7-Eleven. Two scruffy clerks (*Wanted: 7-Eleven clerk, must be scruffy*) were on duty as we roamed the aisles collecting orange wine coolers, Doritos, bean dip, Milk Duds and those really gross pink snowball thingies for Mona. Laundry night always required generous amounts of cheap alcohol and junk food.

Mona poked her sister with a bony finger and, nodding toward the scruffiest clerk, said in an undertone, "Hey, Margo, there's your boyfriend."

Margo rolled her eyes in disgust, not even bothering to answer. Now that we were properly provisioned, we headed next door to the laundromat. As Margo and I staked out our machines and began to load, Mona pursed her lips at the country song coming through the wall from the bar. She went outside to the car, returning with her boom box, a shoebox full of tapes and a fifty-foot orange extension cord. She got it set up to her satisfaction on an unused washer and cranked up Split Enz, drowning out the cowboy crap.

By this time, Margo was already slumped in a molded plastic seat, slurping down a cooler and lighting another cigarette. Waving her hand in front of her face through the smoke she had just exhaled, she addressed us. "I thought you guys wanted to see that band at the Mongol tonight."

"We did, but the tickets were too steep," her sister replied.

We had discussed going to see Geographic Tongue when we saw the gig announced in the paper a few weeks back. They were a wildly popular trio from San Francisco whom we'd seen once before. I liked them, Mona liked them, everybody liked Geographic Tongue, which resulted in the ticket prices being too high for us poor folks. I'd heard their name came from an actual disease in the medical dictionary. Gross.

I was already opening my second California Cooler. Normally, I didn't really like wine or wine coolers or froo-froo beverages of any kind, but God, I loved those orange California Coolers. They tasted just like baby aspirin.

"Isn't your brother coming down this weekend?" Margo asked me through another exhalation of toxins.

"Yeah," I said over my shoulder from my washer. Now how did she know that? I must have mentioned it to Mona, I thought as I shoved the last of my underwear into my seventh machine. I admit some were white and some were colored, but, hell they were just cheap polyester panties from Penney's and it wasn't likely anybody was going to see them the way things were going. I never had much patience for the sorting process and have found that women who obsess about this are often ill-tempered and prone to all sorts of other bad habits, like fake fingernails and the ownership of small rat-like dogs. I stuck in thirty-five cents and joined Margo in the truly uncomfortable seats. Mona was still loading her machines.

"Yeah," I said to Margo again, "I talked to him last week. He's supposed to be at my place tomorrow morning. I think he was going to stop in Cucho tonight and have dinner with one of his buddies."

"Fuckin' Cucho," she growled for no reason that I could see.

Cucho was a tiny beach town a few miles up the coast from San Tomas, known for its big waves. J. D. had "car" buddies and friends from high school scattered over much of northern California. He'd actually been a little vague about which buddy he was going to have dinner with, making me wonder if it was a he or a she. I didn't really care as long as he gave me an ETA. This was to be one of his occasional visits to see me (not to mention the Camaro), plus do some surfing.

Margo seemed to have slipped back into her funk. She'd slumped even further down in her chair and was puffing furiously with a scowl darkening her delicate features. Being used to her moodiness, I knew she'd work it out herself eventually and would not welcome overtures of sympathy or inquiries from me. She jabbed a Dorito into the tiny can of bean dip, where it promptly broke.

"Fuck," she said under her breath.

I glanced over at Mona. It was taking her longer to load her laundry in the washers because she was simultaneously shaking her booty to "What's The Matter With You," plus frequently pausing to take a swig of wine cooler or bite off a chunk of pink snowball thingy (shudder). She shook some powdered detergent into the machine in time with the song, then made sure to close the lid on the downbeat, swiveling her bony little hips the entire time and singing along, which entailed some spitting of pink coconut flakes.

Grabbing her wine cooler, she meandered over to us as the song ended. She sat down on the other side of her sister, then leaned forward and gave me a smartass look. "So, Hev, heard from Flaco today?"

I don't think I blushed. Much.

Even Margo evinced interest, sitting up a little and saying, "Flaco? That guy who's always with the Romanoff? The one with the tattoos?"

Like there were so many Flacos littering the landscape that we had to narrow it down to the one with the tattoos. Like we hadn't just seen him the night before. "Jesus, how stoned were you last night, Margo?" I asked her.

Margo took a long look at me and then burst out laughing. Well, criminy, so glad I could help lift her spirits.

Mona was saying in a high-pitched voice, "Fuh-laaaaaaaaaa-co...Fuh-laaaaaaaa-co..."

And this was my support system. Unchanged since the second grade, when Mona had loudly announced to the rest of the class, "Hev, it's okay 'cause you can hardly tell that you peed in your pants."

Oh well, I'd overcome incontinence without any help from the two of them, so perhaps romance was next on the list. "Just shut up, both of you," I said. "I only danced with him. No big deal."

"I thought he kissed you on the cheek," Mona challenged.

"Well, just on the cheek. And on the hand. But not like a big-time actual kiss," I told them, remembering the feel of his breath on my cheek just before his lips brushed it. And how his hand had felt on the small of my back. And then flashed to that odd moment when Jules had asked me to dance. I noticed both Murdocks were sitting up straight in their chairs and staring at me intently.

"I don't even know if he'll call me," I said defensively, trying to close the Flaco topic.

"That might be hard without your number!" Mona cackled.

"Well, yeah," I admitted.

Margo chimed in, "I wonder if Latin guys are as hot as they say. You'll have to let us know, Hev."

"Hey, I just danced with him!" I protested in vain, as ribald discussion of Flaco's sexual potential ensued. How embarrassing. As if I hadn't been thinking the exact same thing all day in some dark corner at the back of my mind. Ay yi yi.

We ended up going next door for more California Coolers while the washers were in the spin cycle. I don't know why laundry night and extreme tipsiness went so well together, but it always seemed to happen that way. Margo even wanted to go in the country bar and do some shots, but Mona and I physically restrained her.

Once we got the clothes into the dryers, Margo and I returned to the tortuous seats while Mona fired up The Motels, one of her favorite bands. She adored Martha Davis, the lead singer and songwriter. We still had the laundromat to ourselves. Margo got up and checked all the dryers, touching the glass window in each door to make sure it was at least warm. The last time we'd done laundry, she'd gotten stuck with a dryer that spun, but never heated up, and didn't realize it until she went to retrieve the cold, clammy load. True to our sensitive natures, Mona and I laughed our butts off at that one.

"Seriously, though, Hev," Mona said to me. New topic, I hoped. "What do you think about all that shit at your apartment building? Do you want to move again?"

"Oh, no," I replied instinctively, with the horror of one with all too fresh memories of packing, moving and unpacking. Well, some unpacking.

A very small and mean part of me wondered at that moment who would move in next door now that Werner was gone. Small, mean and apparently incredibly resilient! I repressed that thought and voiced another.

"I just keep thinking about Jackson Miller," I said. "I wonder what happened to that guy. How could he just disappear and nobody even cares?"

"If I disappeared, would you care?" Mona asked her sister, who had sat down next to her.

I thought Margo was going to make some typically cutting remark, but instead she merely said, "Yes, Mon."

While they hugged it out in one of their infrequent displays of affection, I opened another California Cooler. "Tragic Surf" was blasting from the boom box.

"I just wonder where he is, right now..." I said.

* * *

In retrospect, I hate to think how often we drove drunk in those days. The hell of it was, everybody did it! Makes me squeamish now to think about what was socially acceptable then. We never hit anybody, thank goodness. Lord knows we might have survived just about any crash in the tank that was the Monamobile, but I doubt the other party would have.

Anyhow, laden down with fresh laundry and awash with California Coolers, we managed to make it home safely. Once back at my apartment, I went to bed immediately where I drifted off into a dream of Jackson Miller chasing me through a vast and gleaming all-white laundromat of the future. He wore an oversized cowboy hat which concealed his face, but I knew it was him. I tripped over a bottle of baby aspirin and fell down, down, down.

CHAPTER NINE

Saturday

Ah, Saturday morning. I woke up feeling happy and had no idea why. Oh, yeah—clean laundry and J. D. coming to visit. By the time I was showered, dressed and prepared to face the world, or at least my brother, it was a little after eight. I grabbed a Coke, then stepped out onto the veranda or second-floor walkway or whatever you want to call it. It promised to be another fine day in San Tomas. The sun was shining and big, white, fluffy clouds slowly scudded about in the blue sky, propelled by a gentle sea breeze. Standing on the veranda, I faced north, but if I craned my neck and looked carefully between two chimneys down the hill toward the west, I could just see a patch of surf rolling up on the beach.

The neighborhood was pretty quiet at that hour on a Saturday morning. A few people were strolling down Highland and the guy across the street was washing his car, which made me recall Werner washing his Mercedes the previous weekend. I involuntarily glanced over at his apartment, but there was nothing to see, of course. The cops had put an official-looking seal on his front door at some point and it was still there, intact. I hadn't seen his car since, well, since before. I presumed it was in his garage.

I walked over to take a look at the police seal and heard some muffled barking from inside Werner's apartment. Good golly, was that poor dog still in there by himself? I thought the cops were going to take care of that. Well, he sounded lively enough. Although as soon as I thought that, the barking stopped. I looked around— no one appeared to be watching me, no police cars to be seen. There was a kink in Werner's mini blinds that I could just peek through if I stood on my tiptoes and craned my neck at a forty-five degree angle. There. I could see the dog lying placidly on the living room floor. A Rottweiler. That explained those big boy barks. He didn't seem aware of me outside his window. As I watched, he got up and went into the kitchen for a moment, then came back. He turned three times and lay down on the same spot. He didn't seem to be in any discomfort. Not to be gross or anything, but let's face it, I figured he had water to drink from the toilet, at least, if there wasn't a bowl for him in the kitchen. Despite the untouched seal on the door, I felt sure the cops must have been taking care of him in some fashion. They wouldn't just leave their fellow officer's pooch to languish. Heck, with no Werner there to bitch at him and plenty of toilet water to drink, he might have been in puppy dog heaven.

The sound of a truck pulling into the driveway below and behind me cut my canine observations short. Actually it was the sound of "Tainted Love" blaring out the windows of my brother's pride-and-joy Toyota 4 x 4 pickup. I could also hear him attempting to sing along, which was not pretty. His automotive skills far outweighed his musical ones. He gave me a wave as he pulled in behind the Camaro. I'd pulled it right up to the garage door the night before in anticipation of J. D.'s arrival. I knew I'd have to park my car in the garage sooner or later, but for now, I was opting for later until I could get over my newfound garage door phobia.

"Hey, Hev!" he shouted cheerfully as he jumped out of his truck and slammed the door shut. I hoped all the neighbors were already up.

"Come on up," I called back in gentler tones, pointing to the stairwell at the other end of the veranda. "I'll give you a tour of my new place."

Which took all of thirty seconds. It was a very small apartment. "Cool," he pronounced it. "I can't believe you're only two blocks from the beach. That is so killer."

He looked pretty beachy himself in flip-flops, Birdwell's and a ratty-looking Pep Boys T-shirt, with a backpack flung over his shoulder. We shared the same light brown hair, though he kept his fairly short so it wouldn't get in his face when he worked on cars. He was four years older, six inches taller and had always been there for me. My brother, J. D.

"Oh, hey," he said, "before I forget, I brought you a housewarming present." He pulled a paper bag out of his backpack, then pulled a large bottle of Kahlua out of that.

"Wow! J. D.! That stuff is expensive," I said, both impressed and taken aback. Super expensive—and super good! I had discovered White Russians (Kahlua, vodka and light cream, for the uninitiated) just that year, although I had to limit my intake of them, as they induced most unladylike shivers of ecstasy as they slid down my throat. Loss of inhibition and/or hurling then followed. At that point in my life, there was no doubt that a White Russian was better than sex. Way, way better than sex. At least any sex that I'd had. Sigh.

Take kissing, for example. Girls in romantic movies went weak at the knees from a single kiss, but all the kisses I'd had felt like… well, just lips. Like kissing my own arm. Or a department store dummy. I was severely disappointed to find out that's what kisses actually felt like. At least for me. But I played along and tried to fit in whenever the topic or activity came up—what else could I do? Hope that my luck was so bad that I'd just been kissing the wrong people? Yeah, right. Come to think of it, though, they lied about almost everything else in those movies, so maybe I shouldn't have been surprised about the duddiness of kissing.

Hell of bummer though. And it wasn't like I could even talk to anyone about it. Not even Mona. What could I say? Hey, guess what, I'm a fuckin' freak…

My brother was looking at me with his eyebrows raised. "Hello?" he said. "I'm trying to give you a present here."

"Sorry!" I said, snapping back to reality. "It's wonderful—but so expensive…"

"Didn't cost me a dime," he told me with a dismissive wave of his hand. "I won it off Gator playing poker. He just got back from surfing Rosarito."

Gator was one of his Cucho buddies. "You're sure you don't want it?" I asked, trying to be a grownup, while my childish brain yelped, "I want it! I want it!"

"I'm more of a Budweiser guy," he said, looking dubiously at the bottle he still held in his hand. "It's girly booze anyway."

"Well, isn't there some girl you could give it to?" I teased him.

"She doesn't like Kahlua," he muttered. "Besides, you're a girl, right? Just take it," he said authoritatively, putting the bottle in my hands.

I put it on the kitchen counter, thanking him profusely. I added vodka and cream to my mental grocery list. White Russians later, woo hoo!

We decided on breakfast first and oil change second since we both were starving. I never had checked my mailbox the day before, so I took a look in there on the way to J. D.'s truck. All junk for me and nothing for Jackson. I left it in the mailbox to deal with later.

"Can we go now?" J. D. called from the driveway with mock impatience.

"Yeah, yeah."

We headed for the mall and Ed's Café. On a busy Saturday morning, we had to wait for a table, but it was worth it. Ed's was an unabashedly local joint with no decor beyond mismatched tables and chairs, no menu other than what Ed felt like writing on the chalkboard, a scuffed up linoleum floor you didn't want to look at too closely and the finest blueberry pancakes on the West Coast. (The secret, per Ed, is to use the waffles recipe on the side of the Bisquick box, not the pancake one. You're welcome.) That was my order, but J. D. went with the breakfast special, Ed's version of huevos rancheros. He looked a little hungover, actually, and after downing a few cups of coffee, he ordered a Bud from Ed. At nine o'clock in the morning.

"Too much fun in Cucho?" I asked, skimming my forkful of pancakes through the syrup on my plate.

"Yeah, something like that," he said.

Not the most forthcoming of men, my brother J. D. He and his buddies had probably spent all day Friday surfing and drinking on the beach. I wondered if there'd been any girls there—maybe the one who'd turned down the Kahlua? (Clearly a bonehead.) I hadn't heard about any particular woman in J. D.'s life since he'd broken up with his last girlfriend a few months before. "So how's your love life, J. D.?" I asked.

"What?" He choked and sprayed a few bits of huevos on the table. Gathering himself after a swig of Bud, he said, "None of your business, Miss Nosey Butt. And it's fine. Just fine."

"Geez, I didn't know it was such a sensitive subject."

I couldn't help but tease him a little bit (as outlined in the Little Sister's Handbook, Part One, Chapter Seven). He shook his head and growled one more, "Fine," then dove back into his eggs and potatoes, attempting to ignore me. I tried not to laugh. Then he looked up and said, "How's yours?"

Oh. The urge to laugh went away and quite quickly too. "Oh. Uh…It's fine too," was my smooth reply.

"Uh-huh. I heard you met some new guy."

"Now how in the hell did you hear that?" I asked. How does family always sniff these things out? Some kind of genetic radar?

"I don't know, maybe Mom said something."

I hadn't even spoken to my mother that week. Ooh, I felt a small pang of guilt as I realized I hadn't even spoken to my mother that week. Oh, well, I'd call her later. Or maybe tomorrow.

"Who is he? Some college puke?" That big brother protective streak was never far from the surface.

"No, he's…" I paused, gesturing with my fork while I tried to think how to describe Flaco. He's…tattooed. He's…employed? Hmmm, I didn't know what he did for a living, unless it was painting. He's not an illegal alien or Mrs. Romanoff's lover…I decided this was not a conversational path I wanted to pursue at that particular time.

"Okay, well, how those huevos rancheros treating you?" I asked, grinning to acknowledge my obvious changing of the subject.

He grinned back, shaking his head at me. We spent the rest of our breakfast talking about our parents, my job, his job as a mechanic and other catching up kind of stuff. I didn't tell him anything about Jackson or Werner, because (a) he would just worry and (b) he would likely tell our parents. Which would probably lead to the "when is Heavenly moving back home?" speech, which was not one of my faves. Easier to just skip that topic, as riveting as it was to the rest of the family.

I didn't tell him about Jules either. I mean, what was there to say, really? Nothing. I did tell him about Mona's big gig coming up, although he wasn't particularly interested.

"The Fabulous Murdock Sisters," he muttered under his breath, picking at the last bits of huevo on his plate.

Our father had coined that term. It was Halloween in 1970. I think I was a cowboy that year, having flat-out refused to don the "buckskin" cowgirl skirt that came with the costume. Jeans were definitely more my style, especially when my mom was cool enough to reengineer the skirt into some chaps. Ten-year-old Mona and nine-year-old Margo appeared on our doorstep dressed as some kind of generic superheroes, ready to walk with me over to the elementary school carnival, trick-or-treating along the way. Dad opened the door, saw them there in matching tights, rain boots, homemade capes and masks, and said, "The Fabulous Murdock Sisters are here to save the day!" The nickname stuck, at least in our household.

J. D. had never cared for either Murdock sister, to be honest. Which was understandable—what ten-year-old boy would want three little girls (ages six, six and five) dogging his every footstep? He was obligated by blood to tolerate me, but clearly thought the Fabulous Murdock Sisters were nothing but obnoxious brats.

We drove back to my place after breakfast. As J. D. pulled back in behind my car, I saw that someone—probably the property manager—had hosed down the driveway that morning, washing away most of the stain by Werner's garage door. I tried not to look at that. A few damp patches and puddles remained on the concrete, but were burning off fast in the already hot morning sun. I wasn't sure when I'd feel ready to open up my garage door again, even though it was Werner's door next to it that had done the deed.

While J. D. worked on the Camaro, I watched from my beach chair on the west side of the driveway, in the shade under the one small tree in the grassy area. By this time, I was drinking a beer too. It was very pleasant there, drinking a cold one and watching someone else do the hard work. First he changed the oil, mooning over the engine like it was solid gold sprinkled with diamonds. Then he changed the spark plugs too. What a guy. He gave something a final swipe with a rag and was about to close the hood when a police car pulled into the driveway on Werner's side. It was Officer

Pacheco, looking buff in his uniform, but merely there on doggie duty as it turned out. I didn't get up. I was still nursing a grudge over our flashlight-in-the-retinas encounter.

He was bonding with J. D. anyhow, enthusing over the V8. He finally glanced over at me and gave me a lukewarm smile and a, "Hey."

I responded in kind, but didn't join them. I didn't want to get into a conversation about Werner with my brother standing right there. Thank goodness Pacheco hadn't said anything on his own. J. D. closed up the hood as Pacheco went upstairs to Werner's front door.

"Nice guy," J. D. said to me, wiping his hands on the rag and packing up his tools.

"For a cop," I said.

He smiled at his little sister's tough-guy attitude. Then frowned as he caught sight of some dirt and oil on his shirt. "Shit, I was trying not to do that."

Since he was a mechanic and begrimed was his natural state, I didn't think it was that big of a deal. He surprised me, however, by asking if I had a clean shirt that would fit him. As J. D. was a muscular six foot one, we didn't exactly wear the same size, but I thought I could dig up a T-shirt that would do the job.

I got up from my beach chair, which was not as easy as it sounds, and ran upstairs to check. My Go-Go's tour shirt was right on top of a pile of clean laundry. It was a large, more than roomy on me, but that had been the only size left when I'd bought it at the concert. It was snug on J. D., but at least it was clean. He looked unhappy, however.

"Don't you have anything else?" he asked, looking down at the logo on his chest. "Like a polo shirt maybe? Something less gay, at least?"

"Well, excuse me, Mr. Fashion! And no, not in your size."

Why did people always say stuff like that, I thought in passing. Even J. D., my cool brother, always said stuff like that. Why was it "gay" for him to wear a Go-Go's shirt? I knew he liked their songs. I'd heard his hideous, tune-free rendition of "Our Lips Are Sealed" the last time he had visited. And why did people even care who other people slept with? Why did that even matter? I mean, if we all really knew what everybody else did behind closed doors, probably nobody would like anybody. So maybe everybody should just give everybody a break. You know what I mean?

"Okay," he said, kind of glumly. "I guess it's all right—I mean, it's clean at least. Thanks, Hev. Hey, I'm gonna take off now—I've got some stuff to do."

I gave him a quick hug, saying in a singsong, "Thanks for breakfast, thanks for the Kahlua, thanks for changing the oil, thank you, thank you, thank you!"

"You're welcome, butthead," he said with equal parts affection and irony. "I'll see you later. Don't forget to call Mom and Dad, all right?"

"Yeah, yeah."

He gave me a wave as he drove off with "Tainted Love" again shattering the peace of the morning. Rather late morning by then, which appeared to be turning into an overcast afternoon. Those big, white, fluffy clouds had gotten together to form a woolly gray covering. Instead of cooling down, however, it was still determinedly hot and getting stickier by the minute.

As I folded up my beach chair, I was contemplating the joys of an afternoon nap, but my reverie was interrupted by the unmistakable noise of the Monamobile coming down the street from the opposite direction J. D. had just taken. Yup, thar she blew—the ginormous car, packed full of people, was blocking traffic at the corner of Third and Highland with Mona's stick-like arm protruding from the open window to communicate her desire to turn, since she could never be certain if the turn signals were working.

There was no way she could park on the sand—it would take multiple tow trucks and/or the National Guard to get the Monamobile out of there. Since the Camaro was already nosed in right up against the garage door, her vehicle could just fit behind mine. Mona pulled in with only the usual ominous noises from the steering, transmission and exhaust systems. With the cop car on the left side of the driveway, everyone exited from the right. It was a little like the clowns in the circus: first LeClaire got out, then Petey, then Handsome Pete, then Margo and finally Mona. Hail, hail, the gang's all here.

But not quite, Mona informed me. Seemed Flaco had pulled up as they were leaving their apartment building, one thing led to another and he was expected any minute. Well. How did I feel about that? I didn't know.

I wasn't surprised or put out that the five of them had shown up unannounced. That's the way we lived in those days. Besides, nobody in our circle had an answering machine in 1982, let alone a cell phone, so even if they had called, I might not have heard the phone ring from the driveway. They knew, I knew, we all knew none of us had anything better to do than hang out all day anyhow. God, I really miss those days.

Anyhow, here came Flaco in his white van. There was a seal on the passenger's side door that I hadn't noticed the other night. I saw now that it was remarkably similar to the one on the coroner's van they'd taken Werner away in. As Flaco pulled onto the sand, I realized it was the seal of San Tomas County, but his door was further emblazoned with the words "San Tomas Unified School District."

He popped out with a six-pack of Coors and what looked like a videotape in its black plastic case. Since the other five had brought beer as well as herbal remedies, it looked like we were more than set. And the videotape was fine and dandy, but I didn't own a VCR. I didn't even know anyone who owned a VCR. What were we going to do, pull out the tape and hold it up to the light? We could rent a machine from the video store downtown, but that would cost more money than if we went to the movies.

But I had underestimated Flaco. Turned out he was a full-time employee of the school district's audiovisual department and had a veritable treasure trove of equipment in that white van, including a VCR.

"But it's Saturday, right?" Petey asked, looking a little confused, which made us all laugh.

"It is," Flaco agreed, "but I have to do some work on the high school auditorium's sound system later today. That's why I have the van. We do a lot of the maintenance work on nights and weekends, so we're not disrupting classes."

He was looking good that day in khaki shorts and a tucked-in white T-shirt from a band I hadn't heard of, but of course, Mona had. They discussed the Blasters while we all trekked upstairs. Flaco had another tattoo on the back of his left calf that I hadn't seen before—a pair of dice. At least it wasn't another snake.

Everybody found a place to sit in my tiny living room while I went into the kitchen to see if I had any snacks. I didn't, unless someone wanted a raw potato. Seeing the bottle of Kahlua on the countertop, though, I stashed it in the back of a cabinet. I'd be happy to share it with the Murdocks later, but I didn't want the band to suck the whole bottle down in one sitting, which they were fully capable of doing.

I took a moment to breathe before I dived back into the social whirl that awaited. I wondered if Flaco was there to see me. He was, right? I rejoined the group in my now very crowded living room, which was only about eight feet by fifteen. The front door and all the windows were wide open to permit some of the sulky afternoon air to circulate.

Flaco stood talking to Mona, who was perched on the footlocker. Three people were squeezed in tightly on the love seat: Margo, Handsome Pete and LeClaire. Petey was sprawled on the floor close to the open door. LeClaire was telling him about some new band she liked called the Stray Cats.

Handsome Pete had his right arm on the back of the love seat behind Margo with his beer in his left hand. As the two most beautiful people in the room, they seemed to be enjoying their close proximity, but oddly, Margo wasn't flirting with him. Maybe Mona had told her not to. There had to be some reason, because Handsome Pete was one of those appealing guys *every* woman flirted with. Well, except me, I guess. I never was any good at that stuff. I could never seem to get the hang of it. The few times I tried, it just felt dumb.

Mona had, of course, commandeered the stereo as soon as she'd entered and they were all having to talk pretty loudly to be heard over the Clash. Everybody had a beer and Handsome Pete was digging down in the pocket of his cut-offs for the lighter and the baggie when a shadow fell across the open doorway.

It was Officer Pacheco, with the Rottweiler on a short leash. If London had not been calling, I'm sure I would have heard multiple gulps from the assemblage. In his uniform, with the big dog, not to mention appearing out of nowhere, Pacheco looked pretty damn imposing. I stepped over to the stereo and hit pause. In the sudden silence which followed, the dog licked his chops noisily.

I said, "Can I help you?"

Handsome Pete still had his hand crammed down in his shorts pocket, LeClaire was gazing at the officer avidly, Petey had his head awkwardly craned around from his sitting position and the Murdock sisters appeared frozen. I was suddenly aware that Flaco was now right behind me, at my elbow. A little too close for comfort, in fact. I took half a step forward.

The dog gave a big sigh and sat down on one of the cop's feet. Pacheco looked down at him with mild exasperation, but didn't bother to move his foot. He said to us, "Hi, guys. I was wondering if you could maybe watch the dog for a while? I got a call and I've got to leave in a few minutes, and I hate to just lock him up again."

Pacheco as Animal Lover cast a new light on the situation. The air itself seemed to lighten a bit and all the occupants of the love seat shifted slightly, including Handsome Pete who casually withdrew his empty hand from his pocket and returned it to the back of the love seat.

Margo glanced at me and Mona. We, in turn, gave her the look we'd been giving her since we were thirteen and she was twelve. The look said, "Work thy sinister magic on this cad and make him begone."

As she rose from the love seat, resplendent in navy blue Dolfin shorts and a tight-fitting, sleeveless polo in the same shade, the dog arose too and strained forward a step or two on his short lead to lick the back of Petey's neck, who had turned around for the room's response to Pacheco's request.

"Man!" Petey yelped, startled, then turned to pet the pooch, who was happy to find a new friend. He vigorously lapped Petey's face. Apparently the front was as good as the back. Luckily, Petey liked dogs. The two of them communed.

Pacheco was all eyes as Margo approached, drinking in the long lovely legs, the perfect body, the red hair. The rest of us could only see her back, but we knew her front was even better. I glanced back at Flaco—he was looking at me. Five points for him.

"We'd love to, wouldn't we, guys?" Margo said.

She didn't even bother to glance back at us. She took the leash from Pacheco's hand, brushing his in the process. Turning around, she leaned down and wrapped the leash around Petey's outstretched wrist, since the dog had him pretty much pinned to the floor now. Pacheco was digging the bent over rear view, no doubt about it.

Turning back to him, she maneuvered him a step back onto the walkway. "I'm Margo. And you are—"

"Rich. Rich Pacheco. How ya doin'?"

He was eager. They walked off together down the veranda. (I don't care, I'm calling it the veranda, whatever it was, I'm calling it the veranda.)

I turned the volume knob down some, then released the pause button to get the music going again. Flaco was still right there, extremely close to me. "Well," I said to the group, "that was exciting."

"Very," Flaco said in my left ear.

It was our first verbal exchange since he had showed up—since he had so abruptly left the dance floor on Thursday night, actually. I looked into his eyes. He looked back unwaveringly. I'm not sure which one of us broke off the eye contact, but I lightly poked his rib cage with my index finger to push him back half an inch and somehow also acknowledge the moment. He moved back the half inch and slugged his Coors in a satisfied fashion. I wished we were alone for half a second and then was incredibly grateful we weren't. It's really sad to have such a fucked-up brain. It takes up so much time and energy.

I decided to go sit on the love seat in neutral territory next to Handsome Pete. Mona was fooling with the videotape Flaco had brought. Turned out to be one of those surfing videos, with guys biting it on forty-foot waves around the globe. Fun for the whole family.

"Hey, Flaco-man," she asked him, holding up the tape, "when are we going to watch this?"

"Oh, let me hook up the VCR—wait, I left the cable in the van." He cast a glance at me. "Want to come along?"

To help carry a one-ounce cable? Oh. He wanted to talk. Or...? Down at the van, Flaco quickly found the cable he wanted, then slid the door closed. He turned to face me, saying, "I want to apologize for my quick exit the other night, Heavenly."

About time, I thought. "Oh, psssh," I said, making one of those dismissive mouth noises like I was all footloose and fancy-free, not a care in the world. Yeah, right.

"No, really," he said. "I didn't want to leave, but I had to. I really liked dancing with you." He was going for the major sincere eye contact.

"No biggie," I said casually and glanced off toward Highland, as if the passing traffic were of interest. He shifted the cable from one hand to another, then reached out and lightly touched me on the arm. I looked back at him.

"Maybe we can dance again," he said with a tentative smile.

"How do I know you won't 'have to leave' again?" I asked, doing the air quotes thing. Smiling, but giving him the hard time he totally deserved.

"It was just a one-time thing. A business thing. I assure you it won't happen again," he said fervently, reaching out to take my hand in his.

It was unexpectedly warm. I wondered what the hell kind of "business thing" he'd had at close to midnight on a Thursday night. My expression must have been skeptical because he released my hand and tried again to explain.

"Really," he said. "My aunt, you know, my aunt Magda Romanoff? She and I are, um, starting a business together and we had a one-time opportunity to meet with a vendor on Thursday night."

This apology was getting stranger and stranger. "You're in business with the Ro—I mean, your aunt?" I asked. "I thought you worked for the school district." I gestured at the van.

"I do," he said, "but it doesn't pay that great. I'm never going to get anywhere with only the one job. That's why I'm always looking for other opportunities, like the painting and this thing with my aunt. I hadn't even seen her in years, since my uncle died, but I ran into her downtown a few weeks ago and we got to talking. She thinks we could make a lot of money with this business."

"So what's the business?" I asked.

He blushed a little, which surprised me. He'd sounded so confident and ambitious a moment before when he was laying out his plan for world domination. "Well, we're still, uh, working out all the details. But it'll be something where she can work out of her apartment and I can handle the sales. She's got an extra bedroom with nothing in it that's going to be like the office. Sort of."

His voice trailed off. I guessed those boxes he'd been unloading the other night must have been for their new business, whatever that was.

"Anyhow," he went on, "I just wanted to say I'm sorry about the other night. Okay?"

I decided to give him a break. It was a pretty decent apology, after all. "Okay," I said, smiling.

"Good," he replied, with evident relief. We stared at each other for a moment, neither one of us seeming to know what should come next. "Well, I better lock up the van," he said.

"Yeah, okay, I'm just going to get my mail."

He turned to the van, and I went over to my mailbox to finally retrieve my collection of junk mail. Surprise! It was empty. That was weird. I took a step back and surveyed the area. Nothing on the ground, although how it could have fallen out was beyond me. Except for Flaco, I didn't see anybody else around, but Margo and Pacheco were coming down the stairs.

"Hey, Mars, you didn't grab my mail, did you?"

"No," she said, giving me a look which left no doubt as to her evaluation of the intelligence of my question.

"Well, it's gone," I said in defense and explanation.

Pacheco was interested. "Somebody took your mail out of your mailbox? That's a federal offense."

Well, jump all over it, G-man, I thought. Flaco came up and all four of us looked into the empty mailbox. It was one of those big corrugated metal jobs, better suited to a life out on a rural route somewhere. Its flag thingamabob was permanently rusted into the down position.

"Well, it was just a bunch of junk mail anyhow. I checked it earlier this morning, that's how I even know it's gone," I explained to everybody.

"Why would someone take your mail?" Flaco asked me.

"Maybe he was looking for his mail," Margo said with a cocked eyebrow, then tugged at Pacheco's sleeve to keep him moving toward his squad car. She was already bored with the subject. And probably not keen on losing his attention to me, crime or anything else.

"Who?" said Pacheco and Flaco simultaneously.

"Long story," I said, mostly to Flaco.

Margo said to Pacheco, "So, you'll be back around four?"

They moved off to the patrol car for a final farewell. I closed up the mailbox, shrugging off the loss of my not so valuable mail.

Maybe some stupid kid took it. Or maybe Margo was right and Jackson Miller had just been there, right where I was standing...A tingle ran through me as I imagined it.

"Come back," Flaco said.

"What? I'm here," I replied, looking up at him.

"No, you were somewhere far away for a moment there," he said, smiling. He had a nice smile.

"Well, I'm back now," I assured him.

He took a step closer. The same tingle ran through me. His free hand reached up and smoothed the hair back from my brow, then traced a line down my cheek. "I see that," he murmured as he moved in for the kiss.

I swear, we were that close to our first, actual, big-time kiss when Mona came busting down the stairs, bellowing, "Hey, Hev!"

At the foot of the stairs, she turned and saw us by the mailbox, not in flagrante delicto, but not for lack of trying. Flaco's hand was still on my cheek, but he withdrew it and stepped back as my best friend, God bless her, interrupted us. I could have kicked her ass.

"Oh," she said. Pause. "There you are." Pause. "Sorry."

Flaco looked like he was trying not to laugh. He said something about taking the video cable upstairs and went on up.

"Well, what the hell do you want anyhow?" I contentiously asked Mona. I wasn't getting so many kisses that year that I could afford to waste opportunities. I kept thinking maybe the next one might be like the movies...At least a little bit.

"Jeez, you guys are getting along, aren't you?" she said with interest.

"I'm trying!" I said.

Margo ambled up to us as Pacheco drove off. "What's going on?" she asked.

Both of us ignored her. "All right, all right, I'm sorry," Mona said to me. "I didn't realize you were making out down here. I was just trying to find your Prince tape and I don't see it anywhere. Is it in your car?"

"I've got the record, not the tape, remember?"

"Oh, yeah."

Somebody else had evidently found it since I heard "When You Were Mine" coming out the open door to my apartment. As Mona, Margo and I climbed the stairs, I felt a twinge when I realized we would never have been able to play the music that loud if Werner was still next door. I hoped we weren't bugging Jules and Ashley, but I figured they'd let us know if it was too loud.

Prince music always made me want to dance. I felt the urge to boogie down the veranda, but was constrained by Flaco's proximity. What if he looked out the doorway and saw me? Well, shit, I thought, if my boogie-ing was going to be the determining factor, let it be. Whoever is destined to love me must accept that I'm a dork. I shook my groove thang to and through the doorway. And immediately fell over the dog who was lying there. Did I mention my innate dorkitude? To his credit, the Rottweiler regarded me calmly and without reproach, his tongue hanging nearly to the floor.

A serious haze hung in the air over the band, who were laughing heartily at me. The Murdock sisters stepped over me gingerly, laughing as well.

"Yeah, yeah, yeah," I said, getting up and dusting myself off. "What the hell is this dog's name, anyhow?"

"Chopper!" cried Petey, which sent them off into more peals of pot-induced laughter.

"What?" I squatted down and patted the dog on his head, which he graciously accepted and then rolled onto his back, inviting the ever-popular tummy rub. For such a tough-looking monster, he seemed to be just a big sweetie pie. If I haven't mentioned it before, let the record show that I love dogs.

A metal tag hung from his leather collar and glinted in the sunlight leaking through the mini blinds. Sure enough, the tag proclaimed his name to be Chopper. I whumped his belly a few times, earning his obvious approbation. "Chopper—is that your name, Chopper? Are you a good doggie, Mr. Chopper?"

Chopper assured me he was by giving my kneecap a big slurp. I looked up to see Flaco watching me with a benevolent, tolerant expression. Like an aw-isn't-she-cute expression. How long before that started to bug me? Be cool, Hev, don't judge, don't judge... You like this guy. Maybe. Sort of. Don't you?

Anyhow, I canned the doggie-talk and went to the kitchen to wash my hands. I liked the dog, but no need to smell like the dog. When I got back to the living room, Mona was explaining to Flaco and the rest of them about Werner, the Mysterious Disappearance of Jackson Miller, etc. Flaco stood to one side, apparently waiting to see where I would sit. The love seat was the obvious choice as LeClaire and Handsome Pete were now sitting on cushions on the floor.

As I passed Flaco, I lightly snagged his wrist, leading him to the love seat where I sat in the middle, which put him on the opposite end from Margo (no need to tempt Fate, says I). He put his arm up on the back of the couch, which brought his right side pleasingly in contact with my left side. At least the warmth of him felt pleasant. Although the slightly prickly hairs on his bare leg were touching my bare leg, which was not so pleasing. And Margo's bare left leg was also somewhat in contact with my bare right leg on the other side, which to tell the truth, was all a little too much information for my overloaded nerve endings. There is no doubt that I am a woman who needs her space. Not to mention the heat, the humidity, the smoke, the too many people and one large canine in too small a room. But I tried to assure myself I was having a good time. This is how people have a good time, I told myself. And I was a people, so, ergo, I must be having a good time. Right?

I swallowed my doubts along with a large slug of Coors. Handsome Pete had rolled a joint, which was making its way around the room. Margo inhaled, started to pass me the joint, remembered I didn't do that kind of stuff and handed it on to Flaco. Flaco took a toke, then forwarded it to LeClaire.

In that special talking-without-breathing voice pot smokers use, Flaco said to Handsome Pete, "Dude, I know where you can get some killer stuff, if you're interested."

I missed the rest of that exchange, because Jules appeared in the doorway, my screwdriver in one hand and her mail in the other. Chopper, who hadn't moved from his spot near the door even when I fell on top of him, sprang to his feet and went to her, head down, stumpy little tail wagging madly, his whole body wagging, actually, expressing much doggie joy.

"Hey, Puddin'," she said to him with affection and surprise. "What are you doing here?" She went down on one knee to hug him.

I got up and went over to her, turning the music down on my way. I hadn't talked to her since Thursday night at the Mongol. Since she asked me to dance...

She stood as I approached. Chopper did a little tap dance between her and me, looking up at both of us hopefully. I smoothed the fur over the broad space between his ears. He turned his big head and licked my hand, then went back to slobbering on Jules, who didn't seem to mind. She petted him absently as she spoke to me.

"I brought back your screwdriver," she said, handing it to me. "Thanks again." Polite, but not her usual smiling self.

"You're welcome," I replied evenly. I could do polite too. I turned to the group. They were all looking at us anyhow. "Hey, everybody, this is—" I turned back to her. "I'm sorry, I don't know your last name."

"Talbot," she supplied.

"This is Jules Talbot, my neighbor from downstairs."

A chorus of, "Hi, Jules" filled the room.

She smiled and did one of those little waves to acknowledge all of them. I watched her take in the room. She nodded at Mona and had no reaction to LeClaire, who was busy relighting the joint in her mouth. Her eyes slid over Petey, Flaco and even Handsome Pete without hesitation, then paused on Margo for a long moment. Margo gazed coolly back. It reminded me of a nature film I'd seen in high school with a lion and a cheetah staring each other down from different sides of the watering hole.

Jules turned her attention back to me. "Can I talk to you for a second?" she asked. Still no smile.

"Sure," I said. Uh-oh, I hoped this wasn't about us being too loud. I saw the Murdock sisters exchange a look in my peripheral vision.

Jules turned and stepped out onto the veranda, a few paces away from my open door. Chopper and I followed. Someone inside turned Prince back up.

"That was awful about Werner, eh?" I said.

She nodded, but then surprised me by abruptly asking, "Why is Chopper here?"

I explained about Pacheco and my temporary babysitting duties.

"Oh," she said. The dog licked her dangling fingers and she caressed his muzzle. She seemed to realize her tone had been a little terse. "Sorry," she said. "I've been worried about him, wondering what was going to happen to him after Mr. Werner died. Ash and I looked after him for a couple weeks last November when Mr. Werner's mother died and he had to go back east. I really bonded with him then."

She obviously meant the dog, whose ears she was fondling. The two of them exchanged looks of mutual devotion.

"Last November?" I asked. Something clicked in my brain, but I wasn't sure what.

"Yeah, right around Thanksgiving," she said. "I took Chopper with me to my folks' place up in the mountains for Thanksgiving dinner. They have a huge lot, and he was loving it up there, running around in the redwoods. Didn't you, Puddin'?"

Chopper barked in response to her question and wagged his tail, clearly in agreement.

"I wish I could adopt him now," Jules said to me, looking sad, "but there's no way Ashley would go for that. And we really don't have the room."

I told her Pacheco had said one of the cops was going to adopt him and she brightened some at that. She was wearing her gray gym shorts again, with a white UCST T-shirt with the sleeves rolled back a couple turns and some serious looking running shoes. She looked like a runner, come to think of it, with those legs. I myself was dressed in blue denim shorty overalls and a white Mickey Mouse tank top, hoping I looked at least semi-cute.

"Anyhow," Jules said, serious again, "That's not what I wanted to talk to you about."

Gulp.

"I just wanted to say I was sorry if I freaked you out at the Mongol."

"Oh," I said, a bit startled. "You didn't freak me out." Much.

"Well, that's good," Jules said. She seemed relieved. There was the smile. That was better. "I wouldn't want our friendship to get off on the wrong foot. I wasn't sure if you were…" Her voice trailed off as if she suddenly weren't sure how to end the sentence.

"Were what?" I prompted.

Her eyes locked on mine for a moment, then she said, "A dancer?" And smiled.

"Not much of one," I said, smiling back at her and relieved we seemed to be past the awkwardness. "Hey, why don't you come hang out with us and have a beer?"

I nodded toward my apartment and she followed me as I walked back to the door. The Prince album ended just as I got there and conversation within returned to a normal volume level. Chopper hurried ahead of me as if he had suddenly remembered a pressing engagement, but his only mission was to flop back down on his previous spot just inside the door as if he were afraid someone was going to steal it. This resulted in me stopping suddenly so I wouldn't step on him. Again. Jules bumped into me from behind and put a hand on my waist for a second to steady herself, then took half a step back. Her touch felt odd. Almost…familiar?

Mona was riffling through my records, looking for the next selection. Flaco and LeClaire were talking about Lord knows what, while Margo stared off into the distance. Stoned again. Handsome Pete and Petey were laughing at the cover art on the Prince album.

"What a homo," I heard Petey say. Handsome Pete snickered.

Jules stirred behind me. I turned and her blue eyes met mine and held. My mind went perfectly blank for a moment. She scanned the group behind me and seemed to reach a decision.

"You know what?" she said. "Thanks for asking, but I really need to go do my run." She gestured at her running shoes. I don't know why I was disappointed when I already had more guests than I could handle. "But maybe we can get together for a drink sometime," she said to me.

Margo coughed on the love seat. I shot her a look, but she was staring at her nails.

"Oh and this is yours," Jules said, offering me the handful of mail she still clutched. She laughed at my bewildered expression.

"Why do you have my mail?" I asked her, confused.

"Well, when I went out to get my own mail earlier, there was this strange guy hanging around the mailboxes. I saw him look in Werner's box and then yours, Hev. He took off like a scared rabbit when he saw me, but I thought I'd better grab yours for safekeeping."

"Oh, my God!" I said. "Was it Jackson?"

"Jackson Miller?" Jules exclaimed, then laughed again. "No. He's been gone for months."

It belatedly occurred to me that not only would she have recognized him, she might have known him fairly well. They'd been neighbors after all. I'd have to ask her about him later, when we had a chance to talk privately. The gang had been following our exchange—especially Mona, Margo and Flaco. I felt a little self-conscious in the face of their interest, but I still wanted to know about the strange guy who'd been snooping around my mailbox.

"What did this guy look like?" I asked Jules.

"Just kind of a skinny guy," she said unhelpfully, but then went on with more detail. "A white guy, about thirty, I guess. Kind of scraggly-looking."

Scraggly? Mona and I exchanged a significant glance. But what would the assistant marina manager want with my mail? I quickly sorted through it again to see if anything was missing. Nope, all there. And it was all junk mail anyhow, stuff addressed to "Occupant" and "Our Neighbor At." Except one from the UCST Alumni Association, who were always after me for a donation, even though I was a dropout, not an alumnus. That envelope had my name on it. Oh, my God. My *name*. Maybe that's what he was after.

Neither Mona nor I had told him our names during our brief conversation the other night, although he might have got Mona's from the Cap'n Cino's gig, since he was there too. Had he followed us back to my apartment that night? And come back later to find out my name? My mind was racing, but I was still more confused than anything.

"Hey?" Jules looked at me inquiringly. "Is everything all right?" she said, touching my wrist with her fingertips. They were cool. Or maybe I was growing feverish.

"Do you know the assistant manager down at the marina, by chance?" I asked her.

"No," she said. Now she was looking confused.

I decided I would talk it over with her later, if at all. "It's fine," I assured her. "Thanks for the mail."

"You're welcome," she said, smiling. "I'll see you later, okay?"

"Okay."

Margo and the group started rehashing the topic of Jackson's disappearance, but Mona joined me in the kitchen as I got another beer. Of course, she put another record on the turntable before doing so (Robert Palmer's *Secrets* album), but at a low volume. For her.

"Why would that marina guy want your mail?" she demanded.

"Maybe it wasn't him," I suggested.

"Oh, yeah, right, now you've got *another* mystery man in the mix?" she said caustically.

"Well, shit, I don't know," I answered. "There are a lot of strange people running around loose in San Tomas, that's for damn sure."

"It would make a little bit more sense if the guy was Jackson," she grumbled.

"I know, but Jules knows him and she said it wasn't him."

"What if…" Mona had a speculative look in her eye as she took a hit of her beer. "What if Jackson bribed the scraggly ass marina manager to let him know if anyone asked about him or his boat? Jackson's rich, right? So he'd have plenty of money to spread around to help cover his tracks when he disappeared."

Hmmm, if that were true, he might have paid off the parole office chick too, I thought. "So you're saying he wanted to disappear?" I asked. "I thought he was dead under my trapdoor." I couldn't resist needling her about her former theory.

"Maybe the scraggly guy killed him and he doesn't like you nosing around."

Yikes! That one actually sounded more plausible than anything else we'd come up with so far. Except why in the world would the scraggly guy have killed Jackson? I guessed they could have argued about something. Although all the marijuana smokers I knew were more on the mellow side. Hard to imagine a pothead getting that worked up about anything.

The potheads in my living room were still on the same topic. "So, Hev," Margo was saying, "do the cops think it was an accident?"

I assumed she meant Werner. "That's what they said. The garage door came down on his head and boom."

Flaco listened closely. Margo had another question. "Isn't that kind of weird that the guy who lived here disappears, then the guy next door kicks it?"

"Yeah. But I don't think they're investigating either one. I mean, there's no crime in an accident and there's no crime in someone just taking off. And that's what they think has happened."

Flaco interjected, "Did your neighbor and the man who lived here know each other well?"

"I guess," I said. "They were next-door neighbors. And I read something about them planning to go on a fishing trip together." Although that might have been bullshit.

Petey chimed in from the floor, "Maybe there's some clues in the dead guy's apartment."

General derision, accompanied by hooting, greeted this declaration. Chopper even roused himself to sit up and bark once.

"Well, there could be," Petey protested.

"Don't you think if there were any clues, the cops would have removed them by now?" drawled Margo.

"Not if they're not investigating," Petey responded.

Good point. We all mulled that one over.

Jokingly, Mona said to her sister, "Hey, Margo, maybe Serpico will let us in and give us a tour of the place when he gets back."

For no reason whatsoever, except that my mouth is occasionally disconnected from my brain, I said, "I know how to get in."

Everyone turned and looked at me.

I felt myself flush, but said defensively, "Well, not that we're actually going to try to get in, but the crawl space in the kitchen goes over to next door."

Everyone turned and gazed upward at the trapdoor in the ceiling of the living room. At the same time I said, "Look, this is ridiculous," Mona said, "We should totally do it."

There was brief pandemonium while everyone stated his or her opinion and the dog barked some more. Then, in one of those moments where everyone is suddenly quiet, Flaco said, "I've got a video camera in the van."

More opinions, more barking, me vainly protesting this was stupid, we couldn't possibly be thinking of doing this. God, I hate peer pressure. Especially when I cave. And I hate decision making by committee. Especially when the committee is wasted on domestic beer and weed. Flaco was really into it. What was up with that? Did he think he'd be my hero or something? Sheesh. I didn't even want to do it.

And yet somehow, I found myself in the kitchen with the rest of them, the dog wagging his stumpy little excuse for a tail in appreciation of all this merriment. The Petes figured they'd give Flaco a leg up into the crawl space, then hand him the camera, which he'd retrieved from the van. A big-ass clunky camera as this was 1982. With a little metallic sticker on it proclaiming it to be the property of San Tomas County Unified School District. No doubt this would all end up in my permanent record somehow, further besmirching that sorry document.

With a heave and a ho, the boys hoisted Flaco into the space vacated by the pushed aside trapdoor. Margo watched the testosterone closely, with what was left of the joint firmly clenched between her thin upper lip and fuller lower lip. She looked like she was either about to hurl or start quoting James Joyce, but I knew that was just her ganja face while she held her breath. Mona stood next to Petey, holding the video camera at the ready. LeClaire was perched on the kitchen counter, moodily turning the cold water faucet on and off. She reached over to take the roach from Margo's outstretched hand.

Done with the verbal protests, I still physically distanced myself from the criminal element by hovering at the junction of the kitchen and the living room, uttering useless, hand-wringing phrases like, "You guys…"

Flaco was fully ensconced now.

"Do you see anything?" asked Petey.

The sound of coughing. A dusty hand reaching down. "Nah. Couple of dead spiders. Gimme the camera."

Mona handed it to Petey, who passed it up. We heard Flaco easing his way east toward Werner's kitchen, twin to my own on the other side of the wall. Was there a trapdoor there too? "Hey, there's a trapdoor here too, people."

Small noises were heard as Flaco presumably moved aside Werner's trapdoor. We waited for his next announcement. Margo moved to my side and said quietly to me, "So, Hev, where's your brother? You said he was coming down this weekend, right?"

"Yeah, he left right before you guys showed up."

"Oh."

She turned her attention back to the Petes, who were calling out questions and encouragement to Flaco, whose muffled replies I could not make out. Although I think I heard one curse in Spanish. Hijo de something or other. I fervently hoped he would not drop the camera or fall out of the trapdoor, or even worse, crash through the non-raftered bits of ceiling into Werner's place. What a dumbass idea this was. We could all get in a lot of trouble. Especially me.

But thank goodness—Flaco was back. He lowered the camera to Handsome Pete, then swung agilely down to the floor. Smiling, he wiped his hands on his shorts and ran a hand through his hair to wiffle out the cobwebs and dust. His formerly white T-shirt was now filthy, as were his shorts and knees.

"Whew!" he said and sneezed prodigiously. "Let me shake off this dirt outside."

We all moved back to the living room and sat down. Flaco walked out on the veranda with Chopper interestedly following. He slapped the dust from his clothes, which then made it Chopper's turn to sneeze. He shook his head so hard I heard his ears flap. Margo got up and ran some water in a cereal bowl and took it out to the dog. He lapped it up vigorously. I made a mental note to eat my cereal from the other bowls in the future.

"Well," demanded Mona when both her sister and Flaco returned to the living room. "What did you see? Did you get any clue footage?" This last remark was obviously aimed at Petey, who was too enthralled or too oblivious or too used to Mona's sarcasm to care.

"Let's check it out," responded Flaco.

He took the camera back from Handsome Pete, popped out the videocassette and put it in the VCR. He briefly rewound the tape, then pressed play. After a few seconds of blue screen, a shaky picture of...darkness appeared on the screen. Oh. Now we were looking at Flaco's leg and the hem of his shorts. The view then whirled to reveal the dim interior of the crawl space and Flaco's hand opening Werner's trapdoor. Light flooded in. More shaky shots of nothing much while he maneuvered himself and the camera into position to tape my dead next-door neighbor's kitchen. He must have wedged himself into a pretzel to get those shots. I considered, for a moment, the possibilities inherent in such flexibility. Then gave myself a little shake and returned my attention to the TV.

The camera slowly panned to give us a bird's-eye view of the room. Flaco had apparently leaned down as far as he could, holding the camera with one hand and then slowly turned it full circle. Looked pretty much like my kitchen. Same linoleum floor, white countertop, curtains, cabinets and appliances. A trash can with a plastic bag in it and no visible trash. A glimpse of Chopper's food and water bowls on the floor. There were a few dishes set to dry in the wooden rack on the sideboard. Either Werner had thought to do his dishes and take out the trash before lying down to die in his driveway, or maybe one of his cop buddies had done it postmortem. Would they do that at a crime scene? I mean an "accident" scene? He even had the same cheap dish soap I had, in the big, yellow, cylindrical bottle. It felt odd to think he would never finish that bottle now. No more dirty dishes for you, Mr. Werner. No more dishpan hands.

The screen showed the doorway of the kitchen with a glimpse of the living room beyond. Flaco paused it there, so we could study the freeze-frame. I saw the end of Werner's couch and a rug on the floor. There was a large framed picture hung on the wall, but the sunlight reflected off the glass so I couldn't see what it was. As if that would be of any help anyhow.

No clues being obvious from the slice of living room we could see, Flaco hit play again. The picture slid along the back wall of the kitchen, with wood paneling halfway up, then glossy off-white paint. Just like my kitchen. I had adorned my paneling with a tasteful selection of Lynda Barry cartoons torn from the *San Tomas High Society*, the cooler alternative to the stodgy *Bay Reporter*. Werner had left his walls unadorned, but had gone to town on his refrigerator door.

Flaco froze the shot again. All kinds of papers were stuck to the fridge with magnets or tape. It was hard to see details, though, what with the graininess of the freeze-frame and the odd perspective of the video camera being about eight feet up in the air and pointed downward. Looked like takeout menus, some business cards or maybe they were medical appointment reminders, a snapshot of Chopper, coupons, postcards, a newspaper article, a parking ticket. He had his whole life stuck up there.

"Clues," Petey breathed out hopefully. He was sitting on the floor again, propped up against the couch. Mona, seated on the couch behind him, flung a leg over his shoulder and pulled his hair musingly.

"Flaco, can you zoom in on any of that?" asked Handsome Pete.

With all the amused tolerance of the professional for the amateur, Flaco informed him, no, he could not, not with this technology since he worked for the unified school district, not the CIA.

We all pondered the stuff on Werner's fridge some more. One of the takeout menus was clearly for the deli just down the street. The other one was too fuzzy to read. The print on the business cards was too tiny to make out, so they were a wash. The coupons looked like the ones I had so recently tossed for local merchants.

Handsome Pete had crouched down right next to the TV to get a closer view. "Is that a naked lady?" he said, pointing at the postcards.

Yup, no doubt about it. Upon further review, all of the postcards featured nude women, mostly from infamous strip bars up in San Francisco. Gross. The points I'd given Werner for having a photo of his dog on the fridge were immediately deducted.

I crinkled up my eyes to stare at the newspaper clipping. It didn't look like it came from the local paper, but without the heading or other hints, it was impossible to guess its source. There was a small photograph with the article, a little blurry on the freeze-frame, but obviously a man's face. Looked like a mug shot or driver's license photo. The whole piece of paper couldn't have been more than two inches by three. The bold headline read: EX-CON WINS LOTTERY. The rest of the text was too little to be legible. Somebody Werner had once busted, maybe? Or just irony so rich as to warrant posting on the fridge door?

The parking ticket I definitely recognized as being from the city of San Tomas, having some expertise in that area. Couldn't make out the date, the specific offense or the amount of the fine. He had probably planned to have that fixed by one of his former colleagues.

Flaco hit play again, but after a few more feet of paneling, the circle was complete. The tape ended there. Flaco explained it a little differently, but basically, he chickened out and didn't even try to get to Werner's living room trapdoor. That was fine with me. I expected Pacheco to show up any minute and arrest every single one of us. But of course, those things only happen in my mind. Some people say I worry too much.

He rewound the tape and we watched it a couple more times, but it still looked the same. Looked like the Great Crawl Space Camera Caper was a dead loss.

Margo, Handsome Pete and LeClaire decided to take Chopper for a walk around the block at that point. Mona and Petey grabbed fresh beers, then stepped out on the veranda to discuss (what else?) band business. That left me and Flaco and a suddenly embarrassing silence. He spoke first.

"Say, we better close up your trapdoor."

"Oh, my God, you closed his, right?" A sudden jolt of anxiety raced through me.

"Of course," Flaco said reassuringly.

Whew. In the kitchen, with Flaco close behind, I grabbed the broom I kept beside the refrigerator and tried to move the lip of the trapdoor cover back into place. It stubbornly resisted. I kept a-pokin'.

"Here, let me help," he said.

Standing behind me, he reached up and grabbed the broomstick handle at a point about a foot above my hands. Together, we finally got the pesky thing back in place. It settled into position with a little puff of dust. I felt better already knowing that the portal from Creepy Crawly Land was sealed off.

Lowering the broomstick together brought Flaco's arms around me, loosely encircling my waist. Which was obviously his plan, but I didn't mind too much. I took a step toward the fridge to stow the broom and he took it with me without breaking his hold. Once more, I was keenly aware of his ultra close proximity and body heat.

I set the broom aside and slowly executed a one-eighty-degree turn which brought me face-to-face with Flaco. We exchanged a serious gaze. His lips started toward mine for our first, actual, big-time kiss. Maybe this would be the one…

Nope. Dang it. Dummy lips again. Some remote part of my brain registered my bitter disappointment, while the rest of me focused on not letting it show. He was still kissing me. He seemed into it. I didn't want to be rude, but…

I heard Mona before I saw her.

"Hey, Hev, do you—" She came around the corner full tilt, only to come to an abrupt stop, rocking back on her heels. Damn the woman! What did she have against me anyway? "Oh," she said.

I clumsily pulled away from Flaco. "What?" I said curtly to Mona.

Flaco sighed. Audibly. Then stepped gracefully around Mona back to the living room and the promise of less immediate humiliation.

Which gave me the chance to hiss, "Jesus, Mona! Fuckin' good timing again."

"Well, excuse-ay moi, I thought you'd be back to your usual thirty-day gradual approach by millimeters plan." But even with that cut, I could tell she was sorry. Sort of.

And that little part of me, you know that really annoying part that constantly, objectively observes without offering any helpful suggestions, seemed to think I was...relieved? Not actually that upset? Off the hook?

Flaco reappeared in the doorway and told me he needed to get going, he had that work to do on the auditorium he'd mentioned earlier and he'd pick up his stuff later. He was leaving it behind so we could all watch the surfing video, if we wanted. His abrupt departure seemed like an easy out from an awkward situation, but God knows I'm a fan of those. And I couldn't hardly blame him after he'd been shot down twice.

I walked him out to the veranda, where we finally exchanged phone numbers. "Thanks for coming by." My voice sounded deeply insincere, even to me, and I was actually trying to *be* sincere.

He reached out his hand, but somehow ended up lightly cuffing me on the shoulder. Kill me. Kill me now.

I won't blame it on my subsequent foul mood, but the party did break up shortly thereafter. Margo too said she had to go to work. The band had practice. Me? A beer-induced nap on my trusty love seat was my plan.

Mona was the last one out the door. She paused there, looking me over. "You all right?" she said.

"Yeah...You don't really think that scraggly guy's after me, do you?" I asked her.

"That little worm? Naw. Probably wasn't even him. Probably just some weirdo, like you said."

"Yeah, you're probably right."

"You can come to band practice with us if you want, Hev," she offered.

A nap sounded far more enticing than that. I told her I was fine and I would see her later.

"Okay," she said. "I'll call you when I get home from practice. And lock this door behind me, all right?"

I did and then succumbed to a first-class siesta on the love seat, with the dog asleep in the corner too. But just one short hour later, I was awakened from a deep sleep. Turned out it was the shrill ring of the telephone, not the growls of polar bears as they ate my liver. Whew. The dog looked at me and gave a grunt like I was to blame for those loud ringing sounds.

"Hello?" Nothing. I tried again. "Hello? Mona?" Just the wind in the wires, then a click as whoever was on the other end hung up.

As annoying as that was, I was glad for the wake-up call when I realized it was almost four. Pacheco was due back any minute. I roused myself and took Chopper downstairs to visit the sand patch masquerading as lawn. He was humbly squatting near a clump of grass when Pacheco showed. We all three walked upstairs to Werner's door, where Chopper capered a bit, obviously happy to return to his own digs. I noticed the seal and all the yellow police tape was gone.

Pacheco produced the key and let the dog in. Closing the door and relocking it, he said, "He's got plenty of food and water in there. Don't worry about him."

"No problem," I said, a mite too truthfully.

"Well, thanks again, Heavenly," he said.

We parted ways. I had nothing more ambitious in mind than returning to my nap. Somewhere between Werner's door and my couch, however, something clicked in my cerebellum. I found the two microfiche prints from the library and plopped down in front of the TV. I rewound Flaco's tape and watched it again. Something was nagging at the edge of my brain. I concentrated as the camera panned over to the fridge and held there for about ten seconds. Without the freeze-frame, the picture was much clearer. The man pictured in the newspaper article on Werner's fridge looked a hell of a lot like the photo in my microfiche article—Jackson Miller. I felt a sickening thrill of recognition.

I wasn't one hundred percent certain. But there was a definite resemblance. If I could just see the actual article instead of a few seconds of videotape, I thought I would know for sure.

But doubts were already beginning to assail me. Maybe it was just a coincidence. Too many of those recently, though. Maybe I was wrong. I rewound the tape and checked it again. No, I was right.

It definitely looked like the same guy. The fridge version didn't look as clean-shaven as the microfiche man, it was true. I grabbed a pencil and shaded in some stubble on one of the microfiche prints. I made his hair messy too. I held it up to compare to the screen. I was no artist, but they looked identical to me.

Something about the drawing triggered another memory. I carefully erased the stubble and messy hair, then drew a moustache, glasses and a baseball cap. Voila! The Staring Man from the Mongol!

Holy crap. I had no idea what all of this meant. Jackson was an ex-con who'd won the lottery somewhere? But he'd told the property manager he'd come into an inheritance from his grandmother. On the other hand, if I were an ex-con, I might lie about a lot of stuff.

And wait—he wasn't missing, he was at the bar at the Mongol? I really wished I could read that fridge article and see what it said, but it was too tiny and blurry on the video. How in the world had Werner ended up with the article?

I heard Chopper barking next door. Dumb dog. Barking at nothing. Too bad he wasn't smart enough to open the front door for me, so I could pop in there and read the article. Ha.

There was no way I was going to attempt the crawl space, either. Without a ladder on both ends, my chances of making that trip successfully were zip and nada.

I sat on the floor in indecision. Werner had plenty of naked women on his fridge door, but only one newspaper article and nothing else pertaining to a man. It must have meant something to him. From my brief acquaintance with him, he didn't strike me as a big fan of irony, either. No cartoons at all.

I tried to think like Jackson. If I were an ex-con who'd apparently lived back east somewhere and I won the lottery, what would I do? Move out to sunny California and start a new life, luxury style, my brain answered. Okay. That made sense.

I then tried to think like Werner. If I were a cranky, middle-aged, retired cop who somehow found out my new next-door neighbor was an ex-con who'd won the lottery, what would I do? Uh…rail at the fates for being so unfair? Tell the neighbor that I (the law-abiding cop) would be keeping an eye on him (the criminal element) and let it go at that?

Shaking my head, I got up and dusted my hands off on the seat of my shorts. It was no use. I had no idea how Werner's mind had worked and trying to think like him was giving me a headache. As I bent over to turn off the TV and VCR, the phone rang again.

"Hello?"

Breathing. Faint background noises. This was getting annoying already.

"Hello?" I tried again. "Who is this?"

"Miss Wilcox?" a quiet voice said.

"Yes?"

"This is Jackson Miller."

I held my breath and froze for a moment. Even the dust motes seemed to slow down in the sunbeam arcing from the windowpane to the floor. "Who?" I tried.

"I think you know who I am. Especially since you called the parole office about me."

Why did I give those people my name? I swear I'm so stupid. But still, how did he get my home number? The San Tomas phone book lay on the footlocker next to the phone. I flipped the slim volume open to the Ws. Oh. There were no other Wilcoxes listed. Which meant my new number was quite likely the only Wilcox listing Directory Assistance had. Duh. Probably should have got an unlisted number. This is what comes of growing up in a small town.

"You're the only Wilcox listed, did you know that?" he asked, reading my mind.

I do now, I thought. "What do you want?" I said. "You know people are looking for you, mister."

"That's just a misunderstanding," he said dismissively. His tone changed to a persuasive one. "Look, I left something there in the apartment."

How did he know I was living in his old apartment? Now I felt completely freaked out. Not to mention scared shitless. For all I knew, he was just down the street on a pay phone. With a machete, duct tape and a coil of rope.

"What apartment?" I tried. My voice sounded weak and wobbly. A trickle of sweat made its way down my lower lumbar region.

"Hey, come on, Miss Wilcox," Jackson said cajolingly. "You're looking for me, right? And I need to see you. I know you rented my old apartment. Let's meet somewhere and we can talk. I just want to talk."

As an aside, I will mention here that he did not sound like a crazy person. His voice was soft, tenor, well-modulated. Not threatening at all. But still...I made a snap decision to play along, at least for the moment. I was curious about the guy, but there was no way I was going to meet him in some dark alley.

"All right," I told him. "How about the front bar at the Moonglow? Say Monday at six?"

There was some noise in the background. It *did* sound like he was on a pay phone, which was not helping my freak-out. "Sure, okay, see you there on Monday at six o'clock," he said hurriedly.

"What did you leave in the apartment?" I asked, but he'd already hung up.

I stared blankly at the receiver in my hand. It felt as though the air around me had gone electric. I tried to think calmly, but my mind was going a million miles an hour. One thing I was certain of—whatever he had left behind, it wasn't in the apartment now. The property management people had done a bang-up job of cleaning the place out and moving all his stuff into storage somewhere. I hadn't found so much as a paper clip left behind.

But what if he thought it—whatever *it* was—was still there? I felt a powerful urge to get out and seek haven elsewhere. Immediately. Should I call the cops? No, I should get the hell out right now.

I hung up the phone, grabbed my keys, my backpack and my sunglasses. Despite my urgent need to flee, it somehow felt crucial to also take the videotape with me. Like Petey said, it was a clue and God knew I needed one of those. I ended up just stuffing Flaco's surfing video and my microfiche prints in my backpack. The VCR with the tape still in it and cables wrapped around it was under my arm.

Less than two minutes had passed since I'd hung up the phone. I scanned the veranda for enemies through the peephole, slowly opened the door, then practically bolted for the car. I felt exposed, as though a sniper might be aiming at me. And here it was, just another lovely afternoon at the beach with people out walking their dogs and traffic going by. Unreal. I got in the Camaro and locked the door. Whew.

I headed (where else?) to the Murdocks'. My basic plan was to spend Saturday night there and think. Even if Mona and Margo were both out, I could always hang with the Nigerians or at Freddy's restaurant until one of the sisters returned.

CHAPTER TEN

Sunday

Sunday morning. I didn't feel like I'd slept a wink, but I must have because at some point, I woke up on the couch at Chez Murdock. It felt early, which my wristwatch confirmed. The curtains covering the west-facing living room windows were drawn, but sunlight struggled through the south-facing kitchen window.

The night before, Mona and I figured out how to hook up the VCR to her TV and watched the video again. I brought her up to speed on my unexpected conversation with Jackson and my "date" with him on Monday.

She was skeptical about the whole thing, but agreed the microfiche man and the video man did look pretty similar. She hadn't seen the Staring Man, so she had no comment on that part. She had no better idea than I did what it all meant. By then, it was past dinnertime, so we ordered a pizza (not from Rocco's). Both Mona and I drank way too much, talking until midnight, until I finally passed out exhausted on the Benny Hill couch.

I could hear the shower running. I sat up and put my feet on the floor, the chenille throw still covering my lap and legs. I ran a hand over my face and through my hair, which had alternating flat and protruding sections. I felt like crap—hung over, hot, sweaty, sticking to the leatherette, cranky because I couldn't be in my own place with my own bed and my own bathroom. Plus, upon reflection, I could have sworn I had heard various comings and goings in the night. Maybe even the sounds of someone getting some action and it sure as hell wasn't me. Or was that just a dream?

Turning toward the kitchen, I realized Margo was sitting at the counter. She was drinking a cup of coffee and seemed wholly focused on that occupation. Feeling my gaze upon her, though, she glanced up. "Mornin', Hev," she said.

She didn't even have the decency to look bad in the mornings. Her pale skin was gently aglow, her blue Murdock eyes luminous against the flame-red hair which tumbled about her shoulders.

"Mornin', Mars. Mona's in the shower?"

"Ummmm…no."

I sat up a little straighter. "Really? Who's in there?"

Before she could respond, the white-painted door to Mona's bedroom, which was immediately off the living room, opened. Mona emerged, carefully. She looked about as good as I felt, clad in a faded men's plaid flannel shirt which I knew to be hers. It hung down to her knees. The sleeves were rolled up in bunches at her elbows. It was so old and faded, you could only see a hint of the original shades of black and red at the seams.

Margo, of course, looked fabulous in a short, forest-green, belted silk robe which set off her hair and skin nicely. The robe was a thrift shop find, but Margo always made her clothes look good no matter what she wore.

I, at the other end of that spectrum, was wearing my panties and Mickey Mouse tank top from the day before. It disturbed me from time to time that I was still basically dressing the same as when I was eight years old. I cast about for the rest of my garments, which were in a wad on the floor by the couch. I slid into my shorty overalls as I stood. The couch made an impertinent noise as its cushions recovered from my weight.

The shower was still running. It was time for the Mystery Guest to sign in, because I needed in that bathroom in no uncertain terms. "Margo," I said, "you better get your boyfriend—" Unexpectedly, she started so badly at my words that she actually slipped off the barstool. I kept going. "—out of the bathroom pronto 'cause it's that crucial time, baby."

She clambered back onto her stool as gracefully as one could while gathering her robe about her and regaining her equanimity. "*My* boyfriend? Whoever's in that bathroom, it's certainly not *my* boyfriend," she declared with an eyebrow arched at her sister.

Mona was pouring herself a cup of coffee as if her life depended on it. She took a sip, then set the cup down on the counter, then used both hands to push her hair behind her ears. Firmly. "Well, Hev," she said, "I expect you'll be wanting to get on home now."

"What? Can I at least pee?" I exclaimed in outrage. The Murdock sisters exchanged a cryptic look. Both went back to close study of their coffee cups. "Hello!" I waved my arms to get their attention. "Girl who needs to pee here! Little help!" I headed toward the bathroom, only to find my way barred by Mona.

"Look, Hev—"

"Mona, I don't give a damn who's in there, just get him out!"

The shower stopped. The bathroom door opened. Mona's face, looking up at me, was screwed up in the expression of one who knows the balloon's about to pop and is powerless to stop the bang from happening.

Petey Houlihan stepped out of the bathroom into the hallway, clad only in a towel. He looked as fit as he was pale. Only the dyed black hair and the black nail polish stood out. "Oh, hey, Hev," he said as he passed by on his way to Mona's bedroom, where he closed the door behind him.

I looked at Mona, then at Margo, then back at Mona. "You? Him?" was about all I could get out.

"Oh, hell, when's the last time you got laid?" Mona said, abandoning all pretense and returning to the kitchen. "Go pee already."

My bladder was forgotten in the midst of my dumb amazement. I followed Mona back to her coffee cup and grabbed her arm before she could lift it to her lips. In an undertone, I hissed, "You slept with *Petey*?"

In the moment of silence which preceded her answer, I clearly heard the back bedroom door—Margo's bedroom door—open and the bathroom door close. I let go of Mona's arm and whirled around to look at Margo. The smirk she'd been wearing due to her sister's discomfiture was suddenly wiped from her face like chalk from the board.

Realizing somebody else was now in the bathroom made me remember how badly I needed to pee. "Crap," I said with feeling. "Now who's in there? Margo?"

Margo looked like she was experiencing some trepidation, which was very unlike her. She rose from her stool and took my elbow, trying to guide me toward the front door. "Hev, come on, I bet you can use Winston's bathroom, hey, let's go see." She said this like she was proposing A Fun Adventure for the two of us.

"I'm not using the neighbor's bathroom, for chrissake," I said, incensed. "What the hell is wrong with you guys this morning?"

"But you really have to pee, don't you?" said Margo cannily. "Niagara Falls? Water slowly dripping from a faucet? The tide washing up on shore?"

"Damn it," I said, resisting the urge to clutch and dance.

The toilet flushed, and I heard the sounds of someone washing his or her hands at the sink. While singing a familiar tune…about tainted love.

Oh. My. God. I brushed past Margo and wrenched open the bathroom door.

"…woh oh oh—oh, hey, Hev," I heard for the second time that morning. J. D. stood there in a pair of droopy boxer shorts and my Go-Go's T-shirt, in the act of adding toothpaste to a toothbrush I happened to know was Mona's.

I couldn't speak. I felt literally stunned—concussed and astonished. I reached out and grabbed the front of his shirt—my shirt!—and hurled him out into the hall, toothbrush and all, then slammed the bathroom door shut and locked it behind him. Both my brain and my body needed a few moments of solitude to sort things out.

My brain was in a whirl, but at least my body felt better a few minutes later. I threw some cold water on my face and slapped myself a couple of times just in case my subconscious was pulling my leg and I was still asleep. Nope, wide awake. As I stared at myself in the mirror, I considered my options. I could spend the rest of the morning in denial, locked in the bathroom…or pull myself together, act like an adult and go take stock of this new world order. And since I was cotton mouthed and dying for a Coke, I decided to pretend I actually had some dignity. No doubt they were all waiting for me anyhow to see my reaction. I unlocked the door and opened it. Nobody there. I heard some music playing at a low volume from the living room—Rickie Lee Jones. Perfect for a Sunday breakfast with friends.

I took a seat at the counter, the one Margo had been occupying. No one seemed eager to make eye contact except Petey who was now dressed and looking mighty pleased with himself. He was drinking orange juice straight from the carton and gave me a big, beaming smile from his barstool as my gaze raked the room. J. D. was at the stove frying up scrambled eggs and bacon. Margo, ever the bartender, pulled a can of Coke out of the fridge and plunked it down in front of me, then returned to slicing a cantaloupe. Mona was at the front window looking down at the street below, having opened the curtains. She cracked open the window to let in a little fresh air.

Rickie Lee suggested I hold on to my special friend. Yeah, right. Special.

I opened the can and took a slug of Coke. "So who wants to go first?" I asked the room.

"Well, I—" said Petey as Mona simultaneously said, "Shut up, Petey," without turning around.

J. D. looked over at me and gestured with the spatula. "There's no reason to be mad, Hev. Everybody here's a grownup."

Of course, the hell of it was that he was right. Did that make me one iota less mad? Of course not. I didn't even know why I was mad, which didn't help either. Guess I just felt...left out. Left behind. Stupid that I hadn't seen any of this coming. J. D. didn't even like the Murdocks! Ever since we were little, he'd thought they were brats and hated them tagging along and constantly being in our house. Of course, that was before Margo got game. And knowing I was wrong did little to explain the irrational sense of betrayal I felt. Damn. I hate feeling stupid and angry and out of control, especially all at once.

J. D. wiped his hands on a dishtowel and handed the spatula to Margo. "Here, you take over, babe."

Gag.

He headed back to her bedroom, hopefully to put some pants on. Mona was heading toward her bedroom too. She closed the door behind her.

Petey smiled at me again. If he'd had a tail, it would have been wagging.

"So, Hev—" he started.

"Oh, shut up, Petey," I said.

He frowned at me, then perked up again when Margo handed him a plate of food and a fork.

J. D. came back out, fully dressed and with his backpack over his shoulder. He wore his ratty Pep Boys T-shirt again. He handed me my folded up Go-Go's shirt. "I'm heading out," he said. "Hev, I'll talk to you later, okay?"

I gave him a look, but didn't answer.

"Hev?" he said again, with a little edge to it. The big brother voice.

"Yeah, okay, whatever."

Margo walked him out. I took the opportunity to make up my own breakfast plate. I took an extra piece of bacon, figuring it was comfort food and hoping I was depriving Mona or Margo of her favorite breakfast treat. If they got to have sex, then I got to have cholesterol. Not seeing all four food groups represented, I found some wheat bread in the fridge and made toast for me and Mr. Smiley, aka Petey Houlihan. I really didn't have any grudge against him and couldn't help but feel a little happy for him, he was so damn happy for himself. He shoots, he scores!

Margo came back in and busied herself about the kitchen. I noticed Petey checking out her ass in that short little robe when she put something back in a high cupboard, but I could hardly blame him. She finally sat down next to Petey with a small plate with just two slices of cantaloupe. That's how a perfect woman eats, my brain observed. And you have failed again, it added as I slathered more apricot-pineapple jam on my toast.

Petey finished his food, still grinning at me like a maniac. Like he was Santa and I was his favorite freakin' elf. Ho ho ho.

"Stop smiling," I told him repressively. "Don't you have somewhere to be?"

"Yeah," he replied happily through a mouthful of toast, "band practice at noon."

Did I have somewhere to be? I wasn't feeling too inspired to go home. Guess I had to eventually, though.

Rickie Lee's Side A concluded and the tape player clicked off loudly. Mona emerged from her bedroom clad in black, low-top Chuck Taylors, black running shorts and a black tank top from San Tomas's Harley dealership. Way to color coordinate. Her backpack was slung over one shoulder, and she clutched her mike stand in one hand. Still avoiding my gaze, she said to Petey, "Let's go. I'll give you a ride to practice."

Petey protested, "But practice isn't until noon!"

Mona replied, "So we're starting early."

"But that's like three hours away! I thought we could—"

"Could what?" Mona's tone could have peeled the paint off a car.

Petey's desire to protest seemed to wither on the vine. Welcome to the morning after, big boy. Shrugging, he got off his barstool and polished off the last of the orange juice. He took the mike stand from her hand as they went out.

From the doorway, Mona said, "Hev?"

"Yeah."

"I'll call you later."

"'Kay."

"'Kay."

The door closed, leaving me alone with Margo. Silence hung heavily in the air, not that she was ever bothered by awkward silences. Those were for other people to worry about. She really did look beautiful in that green silk robe. A single "diamond" on a gold chain hung around her neck. Fingering it, she eyed me, then said with typical directness, "Look, your brother's cute and I did him. Are you gonna get over it or what?"

Always with the sensitivity, that Margo.

"He's not...cute, for God's sake. He's...He's..." Words failed me. Always with the articulateness, that me.

"He's what?" she said, prompting.

"He's...he's just J. D. I can't believe the two of you hooked up. Jesus, Margo."

She took a sip of her coffee, a secret smile like the Cheshire Cat's playing on her lips. "Guess I'm not such a brat anymore, huh?" she said, running a fingertip around the rim of her coffee cup. Her eyes were dancing.

"You wish. Is this going to go on or was it just a one-time thing?"

"Would you mind if it did?" she replied.

"Honestly, Mars, I don't know what to think. I guess it's none of my business."

"Well, just to let you know, despite the grimy mechanic's fingernails, he was quite the gentleman. Very...considerate, if you know what I mean."

"Oh, my God, shut *up!*" I flung a forkful of scrambled eggs at her to emphasize the point, which she dodged, now openly laughing at me.

"You can clean that up while I take a shower," she said. Still laughing, she went off to the bathroom.

I took the opportunity to put the Cars in the tape player. Needed a little more energy to get going. I cleaned up the eggs and went ahead and did everyone's dishes too, just to keep from thinking too much. When I was a kid, it had seemed like everything had its place and fit perfectly into it. Now it seemed like things just kept getting messier and messier. I wiped down the stovetop and the counters with a damp paper towel. There. All non-messy. Until lunch.

Margo was done with the bathroom and getting dressed in her room, so I grabbed a shower and put yesterday's clothes back on. When I came out, Margo was back on her barstool, talking to somebody on the phone. "Yeah, she's here," she said. "Just a minute." She held the receiver out to me, a mocking look of amazement writ large upon her face.

I mouthed the words, "For me?" to her and she mouthed back, "Flaco."

Flaco?

"Hello?" I said.

"Hi, Heavenly, this is Flaco. Flaco Gutierrez."

I got a little flutter in the pit of my stomach from the way he rolled those Rs ever so slightly. "Hey," I managed.

"Hey. Hope you don't mind I tracked you down at your friends' place. I thought you might be there when I couldn't reach you at home."

And how did he have the Murdocks' number? Oh. They were listed too. How many "M & M Murdocks" did I think there were in the phone book? Plus, no doubt the Romanoff had their number on file. I murmured something noncommittal as he continued talking.

"Listen, I'm calling to see if you'd like to join me for dinner tonight."

Margo wasn't even trying to fake how much she was eavesdropping on this conversation.

"Um… Dinner…" Frankly, I wasn't sure if I liked that idea or not.

"Yes, my whole family gets together for a big family dinner once a month and tonight's the night. My mom and my aunts really cook up a storm, and it's a lot of fun."

Whoa! Stop the presses. Big family dinner? I don't think so, buddy. "Big family dinner—wow…That sounds…really big," I said. God, I suck at small talk.

Margo was semaphoring me some advice or comment which I couldn't decipher, but it didn't matter. I hadn't even had one real date with Flaco yet. No way in hell I was going to expose myself to family scrutiny at this point. Although a home-cooked meal from the mom and all the *tías* did sound good…

"So what do you say?" Flaco pressed me for an answer.

"Uh…Yeah, I mean no, I don't think I can make it tonight, Flaco. Sorry."

"Oh." He sounded genuinely crestfallen.

Margo made a rolling motion with her hand, like c'mon-c'mon-don't-lose-the-momentum. I nervously wound the phone cord around and around my index finger.

"Maybe we could get together during the week?" I asked him. Shit, why did I even say that? Sometimes I think my ingrained good manners really hold me back in this life.

"Yeah, well—I have to work tomorrow night and the next night too," Flaco said apologetically. "My buddies and I are painting a restaurant and we promised to have it done by Wednesday morning."

"Oh." My turn to be crestfallen. I mean relieved. I mean, oh hell, what did I mean? Margo was making googly eyes and flapping motions now. I had no idea what that translated to. "What?" I mouthed at her.

In my ear, Flaco said, "But how about Wednesday night? We could get a drink at the Mongol."

Man, he was not giving up. And I couldn't think of a reason to say no. At least not one I could say out loud. Plus, Margo was killing me with peer pressure, albeit nonverbally. "Okay, um, I guess that sounds good. So...seven o'clock?" I said to Flaco. I felt like I was sweating and I'd just gotten out of the shower.

"Excellent!" he said enthusiastically. "I'll meet you at the front bar at seven, all right?"

"Okay, see you then," I said. My gaze fell upon the VCR, still hooked up to the Murdocks' TV. "Oh, and Flaco, I've still got your VCR and stuff, remember? It's here with me at the Murdocks', actually."

"Do you mind dropping it off at my aunt's? I can pick it up from her later," he said.

"Sure, no problem," I told him. "See you Wednesday." I hung up. I handed the phone back to Margo, who was smirking like she'd had something to do with it.

"So?" she said.

"So, we're having a drink on Wednesday at the Mongol. No big deal."

"Oh, Fuh-laco," she said in a high, obnoxious voice, licking the receiver with a pink and pointy tongue. Gross—I was just using that.

I rolled my eyes at her and adopted an attitude of breezy composure, even though my insides were jumping all over the place. I had a date! Holy shit! Just like a real person! Even the thought of having to go back to my apartment and deal with the whole Jackson Miller thing couldn't entirely extinguish the giddiness/alarm generated by the thought of Wednesday at seven p.m. Fuckin' egg, as Petey would have said.

Margo was talking to me. Apparently, Mona had filled her in on everything, including the phone call from Jackson, at some point. "Hey, I don't think it's safe for you to be in your apartment by yourself," she said.

"Yeah, well, thank you for your support," I replied, ever the smartass.

"No, seriously. What if the dog moved in with you?"

"What? The Rottweiler? That's your suggestion?"

"Yeah, when I was talking to Rich yesterday—"

"Who the hell is Rich?"

"The cop, Heavenly," she said, exasperated. "Rich Pacheco. He said they're going to have to put him in the pound if somebody doesn't adopt him soon. He and some of the other cops are going to clear out Werner's apartment next week since he didn't have any family here, but none of them can take Chopper. So he needs a home and you need a guard dog."

I studied her, trying to figure her angle.

"I could call Rich and ask him, if you like. He gave me his number yesterday," she said, sweet as pie.

Aha! There it was. "Let me get this straight," I said. "You just slept with my brother and now you want me to help you hit on a cop. Is that about right?"

Still sweet as pie, she said, "But Hev, I thought you didn't want me to sleep with your brother."

That was actually true. Disturbing, but true. And now that I thought about it, Pacheco might let us into Werner's apartment to get the dog and his doggie gear. Which might give me a chance to check out that article on the fridge…As much as I love dogs in general, I wasn't crazy in specific about taking Chopper into my home, but there was no doubt I would feel safer with him there. And I certainly couldn't consign him to the pound in good conscience…

Margo watched my wheels turn. It was truly unfair how she got to look like an angel when she was actually pure evil, but that's how it goes.

"All right," I said, "it's a deal. Call him up."

"Really?" She smiled.

"Yep. We can meet him there in ten minutes."

Chalk it up to Margo's sexual wiles or the low crime rate in San Tomas (my recent experiences not withstanding), but ten minutes later, we stood with Pacheco at Werner's front door. I heard Chopper whining, yelping and ponderously frolicking about behind it. That was my new one-hundred-and-twenty-pound roommate. Yikes. I wasn't even sure if my lease allowed me to have a pet. Oh, well. I guessed that was the least of my problems.

We'd dropped off the VCR stuff with the Romanoff on our way out. Then, in my car on the way over, I'd worked out with Margo that she would keep Pacheco occupied while I got the dog's food and stuff from the kitchen.

When Pacheco opened the door, Chopper shot out, caromed off the railing and hurried down the stairs to the sandy patch in front of the building to do his business. I left Margo and "Rich" unconcernedly following him down to the lawn while I went for the kitchen. My palms were sweaty. I'm really not cut out for this espionage stuff.

I doubled back to the door and nervously checked that Pacheco was still spellbound by Margo. He was, of course. She was alluring in a close-fitting pair of her own shorty overalls (they were big that year) that showed off her long and lovely legs. Pacheco appeared to be closely inspecting the hooks on the straps of her off-white overalls which overlaid her close-fitting, orange, French-cut T-shirt. Suede work boots laced up to her ankles completed the outfit and I'll be damned if she didn't make those look good too.

In the meantime, here I was perspiring in my dead neighbor's kitchen, grabbing a fifty-pound bag of smelly dog food for a dog I didn't want while wearing yesterday's wrinkled, dirty clothes. She got to be beautiful and dashing and flirty. I got to be smelly and wrinkled. That's apparently the way the Universe wanted it.

First things first. I put the dog chow, food and water bowls and a leather leash by the front door, ready for a quick getaway. I then turned my attention to the article on the fridge, consciously averting my gaze from the superhumanly endowed, naked, postcard women. Did I really dare to take it? But if I didn't, they were going to throw it out anyhow when they cleaned out his apartment the next weekend. A sane woman probably would have just told Pacheco or another one of the cops about the clipping instead of taking it herself. But, my little voice rationalized, if they don't believe you because you're just a stupid, college dropout chick and then they throw it out, you'll have missed your chance to take it.

Still, I dithered. I couldn't decide and felt myself chickening out already. You'll get in trouble if you take it, sang the angel on my right shoulder. Just grab it and stop being so damn feeble, demanded the devil on my left, jabbing me in the collarbone with her tiny pitchfork. Ow.

The article was so short, I couldn't help but read it while I stood there deliberating:

EX-CON WINS LOTTERY

FAIRFIELD—Lottery officials confirm that the winning ticket for Wednesday's $6,000,000 jackpot was purchased by William Sikes, 29, of Fairfield. Sikes was released from state prison last May after serving a term for vehicular manslaughter while driving under the influence. He was convicted in 1976 for the deaths of Jacques and Emily Bastille and their two young daughters, Courtney and Brooke, after running a stop sign on an icy winter road. Witnesses reported seeing Sikes drive away from a local roadhouse at a high rate of speed prior to the crash. State troopers recorded his blood alcohol level as .12. Neither Sikes nor his mother, Nancy, of Fairfield, could be reached for comment following Wednesday's lottery drawing.

My initial reaction was shock. What a horrible story. Drunken asshole wipes out an entire family in one fell swoop. Awful. Those two little girls…

The fact that I now heard far too many horrible stories on a daily basis at the Public Defender's office hadn't desensitized me to the awfulness of the world—in fact, the opposite. It seemed like each one hit me harder and harder, right in the gut. And this one in particular—I mean, how many times had I driven drunk since coming to college? And Mona too. I shuddered to think of how a similar fate could have befallen us. No doubt Jackson hadn't set out that night to commit a crime—to kill a family. But he did. Not out of malice, but out of drunken stupidity. Maybe that capacity to be a villain lurked somewhere in all of us, just waiting for one bad decision to bring it out. With a shudder, I willed myself to smother those dark thoughts and refocused my attention on the article.

The photo was a mug shot, showing a thin young man with disheveled dark hair, stubble on his face and a surly look in his eye. Jackson Miller. AKA William Sikes. His fellow citizens must have hated him for his crime, then hated him even more for his dumb luck and instant riches. But why did Werner have the article in the first place? What was the connection?

The sound of Pacheco's heavy steps coming up the stairs snapped me out of my reverie. Decision time—I wavered for an instant, then my devil won again. I grabbed the article off the fridge and moved some of the postcards around so the empty space wasn't obvious.

I didn't want to mess up the article by folding it and putting it in my pocket before I'd even had a chance to really study it, but where else could I put it? Pacheco was on the veranda now. Panic! Flustered, I stuck the article down the front of my shirt in my bra (plenty of room there), ran to the front door, threw the bag of kibble over my shoulder and grabbed the bowls just as Pacheco stuck his head in.

"Oh, here, let me help you with that," he exclaimed, taking the bag off my shoulder. Which was fine with me. Stepping back to let me pass, he said, "Whew, it kind of stinks in here."

He was right. In contrast to my sunny (and hopefully sweet smelling) apartment, Werner's place was dim and cobwebby-looking. The smell was probably at least partially due to Chopper being shut up inside there, but it was undeniably fuggy. Some sort of cigarette smoke, middle-aged white guy's hair product, Chinese food, dog chow and eau de Rottweiler combo. I was glad to be out in the fresh air again.

I headed down to my door where Chopper was vigorously lapping Margo's left calf, hoping the sound of paper crackling under my shirt wasn't as loud as it seemed. Margo was laughing, bending down to pet the brute's head. Pacheco followed, probably hoping he'd get to lick Margo's other calf. We all went in my apartment, where Pacheco and I dumped the doggie stuff on my kitchen counter.

"Thanks," I said to him.

"No, thank you for taking him," he said earnestly. "I was really worried he wouldn't find a home, so thanks."

Margo joined the thank-fest by putting her hand on his bicep and telling him she *really* appreciated his help, with overtones that would make any man hopeful at the true extent of her gratitude. He asked if he could give her a ride somewhere. She regally accepted. I walked them out to the veranda. Margo looked back over her shoulder to give me a smartass nod with one eyebrow cocked. I watched them drive away with the big dog at my side, shaking my head. Margo and I were so different, she made me feel like a different species.

I had to admit I did feel safer with the dog there. He yawned, giving me a comprehensive view of his many sharp teeth. I wouldn't have wanted to mess with him, that's for sure. I turned to go back inside, but he beat me to it.

He did a comprehensive olfactory tour of the joint, snorting and sniffing at every corner and object. I let him roam and followed in his wake, thinking it was probably wise to check the place out myself—I had been gone all night, after all. I didn't really think Jackson or anybody else had broken in overnight—everything looked fine—but it never hurts to double-check.

We ended up back in the living room. I looked at Chopper, who was eyeballing me with his tongue hanging out of the side of his mouth. I was glad he was there, but it was hard to tell which one of us was less comfortable with the situation.

I got an old Mexican blanket previously used for camping and beach bonfires out of the bedroom closet. I arranged it on a corner of the living room floor for him. He came over to stand at my side, looking up at me, brow furrowed.

"I now pronounce us man and wife," I said to him.

He made a noncommittal noise in his throat, but settled down contentedly enough on the blanket, appearing ready for a snooze.

I sat down on the love seat and pulled the article out of my shirt, smoothing it out on my thigh and reading it again. I kept a pen and a pad of paper handy on the footlocker/coffee table for grocery lists and other important notes. I jotted down some thoughts about the article, none of which were earth-shattering, like the fact that although I had no idea what newspaper the article came from, it wasn't from the local paper. Totally different typeface, for starters. There was a town called Fairfield not too far away—on the way to Sacramento, actually—but clearly the story hadn't taken place there. For one thing, we didn't have a lottery in California. Maybe someday. There was probably a Fairfield in every state in the union, I thought. This one sounded like it might be back east somewhere with its mention of icy winters, state troopers and a "roadhouse." Werner was supposed to be from back east somewhere…

Oh, hell, what did I know? The only state I could rule out for sure was California. There was no clue as to when the events had taken place, either. Where was Nancy Drew when I needed her? I looked at my grocery list pad, trying to think of anything else significant. The actual grocery list itself had only two items on it at present: vodka and light cream. Apparently, I was no better at nutrition than I was at solving mysteries.

CHAPTER ELEVEN

Monday

The rest of Sunday passed uneventfully, although with the addition of some walks around the block to my usual routine. I would not normally have been at ease strolling about the neighborhood in the pitch black late at night, but I must say with Chopper at my side, I felt pretty tough. I wasn't sure if he would actually come through with tooth and claw on my behalf, but he certainly looked the part. The few other late-night strollers we encountered gave him a wide berth. Nothing like a Rottweiler at your side to stop you from making new friends. Anyhow, he peed upon the neighbors' mailboxes and bushes with gusto. Since I didn't know any of them and it was dark, it was all fine with me. I was just hoping to get through our temporary domestic arrangement without him peeing on anything belonging to me.

And how temporary was that, anyhow? I did feel better with him at least playing the part of my protector. The whole situation felt unreal. I felt like I should be afraid, but I wasn't. I was always concerned I wasn't feeling what I should have been feeling in exactly the right proportions, whether it was fear, lust, empathy…

But back to the point: I had a tiny apartment with a very large dog. Who didn't smell that great. I could barely afford to take care of myself. I had never had a dog before, to tell the truth, or any pet. My parents didn't believe in pets, stating it was contrary to the laws of nature for man to constrain a wild thing. Yeah, whatever. The hamsters, kitties and pooches held in constraint by my friend's families all seemed relatively happy with the scheme of things. Especially the dogs, who appeared to be full-fledged members of their families. Even the Murdocks had a scruffy mutt at one point in their childhood. Grandmother Murdock, so intolerant of the foibles and screw-ups of little girls, would actually kiss that mangy cur on the lips even though we all knew its main and oft-achieved goal in life was to get in the garbage.

But I do like dogs. No doubt my parents' refusal to provide me with a pet instilled me with a burning desire to have one. Just like their unflagging devotion to Colgate drove me straight to Pepsodent as soon as I had a choice in the matter. It's hard to rebel when your parents are hippies.

This was a problem shared by the youth of San Tomas, as so many of their parents were granolas. This probably explained why all the high school kids were absolute preppies that year. In response to their parents' liberal views, they'd swung all the way back to the far right. In fact, I happened to know the president of the Young Republicans club at San Tomas High was one of Carmen's clients—he'd been busted pursuing a favorite hobby of the townies, namely fag bashing.

His single mother, who was the cashier at a shop on the mall selling crystals, incense and other San Tomas necessities, lacked the funds to hire a lawyer, although I partisanly believed there was no better attorney on the face of the earth than Carmen, free or not. With three of his buddies, this clean-cut, handsome young man had bravely beaten to a pulp another young man whom they'd caught on a side street on his way home from the Avalon, a small gay bar just up the street from the Mongol. After leaving him unconscious in the gutter, they'd all but killed a vagrant who'd also had the misfortune to cross their paths that night. The kids called the latter "troll bashing" because so many of the homeless lived under bridges and highway overpasses.

I'd overheard Carmen on the phone while I was in the hall filing one day. Despite her best efforts, it looked like eighteen-year-old Mr. Prep was on his way to state prison in the fall instead of college. There were times when I regretted the dark window my job at the Public Defender had opened for me on the previously guileless streets of San Tomas.

Anyhow, Chopper and I passed a peaceable Sunday evening together, as I reported to Mona when she called. And he was darn glad to see me when I got up early on Monday morning, although I suspected this was due to biological needs more than burgeoning affection. I took him down to the beach, two blocks away, to run and play in violation of the many posted signs banning dogs from the beach. Several other dogs and their owners were out in the early morning sun and everyone seemed to be having a grand time. I drank my last can of Coke while I watched them. Nothing like getting up early, getting some exercise and blowing off municipal codes to start your day right.

By the time we got back to the apartment, it was past seven, so I really had to hustle to get ready and make it to work on time. Which I did on a wing and a prayer, having left Chopper locked in the apartment, licking himself on the Mexican blanket. He seemed resigned to the plan, perhaps due to Werner abandoning him daily in a similar fashion. I hoped he would deter any would-be intruders while I was gone.

The night before, while locking up after the last of our evening rambles, it had finally occurred to me to wonder if the landlord had changed the locks since Jackson Miller lived there. That gave me pause. I hadn't thought to ask. Ever. I had trusted with this landlord and all previous landlords that I was moving into secure premises. A chill ran through me when I imagined Jackson having a key to my apartment.

But, I'd reassured myself, I had a chain lock on the front door. And Chopper. And my trusty Louisville Slugger propped up in the corner. Feeling paranoid again, I'd done another quick security check of the apartment, bat in hand and Chopper by my side, to make sure no one had broken in while we were at the beach. Nope, no murderer in the closet or shower.

I suppose I could have spent the night at the Murdocks' again, but frankly, after all that drama, I couldn't stand the thought. I needed some alone time. And the comfort of my own space, my own bed, my own shower. Maybe, in retrospect, I was foolish. But all the dangers swirling about me that I sense so keenly these many years later were nothing more than beach fog to me then.

So Chopper and I passed the night without disturbance and the morning at the office passed much the same way. The usual rush of Monday morning work kept me busy until noon, when I had to run home and liberate my roommate for a lunchtime poop run. I wondered if this was anything like having a baby. Part of me kind of liked being responsible for another living thing, while the rest of me was already thinking what a pain in the ass it was. Everything is always so complicated.

Back at work, my afternoon assignment was to (wo)man the front desk, which was slow until the afternoon court session started letting people out around one thirty. Then it was reprobate city. But just like always, we got 'em all processed, assigned and interviewed so both the guilty and innocent alike could be home in time for supper with their loved ones.

Strange to think of the sinners having just as nice a dinner as the saints.

Unsure, as usual, as to my status in either group, I didn't have dinner. Instead, I jammed home, let Chopper out for five minutes to do his thing, then found myself apologizing to him for locking him right back up in the apartment. He seemed unmoved by my promises to return ASAP.

I picked Mona up in front of her place. She had insisted on accompanying me to my "date" with Jackson. And since no one can insist like Miss Mona Murdock, she was there. Besides, it was happy hour and they had free hors d'oeuvres in the Mongol's front bar on Monday evenings. Intrigue, appetizers and cheap booze—who can resist that combo?

"So, what's the plan again?" she said in the car.

I was glad to have her along, even if she did weigh only ninety-seven pounds. I could tell she was into her self-appointed role of bodyguard/backup—she was dressed in all black again: black boots, raggedy black jeans and a black Scorpions tour shirt with the sleeves cut off. She was wearing her trout lure earring again and even the spikes in her hair had a menacing look about them that evening.

My plan, if you could call it that, was to get there prior to the designated rendezvous time of six o'clock and scope out the sitch. Kind of funny to think I had this meeting with Jackson on Monday night at the Mongol's front bar, then my date (gulp) with Flaco on Wednesday night in the exact same place. My list of places to meet men of whatever stripe for a drink was pretty short. And getting shorter.

The front bar was a large rectangular room, maybe sixty feet by one hundred. Many small tables with two to four chairs dotted the interior. We snagged one in a corner that had a good view of the entire room. I didn't see Jackson anywhere. There was a long bar at one end of the room and the periphery was marked by large potted palms. The high ceilings with their broad-bladed fans added to the *Casablanca*-ish feel. I had a sneaking suspicion I was more Peter Lorre than Bogart or Bergman in this particular drama, but we don't always get to pick. And who did that make Mona? Dooley Wilson, of course.

The bar was about half full when we arrived. By six o'clock, it was full and the joint was jumping. Happy hour at the Mongol was a San Tomas tradition. There was no live music in the front bar other than solo or duo acoustic acts on Sunday afternoons. James Taylor kind of stuff. Mona had yet to crack that room, but her time was coming. I knew it. Anyhow, the stereo system that evening was pumping Talking Heads.

By unspoken agreement, neither Mona nor I had mentioned the events of Sunday morning. It helped that the loud music was discouraging to thoughtful conversation. I had decided the subject was best relegated to the furthest back corner of my mind for now. Why did I even care who was sleeping with whom? I didn't really, except it seemed like if everybody else was doing it, why wasn't I? Was I such a monster? Doomed to a lifetime of loneliness and spinsterhood, whatever the hell that means? I had tried to think about it objectively a few times during the day, but that only brought on fleeting dizziness and nausea. At least the avoidance of the topic of romance kept Mona from teasing me about my date with Flaco. Instead, she scanned the crowd intently, on the alert for any sign of Jackson Miller. I felt pretty damn alert too, wondering (a) if this meeting was a really rotten idea and (b) what he might have in mind.

Mona said, "Lemme see those pictures again."

I handed them over. She studied the pictures carefully, then scanned the crowd again. "He's not here," she said, handing the papers back to me.

I nodded. I hadn't seen him either. But it was only ten minutes after six. Maybe he was running a little late. We decided to wait until at least half past the hour. In the meantime, we hit the buffet. There are few two-word combinations sweeter in the language than free appetizers, I must say.

He never did show. We ended up seeing some friends from school, plus one of Mona's (adult) piano students and two of the Public Defender's better known recidivists, but no Jackson Miller. Heck, I even saw Leo the defense attorney at the bar on my way back from the restroom. He appeared to be alone and was drinking with steady purpose. He didn't notice me, thank goodness.

By six forty-five, we'd finished our last drinks and were ready to move on. Not a total waste of time, what with the free food, but I wondered why he had stood me up after he'd seemed so eager to initiate the meeting. Oh, well. Just like with Flaco, I couldn't tell if I was relieved or disappointed.

We left the Mongol and walked to where I'd parked my car a few blocks away. There was still plenty of daylight left and the air felt soft and warm outside. The sidewalks of the mall were still busy with shoppers and other pedestrians.

People who didn't know me and Mona that well might assume I was the more practical of the two of us. Actually, her well-developed sense of survival forced her to be extremely practical. I could afford the luxury of being an idiot from time to time, with the safety net of my parents and their home always just a phone call away. Since Grandmother Murdock tended to be about as helpful and sympathetic as a bag of last week's zucchini, Mona and Margo had learned to be self-reliant.

Thus, it should have come as no surprise to me that Mona was vehemently arguing with me that I should spend the night at their place (as if she was capable of arguing non-vehemently). "Look, Hev," she said, "this is no joke. This guy could have a serious screw loose. I don't think it's safe for you to stay at your apartment for now."

I explained my chain on the door/Rottweiler/baseball bat theory of personal safety as we drove to the beach. With little effect. She was still going on about it when we pulled up in my driveway.

Chopper was sitting in the yard, carefully scratching an ear with a hind foot.

I had my hand on the key to turn the engine off, but I didn't turn it. I was experiencing that weird break from reality sensation, like the universe had just tilted on its axis about five degrees. I had left the dog locked in the apartment. So how had he gotten out?

Mona looked back and forth from the dog to me, and up to the apartment door, which appeared to be shut. There was no one in sight. Once again, her practical nature came to the rescue while I still sat there trying to process.

Opening her door, she leaned forward and pulled the lever to make her seat flop forward as well. "Chopper!" she yelled. "Get your furry buns in here!"

Chopper leapt to his feet at her stentorian tones, then ambled amiably over to the car, peering in interestedly with his tongue lolling out. After about sixty long seconds of both me and Mona entreating him to enter, he finally got the idea and maneuvered himself into the small backseat area of the Camaro. Once he was in, Mona slammed her seat back, the door shut and told me to "hit it."

I stole one more glance up at my apartment door. Still shut. No one in sight. Checking over my shoulder, I got a face full of meaty-smelling doggie breath from Chopper, but managed to back out into the street without incident even though he was blocking most of my view. We didn't go far. I drove the two blocks to the little corner minimart where Mona took charge again, calling the cops on the pay phone. When I saw the patrol car roll by fifteen minutes later, I pulled my car out and returned to the apartment. The cop had parked in the driveway on what I still thought of as Werner's side, so I parked on my side.

I'll be darned if it wasn't Pacheco again. Maybe there were really only, like, five guys on the whole San Tomas police force and all the criminals had very little to worry about. Which worrying thought was actually supported by the actions of the clientele at work. Shaking that thought off, I got out of the car as Pacheco stepped out of his.

"What's up?" he said. Mr. Warmth.

Briefly, I explained that I was afraid someone was in my apartment. He asked who else had a key. Nobody, I said. Just the landlord and me, as far as I knew.

"Boyfriend?"

Didn't I just say nobody? "No," I told him. "But…"

"What?" Pacheco asked.

I told him I thought it might be the guy who used to live in my apartment.

"What, that guy who took off?" Pacheco said skeptically. "Why would he break in? The landlord's got all his stuff in storage, right?"

"You know about Jackson?" I asked, surprised he seemed to know all about it, but I was glad I didn't have to go through the whole explanation. And this was his beat, after all. Perhaps I had underestimated him.

He nodded impatiently, so perhaps not. His body language seemed dismissive somehow, as if he had already shrugged off my theory without even thinking about it. Hysterical females— what are you gonna do with 'em? He told me to sit tight and he would check out the apartment. I gave him the keys, then got back in the Camaro with Mona to watch. I wondered if the door was indeed still locked. Sure enough, I saw he had to use the key on the doorknob, but the deadbolt was unlocked. I knew I had locked them both, as I always did.

With his hand on his holstered gun, he entered, leaving the door wide open behind him. I couldn't see much from my vantage point down below. After a couple of minutes during which I found breathing difficult and Chopper licked my ear twice (yuck), Pacheco emerged, gun in holster. He waved us up.

On the landing, he declared, "There's nobody in there. No sign of forced entry, either."

Mona asked, "Did you check the closets?"

He smiled knowingly. "There's no one in there, miss. I've been thoroughly trained in search procedures, I assure you."

Mona said, "Did you check the crawl space?"

That got rid of the smile. Pacheco turned to me and gave me my keys back. "Do you want to see if anything's missing? As far as I can tell, it doesn't look like anybody was in here."

He was right. If Jackson had rifled through my stuff, he'd been careful about it. Nothing looked out of place. I walked through the apartment with Pacheco, Mona and Chopper all following behind me like a little parade. I had nothing of value. Sad to say, all my stuff was crap. Even the TV and the stereo were aged hand-me-downs from J. D. I couldn't see that anything was missing or had even been moved. Except the dog. I looked at him. Nope, definitely not smart enough to unlock two locks, open the door, and lock and close the door behind him. He wagged his stumpy little tail as he happily returned my gaze. My new best friend.

Shit! Realization struck me—Jackson was probably his friend too. So much for hoping the beast would tear him from limb to limb. No wonder Chopper looked so happy. He'd probably just been fed a bunch of doggie treats by the very intruder I was hoping he'd protect me from. Meaty-breathed traitor.

Pacheco, with exaggerated patience, was explaining to Mona that no, he wouldn't be calling the crime scene techs to fingerprint the place because he didn't see any evidence of a crime. Clearly, he thought I had somehow let the dog out, forgot about him and forgotten to lock my deadbolt as well. Probably memory loss from all that pot smoking—dang college kids!

In response to her nagging, however, he did check the crawl space, getting up on a chair and shining his flashlight up and down the tunnel much as I had done.

"All clear," he told us, getting down. His tone and body language indicated he was ready to go. "If you're feeling uncomfortable here, you might want to spend the night with friends, miss," he told me. "Or have someone stay here with you. But I really don't think there's anything to worry about. You can deadbolt the door behind me when I go, plus you've got the dog, right? Give us a call if you have any trouble, of course."

I noticed we were back to "miss." No more Heavenly. Fine by me. I thanked him sincerely and locked the deadbolt when he left. I then immediately went to my bedroom and started packing my backpack with a few clothes and other essentials. Mona came in behind me, now sporting the bat over one shoulder and drinking one of my beers.

"Good," she said, approving of my activity. "You're definitely staying with us tonight."

"No argument there," I replied.

I stepped into the bathroom and grabbed stuff like my toothbrush and deodorant. My swimsuit hung from a hook in there, now completely dry. I threw it in the backpack too, for no particularly good reason except I wasn't thinking completely straight.

It was still daylight outside, but I felt a strong compulsion to get out of there quickly. Who knew if he was lingering nearby, waiting to come back for whatever he was seeking? If he hadn't found it the first time, whatever it was. Had he hidden something in the apartment when he lived there? Or left something behind on purpose or by accident when he fled? I didn't want to be there to find out. I didn't care what Pacheco thought—I *knew* Jackson Miller had been in my apartment. I could feel it in my gut, which was twisted with anxiety.

"Do me a favor," I said to Mona. "Put some dog food and his bowls and leash in a trash bag—the big bag of food is under the sink in the kitchen. Trash bags are there too."

"Oh, hell no, I don't think so," she said. "He's not coming with." She pointed her bottle at the dog while leaning on the bat like a cane. She was such a shrimp it was almost the right height.

"Oh, come on," I said. "I can't lock him up in here all night. He'll mess on the floor, for one thing. Besides, I feel better with him along." I did, even if he was just a big doofus.

She complied, albeit reluctantly, leaving the bat on my bed. I finished packing and went to check the veranda through the peephole. Empty. Mona emerged from the kitchen, with a kibble-enthralled Chopper in her wake. His eyes were pinned to the trash bag in her left hand. Her mostly full beer was in her right.

"Let's go," I said.

She hesitated, glancing at her beer bottle, condensation beading its exterior. Here I was, running for my life, and she was worried about maintaining her buzz.

"Jiminy Christmas, just bring it with you!" I told her, exasperated. "Here, I'll get you a cup." The last thing we needed was for her to be spotted drinking a bottle of beer in my car.

I went into the kitchen and found a plastic tumbler that would conceal her offense from prying eyes. I closed the cabinet door. Wait—something was different. The Kahlua was gone! "Son of a bitch! That asshole stole my Kahlua!" I called out indignantly.

"Who, Pacheco?"

"Not Pacheco, ya bonehead—Jackson! Jackson stole my Kahlua. And I hadn't even opened it yet. Damn." I had really been looking forward to a White Russian or two. Dang. Now even that small dream had been crushed.

"So are we going?" Mona said.

"Yeah, yeah, here's your cup."

We made it to the car safely, my head on a swivel looking for Jackson in the driveway, across the street, everywhere. Chopper was right by my side, with Mona bringing up the rear, reminding me that pets were not allowed in her building and we'd have to elude the Romanoff at all costs.

"He's not moving in, all right?" I said with some irritation borne of anxiety. "Just give me a night and I'll figure something out, but for now, let's just get the fuck out of here, okay?"

We piled back into the Camaro and made good time to her place. Chopper liked standing up in the backseat to look out the back window with his hind feet on the floor and his front feet on the seat, so every time I glanced back there, I was treated to a close-up of Rottweiler heinie. Not a pretty sight, let me tell you. Better than a little yappy dog running wild all over the car, though. I hate that.

The closest parking space was three blocks away from the Murdocks' front door. The sun was starting to go down as we made the hike, with Chopper marking every parking meter, signpost, mailbox and hydrant he came across. He was having a big day, I could tell.

Thankfully, there was no sign of the Romanoff when we entered the building. I could hear her TV blasting a game show as we climbed the stairs. I'd like homicidal maniacs for fifty, please, Alex.

Chopper scampered up ahead of us without urging and we made it into the apartment without encountering anyone. Margo was slouched on the couch, talking on the phone. She mumbled something and hung up as we came in.

No lights were on, but the waning daylight outside still provided a little illumination. The dog bounded over to her and she started petting him, questioning us with her glance. Mona sat down on the coffee table, facing her sister, and launched into a lively explanation. Nothing seemed required of me, so I slung my bag on the floor, scavenged a beer from the fridge and made myself at home on the other end of the couch.

"So, they're spending the night here," Mona finished. Oh, great. The dog and I were now "they." A couple!

Margo gently stroked Chopper's forehead as he sat panting adoringly at her feet. "Fuckin' egg," was her thoughtful comment.

CHAPTER TWELVE

Tuesday

So I woke up on the Benny Hill couch again. It was still dark, but close to dawn according to my inner clock. I heard horrible snoring coming from about a foot away, which disoriented and alarmed me. For a second, I dreaded I had somehow awoken in a strange bed with a strange man with a terrible sinus deformity. Then the world rearranged itself and I realized I was back on the Murdocks' couch, in their apartment, with a congested Rottweiler asleep on the floor just beneath me. Whew! Big relief.

I don't know why my subconscious always suspects this secretly promiscuous side to me, just waiting to come out. The truth was, I'd only slept with one other guy besides the aforementioned Kyle and that had been just the one time on an ill-fated camping trip with Mona and a bunch of her musician friends about a year prior. Shudder in retrospect. I am never drinking Yukon Jack again in my life, I swear.

Celibacy was actually not that daunting a prospect when you thought about all the details involved with the alternative. Fluids. Smells. Conversation. Yikes. I wasn't against the prospect of someday latching on to the right person, but the awkwardness of the process was certainly tiresome. I was fine waiting it out for now. Maybe it was just easier not thinking about that stuff. As if I could stop the part of my mind that thought about it All The Time.

Of course, then there was Flaco. I liked him. Didn't I? I kind of liked touching him, feeling the heat of him. Or maybe that was just some longing for a little contact, the feel of another warm body. I wasn't entirely sure it was Flaco-specific. I liked the idea of having someone to hang out with, go to the movies with, go to dinner with. What did he like the idea of? What the hell did he see in me, anyhow? The creepy thing, as I got older, was that I was starting to figure out how much of the time we simply fill some role for the other person, with one's true character simply not a factor except as it contributes to the breakup.

All this predawn and not even on my own couch. Argh. I leaned over and gently patted Chopper until he snorted and turned over, which stopped the snoring, thank God. I turned over myself and vowed to think only good thoughts until I fell asleep again.

"Hev. Hev."

Somebody was gripping my upper arm and shaking me. The light was blinding now. Somebody licked my cheek. What the heck? I opened one eye to see Chopper moving in for another lick and Margo walking away, calling over her shoulder, "Wake up, bonehead! You're late!"

Damn, she was right. My watch said nine thirty-eight. Fuck. Fighting Chopper off, I sprang to my feet. The couch made a low, tortured moan behind me as I sprinted for the phone to call Stephanie. She was lukewarm, to say the least, at my profuse apologies, but I assured her I was on the way. Damn, she was going to make me pay for this, for sure, I thought. But since I was already super late, I took a quick shower. Thank God I had a clean shirt and underwear in my backpack to go with the khaki pants I'd worn the day before.

The Murdock household was late rising as a rule. Mona was still asleep when I flew out of there. Margo was drinking a Coke and smoking a cigarette in the hall in her robe, but promised to look after Chopper for the day. God bless her for pulling another cold can of Coke out of her robe pocket and passing it to me like the baton for a runner in a relay as I passed. I ran down the stairs and then galloped down the street to my car, calling out a good morning to a bemused Freddy who was sweeping the sidewalk in front of his restaurant.

I rolled into the office at two minutes after ten, avoiding the steely gaze of Stephanie, muttering regrets and contritions under my breath as I scuttled to my corner. Fortunately, it was a busy Tuesday morning and the office was in full swing, so she didn't have time to spare for me beyond a terse reminder that I was on phone duty that morning. She had made the mail run herself earlier that morning and dumped the calendar info on my desk. I powered up my computer and tried to drag my wits together to plan my workday. I slugged down the Coke remaining in the can Margo had given me and wished I had another one, but I didn't dare cross Stephanie's line of vision for a while.

"Hey, Hev," Tasha stuck her head around the corner. "Some guy's been calling for you this morning. Won't leave a message, just says he'll call back."

I couldn't imagine who it could be. Then wondered if it might be Flaco. Had I told him where I worked? Maybe he'd call me at work if he couldn't get me at home or at the Murdocks'? I felt a little warm flush creep up my cheeks at the thought of this possible telephonic pursuit. Or maybe he'd come to his senses and was calling to cancel.

I asked Tasha, "Did he have a little bit of an accent?"

She shook her head. "Nope. Sounded all-American to me. Had an all-American name too—Wilson or Miller or something." She went back to her desk, not seeming to notice my poleaxed state.

Miller. Gulp. My mouth suddenly felt even drier.

How did he know where I worked? Werner had known, but I'd assumed that was because Terry's questions to some of his former fellow cops had tipped him off. How did Jackson know? I suddenly had a clear mental image of the top of my dresser: framed picture of my family, earrings, loose change, one of those hula girl dolls on a little stand...and my most recent pay stub from the temp agency which had "San Tomas County Public Defender" listed as my assignment. If he had been in my apartment—and I knew he had—he could have easily seen that. Shit.

Plus there was my boneheaded call to the parole office when I gave them my name like a doofus. Maybe Mona was right and

Jackson had not only paid off the scraggly assistant marina manager, but someone at the parole office as well. Maybe he had a whole network of spies in place to alert him if anyone asked about him. Or…could Werner have set up the spy network as he tried to track down Jackson? As a cop, he'd know the value of having snitches on the street to keep him informed. My brain was in danger of shorting out as I juggled all these conspiracy theories. The only thing I knew for sure was that I did not know what was going on. What else is new?

Stephanie emerged from her office and told Ethel she had business across the street at the courthouse, but would return shortly. I waited until the door closed behind her, then counted to ten to make absolutely sure she was gone. I asked Ethel if she could cover the phones for just a minute while I zipped down the hall to get a Coke and she docilely agreed.

Libation secured, I was back at my desk a few moments later. I popped the top while I considered my next move. Which should have been to get to work and assemble the calendar, but instead I got my little address book out of my backpack and looked up the number for my landlord. Or rather, the property manager. She answered on the first ring.

I said, "Um, hi, this is Heavenly Wilcox, the tenant in the number three apartment on Highland."

"Oh, hi, Heavenly," she said. "How are you doing? Wasn't that just terrible about poor Mr. Werner?"

It was, but that wasn't why I was calling. After a few comments back and forth about the terribleness, I got to the point. "You know, I just wanted to check—was the lock changed on my apartment before I moved in?"

"Oh, I'm sure it was, hon," she said. "We routinely have the locks rekeyed when a tenant leaves. Let me just check the files here and see when that was done…" There was a pause while she shuffled through some papers. "Oh, dear," she said.

Uh-oh, I thought.

"You know, the circumstances of Mr. Miller's disappearance were so unusual…I don't see that we did have the locksmith come out. There's no note in the file…But I'm sure it's not a problem, dear—I mean he's long gone, right?"

Little did she know, I thought. We proceeded to work it out that she would have a locksmith come by that very afternoon to rekey the lock if I could meet him there.

"At five fifteen?" I suggested.

She told me to plan for that and if it was going to be a different time, she would call me back. I gave her the office number, thanked her and we hung up.

I'd been extremely fortunate that there had been no incoming calls during my brief conversation, since I was on phone duty. I hoped the dry spell would continue and turned my attention to assembling the calendar. I had barely started, though, when the phone rang. I jumped about a foot. I couldn't let it just ring because I was on phone duty. This was before voice mail too, so chickening out to let that pick up wasn't even an option. And, yes, this was way before caller ID and star sixty-nine.

It had now rung three times. I had no choice but to pick up. "Public Defender," I said warily. I heard breathing. I waited.

"Heavenly Wilcox?" he said.

There didn't seem to be any point in denying it. The man knew where I lived, knew where I worked. "Yeah," I said in a flat voice. "What do you want?" Hoping to get it over with. Make this all go away.

"You know what I want," Jackson said. "You took it from his apartment. I want it back."

For a second, I was confused, as well as terrified. For that split second, I thought he was talking about the dog.

He said, "I want the clipping, Heavenly. You got that?"

"Oh," I managed.

Right. The clipping. Really, I didn't know what was more in danger of seizing up—my brain, my heart, my lungs, my extremities. None seemed to be functioning properly. I felt sweat pooling in the small of my back. I could also feel the newspaper article crinkling in the back pocket of my khakis, right where I'd left it last night along with the microfiche print.

"The clipping," I repeated.

"Yeah, the clipping," he mocked my dull tone. "The one you stole off Werner's fridge. I know that's where he kept it. He showed it to me himself on Thursday, before he had his little accident. I went back for it yesterday and it was gone. You're the only one who's been asking questions about me. You're the only one who would have taken it. And now you're going to give it to me."

Oh, my God, I thought. Jackson had been there with Werner on Thursday? Why? Had he played a part in Werner's death? Worse and worse.

"How'd you get into Werner's apartment?" I asked, stalling for time. And genuinely curious too. Having just confirmed he had a key to my apartment, I wondered if he had Werner's too.

"The crawl space, genius. Haven't you figured out you've got a nice little tunnel connecting you to next door yet?"

A part of my brain noted I really didn't care for his tone. The rest of me was pretty frightened.

"Look," he said, "just give me the fucking clipping and we can put this whole thing behind us. Okay?"

I was wholeheartedly for that, although I wasn't sure I believed him. I could give him the clipping, but we both knew I would still have the information I'd gained from it. Which wouldn't matter as long as he was both innocent and sane. Yeah. How did I get myself into this?

"Okay," I said, stalling some more. "So how come you didn't show up at the Mongol last night?" Might as well get all my questions answered while I had him on the line.

"Something came up," he said shortly. There was noise on his end—a voice in the background. "Do you mind?" he said, apparently not to me.

Was he on a pay phone? Hopefully not one across the street at the courthouse. Although the courthouse was full of cops…

The voice on his end spoke more loudly. And clearer. Something about "not supposed to be using that phone." I could hear other noises, faintly, in the background, I realized. Sounded like somebody being monotonously paged. And beeping, like some kind of machinery. Was he at an airport? The nearest big airports were San Francisco and San Jose. That would be good, since both of those places were at least an hour away. He responded curtly to whoever had spoken to him with his hand muffling the receiver. Sounded like buzz off or something even ruder. At least the interruption gave me a second to think. When in doubt, make something up.

"Hey, Jackson." I really felt we were on a first-name basis by now. "Maybe I gave the clipping to the cops. Maybe you should go ask them."

There was a pause. Heavy breathing. I clearly heard the page in the background this time: "Dr. Lincoln, please call one-two-five. Dr. Lincoln, one-two-five."

Then he spoke. Softly. "You're dead, bitch."

There was a click and that was it. The call was over.

My hand shook as I hung up. This was way out of control. Maybe I should give the clipping to the cops. A little voice in my head sang, *you'll get in trouble!* True. I really shouldn't have taken it. Why the hell did I take it? *Curiosity killed the cat*, sang the voice.

Oh, shut up, I replied. If you're not going to help, just shut up.

The phone rang again, but thankfully this time it was a real client, whom I transferred to his attorney. In quick succession, I took three more calls from clients, answering basic questions, transferring and/or taking a message as the situation warranted. After concluding the last one, I pulled the clipping out of my pocket and smoothed it down on the desk. Jackson Miller's unsmiling face stared up at me from it. The little square of newsprint was looking pretty crumpled from having been folded, refolded, stashed in my pocket and sat on. Lieutenant Stokes's card was still in my backpack—I could call him right now and say…what?

Okay. Once again, when in doubt, make something up. So what if I gave the clipping to the cops, but told them I had somehow blamelessly and accidentally acquired it? Like…My powers of invention failed me. I doodled on my yellow phone message pad, but inspiration was not forthcoming. Although it looked good when Stephanie stalked back into her office. Fortunately, she stalked right back out again with paperwork under her arm, heading down the hall to an attorney's office. Taking advantage of her further absence, I made a quick call to Mona even though I knew it was too early for her.

She answered with a sleepy, "What?"

"Mona, wake up, it's me."

"What?"

"I need your help with something. Are you awake?"

Yawning. "Yeah. I guess. What's up?"

She sounded semialert now. I filled her in on the latest and told her I was seriously thinking of calling the cops.

"Good. Do it. Good night."

"No, wait!" I explained my fear of getting in trouble for removing the clipping from Werner's apartment in the first place.

She thought it over. "Well, just put it back, ya bonehead. How hard is that? You read it while you were in there getting the dog food and you just now realized its significance. They'll buy that. Why would they even suspect such a sweet college dropout girl as you anyhow? Can I go back to bed now, please?"

"Okay…but it's awful wrinkled."

"What?"

"The clipping—it's really wrinkled from being in my pocket."

"So, iron it, genius! Call me later. I'm going back to bed." She hung up.

I had now been hung up on and sarcastically called a genius by both my newfound nemesis and my oldest and best friend in the space of fifteen minutes. What did that say about me? More importantly, could I iron the clipping without burning it up? Maybe if I put a pillowcase between the paper and the iron…Was that what Heloise would advise?

A steady stream of incoming calls from clients kept me busy for a while. Until it suddenly occurred to me I was in possession of an actual clue. Somebody, somewhere was paging Dr. Lincoln. If that call was local, so was the good doctor. If I knew where Honest Abe was, I'd know where Jackson was, at least for the moment. Sometimes I am so smart I can hardly believe it. I borrowed the phone book from Ethel when Stephanie took a bathroom break. Good job he wasn't named Smith or Jones. And there he was—the only Lincoln listed: Harold Lincoln, M.D., internal medicine, with an office address downtown. But wait. They wouldn't page him at his own office, right? How big could his office be?

I dialed the number.

"Doctor's office," a motherly sounding woman answered.

"Is Dr. Lincoln there?" I asked.

"No, he's not in the office today. Can I take a message?"

"Uh…is this his office or an answering service?"

"It's the office, dear—can I help you with something?"

Hazarding a guess, I asked, "Is he at the hospital?" The hospital wasn't that far from downtown, so I was hoping for a no on that one.

"No, today's the day for his rounds at the Meadows."

The Meadows. Never heard of it. Sounded like some pricey mental asylum or rehab clinic for rich people. Or maybe a nursing home. I was already flipping through the phone book looking for it. The nurse, or whoever she was, was getting grumpy and asking again if I wanted to leave a message. I thanked her and hung up without further ado.

I couldn't find any listing in the San Tomas phone book. I tried information, but they had no number for the Meadows in San Tomas. It might be located in any of several nearby towns, for all I knew. Or even San Francisco.

Stephanie still hadn't come back, so I wheeled my chair over to a spot where I could see Tasha at the front desk, conferring with Leo about something and Ethel at her computer. "Any of you guys ever heard of the Meadows?" I asked them.

Tasha looked blank, Leo stiffened and Ethel, surprisingly, pinked up with a blush.

"Ethel?" I asked.

"Well, yes," she admitted. "It's down toward Monterey—a private treatment facility for alcoholics in Sea Shell," she explained, mentioning a small community down the coast from San Tomas.

Leo, not liking this turn to the conversation, headed back down the hall to his office. Tasha eyeballed Ethel speculatively, causing her to blush a shade deeper. I turned back to her too. Could boring old Ethel, with all the pizzazz of a sack of cement, be harboring a Dark Secret?

"My uncle Elbert spent some time there a few years back," she explained primly.

"And?" prompted Tasha.

"And the only time they could keep that man sober was when he was locked up in there. My aunt spent a fortune trying to dry him out."

I heard Stephanie's voice in the hallway as she belabored Leo about something. Her voice got louder as she came closer to us. Ethel heard her too and firmly returned to her work. I wheeled on back to my desk to fake some more work too.

At least I knew where the place was now, so I could get the number from 411. Best of all, it was far enough away that I didn't need to worry about Jackson showing up for at least an hour or so. And if he was locked up in there...but if he was locked up, how'd he get out to break into my apartment? It was all very confusing.

I resolved to go back to the Murdocks' at lunchtime, try the ironing thing and run this stuff past Mona. Her idea to replace the clipping was better than any idea I had. And if it worked, I could call Stokes after lunch. Hey, maybe I'd have the whole thing wrapped up by five o'clock. Color me optimistic.

At noon exactly, I went out the door behind five of the female attorneys who were off to lunch somewhere. God forbid they should invite me, scum of a temp clerk girl. The gulf between us was unbridgeable, even though they were only a few years older than I was and only making about five grand more a year. And I had a lot less student loans to pay off! Snobby or no, at least they were good cover to get me to my car safely. Wherever Jackson was, I didn't think he was nearby—but I was definitely feeling paranoid and kept an eye out regardless.

Mona was up (barely) and Margo was still there too, when I arrived unannounced for lunch. Chopper came out of Margo's back bedroom and frisked about my ankles, sniffed me carefully, then lay down in front of the front door where he could watch all of us as we talked in the living room.

I told them about my conversation with Jackson, my thoughts about the police and my date with the locksmith. After a brief discussion, the labor was equally divided amongst us. Margo was clearly the best (possibly the only) ironer in the group, so she went to work on the clipping. Please note she did use a pillowcase, without prompting from me. Aha! I knew I'd been right about that.

Mona got the number for the Meadows from the operator and proceeded to call, pretending she was checking them out as a potential place for her uncle with a drinking problem. Poor old Uncle Elbert.

I made good use of my time by preparing and eating a peanut butter and banana sandwich. Across the room, Margo held up the newly unwrinkled clipping for my inspection.

"Perfect! Thanks, Mars," I said, toasting her with my glass of milk.

She sat down next to me and laid the still warm piece of paper on the kitchen counter. Mona hung up the phone and consulted the notes she'd taken.

"Okay," she said. "It's a high-priced drunk tank for rich people like you thought, Hev. They've even got a waiting list of people wanting to get in. The minimum stay is thirty days and they lock you up there for the whole time. If you want the full treatment, you gotta stay for at least sixty days, but some people are there for like six months."

"And you can't get out the whole time?" I asked.

I wondered if this explained Jackson's "disappearance." The timing was about right. But wouldn't the staff realize they had a missing person checked into their facility? Wouldn't the cops check those kinds of places when they were looking for missing people? Maybe he'd checked in under another name?

"Apparently, after that initial sixty days, you can get day passes for once or twice a week if you're good," Mona explained, reading from her notes.

Hmmm. Like for Mondays and Thursdays, the days when he'd popped up in my life? If that was true, I was safe for at least thirty-six hours and had that amount of time to figure out what the heck to do next. If he followed the rules. If he was even there. I shared this line of thought with the Murdock sisters, who mulled it over.

Mona finally shook her head, not really disagreeing, but at the whole situation. "Look, Hev, it doesn't really matter—this is totally messed up, no matter how you slice it. I think you're right about telling the cops about the clipping. Let them deal with it. This is way out of our league. Who knows where the fucker is? Maybe he's in rehab or maybe he's downstairs at Freddy's with a butcher knife, you know?"

I had to agree. I looked at Margo who, typically, shrugged noncommittally and looked down at her hands, folded on the counter. I noticed she had painted her nails a pale, pearly pink. I glanced at Mona's hands. Her black nail polish was starting to chip. Plus, now the words "LOVE" and "HATE" were written on her knuckles in blue ink. Pretty.

My lunch hour was waning quickly. Draining my milk, I told them I'd call Stokes from the office. On my way out the door, Mona said I could come to band practice that night after I was done with the locksmith if I brought a pizza that was not from Rocco's for her and me to share. Deal. She also gave me the spare key to their apartment.

Driving back to work, I thought about my upcoming call to Lieutenant Stokes. Best case scenario was I would somehow put the clipping back on the fridge, then tell the cops about it. But how in the hell could I possibly put it back? Get Pacheco or the property manager to let me back into Werner's apartment on some pretext of getting more dog stuff? I was really clutching at straws and I knew it. I could call Flaco and ask him to help…but shit, give a guy even a little encouragement and he'll think you want to have sex with him for sure. It's very tedious.

If I didn't put the clipping back on Werner's fridge, I'd have to admit to the cops that I had taken it from his apartment. I could really be in trouble for that. I'd seen a few "obstruction of justice" cases come through the Public Defender and they hadn't ended well.

Ay yi yi, I just wanted the whole mess to be over and done with. I was almost back to work and I still didn't know what I was going to do. I considered telling Stephanie I was sick and then heading straight for the police station just to get it over with. Just thinking about lying to Stephanie actually did make me feel a little sick.

Shit. I guess I'd known all along what I was going to do. I didn't have it in me to lie to Stephanie's face, much less tell the cops some story. Either one of the Murdocks could have pulled it off with aplomb, but I'd foul it up for sure. Crap. I decided I would just tell Stokes the truth and let the chips fall where they may. Waste of a hell of good ironing job, though.

I parked in the employee lot and didn't see a soul on my short walk back to the office. I hurried anyway, tension building in me. Things seemed to be closing in and I didn't like it. At all. I stowed my backpack in my desk drawer and tried to think. I was having trouble breathing, let alone concentrating. I wasn't sure if twenty-two-year-olds could have heart palpitations, but it felt like a conga line in my chest.

Stephanie, returning from lunch, made a suggestion which loosely translated to "get off your butt and do some filing." Which I did, but all the while waiting for her to take a smoke break so I could call Stokes. Finally, at quarter after three, she went out the front door, cigarettes and lighter in hand. I scooted down the hall to my desk and dug Stokes's card out of my backpack.

"Lieutenant Stokes's office," a nasal female voice answered after several rings.

"May I speak to Lieutenant Stokes, please," I requested.

"He's not in. May I take a message?"

"Oh. Gosh." I really should have rehearsed this ahead of time, I thought. "Um, would you ask him to please call Heavenly Wilcox?" I gave her my work and home numbers, plus the Murdocks' number.

"What is this in regard to?"

"Jackson Miller. And Mr. Werner."

I realized I still didn't know Werner's first name. I really hadn't had time to know much of anything about him.

"Jackson Miller, Mr. Werner," she repeated phlegmatically. She said she'd give him the message and we hung up.

Well, that was anticlimactic. But at least I had tried.

Now what? Back to work. I couldn't think of anything else I could do about the situation that I hadn't already done. I'd left a message for Stokes, I was getting the lock changed at my apartment, I was ready to bare my soul to the cops and tell them everything I knew and/or guessed if they would just call me back. In the meantime, I'd make sure I stayed away from dark alleys. If I was in the company of other people at all times, I should be safe enough, I thought. I hoped. Besides, what was I supposed to do, hide in a closet until Jackson Miller died of natural causes?

I went back to the filing for the rest of the afternoon. Only another decade or so and it would all be done. I walked out with Tasha at the end of the day and made it to my car without incident. The locksmith, a taciturn old man in his seventies, was waiting at my apartment building. He had parked his van on what I still thought of as Werner's side of the driveway. Since he'd already spoken with the landlord, he knew what was needed and went right to work after I pointed out my door to him.

I felt exposed, sitting in my car on the driveway. Anybody driving by or lurking nearby could see it there. It was high time for me to get over my garage door phobia anyhow, so I put the Camaro in the garage and shut the door. I decided to see if Jules was home, so I could wait in her apartment while the locksmith did his thing.

To my surprise, though, I found Jules sitting at the foot of the steps. "Hey, what's up?" I asked her.

She was dressed for running again, this time in black Dolfin shorts and a gray, French-cut Adidas T-shirt. Her long bare legs and arms looked elegantly coltish. "I'm locked out," she said.

I laughed, inappropriately perhaps, but it just struck me as funny that she was locked out and I was there with a locksmith.

She said, "I thought Ash would still be here when I got back from my run, but I guess we miscommunicated."

"The locksmith could let you in," I suggested.

"Yeah, right," she said with a smile. "For big bucks."

Her tone made it clear that wasn't an option. She added that Ashley would be back soon, she had only gone to the grocery store. I suddenly wondered if I could get the locksmith to let me into Werner's apartment... No, no, bad idea, I told myself. And bad Heavenly. I was going to tell the cops the truth, stop this life of crime and that was that.

I sat down beside Jules on the stairs. She looked at me appraisingly. I'm sure my work clothes weren't too impressive, but at least I'd taken a shower that morning. Oh, well. Give me an "F" in fashion again.

Jules asked, "Are you locked out too?"

"No," I told her. "But it turns out they never changed the locks after Jackson left, so they're doing it now."

I'd never asked her about Jackson, I realized. Or Werner either. Or exactly what her deal was with Ashley... I told her about Chopper being out the night before and my suspicion that Jackson had been in my apartment. She seemed interested, but skeptical. Of course, I hadn't told her the rest of it—how he had called me twice and threatened me during our last conversation. Not to mention the newspaper clippings and seeing him at the Mongol. I could have, I supposed, but it just seemed like too much to go into. I was just getting to know her and frankly, I didn't want to come off like a wacko. Besides, I was more keen on hearing what she had to say.

That faint hint of peach fragrance was tantalizing my nostrils again. Maybe it was her shampoo...or her skin lotion. She was showing a lot of skin in her running shorts and T-shirt. I yanked my mind back to the topic at hand. "So what did you think of Jackson?" I asked her. "Was he cool?" I doubted it, but I was curious to hear her impressions of the man.

"He was okay at first," Jules said, shrugging. "We didn't really have that much to do with him except to say 'hi' in passing. He was kind of braggy about all his money, you know, having a boat and a Porsche and everything. He always found a way to bring that up if you were talking with him. But he was all right, I guess. For a while. Then he started acting sort of weird."

The locksmith clattered down the stairs toward us. He muttered about having to do something in his van. I moved over closer to Jules to let him pass. I figured he'd be back in a minute or two, so I didn't bother to scootch back. It was very pleasant there in the late afternoon sun. The usual ocean breeze danced through the treetops. Traffic was light on Highland despite the fact it was commute time. There really was no rush hour in San Tomas.

"So Jackson was acting weird?" I prompted Jules.

"Well, he was drinking a lot. And I mean a lot. And when he wasn't drunk, he would be all antsy and jumpy. Paranoid, you know?"

"When did he start getting weird?" I asked.

She thought about it for a moment. "Christmas, I guess? Sometime around the holidays. I tried to avoid him as much as possible, but he'd come knock on our door sometimes for one reason or another. Drunk, usually."

The holidays. Thanksgiving was when she and Ashley had dog sat for Werner, when he'd gone back east because of his mother's death. Had Werner found the newspaper clipping during his trip back east? And he'd bought his Mercedes in that same time period too, according to Terry. Had he inherited a big pile of dough from his mother?

I realized that when I'd been trying to think like Werner before, I'd been trying to think like a law-abiding cop. But what if Werner hadn't been so law-abiding and ethical? Terry had mentioned the suspicions that Werner was on the take and had turned on his fellow officers, ratting them out to save his own skin. That kind of matched up with the a-hole I had met. A-hole was certainly a better description than pillar of integrity...

So what if Werner hadn't used the clipping to keep Jackson in line? What if he had used it to blackmail him? He had said he won the money for the Mercedes gambling on football, but he didn't bet. What if blackmail money had bought the car?

Jules was looking at me curiously. God only knows what expression was on my face. I reassembled my features into a more neutral guise and asked her about Werner. "How about Werner? Did he have money too?"

She looked a bit taken aback at this change of subject, but gamely kept up. "Werner? No. He was a cop. They don't make that much money, you know?"

"But he had that Mercedes," I said.

"Yeah," she agreed. I could tell she had wondered about the expensive car as well.

"Did he inherit money when his mother died?" I asked.

"I don't think so," she said. "When he came back and picked up Chopper, he was bitching about all the expense of flying back there and having to clear out his mother's apartment. Didn't sound like she had a dime. But then, he was always pissed about something. He was kind of a cranky guy."

You don't say, I thought.

"He used to bitch at Ashley about playing her trombone too loud," she went on. "But I never really had a problem with him. My uncle's a cop in Los Angeles. After I mentioned that to him one time, he was cordial enough to me."

I couldn't think of anything else to ask about Jackson or Werner. Frankly, I didn't know what to do with the information or suppositions I already had, except to share them with Stokes when he called. I was kind of ticked he hadn't called back by the time I left work, but I assumed he was a busy man. I'd try him again first thing in the morning. In the meantime, the conversational ball was back in my court.

"So...your uncle's a cop in L.A., your folks have a place up in the mountains and you go to UCST," I said, summing up what I knew of her.

"Wow, you've really been paying attention," she said with a grin.

I felt a little embarrassed. I wasn't sure why. I hoped I wasn't blushing. Every time I'd ever hoped that, though, I was.

"Did you remember my major, though?" she asked, teasing.

"Uh...computer science, right?"

"You got it! I'm such a geek, I know, but I love computers."

She didn't look like a geek to me. Not at all. I stood as the septuagenarian locksmith returned with my shiny new key and two copies. We went up to my door so I could make sure they all worked, which they did. I'd have to drop one off for the property manager someday soon. The new key gave me a little peace of mind that Jackson wouldn't be waltzing in and out of my apartment at will. Although as I reopened the door with the third key, I had a scary thought—what if he were in there right now, waiting for me? I glanced in my living room. Nothing looked amiss. Well, I wasn't going in there anyhow. I locked the door and signed the locksmith's paperwork, thankful the landlord was paying.

The locksmith departed. I went down the stairs after him and stopped at Jules's step again. I had nowhere to go until band practice, but I really didn't want to get there too early to minimize the hearing loss. And it seemed rude to just ditch her there on the stairs when she was locked out…but maybe she wouldn't want to hang out with me anymore on a voluntary basis, so to speak. Her dorky upstairs neighbor. My tongue froze up on me again. Always at the worst possible times.

"So, uh…" was about as far as I got when she thankfully interrupted me.

"Where's Chopper?" she asked, standing up. "I take it he's not upstairs."

"No, he's with Margo," I told her.

"Oh," she said. There was an awkward pause. She gave me that appraising look again. It was a little unnerving. "So how 'bout that drink I mentioned on Saturday?" she said.

"Oh. Okay," I said with enthusiasm. Anything to delay my arrival at band practice. "Where do you want to go?"

To my chagrin, though, she grimaced and said, "Oh, no." But then she saw the look on my face and laughed, saying, "Sorry! It's just, here I am, inviting you out for a drink when I don't have any money on me. My wallet's in the apartment. My ID too. Duh."

"That's okay," I said, reassured. "I'll buy this time and you can get the next one."

She looked at me with a curious grin. "You're so sure there's going to be a next time?"

"Well, yeah," I said. "Why not?"

"Why not?" she agreed, sounding pleased about it. She glanced down Highland. "I can't believe Ash isn't back yet."

"Do you want to wait for her?" I asked, praying the answer would be in the negative.

"Oh, God, no," Jules said decisively, which made me happy. "Let's go find a drink."

We strolled down Highland toward the nearby commercial stretch where there were a few bars amongst the shops and restaurants. It wasn't likely she'd get served without her ID, though, so we decided to just buy a bottle of wine at the minimart.

I let Jules pick out the vino. I wasn't much of a wine drinker and didn't know a Riesling from a Gewürtztraminer. We walked back to our building in companionable silence, the bottle in its long, skinny, brown paper bag nestled in the crook of my arm.

Ashley had returned and was unloading bags of groceries from the trunk of her Datsun. I can't say I was super happy to see her. On the other hand, Jules and I wouldn't have been able to get in their apartment without her. And we definitely weren't going in my place. Without Ashley's keys or a corkscrew, we would have been limited to sitting on the steps again and staring at the wine instead of drinking it.

I glanced in their open door with interest for my first peek at their abode.

Jules said to me, "Why don't you go on in and have a seat? I'm just going to talk to Ash for a sec."

She went around the corner to conference with her roommate. Roommate? Margo's hypothesizing reared its head again, but I shrugged it off. What did Margo know, anyhow?

Their apartment was the same layout as mine, but since the living room was Jules's bedroom, it had a very different feel as I walked in the front door. Cluttered was the word. It was very crowded with furniture, books, a little TV and one of those Japanese room divider screen thingies in the far corner, rice paper panes in a dark wooden frame. That was a nice touch, I thought, to allow her some modesty while dressing, yet still giving Ashley access to the kitchen or the front door. Of course, Jules would have to pass through the other girl's bedroom to get to the bathroom, so both of them had given up a lot of privacy in renting this place. I didn't think I would have been willing to do the same, although I heartily agreed with Ashley's preference for the beach.

Even with everything else that had been going on lately, I was still thrilled with having my own place for the very first time with its proximity to the water. Which made me even more pissed that Jackson was keeping me from fully enjoying it. Jackson. Everything seemed to lead back to him. I hoped he was locked up tight in rehab. Forever.

I thought I'd better take a seat before they came in, just to be out of the way. The narrow path from the front door to the kitchen led past the closed door to Ashley's bedroom. A canvas butterfly chair reposed in one corner of the living room, but I'd had trouble with its ilk before. Drinking alcohol and trying to get up out of a butterfly chair is a bad mix, I tell you. The only other option was the couch, a pale blue futon. Its dark wooden frame was a match to the Japanese screen. A tall cylindrical sea grass basket with a lid sat at one end of the futon, doing double duty as end table and hamper, I suspected. An alarm clock sat on top.

Ashley and Jules came in, each toting a paper grocery bag.

"Hey, Ashley," I said, taking the initiative.

"Hey," she said shortly as she trod past on her way to the kitchen.

Jules favored me with a brilliant smile, however, and reached over to pluck the wine bottle from my hands as she passed. "I'll get some glasses," she said over her shoulder.

It was much darker than in my apartment, probably due to my penchant for keeping the blinds open. Which was more appropriate on the second floor than at ground level, what with all the pedestrian traffic on Highland. It smelled good in there, perhaps due to the many candles lining the windowsills, all either a little or a lot melted. Under the windows, shelves made from plywood boards and cinderblocks held a collection of books. A little boom box was there too, a box of cassette tapes by its side. An elderly chest of drawers was on the wall opposite me, next to the bedroom door. A small TV sat on top of the chest, with Jules's motorcycle helmet balanced on top of that. A ten-speed bike was parked in the corner. In lieu of a closet, her clothes hung on nails driven into the southern wall and on clothesline strung between the nails, which created a colorful, kaleidoscopic display of different fabrics and patterns. Hey, who needed art when you could just hang up your wardrobe instead?

The space was definitely cramped, but I kind of liked it. It felt warm and welcoming, sort of like Jules herself. She came back from the kitchen with the uncorked bottle and two glasses. I heard Ashley slamming cabinet doors in there as she put away the groceries. Jules seemed undaunted, though.

"Everything okay?" I asked her.

"Fine," she said, setting the bottle and glasses down on a small oval coffee table in front of the futon. I wondered where the table went when she was ready for bed. Outside the front door? Hung from the ceiling? Or maybe upended against the clothes wall.

Jules turned on the boom box, which picked up in the middle of a Fogelberg song at low volume. She cracked open a window as Ashley skulked by, avoiding eye contact with me. I caught just a quick glimpse of her darkened quarters before she closed the door on us. I made a mental note to thank Mona again for helping me move my dresser over the trapdoor in my bedroom.

Jules sat down on the futon next to me, poured generously and handed me a glass. "Cheers," she said, gesturing toward me with her glass, but thankfully not insisting on us clinking. I hate it when people are fanatical about that. We both took a sip.

"Good?" she asked.

"Yeah," I said. "Very good."

It actually was, plus it was a lovely shade of pale pink. There was a pause while we both sipped again. Muffled thumps and other mysterious noises were coming from Ashley's room. I wondered what she was doing in there.

"Is she all right?" I asked Jules.

"Don't mind her," she replied. "She's not much of a socialite."

I'll say, I thought. The bedroom door opened and Ashley emerged, trombone case in hand. Without a word or even a gesture, she headed out the front door and was gone. I heard her car pull out a moment later. I felt relief mixed with a little guilt. "I hope we didn't run her off," I said.

"No, no," Jules replied. "She said she had to be somewhere anyhow. Don't worry about her," she added, smiling into my eyes. She wriggled into a more comfortable position on the pygmy couch, half-turned to face me, her knee just touching mine.

"So are you and Ash…" My voice trailed off as I realized I wasn't quite sure how I wanted to finish that question.

Jules seemed amused. "A couple?" she asked, her eyes twinkling.

Now that I was in their apartment, it seemed evident that they didn't share a bed. Unless the futon was just a couch and they did. I hated feeling so confused. And since she'd brought it up… "Well, are you?" I said, taking an emboldening drink of wine.

"No," she said with a smile. "We're just friends. We've been friends since high school."

See? Poo on you, Margo Murdock. "Mona and I have been friends since we were seven," I said, just to be saying something.

"And you're just friends?" Jules asked me.

I choked on my zinfandel, but managed not to spew it across the room. Jules seemed even more amused now. She patted me lightly on the back first, then got a paper towel from the kitchen for me when I continued to sputter.

"Yes," I finally managed to croak, red-faced and swallowing the last of my drink to help restore the proper balance to my airway and esophagus.

Jules poured us both another glass while I dabbed at my eyes with the paper towel. Shit, embarrassed again. You'd think I'd be used to it by now.

"Sorry," she said, trying and failing to repress her grin. "Didn't mean to make you choke."

"That's okay," I said. "But no, Mona and I are definitely not a couple."

I was horrified to think she might have thought that, to tell the truth. I mean, if she had at least thought *Margo* and I were a couple, then at least my imaginary girlfriend would be a fox. Wait. That came out really weird. I decided not to share that with her. Or anyone else.

"You didn't really think Mona and I were together, did you?" I asked her.

"No," she said. "I didn't think that. So do you have a boyfriend?"

From one conversational minefield to the next. Boyfriend? No. I had a date with a boy. The next night, in fact. A date I kind of didn't even want to go on…Or did I? "No. Not exactly," I said slowly, then tried to explain as she looked at me questioningly. "There's this guy I've sort of been seeing. I have a date with him tomorrow. One of the guys who was in my apartment last Saturday, actually," I added, remembering she had seen Flaco there. My gut churned for a moment when I thought of the upcoming date.

"Which one?" she asked. "The good-looking one?"

Aha, so she had noticed Handsome Pete. "No," I said, a tad regretfully, "one of the other ones. His name's Flaco."

"Hmmm," was her only comment.

She went over to the boom box and flipped the tape as side one of *The Innocent Age* had finished. She told me she had seen the concert for that album and we talked about music and concerts for a while. And school, and work, and cars and scooters...cabbages and kings. The wine flowed freely. She had half a bottle of the same stuff in her fridge and we drank that too, after the first bottle rather quickly disappeared. It felt good to just relax and have a laugh or two. I felt warm, but not too hot. Just...comfortable, I guess. I felt like I'd known Jules for years, not days. She was very easy to talk to. And a good listener too. Mona, God bless her, did not always fall into that category.

We were down to the last of the wine. It was about seven thirty, so the sun was low in the sky. It was almost dark in Jules's room. She lit a few of the candles, but left the overhead light off. I knew I should leave soon to go get a pizza and meet up with Mona at band practice like we'd planned, but a part of me didn't want to go. I was so comfortable on the couch with Jules. I just wanted to stay there forever. At least until I sobered up enough to drive.

She sat back down on the couch next to me, coming down a little over the center line onto my half of the couch. "Whoops!" she laughed and I did too.

I guess we were both a little tipsy. By this time, I was curled up sideways on the couch with just one foot on the floor. Buzzed and comfy.

She leaned forward to pick up her wineglass off the coffee table and her T-shirt slid up to reveal a few inches of bare back. Slender, strong, tan, bare back. My hand reached out as if of its own volition to touch it, but I stopped myself just in time. What the hell was I thinking? I couldn't touch that. Must be the wine. I silently vowed to stick with beer from there on out.

"Hey, you never told me what your deal was," I said.

"What do you mean?" She peered at me in the dim light.

"I mean, you asked me if I have a boyfriend—so do you have a boyfriend?"

There was a long pause while she studied me carefully. She twirled the stem of her wineglass slowly in her fingers. "I thought you knew," she said finally.

"Knew what?" I drained my glass and leaned forward to set it down on the coffee table.

"That I'm gay, Hev."

Time stood still for a moment in the dark room. My hand was motionless on the glass. Traffic noises from Highland filtered in through the open window. I sat back up and tried to think of something not foolish to say.

"Oh," I said. Like a fool.

"Yeah, oh," she said.

She was right there, so close. I noticed again how cute the freckles on her nose were. "But you're not with Ashley?" I asked.

"No," she said softly, watching me. She leaned in a little closer, squinting as she focused. "You have really beautiful green eyes, you know?" she said in that same soft voice.

I knew they were green, but this was the first time anyone had ever said they were beautiful. I was petrified, or maybe mesmerized was a better word. I couldn't take my eyes off her. I thought about how she'd looked on the beach. How I'd wanted to touch her back a moment earlier. Maybe it was the wine. But when she leaned in one more inch to kiss me, I let her.

And Oh. My. God. There it was—finally. Like the movies. Like they say. Like everything I wanted it to be. Her lips were soft on mine as she kissed me gently. Then she pulled back to gauge my reaction, seeing as how I was too flummoxed to kiss her back. When she pulled back, though, I moved forward, chasing her lips with mine. The second kiss was a mutual effort and more lingering. The third one kicked in with an urgency I felt my body respond to. Somehow, I was now lying on my back on the couch, with Jules's lanky figure fitting neatly against me, softly pressing against me in all the right spots.

I'm not sure how long we kissed, or what might have happened had we not been interrupted, but the sound of a key scraping in the lock brought us to an abrupt halt. Jules managed to halfway sit up, but I was still prone on the couch when Ashley stepped in and hit the light switch by the front door. All three of us froze in the harsh glare of the overhead light fixture. Ashley looked equal parts appalled and traumatized, then quickly lumbered into her room before anyone could say a word. I don't know who was more embarrassed, her or me.

"Well, shit," Jules said cheerfully, running a hand through her wavy hair.

She disentangled herself from me and pulled me upright to a sitting position too. I stood up, feeling a need to flee. My brain was stuck on the phrase: oh my God oh my God oh my God...

"I, uh, should go," I told her, trying to sound cool and no doubt totally failing.

"We could go up to your place," she suggested tentatively.

"No, I'd really better be going," I said in a voice that hardly sounded like my own. "I'm spending the night at Mona's and I have to get a pizza and she'll be expecting me at band practice, so I should go. Now."

Great. Babbling. Why was that option even in my conversational toolbox?

She walked me out to the car. We strode in silence from her apartment to my garage, where she helped me open the door. We both then nervously took a step back to make absolutely sure it stayed up. It did. Which reminded me to glance around for Jackson, but no one was in sight in the gloomy dusk.

Jules took my hand. I jumped from the unexpected contact and my hand slipped from hers. "Hev," she started, sort of helplessly.

"I gotta go," I said, avoiding her eyes.

Smooth, Hev. Real smooth. I darted into the darkness of the garage, fumbled with the car door and the keys, and finally got the Camaro backed out of there. Jules was still standing on the driveway, watching my every move. It seemed impolite to just back on past her, so I put it in neutral and rolled down the window, hoping for a quick escape. She crouched down, her forearms on the door. I stole a look at her. She looked a little worried. But her furrowed brow looked mighty cute, I have to say.

"Look, Jules, I'm sorry, all right? I just need some time to think. Okay?"

She gazed at me wordlessly for a moment, cocking her head to the side slightly. I was suddenly, keenly conscious of how wet she'd gotten me. No kiss had ever done that before. No other person had actually done that before. I hoped she couldn't see my blush in the waning light.

"Okay," she said, seeming to have come to some decision. "But, Hev—"

"Yes?"

"You should know you're a really good kisser," she said.

She leaned in and planted one more on my lips, which were slightly parted in surprise. She stood back from the car and made an exaggerated gesture to wave me out of the driveway, smiling all the while.

I drove around for a while, my brain on fire with too many thoughts. They ranged from "yahoo, I'm a good kisser!" to the more predominant gut wrench of the "oh my God" tape loop. I was lucky I didn't drive into a telephone pole with all the confusion raging in my head. I mean, I wasn't gay. I couldn't be gay. Gay was something *way* over there. Not me. I didn't even know anyone who was gay (okay, with the obvious new exceptions of Ashley and Jules). There certainly weren't any gay role models when I was growing up. Not in books or movies. Definitely not on TV. And no, I do not count Liberace. Although certain aspects of my cousin Ray's behavior and history were suddenly clicking into place…

But not me. For God's sake, I had a date with a man the very next night. That you don't want to go on, my little voice said. Who you don't like kissing, it added helpfully. Not like Jules…

God. Maybe it was the wine.

But in the midst of my confusion and freaked-outedness, some core part of me felt great. Felt wonderful! Hey, I wasn't a freak with abnormal and dysfunctional lips—I could feel something after all! I felt like…like I'd been dying of thirst and I'd just had my first drink of cool, clear water. As if a mist that had veiled my sight, that I didn't even know was there, was clearing away. Like I'd maybe die if I didn't kiss Jules Talbot again at the very earliest opportunity. Those lips of hers…

The car behind me honked. The stoplight I'd been sitting at was green. I needed to park somewhere and get a grip. I'd been driving around in circles and hardly knew where I was at that point. I pulled forward and turned into the first driveway, which was a strip mall on the edge of downtown occupied by a dry cleaner, a liquor store and Sportsman's Pub & Pizza. Good work, subconscious! I parked and went in, drinking a Coke at the bar while they cooked up two pizzas. Mona would only eat pepperoni, bell peppers and onions—she was a despot in this area as in so many others. I ordered a veggie supreme for the band too, just to be nice. Veggie supreme because the guys would eat anything and LeClaire had been insisting recently that she was a vegetarian, although I'd seen her Karmann Ghia at the Arby's drive-through more than once that summer.

Hopefully, by the time I showed up at the practice space, they'd be almost done so we could just eat the pizza and go home. I was ready for the day to be over with. Ready to be alone on the Benny Hill couch in the dark, where I could think this through. Or just shut my eyes and hope to sleep.

Oh my God oh my God oh my God.

Half an hour later, I was rolling down the back alley that led to the practice space. It was the freestanding garage to an old farmhouse up by the campus—a throwback to when the area was agrarian, not academic. The lights were out in the house. A single lightbulb shone brightly above the side door to the garage. It was awfully quiet out there. The band must be taking a break, I thought. I heard a dog barking in the distance.

Hadn't I told myself to stay out of dark alleys? I glanced about somewhat fearfully. It was really dark out there. This is where the coed in the slasher film gets it every time, I thought. I decided to be smart and honked the horn twice. After a moment, the door to the practice space opened and light flooded out. Petey waved, then came over to help carry the pizzas.

My arrival (well, the food's arrival) was heralded with much joy. It was quiet because Petey had been replacing a broken guitar string. Mona, exercising her supervisory skills, stopped the mad dash for the pizza with a peremptory gesture and gathered her flock unto her. Mona believed in preparation like I believed in gravity. She wanted herself and the rest of the band to be ready for any eventuality.

Thus, while I settled on the saggy couch by the door, she made LeClaire and Handsome Pete join her in practicing their "what if Petey breaks a string on stage?" song, which was an a capella version of Joe Jackson's "Is She Really Going Out With Him?" Handsome

Pete could sing—rather well, actually—but since he couldn't sing and play drums at the same time, his vocals were rarely heard. This song, however, was an intentional stunt to distract the audience for the approximately two minutes it would take Petey to change a broken string.

The Handsome One started them off. He had the bass part, so to speak—but sang it doo-wop style. LeClaire produced a tambourine to add a little rhythm while Mona sang the lead. They broke into three-part harmony on the choruses. Mona, of course, refused to change the gender in the lyrics on principle. If that's what Joe Jackson wrote, that's what Mona Murdock would sing. It didn't really matter in San Tomas anyhow. The sexual ambiguity of it probably enhanced Mona's reputation in that town. Meanwhile, Petey quickly and quietly tuned his guitar in the background.

The three of them ended in perfect unison with a flourish of LeClaire's tambourine. Mona looked over at Petey. Smiling, he held up his axe with all six strings intact.

"Perfect timing," he told her. "I just finished." He turned a couple knobs and rattled off the opening lick from Van Halen's "Ain't Talkin' 'Bout Love" to prove it. With a slightly wicked grin at Mona (well, as wicked as Petey could get), he then started playing the "Crazy Train" riff.

"All right, all right, enough," she said. "Have some freakin' pizza."

The band descended upon the food like starving wolverines. Someone handed me a warmish can of beer (as if I needed more to drink that night) and I used it to wash down a couple of slices. I made a few feeble attempts to ferret out info on their top secret new material, but they were uncrackable. Even Petey, who was usually an easy mark. I could tell they were pretty proud of themselves about something, though. Something big was clearly in the works for Dollar Night, but I'd have to find out on Thursday along with the rest of the world.

Mona and I caravanned home to the Murdocks' apartment about ten o'clock, where Chopper greeted me enthusiastically, Margo less so. The three of us took him out for a final spin around the block. Everyone seemed tired. Thankfully, no one had any questions for me about my evening's activities beyond confirming success with the locksmith.

We were all in bed shortly thereafter. Chopper slept on the floor at the foot of the Benny Hill couch. I was glad of his goofy, undemanding presence. His steady breathing and occasional snuffles had a soporific effect, although I grimly resolved to give him a bath at the earliest opportunity.

As I lay there, with the unearthly glow of the streetlights below coming through a gap in the curtains, I tried to empty my mind. I was hoping for instant sleep, but that was not to be. Instead, my busy brain kept sending me Jules-related thoughts, images and sensations. All I could think about was her fingers…and her lips… her curves and her softnesses.

I thought: What the hell am I thinking? What the hell am I doing? Jesus, what would my friends think? What would my parents think? Oh, God…

I remembered a scandal from my high school years. It was discovered that the maintenance man at Grandmother Murdock's church was secretly gay. The man had worked there for eleven years and even lived on-site in a small, furnished room in the basement, providing some basic security for the grounds and being readily available round the clock for any maintenance problems. The parishioners bragged on his skills, which kept their church so clean and pretty (prettier than those uppity Lutherans down the block, at least, with whom they maintained a politely vicious adversarial relationship) and called him "dear Clark" and "a valued member of their community."

Grandmother Murdock was head of the committee which had "had no choice" but to fire dear Clark and put him out on the street after eleven years of service simply because he was homosexual. My parents, I recalled, had commiserated with her over the front yard fence about how sad it was.

Funny. I hadn't thought about that in years.

Oh, God. Oh, Jules.

I thought about how it might feel to put my mouth on that solitary freckle on her stomach. I thought: Maybe it was the wine. I cast aside all thoughts of friends and family. And added wine to my mental grocery list.

CHAPTER THIRTEEN

Wednesday

I slept poorly, if at all, and was up at dawn to take Chopper out to commune with nature. Nature, in this case, being the signposts and parking meters immediately in front of the building while I lurked in the doorway. I wished we were home so I could take him down to the beach for a romp. Poor guy. I felt guilty that he wasn't getting enough exercise. Both of us would have benefited from a long walk in the Murdocks' neighborhood, but I was too paranoid that Jackson might be out there somewhere waiting for me. Calling Stokes was my first priority when I got to work.

Upstairs, I took advantage of being the first one up to grab a shower. I decided I might as well sample the strange, unexplored world of going to work early, so I got dressed, grabbed a Coke from the fridge and left the Murdocks a note on the counter proposing we all three meet for lunch at Ed's Café if they were available. Chopper had already gone back to sleep in his spot by the couch, but I felt oddly energized, in that weird sleep-deprived, yet adrenaline-flushed way.

All was quiet as I cautiously peeked out the front door of the building to where I'd parked my Camaro across the street the night before. No person or vehicle stirred. Maybe I was the only one up in the whole city.

I drove swiftly through the empty streets as the sun's early rays warmed me with a hint of the heat later to come. I felt vulnerable and alone in the car and hurried from the employee parking lot to the Public Defender as if I were one of its wrongdoers fleeing from an inexorable Justice. The office was dark, warm and quiet when I let myself in just before seven. I thought I'd have to pound on the door to get one of the early birds to let me in, but luckily found myself climbing the steps right behind one of the attorneys who had a key. Once inside, I made sure the door was locked behind us, then sighed with relief, feeling secure in my familiar workplace.

I flicked a switch to turn the lights on in my little area, but left the rest of the work area and lobby dark. There was enough ambient light from the windows to navigate by. As I headed down the long, dim hallway for another Coke, I saw that lights were on in two of the offices. The nearer one belonged to the guy who'd let me in. The other was Carmen's. Of course! I resigned myself (again) to the impossibility of living up to her standards.

I hoped I wouldn't startle her when I passed by her open door, but figured she'd be deep into the penal code and probably not even notice. My feet were silent on the worn carpet. I glanced in as I passed and froze at the sight that met my eyes.

Carmen stood behind her desk, one foot on her chair, her skirt and slip hiked up around her midriff as she struggled with a pair of black pantyhose. She was wearing underwear and had the hose eighty percent in place, so it wasn't like she was really showing anything, but it stopped me in my tracks nonetheless. There was an awkward pause as our eyes met. Words failed me.

"Morning, Hev," Carmen said, completely unruffled, pausing in her contortions to civilly greet me.

"Morning, Carmen."

She resumed her struggle while I moved on down the hall to the kitchenette. Of course Carmen was completely unruffled, I thought as I grabbed a Coke. Because (a) she was Carmen and (b) she didn't have to worry if she was gay.

Or maybe she did. Who the hell knows? In any event, the unexpected flash of attorney thigh had ripped the top right off all those Jules thoughts I'd been trying so hard to repress all morning.

Great. Thanks, Carmen's thighs! My brain went right back into "Oh my God, oh my God" mode. Freaked out does not begin to describe my turmoil. I tried to stuff all those thoughts and feelings right back where they'd been and let my subconscious earn its paycheck. Chewing on it incessantly wasn't going to make it any better. And I needed to focus on work, I told myself.

Back at my desk, however, I found myself unable to conjure up any work to distract myself with. It was too early for the courthouse run. The telephone switchboard was set to not let incoming calls start ringing until eight o'clock. I could, of course, have resorted to filing in the hall, but after my encounter with Carmen, I was steering clear of the hall for a while. At least until she had her drawers completely on. Was it too early to try Stokes? One way to find out.

"Lieutenant Stokes's office," the same nasal female voice answered.

"May I speak to Lieutenant Stokes, please," I said.

"He's not in, may I take a message?"

"Do you know when he'll be in?" I asked.

"He's on vacation for two weeks," the voice said.

"Vacation?" Crap. Why didn't she tell me that yesterday? Now what was I supposed to do?

"Would you like to leave a message?" Miss Nasal asked, popping her gum. I hate that.

"Can I speak to, um…" Oh, hell, what was the other guy's name? Sauerkraut…Gravenstein…Steinway…Grausteiner! "Can I speak to Detective Grausteiner?"

"One moment, please."

A few beeps and clicks later, I heard Grausteiner's voice. Unfortunately, it was an answering machine. I left a detailed and probably completed garbled message, including all my various phone numbers and my intention to call him back later that afternoon if I didn't hear from him first. Really, these communication problems were très aggravating.

With a sigh, I headed down the hall for some quality filing time. Stephanie was shocked, but pleased, to find me there when she arrived around seven thirty. The rest of the staff rolled in one by one as the day got under way.

When I returned from my courthouse run later that morning, I found a message from Mona on my desk. She would meet me at the office at noon and escort me to Ed's, where Margo would join us. I had no intention of discussing the Jules thing with them, but planned to seek their counsel on the Flaco thing. Jiminy Christmas—how had I ended up with two things at once?

At noon, I found Mona alone in the Public Defender lobby, leafing through a copy of *BAM* (short for Bay Area Music) magazine that she must have brought herself. There was no point putting magazines out in the lobby, seeing as how the clientele would promptly steal anything that was not nailed down.

There was no sign of Jackson during our short walk to the restaurant, where Margo (and the Monamobile) were waiting. Maybe the "locked up in rehab except for Mondays and Thursdays" hypothesis was valid. Maybe. I remained vigilant, but my self-appointed bodyguard was predictably all het up over Dollar Night which was now just One Day Away! She filled my ear with gig-related plans, preparations and problems.

Margo had been shopping. Paper and plastic bags from various establishments on the mall surrounded her at a table in the corner. As we settled in, Mona finally thought to ask me a non-Mona related question. "Hey, did you call the cops?"

I explained about the phone tag situation. She shook her head, disgusted at this unsatisfactory turn of events. "Well, what can I do?" I said. "I'll call Grausteiner back this afternoon if he doesn't call me first."

The waitress came by with the drinks Margo had precognizantly requested and took our food orders.

"How's Chopper?" I asked the sisters.

"Fine," said Margo.

Mona said, "We can't keep him hidden from the Romanoff forever, though, Hev. Just yesterday she almost caught us on the stairs."

"I know, I know," I said apologetically. "I'll have him out of there as soon as I get it squared away with the cops."

"Plus he stinks," Mona added, truthfully but uncharitably, I thought.

"I wish we could keep him," Margo said unexpectedly.

Her sister stared at her.

"I know we can't," Margo said defensively with a defiant toss of her lank red hair. "I just wish we could. I like having him around. He's a sweetheart."

"Speaking of sweethearts," Mona said with a leer to me, "are you ready for your big date tonight?"

Oh, fuck. I knew it would be a huge mistake to tell them about Jules when I hadn't sorted out those thoughts for myself, but as soon as I'd seen Mona, I'd began struggling with a powerful urge to Tell Her All, as I usually did. I hated having to lie, even by omission. I prided myself (I thought) on being an honest person. Now here I was keeping something major from my two best friends in the whole world. Well, from Mona, at least. Margo wasn't exactly my friend. But I'd known her practically my whole life and she came with the package, so whatever. But Mona—usually, I'd tell her everything. And I mean *everything*. And since I'd been doing that since I was seven years old, it was tough to hold back now. Although she hadn't told me about Petey…or Margo and my brother.

"Hev?" Mona glanced at me a little strangely when I failed to reply.

The awkward moment was covered, however, by Margo saying, "Oh, yeah, tonight's Flaco night, right?"

They both looked at me expectantly. Well, at least I could talk to them about Flaco, if not Jules. "I'm not sure I really want to go," I admitted to them. This was greeted with scorn and disbelief. "I don't know if I even like the guy," I protested.

Two pairs of identical Murdock blue eyes stared at me assessingly.

"Well," said Margo prosaically, "why don't you just sleep with him and figure it out?"

I was shocked (well, a little) but Mona merely nodded, drumming her fingers on the tabletop as she scanned the café for our waitress. I moved my chair closer and leaned in so I could speak more discreetly. "You really think I should have sex with him? Tonight?"

"Sure, why not?" Margo asked, already tired of the topic.

The waitress arrived at this point with our food, so there was a pause while we sorted out who got what, Mona stole my pickle, and we all applied various condiments. I was chewing a bite of my burger when Mona chimed in.

"Maybe you should, Hev. Sleep with him, I mean."

"Really?" I said dubiously. "I'm not sure I want to have a drink with him, let alone jump his bones."

"Well, at least go out with him. It's a little late to cancel anyway. He's kind of cute, he's employed, he seems nice enough and he's more or less clean, right?"

What a ringing endorsement, I thought. But Mona wasn't finished. "And I mean, how long do you want this dry spell to go on?"

Ouch. That was nice. Bring up the dry spell. My inner voice reminded me how not dry I'd been the night before after Jules kissed me. I involuntarily shivered from too many conflicting emotions.

Mona said, "So are you going to go out with him?"

"Fine," I said, somewhat hoarsely. "I'll go out with him. Can we talk about something else now?"

And we did. Mostly, they talked while thoughts ran around and around in my head like rats in a maze. Look, one part of me said, girls go out with boys—you're a girl, he's a boy, end of story. But I don't want to, said another me. Just do it, said the first one. Do what you're supposed to do. Do what they want you to do.

Through no fault of Ed's, his french fries turned to ashes in my mouth. I took a slug of Coke to wash them down, nearly choking in the process. Mona slapped me on the back, hard enough to hurt a little bit. I could only hope my exterior hid the inner turbulence. Nobody wanted any dessert, so we did the math and piled up the needed bills and coins in the center of the table.

I was about to stand when Margo said to me, "Oh, hey! Wait a minute. I've got just the thing for you." She started rooting around in the bags at her feet. I sincerely hoped she wasn't going to pull out some trashy lingerie that wouldn't fit me anyhow. She had the bag from the drugstore on her lap now. "Here you go," she said, handing me an item.

I looked at it—a box of sponges and not for doing the dishes if you know what I mean. "Jesus, Margo!" I hissed at her, quickly sticking it in my backpack so no one would see.

Both Murdocks laughed at my obvious discomfort. Call me a prude, but I was not in the habit of publicly displaying my contraceptives.

"You can pay me back later," Margo said, still cackling happily.

Actually, I was secretly glad I would not now have to go to the store and buy them. I always hated that moment when the cashier would ring them up, then glance at me. Although I was doubting I would be needing them. Not that night, anyhow. Maybe never?

"Let's go," Mona commanded, chewing a toothpick with the little frilly ribbon on the end.

The Monamobile was parked in back of the restaurant. We all three got in the front seat, with me in the middle as usual. Mona wanted to cruise up to the Mongol end of the mall to see if "Bertha's Attic" was on the marquee yet, but I told her to do that on her own time as my lunch hour was close to expiring.

The day was sunny and bright. Birds chirped in the small trees that dotted each block. Jumbo-sized cumulus clouds sailed majestically through the heavens. Only I seemed to feel a pall upon my soul. Was Jackson Miller out there somewhere plotting my demise? Was I really supposed to have sex with a guy I barely knew that very night? Did the fact that I had feelings for a girl—that I'd *acted* on those feelings—make me a...lesbian? What a weird word. Surely that wasn't me. God, I'm such a freak, I thought despairingly.

We paused at a stoplight.

"Hey, Mona, there's your boyfriend," Margo said, looking in the rearview mirror on the passenger side.

I turned my head to see. A sputtering Volkswagen bus was behind us, garishly and amateurishly painted with rainbows, white doves, peace signs and a portrait of either Jimi Hendrix or Buckwheat from the Little Rascals—I honestly couldn't tell.

"What?" said Mona, her attention focused on the stoplight while she impatiently waited for it to turn green.

The VW's driver had exited his vehicle and was walking up toward ours. In his fifties, he wore a tie-dyed T-shirt, cut-offs and Birkenstocks, and had long greasy gray hair pulled back in a ponytail. Classic "there's your boyfriend" material, if I ever saw one.

"Granola off the port bow," I said to Mona.

"What?"

The granola now appeared in her open driver's side window, making her jump, which did not improve her attitude. "Hey, man," he began in a friendly tone.

"Do I look like a fucking man to you?" Mona shot back at him.

He took a step back, which was perilous considering we were in the middle of traffic. "Hey, whoa, whoa," he said. "Peace, sister. I just wanted to tell you both your brake lights are out."

"Yeah, well, they're only visible to people with IQs over eighty," she said, still pissed at being startled by him and probably at being the butt of Margo's joke too.

The light turned green and she stomped on the gas, leaving him open-mouthed at the intersection with cars beginning to honk from behind. Several moments of silence passed.

"Should probably fix those brake lights," Margo said finally.

"Yeah, all right," Mona muttered.

It had occurred to me before that if Mona and I had been born male, I would constantly be restraining her from getting in fistfights. She really was too aggressive for her own good sometimes. On the other hand, if we were guys, think how many other things would be so much easier. Peeing. Clothes. No worries about makeup, nails, shaving body parts other than faces and hell, we could just grow beards if we wanted to skip that. I wondered if I'd make a better guy than I was a girl. Probably. Then hurriedly suppressed that thought as I realized how weird it was. But then thought if I were a guy, having feelings about girls would be no problem and *that* would certainly be a relief.

Why couldn't I just be me and do what I wanted? Why couldn't my outside—for which society had a definition and rules and expectations—match the inside? Why was even the simplest thing—like a kiss, goddamn it—so *fucking* hard for me and so easy for everyone else?

I felt dangerously close to tears, but willed them back with a ferocious effort. I ran a slightly trembling hand over my face and hoped, like I always did, that no one would notice the hell I was in. Fortunately, Mona was concentrating on her driving and Margo was staring out the window.

They dropped me off at the office. Mona walked me up the stairs to make sure I got in safely. She took her bodyguard duties seriously. She reminded me she had band practice again that night.

One last chance for perfecting all their efforts before they took the stage on Thursday. She told me she'd see me later, though, and find out how my date went.

"Oh," she said with a wicked gleam in her eye, "unless you're spending the night at Flaco's, of course."

Man, she was really pushing this sex stuff! As if it were all it was cracked up to be. Sheesh. I grimaced and shut the office door in her face without further communication, then trudged disheartenedly to my desk.

This was one of the rare days at work where the phone schedule skipped over me. As much as I hated phone duty, it was almost worse without it because that usually meant the bulk of an entire day had to be devoted to the soul-killing filing. But that's what they paid me for, so I took a deep breath and girded up my clerical loins. Before I could start, though, Tasha called out that I had a call on line one.

"Detective Somebody," she added quizzically.

I practically leapt for the phone. "Hello?"

"Miss Wilcox? Detective Grausteiner here."

"Thanks for calling me back, Detective. I really need to talk to you."

"Yeah," he said. Sort of ominously. Uh-oh. "I heard your message," he said. "What is this about a newspaper clipping? You took something out of Werner's apartment?"

"Um, well, yeah. I'm really sorry about that. I made a mistake. That's why I want to give you the clipping. Today, preferably."

"What were you doing in his apartment?"

Hello—were we not already past this trifling detail? Apparently not. I sighed, then launched into my slightly edited tale of woe about Pacheco letting me in for dog food, seeing the clipping on the fridge, making the connection between Sikes and Jackson, and taking the clipping, for which I was now very, Very, *Very* sorry. Very sorry. Mr. Policeman, sir. There was a long pause on the other end of the line.

"So, can I bring it to you?" I asked him.

"Trespassing is against the law, you know. As is breaking and entering."

Criminy, this guy was hung up on busting my chops when he really needed to focus on the clue I was trying to give him.

"Officer Pacheco let me in," I retorted. "And nothing got broken."
I breezily skipped over Flaco's little trapdoor adventure. No point
in bringing that up.

Grausteiner said, "What? No, give me another minute here.
I'm almost done."

Clearly, he was talking to someone else. I was losing my temper.
I hate it when people blow me off.

"Look, Detective," I said, with an emphasis on his title, "I
am trying to tell you something funny is going on. Werner had
a picture of Jackson Miller in his apartment, but with a different
name. Jackson's supposedly disappeared, but I've seen him at
the Mongol, and he's called me twice, at home and at work, and
threatened me, and now Werner's dead and I really think you need
to take a look at this freakin' clipping and get this guy off my back!"

My voice had gotten considerably louder as those words
tumbled out. Tasha was giving me the eye from the reception area.
The raggedy looking prostitute she'd been assisting at the counter
took a step back to peer around the corner at me too.

"Sorry," I mouthed to them both. Fortunately, Stephanie hadn't
come back from her lunch yet. I took a breath and tried to calm
down, my heart pounding in my chest.

"All right, all right, don't get your panties in a bunch," said the
detective, sounding amused.

So glad I could brighten your day, asshole, I thought.

"I'm out in the field now," he said, "but I'll be back at the station
by four or so. You're at the PD's office, right?"

"Right."

"So come by the station after you get off work and ask for me
at the front desk."

"Okay. I will," I said, trying to get my temper under control
since he was doing what I wanted him to do. "Thank you," I added
belatedly.

We said goodbye and hung up. Whew. Just a few more hours
and hopefully this whole Jackson Miller mess would be over. Of
course, I then had the Flaco Gutierrez mess to deal with, but at
least he hadn't threatened my life. Yet. I thought of Margo's box
of sponges in my backpack and felt my stomach twist into a knot.
This was not my best day.

By four o'clock, I was so tired of filing I thought I might spontaneously combust. I went to the restroom to splash some cold water on my temples. As I patted my face dry with a paper towel, I looked at my reflection in the mirror. I looked haggard. I felt haggard. I told myself to buck up. It didn't work.

I still didn't know what I was going to do that night. I would go to the Mongol and have a drink with Flaco as agreed, but after that...

Somehow, my swirling and devious subconscious had now cooked up some low-level resentment toward Jules. How dare she get me all screwed up like this. Who was she to me anyhow? Just some girl I'd gotten tipsy with and foolishly let kiss me and make me feel all...damn it. Maybe I should take Margo's advice. Sleep with Flaco and just get it over with. She should know in that department. Just because the sex I'd had with two guys before hadn't been stellar, that didn't mean...well, what did that mean? And stellar—hell, who was I kidding? Better adjectives might be icky, awful, awkward, painful, regrettable...But third time's the charm, right? And then maybe I'd know. Straight, gay, bi, whatever. At least I'd know. Know what? Know if I wanted to sleep with Jules? God, what was I thinking? What would people think of me if they only knew? I looked at myself in the mirror again and groaned.

Stephanie was pouring herself a cup of coffee at the kitchen counter when I exited the restroom. She gave me the once-over. "Are you all right?" she asked with unaccustomed concern. "You look a little pale."

I did feel queasy, but that was because of my all too soon date with Flaco, not my health. However, I could not refuse this gift from the gods—the boss herself suggesting I might be sick! "I think I might be coming down with something," I told her.

I turned my head and coughed quietly into my closed fist. I was aiming for ailing, but dignified. You know, Elizabeth Taylor in the 1944 movie version of *Jane Eyre* as the dying childhood friend? I must have nailed it, because Stephanie sent me packing off home immediately, noting I'd been there early anyhow. Her concern may have been more budget than health-related—overtime was a four-letter word in her vocabulary. Anyhow, with that kind of groundwork laid, now I could call in sick on Thursday without arousing any suspicion and have a much needed mental health day! Woo hoo.

My mood lifted, I wasted no time in bailing from the office, although I carefully looked around as I sped to my car in the employee parking lot. The police station was about six blocks away. Normally, I would have walked there (in theory, at least), but under these circumstances, driving seemed like the better choice.

A scooter zipped past me, going the opposite direction as I drove to the police station. A red one. Not Jules. I had a sudden urge to talk to her, to see her again. Maybe she could help me make some sense of all of this. And she always smelled so good…I caught myself. Shut up, I told myself, just shut up.

At the front desk, a female uniformed police officer looked at me dubiously when I asked for Detective Grausteiner, but she made the call. A few moments later, he popped his head out a side door.

"Miss Wilcox? Back here."

Seated on a straight chair by his desk, I handed him the clipping. I felt relieved to have it out of my possession and waited patiently while he read it. Twice, judging by the movement of his eyes.

"Walk me through this one more time," Grausteiner said finally. "What exactly is it you think has happened?"

His skepticism was evident. I wasn't sure if it was me specifically that inspired it or just his natural cop cynicism. In any event, my hours of filing that day had given me plenty of time to think what to say to him, so I had my pitch ready.

"It started when Jackson moved in next door to Werner. But Jackson wasn't really Jackson—he was some guy named William Sikes from back east and an ex-con to boot. I don't know how Werner got the clipping and found out about it, but somehow he did."

"Well, so what?" Grausteiner interjected. I could tell he was the kind of guy who liked to interrupt. "He'd done his time, paid his debt to society. It's not a crime to be an ex-con."

"But he had money," I countered. "A lot of it, from winning the lottery. There he was, living the high life, with a boat and a fancy car and nice stuff in his apartment. Shooting his mouth off about it too, from what I heard. And there was Werner, living off a cop's pension and watching this sleazebag—right next door—enjoying all the finer things."

"But Miller took off," Grausteiner said. "So if there had been any bad blood between them, it was done at that point. And there was no evidence of foul play—we looked into it when he took off. At Werner's request, actually. The guy was just gone. Happens all the time."

"Why did he take off?" I said.

"Like I said, happens all the time. I think you're dreaming up a fantasy here, Miss Wilcox. Unless you've got some kind of evidence of a crime, I'm a little busy, you know what I mean?" He tucked the clipping into a desk drawer, ready to dismiss me.

I tried again. "What if Jackson left because Werner was blackmailing him?"

"What?" Grausteiner gave a short bark of laughter. "How do you figure that?"

I told him about the letter I'd opened by accident when I first moved into the apartment. The unsigned letter that said "you can run, but you can't hide" and other threatening things.

"So, maybe that was a letter from Werner to Jackson," I postulated. "Maybe Werner thought it was worth a shot, hoping somehow the post office would get it to Jackson and maybe spook him into revealing his whereabouts."

"That's pretty weak, Wilcox," Grausteiner said. He folded his arms and shook his head, but he was still listening. I could tell I'd piqued his interest. "Where is this mysterious letter?" he asked.

"I put it back in the mailbox marked 'not at this address.'"

I kind of wished I hadn't done that now, but perhaps it was just as well I hadn't added mail theft to my growing list of transgressions. Grausteiner drummed his fingers on his desk and stared into space for a few moments, then came back to me.

"What else you got?" he said. "Anything?"

"Well…something's been going on with my mail. I thought at first it was Werner, probably trying to see if anything that came for Jackson would provide a clue as to his location."

"At first?"

"Yeah, at first I thought that and I still do think that was what was going on. But last Saturday—two days after Werner died—somebody else was messing with my mail. My neighbor saw him, though, and scared him off."

"So who was this?" asked Grausteiner.

"I don't know for sure," I replied, "but I think it may have been the assistant marina manager. I think he might be a friend of Jackson's."

"So why would he be looking at your mail?"

Oops. The answer to that was: to get my full name and deliver that info to Jackson. Why? Because Jackson needed it to find out my phone number. And Jackson wanted to talk to me because he'd heard from the assistant marina manager and/or the parole office chick that I was looking for him. And I didn't care to mention to Grausteiner that I had called the parole office under the auspices of my temp job at the Public Defender.

Grausteiner seemed to accept my silence and blank look as ignorance, which wasn't too far from the truth. He mulled it all over and didn't look pleased with what he was thinking. He cleared his throat and said, "Look, Werner was a cop. One of the good guys, you know? He wouldn't stoop to blackmail."

"A cop...on the take? Who ratted out his fellow officers?"

That got Grausteiner's attention. He'd been slouching in his desk chair, but now he sat up sharply. "Where'd you hear that?" he brusquely asked.

I shrugged and said a line I'd heard on TV and always wanted to say myself: "That's the word on the street, man."

It was his turn now to stare at me without responding. I had another question for him in the meantime. I tried to phrase it politely. "Detective, how did Werner afford that new Mercedes he bought last December?"

Grausteiner squinted, looking at me like I was some kind of bug. But he was still listening. Sort of. And I noticed he wasn't denying the on-the-take rumors about my former neighbor.

"All right, all right," he said. "Just for the sake of talking, let's say Werner was—theoretically—blackmailing Miller. But Miller took off, which should have shut the whole thing down. So why didn't it end there?"

"I don't know," I admitted. "Maybe it didn't end? Either way, the next thing that happened was Werner's death."

"The medical examiner thinks that was an accident," he argued. "And the ME don't usually get things like that wrong, missy."

"Well, don't you think it's weird? One guy disappears, the other guy dies and the dead guy has the missing guy's picture on his refrigerator door?"

"Weird things happen all the time. Believe me, I know. I'm a cop." Grausteiner gave me his favorite nasty grin and leaned back in his chair, his fingertips steepled.

I felt frustrated. How was I supposed to get through to this guy? He clearly thought he had all the answers and I was a bonehead. Wait. I was a bonehead. I should have told him up front about seeing Jackson, instead of saving that for last. And him getting in my apartment. And the death threat. Duh!

"But I've seen him!" I said, with not too much exasperation showing through, I hoped.

"Who? Werner?"

"No—Jackson. I saw him at the Mongol, I mean the Moonglow last Thursday night. Then he got into my apartment last Monday. And he's called me at home and at work. He told me he wants that clipping and he threatened me when I told him I might have given it to the police."

Grausteiner looked confused. "But you just gave it to me now."

"I know, I sort of lied to him." I kept my eyes modestly downcast at that admission.

"Did you call the cops about the break-in?"

"Yes. Officer Pacheco came over. Technically, though, it wasn't a break-in because Jackson still had a key to the apartment."

"Was anything missing? Did anyone see him going in or out?"

"Well, no," I said, with the exasperation leaking out just a wee bit. "I mean, no, nobody saw him and yes, he stole a bottle of Kahlua, but that's not why he broke in. He used my apartment to get into Werner's through the crawl space. But when he saw the clipping was gone from the refrigerator, he called me up and threatened me."

"Why?" Grausteiner asked, pointing at me with a pencil. "Why you?"

Oh. Good question. I still didn't want to bring up my call to the parole office, which was one possible way Jackson knew I'd been asking about him. Clearly, improvisation was called for. "I don't know, maybe he saw me going in there with Pacheco and figured I took it."

"Which you did."

"Which I did," I agreed with him.

We both thought about that for a minute. He tapped his pencil on his desk, then on his lips. "So where's the crime here?" he said finally.

"Uh, blackmail?" I said in a regrettably sarcastic tone. Sorry, but he was wearing me down.

"You got no evidence of that. What else you got?"

"Murder?"

"ME says accident."

"So Werner's death really was an accident?" I asked him, hoping for reassurance.

"Well, that's the initial finding. They're still working on it. But unless you got something solid, I'm gonna take their judgment over yours at this point, all right?"

Now who was being sarcastic? I could tell he enjoyed teasing me. He wasn't even ten years older than I was. I'd probably been cast as the bratty little sister in his personal drama. But I tried again.

"What about Jackson disappearing and now he's back?"

"There's no crime in that, Miss Wilcox. I keep telling you that. See, I'm a detective—I investigate crimes. You got a whole bunch of loose threads and supposition and no wrongdoing as far as I can tell. Even your so-called break-in involved no breaking in, no damage, no witnesses and not even anything missing except a bottle of booze that maybe your boyfriend lifted."

I practically writhed with frustration. "But he threatened to *kill* me!" I said, my voice rising.

"Okay, tell me about that part," Grausteiner said.

I went over it again—about the phone call and how Jackson had said "you're dead, bitch" right before he hung up. I told him about hearing the page in the background and my suspicion that Jackson was detoxing at the Meadows. He'd heard of the facility, at least. He said he'd look into it.

"And you'll keep me posted?" I said.

"Yeah, sure. Give me your number," he said.

He clearly thought this was a crank call situation, not life or death. *My* life or death. Asshole. I gave him my assortment of numbers—home, work, the Murdocks'—for what felt like the fiftieth time. He pulled out a pack of cigarettes, tapped one on the desk, then stuck it behind his ear while asking me if I wanted to file a report on the phone threat. He seemed bored with me and my "fantasy." I was suddenly equally sick of him and his flippant response to my concerns. Sick of him and pissed off.

"You know what?" I said tersely. "Forget it. I wanted to give you the clipping and I gave it to you. So we're done. Thanks." I stood and headed for the door.

"Hey, don't be mad," he said, scrambling to his feet. "I said I'd look into it and I will."

He beat me to the door by a pace and opened it for me. I glared at him as I went through. I thought that would be the end of it, but he was apparently determined to walk me out to my car.

"Look, if you're worried about the guy, I understand," he said. "Just give me a little time to check it out and be careful, you know? Don't go anywhere alone. Stay with friends for a few days. Don't open the door to a stranger. Stuff like that."

"Great," I said as we reached the Camaro. "Thanks a bunch." I got in and rolled down the window. He bent down to my level.

"Here's my card," he said.

I took it wordlessly. He withdrew with a windy sigh and watched as I backed out.

"Phone us if you see him," he called.

I gave him a wave to indicate "yeah, yeah" and pulled away with relief. I didn't think he'd heard, let alone believed, half of what I'd told him, but at least I had told him. And now he had the clipping. Really, what else could I do? It was in their hands now. Don't open the door to a stranger—give me a fucking break. What was I, six years old?

I drove back to the Murdocks' apartment in that irritable state of mind. I still had a couple of hours before my date, which would be more than enough time to get ready. Maybe if I showed up looking like crap, he'd run away screaming and I'd be off the hook.

I let myself in with the spare key, not expecting either sister to be there, but found Margo watching TV with Chopper. He dashed over and licked my face when I leaned down to pet him, then raced back to the couch, his stumpy tail thumping against the cushions. Margo told me to get a couple of beers out of the fridge, an order with which I was only too glad to comply. I grabbed Chopper a piece of lunchmeat too, just to be sociable, though the evidence of his recently eaten dinner was on the kitchen floor.

He gobbled down the bit of mystery meat, then looked disappointed there wasn't more. I pushed his butt over to make some room for me at the far end of the couch. I passed Margo her beer over the happily panting pooch, who sniffed it carefully in passing to make sure it wasn't a bone in disguise. She got up and turned the volume on the TV down, but not entirely off. They'd been watching the local news. I glanced at her as she sat back down.

Shrugging, she said, "He likes the weather girl."

Really, she was getting way too close with the dog. Maybe she was the one who needed a boyfriend, not me. "Do you think I need a boyfriend?" I asked her.

She looked at me curiously over the top of her beer bottle, then upended it for a drink. "Don't you want someone to hold onto, Hev?" she asked me. "Someone to say, 'Good morning, baby'? Someone to kiss you just the right way?"

She took another slug of beer. I stared at her and prayed she couldn't read my mind. Jules, I thought. Oh, Jules.

"Besides," she said dispassionately post-swallow, "how the hell else are you ever going to get laid? You're not exactly the one-night stand type, Hev."

Wow. Ask a stupid question and get a Margo answer. I blindly petted Chopper while I took in those pearls of wisdom.

"What are you wearing on your date?" she asked.

"I don't know…jeans and…"

Sighing, she rose to her feet and offered me her hand. Chopper jumped to his feet on the couch as well, enthusiastic for whatever was next.

"What?" I said, but let her pull me to my feet.

"Come on," she said. "Let's pick out an outfit and then I'll do your makeup if you want."

After a brief battle on the topic of sundresses—hers were unlikely to fit me and the only one I owned I had sewn myself in ninth-grade Home Ec class, so you can guess how cute that was, besides the fact that it was hanging in my closet—we settled on my white jeans, white leather sandals with a minimum heel and a blouse of hers that I liked although it was hardly my usual style. It was a tight-fitting, stretchy knit with frilly cap sleeves and a plunging V-neck in a hot red, orange and yellow jungle print.

Kind of like Jules's bikini, my brain supplied helpfully. I wondered if she had tried to call me today. Or maybe I was supposed to call her. How did it work when you were both girls? Or maybe she hadn't thought of me at all…

"Hey!" Margo was speaking sharply to me as I stood in front of her bedroom mirror, lost in thought. I refocused on her. "Ready for your makeup?" she asked.

Chopper and I followed her dumbly into the bathroom where she applied makeup to me with much more skill than I possessed. I'd brought my backpack with me into the bathroom, since I had my hairbrush and some lip gloss in there. Margo disdained my minimalist beauty supplies, though, preferring to work her magic with her own tools and materials. Chopper made good use of my backpack by promptly laying down on it.

After the makeup, Margo proceeded to my hair, which she floofed up with a brush and liberally spritzed with hairspray. This made Chopper sneeze when it floated down to his level. Glancing critically at her work, Margo made a few more minute adjustments, then finally pronounced me done. All three of us looked at my reflection in the full-length mirror on the back of the door. Thanks to her ministrations, I looked pretty damn good. For me.

"Wow, thanks, Mars! You rock."

"Eh, I was bored anyway," she said. But she was smiling.

I shooed them both out of the bathroom to give myself a moment. She wasn't due at work until later that night, so Chopper was in good hands for the next few hours. And it was time for me to head to the Mongol. I couldn't put it off any longer.

Other girls seemed to enjoy going on dates, whereas I always had to steel myself as if for some arduous test. Oh God, I said to myself in the mirror, I am so fucked up. All my confusion and distress welled up inside suddenly. I willed back hot tears with something like a sob, not wanting to ruin the mascara. The box of sponges Margo had given me was in my backpack. Grimly, I opened the box and followed the instructions.

I had to know.

* * *

Plenty of people were out walking and shopping on the outdoor mall, so I felt safe as I walked from where I'd parked to the Mongol. At a little before seven p.m. on a Wednesday, the front bar was mostly empty. I was early, but Flaco was already there, waving to me peppily from a table by a potted palm. I tried to ignore the feeling that I was walking up to a firing squad and hoped the smile on my face didn't look too sickly. He's probably nervous too, I reminded myself.

He stood as I approached. "Heavenly! Wow, you look great!"

"Thanks. Uh, you too."

He did look good, actually, in stonewashed jeans and a raspberry alligator shirt that went well with his coloring. "What would you like to drink?" he asked with a flash of his nice white teeth as we sat down.

The Murdocks had attempted to impress upon me in the past that one should never order beer on a date. But I like beer, I'd protested in vain. Girls don't drink beer, they said. You drink beer all the damn time, I'd protested further. Not on a date, they said, like it was some immutable rule of the social order. How come I never know that stuff?

"How about a margarita?" I said. I had a sense this night was going to require quite a few margaritas.

He jumped to his feet again and assured me he'd be right back, then headed for the bar. Alone for a moment, I scanned the familiar room. No one I knew. Joe Jackson was on the PA, asking if we knew that it's different for girls. Yes, Joe. We know.

Flaco came back with not only a pitcher of margaritas and two salt-rimmed, lime-bedecked glasses, but the waitress in tow as well bearing a large plate of nachos with all the fixings. I guessed we were having dinner after all, but I didn't mind as I was suddenly starving. Although, in my head, I could hear the Murdocks intoning another immutable rule—eat very lightly on a date! Oh, the hell with that, I was hungry. Plus, if I spilled anything on Margo's red, orange and yellow shirt, it was unlikely to show unless it was a jalapeño. Have to be mighty careful of those white jeans, though.

An hour later, I was surprised to find that I wasn't having such a bad time after all. Yes, the tequila was having its usual beneficial effect on my perception of reality, but I'd almost forgotten in all my predate angst that Flaco actually was a pretty nice guy. He kept the conversation going easily with stories about his job, his family, growing up in Holmesville and his hopes for the future. He was very ambitious and money-minded, but nothing wrong with that, I thought.

"So, how's your new business with Mrs. Romanoff going?" I asked.

"Oh, we're still working out the details on that one," he said with a confident smile.

He changed the subject to talk about movies, music and other pop culture stuff. Turned out we both had loved *Raiders of the Lost Ark*, but split on *Chariots of Fire*. Neither of us had seen the new movie *Poltergeist* which was one of the hot ones at the theater that month.

"Maybe we can see it together," he said as he poured me the last of the slush from the pitcher.

I smiled, but made no comment. He said he would get another pitcher and went to the bar. I was pleasantly buzzed already, but knew another pitcher was asking for trouble. I told myself to only drink one more margarita, no matter what. I ate some more nachos, figuring something solid in my stomach could not hurt.

A girl walked in one of the side doors and for a second, I thought it was Jules. My heart leapt. And my face burned to think she might see me here with Flaco. God, I'd even told her I had a date with him tonight. But it wasn't Jules. When she walked past, I could see she didn't even look like her.

Nevertheless, I found my hard-won resolve to have sex with Flaco that night crumbling. The demons of indecision and confusion were back and worse than before, if possible. Why didn't I just call it a night and go home, I thought? Nobody was forcing me to do anything here.

The waitress cruised by and I asked her to bring me a tall glass of ice water, which she did. Flaco returned with the second pitcher, all shining eyes and flashing teeth. He certainly seemed to be having a good time. And with all the charm he was oozing, doing his best to make sure I was having a good time too.

He poured me a drink, smiled when I told him that was my last margarita, poured himself one, then sat down and took my hand. His felt hot and strong. He was kind of cute. Kind of sexy, I guess, with the bad boy tattoos and the trace of an accent. Not like the guys I'd dated before. He seemed more self-assured, older—more like a man than a boy.

I kept waiting for an appropriate break in the conversation where I could insert the "Well, this has been great" line, but it never quite came. I didn't want to be rude and just bolt. Before I knew it, another hour had passed in which we chatted about nothing much. Somehow the margaritas disappeared, yet my glass was never empty. I was a little worried about driving home, but it wasn't far and I figured I could sit in my car for a while and sober up if worse came to worst.

The conversation was finally waning a bit when I took a sip of my now room temperature ice water and said, "Well, this has been really nice, Flaco, but I'd better be going. Got to be at work early tomorrow, you know." I was lying through my teeth as I had no intention of going to work the next day, but this too, was part of the dating ritual, the Murdocks had solemnly advised me in the past.

Far from being disappointed, he seemed to have anticipated this move on my part. He'd already paid for the drinks and the food at the bar, but now threw a few bills on the table for a tip as we stood. "Let me walk you out," he said with a broad smile.

I felt anxious to be rid of him now that the end was in sight. I knew it would be smart to have him walk with me back to the car in case Jackson was lurking, but at that point, I didn't care. I just wanted to be alone, in my car, by myself. Alone.

We paused on the sidewalk just outside the club to do the thanks/goodbye/whatever part of the transaction. Darkness had fallen. A single star shone above in the navy blue sky. I took in some deep breaths of night air in an attempt to speed up the sobering process. I still felt pretty buzzed, but not drunk. Well, maybe a little drunk. At least I hadn't fallen off my white leather sandals on the way out of the bar. Before I could launch into my "I had a lovely time" speech, Flaco asked me a question.

"I hate to bother you," he said, "but would you mind giving me a ride home?"

I was nonplussed. That wasn't in the script. "Uh, where's your van?" I asked.

"It's in the school district parking lot since tomorrow's my day off. My buddy dropped me off here after work."

"Oh. Well. Of course."

As we walked to my car, he took my hand. I started to tell him not to, then realized I kind of needed the help to keep me walking in a straight line. That's when I knew I was in no shape to drive. Flaco seemed a lot more together than I was. Apart from the height and weight difference, I wondered if he'd managed to maneuver me into drinking more of that second pitcher than he had. I certainly felt that way. I cursed myself for being a sucker and a bonehead. As reluctant as I normally was to let anyone else drive my beloved Camaro, this was one of those times.

His eyes lit up when I offered him the keys, as most guys' would. At my insistence, however, he drove slowly and carefully through tree-lined streets to his place, which turned out to be a small garage apartment behind a large blue house.

"I think you'd better come in," he said to me, apparently taking the measure of my sobriety and finding it lacking.

"Okay, but just for a little bit," I agreed. Even to my ears, it sounded like "jush for a lil bit." Shit. I tried to look stern, so he wouldn't get any ideas.

He helped me out of the passenger seat and walked me into his place, depositing me on a beat-up couch. It smelled like pot in there, but that wasn't the worst smell in the world. At least it was clean. I wondered if he had cleaned up in the hope he could entice me back to his lair. Well, here I am, lair. I looked around while he fiddled behind a curtain in the corner. Kitchenette? Not much renovation had taken place in the former garage beyond laying down carpet over the cement floor and putting in the small bathroom I glimpsed behind a partially open door. If it weren't for the eau de mary jane, I bet I would have smelled the ghostly vestiges of motor oil and gasoline.

With a pang, I realized his apartment sort of reminded me of Jules's place—the same compact space absolutely full to capacity with furniture and possessions. Most of the floor space was taken up with a queen-sized bed. A fringed brown velour throw with a huge tan lion's head on it was tossed across it. Subtle. The couch I was sitting on was up against one wall. My knees brushed the side of the bed. Industrial-looking metal shelves lined another wall and held his television, stereo, records and tapes. He'd only turned on one light, a dim floor lamp in the far corner, so other dark shapes in the room were left unidentified.

Flaco appeared from behind the curtain, two cans in his hands. Coke for me, beer for him. He stopped at the stereo and turned on some soft music. Duran Duran. Good thing I was too polite to retch. Sitting down beside me, he handed me the can of Coke, which I grabbed with both hands, savoring its slick chill. He reached down behind himself and came up with a bong and a lighter. He got it fired up, then gestured toward me in a hospitable fashion.

"No, thanks," I said, shaking my head.

He shrugged and took a long gurgling hit, then set it back down. My mouth was dry, but I couldn't bring myself to let go of the Coke can long enough to open it. It was hot in there. Airless. I wished he would open a window.

He kissed me. I let him.

He touched me. I let him.

Well, this is what you're here for, Heavenly, I told myself. This is why you came. But it was nothing. I felt nothing.

We moved to the bed and undressed. He found a condom in some dark recess above the bed and put it on. Thank God it was lubricated. He was sweaty now. Urgent. Awkward. All elbows and knees, it seemed. And quick, too quick. He hurt me a little bit at one point, unknowingly, unintentionally, and I made a small sound, which he misinterpreted. He said my name at first, then was reduced to a painful sounding grunting.

Soon, it was over. The heat was unbearable in there. He kissed me one last time, then rolled over and went to sleep, his arm thrown heavily across me. My head felt preternaturally clear and yet drained of all useful thought. My body was without purpose or energy. I lay there for I don't know how long, gathering myself back to me. And then I left.

* * *

Maybe I need to explain something here. Explain it to myself, at least. You see, when I was very small, the process began. Stories were read to me in which beautiful princesses went through all kinds of shit to hook up with handsome princes. Every show on TV—hell, every commercial—was some version of boy meets girl. Every family I knew had at its core a husband and a wife, or at least the survivors of such a pairing.

It wasn't their fault, I guess. After all, they'd all been through the same indoctrination. How could they know I was different when I looked just the same? And how could I know when a boy kissed me that those rubber lips, that utter lack of sensation was not what everyone else felt? I figured they were all faking it just like I was, just like I knew we were all faking self-confidence, knowledge, maturity. My friends sometimes admitted faking those latter things when we did our all-night marathon talks in our college years.

How could I even imagine I was not one of them, when they were all I had ever known? Like a girl raised by wolves. Until Jules Talbot told me I had beautiful green eyes, leaned in and kissed me good.

I drove back to the Murdocks' about eleven p.m. The streets were dark and deserted at that hour. The wind had picked up again, blowing trash and newspapers down the road before me, caught in the beam of the headlights.

The apartment had that heavy silence that only an empty house has. Chopper was the only one home and for that I was profoundly thankful. The last thing I wanted was to have to face a Murdock at that moment. A note on the counter from Margo said Mona was at practice, Margo was at work and Chopper had been duly walked on her break about a half hour before.

I took a long shower, turning the water as hot as it would go, scrubbing away what was left of Margo's makeup job until my skin felt raw and red. I didn't even bother to comb out my wet hair, knowing it would look like hell in the morning either way and I'd have to wash it again anyhow. I avoided the sight of my murky self in the steamed up mirror. It was after midnight by the time I tiredly pushed Chopper off the couch and wrapped myself up in a clean sheet, drifting slowly off to a stuporous sleep undisturbed by dreams.

CHAPTER FOURTEEN

Thursday

I awoke to a pounding headache in the early a.m. Even if I had been planning to go to work, I doubt I would have made it. I dragged myself off the couch to the kitchen counter, where I quietly called the temp agency and told them I was too sick to work. As a courtesy, since I felt almost like a real county employee, I then called Stephanie's work phone and left her the same message. My conscience prickled, but they could survive without me for one day. With the week I was having, a mental health day was more than justified, I thought.

Both bedroom doors were closed, and I assumed that meant both Murdocks were in residence—and hopefully no one else. I couldn't take any more surprises. I found some aspirin and then went back to sleep. I awoke hours later to blinding sunlight streaming in through the curtains Margo had just yanked wide open.

"Fuckin' egg, Margo..."

"You do realize it's almost noon, right?" she said without looking at me, staring out the window, cup of coffee in hand.

Chopper stood quietly beside her, wearing his leash. Since he wasn't doing the happy dance and gouging chunks out of the front door, I deduced that they had already been out and had just come back in.

"Noon…" I sat up wearily on the couch and squinted at the day.

Mona was at the counter, eating a bowl of cereal. "Did you call in sick?" she asked me.

"Yes."

"Are you sick?"

"No."

"Good," she said, munching.

Margo said, "Hey, Hev, there's your boyfriend."

Irritated that I was now the target of this tired and sorry joke, I nonetheless got up and went to the window to see what street bum or old man with a walker she had picked out for me. Oh. She was pointing at Flaco, who was getting something out of his van on the far side of the street. (Aha—I knew he'd lied about needing a ride!) Looked like lamps or something electrical this time.

"Flaco," Margo said over her shoulder to her sister, explaining.

"He's not my boyfriend," I said with emphasis and retreated from the window before he looked up and saw me there.

I rummaged in my pile of stuff on the couch for some pants, finally extracting some wrinkled khaki walking shorts to go with the faded black Ramones T-shirt I'd slept in. I sensed more than saw the Murdocks exchange a look.

"Not a good date, huh?" said Mona.

I flicked her a glance and shook my head as I went past her into the kitchen. I didn't want to talk about it. Probably not ever. She and Margo exchanged another look, but let it lie. I helped myself to a bowl of cereal and a Coke, then joined Mona at the counter.

"Hey!" I said to her, suddenly remembering. "It's your big day! It's Thursday!"

Her mouth was full of crunchies, but she gave me a smile that was deep in her eyes. I could see how excited she was, despite her calm exterior. Internally, she was clearly doing her version of the happy dance.

Margo drifted over to join us at the counter. Chopper was close behind, alert for dropped cereal.

"So what are we doing today?" I asked them. A wonderful idea came over me. "Let's take Chopper out to Four Mile!"

Four Mile Beach was (wait for it) four miles north of town on Highway 1. It was remote and unmarked, unknown to tourists and not listed in any guidebook. To get there, you first of all had to know where to pull off the highway and park because there was no sign. Then you had to hike a narrow dirt path that led over a hill, through a brussels sprouts field and finally down a steep sandstone fissure to the beach itself. A nude beach was rumored to be close by, but I had never actually laid eyes on that. Thank goodness. Four Mile was gorgeous, untrampled sand right on the Pacific. It was a bit of a job getting out there, but worth it.

The Murdocks burst my bubble, though, when Margo said she had to be at work pretty soon and Mona said she had band stuff to do, including a sound check at the Mongol at three o'clock.

"Well, fine," I said rebelliously, "Chopper and I will just go by ourselves, then."

"You can't, Hev," Mona said firmly. "It's Thursday, remember? That maniac might be out there somewhere."

Oh, yeah. Crap. Fuckin' maniacs always ruining my day.

"Why don't you just hang out here?" she asked. "Relax for the afternoon, then we'll grab some dinner and go to Dollar Night. Heck, you can even go back to sleep if you want to."

More sleep was always enticing, but I really felt obligated to take Chopper out somewhere and let him run. He must have hated being cooped up all the time. Or maybe I was just projecting my feelings onto him. Either way, I knew Mona would argue with me if I said I was going out, so I pretended to acquiesce, shrugging and saying, "Okay, I guess so."

She was all on fire with band stuff anyhow, so she didn't notice anything. An hour later, Margo had gone to the Bowl and I was at the window watching the Monamobile head down the street.

"We're free," I said to Chopper, whose answering bark I felt was clearly a doggie "yahoo!"

Maybe it was dumb to venture out from the safety of the apartment, but I hadn't seen or heard hide nor hair of Jackson Miller since that phone call on Tuesday. With any luck, Grausteiner was locking him up in the jail right now. Besides, I was a big girl and perfectly capable of taking care of myself. Well, semicapable of sometimes sort of taking care of myself. But it was a perfect, sunny day outside and I wasn't about to waste my "sick" day lying on the couch. I'd keep my eyes and ears open and be careful. And after all, it was broad daylight. What the heck was he going to do?

I did heed Mona's words of warning to the extent that I reluctantly bagged the Four Mile plan. That was a little too perfect a place for a quiet murder and hiding the body. No matter—the beach in town would work just fine. I changed into my bathing suit, threw the khaki shorts back on top of that, stuffed the dog's leash in my pocket and we were good to go. During the short drive over, Chopper discovered he could stick his head out my open window from the backseat. He seemed to enjoy the wind in his face immensely and only licked my neck seven times on the way to the beach.

I hadn't exactly intended to drive past my apartment, but the Camaro seemed to head that way of its own volition. I decided I would just slowly cruise past and make sure everything looked okay from the outside. It did. Both Jules's scooter and Ashley's car were gone. I slowed down some more. There was something on my door. Small, white and fluttering. A note?

The guy behind me honked and I waved an apology, then sped up. As soon as I could, I made a left and then another left, steering back toward the apartment. I made the final left onto Third Street and slowed to a crawl down its steep slope. There was no one behind me. I paused in the street. There was definitely something on my door up there. I looked around and saw nothing else unusual or out of place. No Jackson lurking with a chainsaw and a hockey mask. Was it a trap?

A car was coming down the hill behind me. Decision time. I pulled into my driveway and parked the Camaro in the garage. As I sat there for a moment trying to collect my thoughts, it occurred to me the note didn't have to be from Jackson. It might be from (blechhh) Flaco or—my heart did a little pittypat—Jules. Or the landlord or the Jehovah's Witnesses, my brain said. Get a grip, it added rudely.

Suddenly tired of my ceaseless indecision, I jumped out of the car with Chopper hot on my heels, practically threw the garage door closed and ran for the stairs. The dog was at first eager to run with me, but changed his mind when he hit the sandy patch. I left him there doing his thing and raced up the steps, arriving out of breath at my own front door.

I checked the knob first—still locked. Good. I looked around from the panoramic vantage point of the veranda. Man, if anyone was watching me, I must look like a complete wing nut, I thought. The note was a single white sheet of standard typing paper, folded in half and taped to my door. The half that faced me was blank, but I could see there were some words typed inside when the paper fluttered in the breeze. Had Jackson applied an exotic and untraceable poison to the paper that would kill me as soon as I touched it? Probably not, I thought and yet—I held up the top half with my keys and read the brief note inside:

Heavenly,
Please forgive me. I'm so sorry for what I said. I didn't mean it. I apologize if I scared you. Believe me, that's the last thing I want to do. I've been under a lot of pressure lately. I just want you to understand. Anyhow, if you have the clipping, please, *please* bring it to the Moonglow tonight. All I want is the clipping back. Please bring it and I'll explain everything to you. I'll make it up to you, Heavenly, I promise, so please come and bring the clipping.
JM

It was all typed, including the initials at the bottom. No signature. There were a couple of typos he'd whited out and typed over, but the spelling was good, the clerical part of my brain couldn't help but note. If nothing else, the appearance of the note gave credence to the "out on Thursdays" theory, for whatever that was worth. Hmmph. The tone was conciliatory. Did I believe him? It really didn't matter. I didn't have the damn clipping, Grausteiner did. Should I call the detective? Absolutely, I thought.

I left the note where it was and went back downstairs where Chopper sat panting by the mailboxes. I checked my box, half expecting it to be empty again, but there was stuff in there. As I pulled it out, the whine of an approaching scooter came to my ears. I had a sudden urge to flee, which was stupid, because I wanted to see her. Right?

Right.

She came from the south on Highland Avenue, so she didn't see us there until she came around the corner from Ashley's parking spot. She skidded to a stop when she saw me, but then rolled the scooter forward to park it in her usual place beneath the stairs. In the few moments it took her to do that, I quickly looked at the mail in my hands. Junk, a bill and a rolled up magazine. I slid the rubber band off (stashing it in my pocket so Chopper wouldn't eat it) to find it was definitely not for me—GQ. Another piece of unforwarded Jackson mail. I guess he didn't need fashion tips whilst on the lam. It rolled back up into a tight tube on its own when I released it.

Chopper had begun barking and cavorting about when he realized his beloved Jules had arrived, but he kept the cavortage at a safe distance from the scooter—I think he was a little afraid of it. Plus, he kept running back over to me for reassurance and a quick lap of my fingers, kneecap or whatever body part was handy. Finally, he leaned heavily against my leg, quivering slightly from the intensity of his feelings. I patted his big head with the hand not holding the mail and told him I knew exactly how he felt.

Jules cut the engine and came around the corner sans helmet, running a hand through her hair in a gesture that was already familiar to me. The breeze wafted a faint hint of her peach scent over to me. She looked trim and sporty in her white Keds, navy blue tennis shorts and a white sleeveless polo shirt, which set off her tan nicely.

Chopper slunk over, stumpy tail madly wagging, ears back, head down and—I could have sworn—grinning. She greeted him with her "Hey, Puddin'" and made much of him, finally looking up at me.

I was wearing sunglasses, but had pushed them up on my head. I smiled at her, perhaps a little tentatively. I seemed to be having a hard time breathing. After the way I'd run out on her the other night and no communication at all on Wednesday, I wasn't sure where we stood.

"Hey, Jules," I managed to say, almost like a normal person.

She stood and walked over to me. Right up to me. Put her arms around my waist and pulled me in even closer, so we were nose to nose. She considered me for a moment, then spoke. "Hey, Puddin'," she said with a smile so adorable, I felt a little dizzy.

She kissed me then, in front of God and everybody, making me drop my mail. Well, all right, there was no one around, but we were in plain sight of the traffic on Highland and the neighbors. A passing car honked its horn and the occupant yelled something, although at us or another driver I wasn't sure. Nevertheless, I backed away from her, blushing.

"God, Jules, not in public."

"Oh, come on," she said, smiling, "it's 1982." She grabbed my hand and started to pull me toward her door.

"Wait!"

I ran to gather my mail, which the ocean breeze had already scattered about the yard. Give a hoot, don't pollute. Chopper found and "killed" the rolled up GQ, then pranced about proudly chomping on it, shaking his head exaggeratedly. Oh, well, it wasn't like anyone was going to read it anyhow. I collected the rest of the mail and threw it back in the mailbox. The mailman was probably sick of me doing that.

Jules had gone inside her apartment and left the front door wide open.

"Jules?" I said hesitantly as we crossed her threshold, me cautiously, Chopper unselfconsciously.

She was nowhere in sight, but then appeared from behind the Japanese screen wearing nothing but her bikini, nimbly fastening the top behind her back. She looked delectable. I gaped at her.

"What?" she said, gesturing toward my swimsuit while she slid her navy tennis shorts back up those long, long legs. "We're going to the beach, aren't we?"

"Yeah, we are." I felt a warm glow of pleasure in my abdomen at her assumption. "We" were going to the beach! But first I needed to call Grausteiner. Before I could ask to borrow her phone, Jules spoke first.

"Hey, do you know there's a note on your door upstairs? I saw it earlier when I went out." She was on the couch, applying Coppertone to first her arms, then her legs. "Hev?" she prompted when I failed to respond.

I tore my eyes from the lubricating process and met her inquiring look. I could tell she was quite aware of the effect she was having on me. She smiled to herself and went back to the rubbing as I finally answered. "Uh, yeah, in fact, I just read it. It's from Jackson."

"Jackson Miller?" She looked both startled and puzzled, reminding me again that I hadn't told her much, if any, of the story.

"Yeah. Long story. Can I borrow your phone?"

"Sure," she said, pointing to the kitchen.

Miraculously, I got straight through to Grausteiner that time and quickly explained to him about the note. He approved of my not touching or removing the paper.

"Where are you calling from?" he asked.

"My downstairs neighbor's," I said.

I could see Jules quietly talking to Chopper, who had his head in her lap, eyes cast adoringly upward at her. I'm not going to record that conversation here, which was mostly along the lines of "Who's a puddy wuddy duddy…"

The front door was still wide open, which was good from the air and light point of view, but not so good from the security point of view. Although I felt pretty safe with Jules there…In any event, the phone cord wasn't long enough for me to reach the door and close it.

"I'll swing by and get the note," Grausteiner said. "You haven't seen Miller, right?"

"Right."

"Well, you stay safe, Miss Wilcox and we'll check out this note. We'll keep an eye on the Moonglow tonight too and see if we can pick him up there."

Wow, maybe Grausteiner was taking me seriously. About time. "Okay, thanks," I said, but he had already hung up. I strode toward the front door to close it, but Jules forestalled me.

"Wait, where are you going?"

"I'm just gonna close the door."

"Leave it open, will you? I like the air," she said. I must have looked doubtful, because she added, "We're going out in a minute anyhow, right?"

"Well, yeah…"

She held out a slender shapely arm, gesturing me toward the couch. "Come here," she said persuasively.

Like someone hypnotized, I slowly went to her, sinking down on the futon by her side. Chopper was at our feet, content with his "bone." He wasn't eating it, I was glad to see, just systematically shredding it.

"That's better," Jules said to me with a knowing smile.

I felt so unequal to her. She handed me the bottle of Coppertone. "Would you put some on my back?"

She turned around so her back was to me. Her lovely, smooth, tan back. That she wanted me to put lotion on. Is there anything more beautiful than a beautiful woman's back? My hands were shaking.

I started with her shoulders, thinking that was safe. They were slender and strong, like the rest of her. She had a dusting of freckles there too, I noticed, where the sun had punished her. The creamy white lotion felt cool on my hands, no doubt because I was so overheated. She slipped each bikini strap aside, just an inch or so, to make sure I didn't miss anywhere. I ran two fingertips slowly down her spine from the nape of her neck to the horizontal line of her bikini. She shivered ever so slightly. I moved on to her lower back then, with special attention to the sides where my hands fit her shape like they'd been made to order. Another lingering trip down the spine, this time ending just inside the waistband of her tennis shorts. My fingertips, slippery with sunscreen, delved further to find the bikini below and slid just a millimeter inside before retreating. Her breathing was noticeably uneven, which emboldened me.

At a deliberate pace, my hands gently slid up her torso to cup her small, perfect, bikini-clad breasts. As my fingertips traced lazy circles, she squirmed in my grip and arched her back against me. With a stifled but urgent moan, she turned and pulled me forward, into a kiss so sweet and true the grim memory of Flaco's bony awkwardness faded. This was what I wanted. This softness, this roundness, this sense of rightness. This joy, this feeling of belonging for the first time in my life. This was what I wanted. Now I knew.

Holy moly, a part of my brain thought—if the kissing was this good, what would the sex be like? Although...to tell the truth, I wasn't one hundred percent sure how two girls did it. I mean, I had some ideas, of course, but as for the actual, technical, "how to" of it...the rest of that train of thought was lost when Jules's hand started fooling with the zipper of my shorts.

As if from a great distance, I dimly perceived footsteps approaching. Jules's tongue and hands still had most of my attention, but the sound of keys being sharply tapped on wood finally broke through to me. I let go of her and realized with a start that someone was standing right there in the doorway. Someone with a nasty smile and a cheap beige suit. Grausteiner.

"Ladies," he said, with a most revolting smirk.

My face was burning. I turned away for a moment to wipe my mouth with the back of my hand. And check my zipper. I smoothed my hair down jerkily and stood, feigning composure. I said to Jules, "He's the cop I just called. This should just take a minute, okay?"

Her eyes widened when I said "cop," but she shrugged, appearing much more collected than I felt. It wasn't every day I was caught smooching a girl by the police. Criminy. I tried to look as cool and casual as she did for Grausteiner, who was still giving me the nasty smile. I spared a moment to glare at Chopper, still placidly chewing his reading material, for failing to warn me of the intruder's approach, but he only happily wagged his tail at my eye contact. Dumb dog.

"Did you see the note?" I asked Grausteiner as I stepped outside, pulling the door shut behind me.

He nodded and patted his pocket, indicating he had it in his possession.

"So what do you think?" I said.

"I think you should stay away from the Moonglow tonight," he said, serious now.

"But I have to go!" I said. "My friend's band is playing."

He looked like he didn't think that was the most important thing in the world even though it clearly was. "You'd be smart to stay away," he told me. "This guy could be dangerous."

"So you do believe me!" I exclaimed.

"Let's just say I've got an open mind. And I don't like the feel of this note. Most of these guys turn out to be harmless, but some are real crazies, you know? Be smart, Miss Wilcox—stay with a friend tonight and let us take care of Miller."

I poked at a pebble with my toe, my expression probably mulish. I knew he was right, but how could I miss this of all Dollar Nights? I could tell Grausteiner was growing impatient with me. With a return to his former manner, he said sarcastically, "Maybe you can stay with your friend here," gesturing toward Jules's apartment.

"Yeah, well, maybe I can," I shot back obnoxiously. "Either way, you guys will be at the Moonglow tonight to pick him up, right?"

"I'll have a man there," he affirmed.

I guess my hope that they'd send the entire SWAT team was a little misplaced. Maybe San Tomas didn't even have a SWAT team. He looked like he was ready to leave, so I remembered my manners long enough to thank him for all his efforts, which I truly did appreciate. Jules came out with Chopper by her side as Grausteiner drove off in his unmarked black sedan.

"Beach?" she said. She had a towel slung over one shoulder and looked like one million and one dollars.

"Beach," I concurred.

Chopper's leash was in my pocket. He sat on his own as soon as he saw me pull it out, making me smile involuntarily. As I clipped it to his collar, I asked Jules, "So where's Ashley today? Work?" Not that I really gave a shit, but I wanted a heads-up if she was going to suddenly appear in our midst again.

"No," Jules said, "I think she had FemTones rehearsal today. She took off with her trombone a while ago."

The beach was sparsely populated, so I let Chopper go. He dashed off in pursuit of some seagulls, and to sniff all of the flotsam and most of the jetsam within a hundred yard radius, but trotted back periodically to check in with us. With the sun still high in the sky, it was hot but pleasant out there with the breeze off the water. Jules and I sat on her towel, not talking much, letting our senses fill with the sights and sounds of the beach. And each other. A stray mutt wandered by and Chopper romped with the pooch good-naturedly, playing the submissive even though he must have had seventy pounds or more on the other dog, which looked to be a mix of Dalmatian, wire-haired dachshund and weasel.

Jules stood up and shrugged off her shorts, then lay down on her back on her half of the towel, long brown legs stretched out in the warm sand, elbows propping her up above the waistline. She brushed the top of my hand with her fingertips, giving me one of her highly charged looks. I was feeling a little hyperventilate-y, with all that Jules on display right there beside me. I looked around, gulping for oxygen. A few people were about, either walking or sitting on the sand like we were. Too many for what I felt like doing, in any case. I could still look at her, though. The same tiny, golden hairs that adorned her forearms and so pleased me were also to be found on her thighs.

Jules smiled, knowing the power she had over me. She handed me the suntan lotion again. "Here, I think you missed a spot." A wicked grin.

"Yeah, I don't think so." I put the bottle down. Not in public.

"Oh, yeah, right here," she insisted, pointing to that tantalizing stretch of stomach below her belly button and above her bikini bottom.

I thought about the feel of the Coppertone on my fingers and then sliding those fingers across her warm brown flesh...I shook my head at her silently, mouthing the word "no." She sighed and lay back, reaching for my hand again. Even her hand felt so different than a boy's. Softer, smoother, a better fit. Not sweaty or gripping too tightly. Just right. I had never enjoyed holding hands before, had always tolerated it rather than liked it. But now it was nothing short of thrilling. Was it the same for her? I didn't know. I don't know.

I've spent other days on the beach, but I cannot recall any happier than those few hours with Jules. Our idyll was short-lived, however, as she was expected for dinner at her parents' house and I had plans with Mona.

"But I'll see you at Dollar Night, right?" I said as we parted on her doorstep.

"Wouldn't miss it," she confirmed. "And maybe afterward...?" She left the question dangling.

Maybe afterward I could finally sleep in my own apartment, I thought, if the cops picked up Jackson. How killer would that be? Oh. It finally clicked in my brain what Jules was saying. Wow. Really? Wow. Was I ready for that? Another piece of Murdock Advice To The Lovelorn floated up in my brain: when your sweetie says something you're not sure how to respond to, kiss him. Or her, as the case may be. I tried it. It worked.

Back at Chez Murdock, it was cocktail hour. Petey sat at the counter with a six-pack of Beck's beer in front of him. Beads of condensation had formed on the emerald green bottles.

"Hey, classy stuff!" I applauded his selection. I helped myself to one as I sat down across from him. He looked even paler than usual, I thought, and a bit tight about the nostrils and mouth. "Nervous?" I asked sympathetically.

It was their most important gig so far. If you played at the Mongol in San Tomas, you had hit the big time. The trick was to do well, draw a big crowd and get them dancing, then score another gig at the Mongol. And then another…A lot was on the line for Bertha's Attic that night.

Petey shrugged. "I'm okay," he said. And took another drink.

"Well, don't get drunk, for Chrissake," I told him. "Mona will kill you if you can't play."

He nodded, but the thought of Mona's ire only made him paler. I gave up on the self-esteem workshop and fed Chopper, then bullied Petey into taking him out for a walk. Mona was still behind her closed bedroom door. It was ominously silent in there. I hoped she wasn't suffering from nerves too. That would make her just about unbearable. I thought about knocking on her door, but with equal parts wisdom and cowardice, decided to let her come out in her own time.

I took advantage of her hibernation and Petey's absence to get myself ready for Dollar Night. My wardrobe was severely limited and not as clean or unwrinkled as I would have liked, but *c'est la vie*. After a quick shower to rinse off the sand from the beach, I chose black jeans, my aqua and white Vans and a little black tank top that had "Baker From The Forest" across the front in small white script. Dangly aqua earrings completed the look. I fussed with my hair for a while, but as usual, it ended up looking the same way it always did. Oh, well. I added a little pink lipstick, but couldn't be bothered with any other makeup. I'd just sweat it off once the dancing began.

As I sat down at the kitchen counter again to await the next chapter of the evening, I saw a couple of phone messages at the other end I hadn't noticed before. I slid down to check them. Ugh—one was for me from Flaco. Did the guy not get the hint from me leaving in the middle of the night without saying good-bye? Apparently not. Well, maybe I could have been a little clearer. I guess I could have a left a note or something. In my admittedly limited experience, most guys needed to be hit over the head with something dull and heavy to get anything important, relationship-wise, through to them. His message said he would see me at Dollar Night. Oh, shit! I would just have to find a way to let him down easy at the Mongol and get rid of him before Jules showed up.

Petey came in with Chopper. Almost simultaneously, Mona's door opened and she emerged from her bedroom. She must have been in there primping and going to town with the AquaNet. She looked fantastic, a total rock star from head to toe. Her hair was a masterpiece of stiff spikes. Skintight, black, spandex pants adorned her lower half, terminating in her black leather go-go boots. Hers had a modest stacked heel, since spike heels were not conducive to her energetic style of performing. Her top half was a buttoned-up, shiny, silver, sequined vest with nothing under it. A completely unnecessary (from the structural integrity point of view) silver concho belt entwined her skinny waist. Twice. Numerous silver (in color, at least) bracelets, necklaces and earrings (including the trout lure) further adorned her. Exaggerated stage makeup completed her look. She was ready for the cover of *Rolling Stone*, in my humble opinion.

"Wow, Mona! You look fabulous, woman!" I cried out enthusiastically.

She turned to Petey for his reaction. He too was awestruck, but managed to mumble an obviously heartfelt, "Fuckin' egg, Mon…"

She was pleased with both our responses. She swaggered over and helped herself to a beer. She didn't really need to get ready that early—it was barely six o'clock—but I'm sure she'd been dying to get dressed since she woke up. She'd probably had that outfit planned for a month.

In stark contrast to all her glamour, Petey wore a UCST T-shirt and dirty plaid Bermuda shorts. He caught my glance and explained he was going to change at the club.

The three of us finished off the six-pack, which gave me time to fill Mona in on Jackson's note and Grausteiner's promise to nab him at the Mongol. She listened, but I could tell her mind was more on her gig than my melodrama, which was only fitting.

Then it was off to Freddy's for dinner, leaving a disappointed Chopper behind. Mona made Freddy bring her extra cloth napkins so there was no chance of despoiling her outfit with a stray drop of soy sauce. Since I was starving, I delighted Freddy (against my better judgment) by ordering some food. I hoped it wouldn't suck. It sucked, but I glumly ate it anyway, not wanting to face Dollar Night on an empty stomach. At least the Tsing Tao kept my buzz going nicely.

The meal was pretty much déjà vu from the previous Thursday night, except Margo wasn't there. She was again stuck at work, Mona told me, but would try her best to make it to the Mongol in time for at least part of Bertha's Attic's set. Fortunately, several other people had called throughout the day to congratulate Mona and assure her they would be in attendance, so she was stoked about that and able to be stoic about Margo's possible no-show.

We lingered over the meal since the first band wouldn't go on until nine fifteen. Bertha's Attic was the second band and the headliner was the third. It was a sign of the rising stature of Mona's group that their first gig at the Mongol was in the second slot, I thought. The word was spreading. I hoped it had spread enough to ensure a big crowd. A big, happy, drunken, dancing crowd that would spend all their money and ensure a return gig for the band.

Even Freddy knew what a big night it was (probably because Mona had told him about a hundred times—besides, she had asked for and received his permission to put a flyer on his door). Instead of the usual fortune cookies, he surprised us by coming out with Mrs. Freddy and the cook in tow. He carried a small, round cake with a single candle burning in its center. As they presented it to us, they clapped in rhythm and sang a quick peppy song in Chinese. I'm not exactly sure what it was about, but I think it was something along the lines of "we're so happy the crazy American girl from upstairs is experiencing modest success in her chosen profession." All six of us were laughing by the time they finished, with us thanking them profusely and Mona even surreptitiously wiping a tear from one eye, the other eye daring me or Petey to say something about it.

I don't know what traditional Far East dessert I was expecting, but it turned out to be a peach upside down cake. A damn fine peach upside down cake. Mona and I had a slice apiece and Petey ate the rest. Warmed by their affectionate display, we tipped extravagantly and floated off on a cloud of goodwill and sugar high.

Mona drove us slowly past the front of the Mongol so I could see the marquee with "Bertha's Attic" in big letters on the middle line. Petey told me the band had taken a photo under the marquee earlier in the day following their sound check. The opening band—called The Mighty Handful—was accorded smaller letters on the bottom line, while the headliner was biggest and boldest of all across the top. Their name was The Think System.

Because the band would be loading their equipment back into the Monamobile at the end of the night, she parked in the little lot in back of the club. Their instruments and amplifiers had been brought over earlier for the sound check. As early as it was, I found the rest of Bertha's Attic had already arrived. We pulled up next to keyboardist LeClaire's orange Karmann Ghia. Handsome Pete's pickup truck was on the other side. In fact, as we got out, I saw that both of them were in his truck, talking and sharing a joint.

When they got out to join us, I could see there appeared to be a sartorial plan in place for the band that evening, or at least a color directive. Not only was Mona resplendent in her black and silver outfit, but LeClaire and Handsome Pete were mostly in black as well. It was a good thing LeClaire would be behind her rack of keyboards, I thought, otherwise she might just steal the spotlight from Mona. She wore a red tube top under a black jumpsuit unbuttoned to the waist, showing lots of café au lait skin. Jumpsuits were big that year. LeClaire was in black stilettos, plus her beaded braids and mirrored sunglasses as usual (day or night) and all kinds of rings, bracelets, earrings and a cross on a chain around her neck. Topping off all this finery was a charcoal gray fedora with a white hatband. She was chewing bubblegum and popped an enormous pink bubble as I looked her over.

Handsome Pete was understated, but no less fine, in black parachute pants and a tight black muscle shirt showing, well, lots of muscle. He was definitely living up to his nickname that night. His brand-new white leather Reebok high-tops gleamed in the dwindling rays of the San Tomas sunset.

I glanced at Petey, the poor relation in his shorts and T-shirt. He caught my worried gaze. "Don't worry, Hev," he told me with a laugh. "I got it covered." He patted his backpack confidently.

We hung out in the parking lot as the day faded, waiting for eight thirty when the front doors would open. At the appointed time, we trooped around to the front where the band sailed grandly through since they didn't have to pay that night. I coughed up my one buck at the box office, visited the bouncer on his barstool by the entrance and was then allowed to pass as well.

I could hear "Abacab" by Genesis thundering in the main room as I hurried to catch up. The guys were pushing together two small tables under LeClaire's supervision and Mona was signaling for the waitress. I bought the first celebratory pitcher and when it came, we toasted Bertha's Attic.

Hardly anyone else was there at first, but soon the club was filling with first a trickle, then a bona fide stream of people coming in. I felt safe in the shelter of the band, but kept a wary eye out for Jackson and/or the cops. I didn't see either one. (No Flaco either, thank goodness.) Maybe Grausteiner had sent an undercover policeman? Hmmm. I eyed my fellow Mongol patrons with even more interest to see if I could spot any hidden law enforcement personnel. Nope—everyone I saw either looked normal or San Tomas-y, and both groups fit right in at Dollar Night. If undercover cops were there, they were well hidden from me and everyone else.

Genesis gave way to Tom Petty, reminding us we didn't have to live like a refugee. Jackson was a refugee of sorts…or a fugitive. He'd tried to run away from his past, but instead had run smack-dab into Werner. Maybe you could never really escape your past, no matter how far you ran. If I had killed an entire family by accident, I don't know what I would have done. The guilt and shame would have been overwhelming, I thought. I shuddered and took a long drink of cold beer, thankful I wasn't driving that night.

I was sandwiched in between Mona and LeClaire on the wall side of the table, which was near the foot of the stage. I asked Mona about the Mighty Handful since I'd never heard of them before. The name sounded borderline dirty, but who knew with all these bizarre band names? I had heard of the headliner—the Think System was a tuneful, pop rock quintet from Monterey. I'd seen them play at a dance up at UCST once and liked them. Sort of Split Enz meets Elvis Costello meets the Cars, if that makes any sense.

"What?" Mona said to me.

"The opening band—what are they like?"

"Awful," she said with a curled lip. "Avant garde, techno-funk crap with a chick singing Japanese on top of it. Total pretentious shit. Fuckin' music majors," she said, adding with a snort that even the band's name was some kind of music major inside joke.

Since her own band's name was an English major inside joke, I thought that was a bit harsh. I kept that to myself. The lights dimmed for a moment, a sign that the first band was due to start any minute.

"Whew! About time," I heard Mona say.

I heard the relief and anxiety, the anticipation and exhilaration, mingled in her voice. I held up my beer and we clinked glasses, sharing a smile. Her big night was finally here. And she was right (of course) about the avant garde techno crap. Man, they were bad. Even the leggy Asian chick in a diaphanous gown couldn't save them from their extreme crappiness. Her vocals, unfortunately, weren't any better than Mrs. Freddy's. Although her legs were top-notch. Well, if nothing else, they'd make the crowd that much happier to see Bertha's Attic and hear some music they could actually dance to, I thought.

Petey disappeared with his backpack about halfway through their painful set, presumably to change clothes. I couldn't wait to see what he'd be wearing. I was sure Mona had preapproved his outfit, so it had to be good. When the Handful's guitar player announced their next song would be their last (to scattered rude applause), Mona and her remaining band members stood up from the table.

"Time to head backstage," she said to me, her eyes gleaming with excitement.

"Knock their socks off," I told her and held out my hand, palm up. She nodded, low-fived me and led her troops off to battle.

With the band gone, I was suddenly all alone at the table. I looked around again for Jackson and saw nothing. Grausteiner's warning echoed in my mind, but I was in a public place, surrounded by other people and trying to be vigilant. Still, I hoped Margo would make it on time so I wouldn't be sitting completely alone. I wondered if I could interest her in Flaco. Anything to get him out of my hair.

I decided to hit the ladies' room in the interval before Bertha's Attic came on. Maneuvering through the growing crowd, I dodged around people to make my way toward the foot of the stairs. Where I came face-to-face with Flaco. Ugh.

"Heavenly!" he exclaimed with a big smile, then pulled me in for a hug.

I slithered out of that as quickly as possible, in part because he again smelled of pot. Could the guy not go one day without lighting up? Really, if I were going to be his girlfriend, I'd have to nip that in the bud. So to speak.

"Hey, Flaco," I said neutrally as he beamed at me.

"I'm so happy to see you," he said, not seeming to notice the neutrality.

"Yeah, well, we need to talk," I told him, "but my friend's band is about to go on, so can I catch up with you after their set?"

The first glimmer of doubt seemed to enter his demeanor, but he manfully shook it off. "Of course," he replied with enthusiasm. "Where are you sitting?"

Oh. Crap. Now he was going to sit with me. Well, I'd brought that on myself. And with Jackson potentially in the club, I would feel safer with someone, anyone, sitting with me. I pointed out the table and said I'd see him there after I visited the ladies' room.

After taking care of business, I paused for a moment in the lee of the staircase outside the room of rest. I needed to brace myself to endure Flaco's presence for the next hour or so. Any meaningful conversation would have to wait until we were outside. It was going to be bad enough to break up with him at a normal volume level—I wasn't about to yell my way through it.

People brushed past me in both directions as they rushed to get drinks, use the bathroom, or go outside for a smoke in the pause between bands. I could only see the table in brief flashes through the crowd. Flaco sat there patiently. In this busy ebb and flow, someone came up alongside me from behind, and before I realized it, slipped an arm through mine. I started and tried to pull away before I realized it was Jules.

"Jules!"

Now *her* hug was welcome. Her body felt good pulled in tight against me. I didn't want to let her go. She turned her head and kissed me on the cheek, ending with a mischievous little lick. I pulled back blushing, I'm sure.

"I didn't miss anything, did I?" she asked me, her hand reaching out to mine.

I moved back slightly to avoid the touch. "No, no," I said, not sure if I meant the opening act or the public affection. "But come on, they're gonna start any minute now." I pointed toward the table, then dived into the crowd with Jules close behind. Very close—I felt her hand on my rear as we neared our destination. "Stop," I commanded.

Her eyes danced, but she acquiesced. "Okay, okay," she said, shrugging and holding up her hands in mock surrender.

We finished our journey to the table like casual acquaintances, with a foot of air between us, just like our tongues had never touched. I said to Flaco, who had politely risen to his feet as we approached, "You remember Jules from the other day?"

"Of course. Nice to see you again," he said to her.

She nodded without saying anything.

There was an empty chair next to the one Flaco had taken. He held the empty for me invitingly. I didn't really want to sit next to him, but I couldn't see any way out of it without appearing rude. "Thanks," I mumbled as I slid into place.

He kept an arm around the back of my chair as he sat down.

Jules sat down opposite me, leaning across the table to say, "Ashley's around here someplace. Is it cool if she sits with us too?"

"Sure, no problem." The more the merrier, I thought.

The sound guy put on the Men At Work album while we tried to carry on a conversation. I could hardly pay attention to what anyone was saying, what with Flaco hanging on me from the left and Jules flicking me occasional amused and yet highly charged glances from across the table. She looked good (when didn't she look good to me?) in blue jeans, white Keds and a men's short-sleeved, plaid, western shirt which fit her quite well. And by quite well, I mean quite snugly in all the right places. The shirt had those little pearl snaps instead of buttons. Which made me think about unsnapping...The green, blue and white in the shirt brought out the blue in her eyes.

A small gold heart with a tiny pearl in its center hung around her neck on a slender chain. Focused on her necklace, I saw her chest rise and fall with the regular rhythm of her breathing as I said, "Uh-huh" to whatever Flaco was trying to say to me. All the while trying to lean away from him—he seemed totally oblivious to the energy flowing between me and Jules. Energy which went to a whole new level when her Keds found my right foot under the table and trapped it between them.

Above the table, all appeared normal as she calmly chatted with Flaco about the weather, the band, his business plans...She gazed directly at me only occasionally. Meanwhile, I struggled to keep my composure and to keep my breathing steady as she ever so slightly would shift first one Ked, then the other, as she gently played with my foot. I could feel her warmth right through my shoe. I actually could not believe the rush of feeling she was creating. I'd heard of people playing footsie before, but it had always sounded dumb and nothing like the sensations she was bringing out in me. It was maddening to have her so near, just two feet away from me, and not be able to touch her or even acknowledge her, while down below the table, a highly intimate interaction was taking place.

I swallowed convulsively. One of my hands was around my beer glass, but the other was clenched around a wadded up napkin, tighter and tighter...I darted a glance over at Jules, who returned it bemusedly, a smile playing about her lips. She knew I was putty in her hands. Or feet.

Suddenly, the lights and the PA music were cut. The soundman's baritone voice boomed in the pitch black. "Ladies and gentlemen, please welcome...Bertha's Attic!"

The club was more than half full now—at least a couple hundred people—so the cheers, whistles and applause that rose up out of the darkness were substantial. I pulled out of the footsie game and jumped up, away from Flaco's arm on the back of my chair. I was on my feet, woo-hooing with the best of them, as blue and white spotlights lit up the stage.

Mona, front and center, looked terrific in her spandex and go-go boots. Her white bass practically glowed in the spotlights, in stark contrast to her black and silver outfit. Off to her left was Petey, who had simply outdone himself. Never before seen black leather pants were on his skinny legs, looking almost as tight as Mona's spandex. Black Chuck Taylors on his feet. A long-sleeved, pure white, dramatic-looking button down shirt of silk—or more likely, rayon—with a skinny black leather tie. LeClaire was in her usual spot with her keyboards on stage right, while Handsome Pete and his drums were directly behind Mona.

In the half second before they began, I wondered what they would play first. An original? A cover? The top secret new stuff they'd been keeping under wraps? I knew how Mona agonized over her set lists, always wanting everything to go just perfectly. She had bemoaned the dilemma bands face when choosing the first song—you wanted it to be a great song that would grab the audience, but the first song was also when the sound man was making adjustments. If he didn't make all the right split-second choices, the first song might be lost in a blare of feedback, or the vocals could be muffled, or a dozen other things could go wrong.

But here they went.

Handsome Pete counted it off behind his drum kit, yelling out, "One! Two! One, two, three!"

Aha! A new song. And a rocker at that—two fingers on Mona's right hand were flying as she strummed an urgent, single low note over and over at high speed, while Handsome Pete's kick drum kept thunderous time, his hi-hat matching her flying fingers. She stepped up to the microphone to sing the opening verse:

> I wanna be an Amazon woman
> Rule the jungle as its queen
> I wanna be an Amazon woman
> And don't think I don't say what I mean

The rest of the band kicked in for the second verse and the crowd followed suit as dancing broke out like a virus on the floor.

> I went to see a voodoo child
> She told me all I need to know
> Vitamins, exercise, an evil curse
> And I think I'm really starting to grow

Petey and LeClaire joined in on the chorus, with Mona singing every other line by herself. The crowd loved it, feeding off her energy as she sang her little heart out.

> AM-A-ZON!
> Ten feet tall and that ain't all
> AM-A-ZON!
> I'm tired of being cute and small

Petey jumped forward to rip off a solo, skinny tie flailing as he rocked the house on his Stratocaster. The dancers were totally with them, with more couples surging onto the floor as the song continued. As far as my amateur ears could tell, the sound guy was doing a good job this week. No feedback, at least.

Not wanting to lose momentum when it ended, they launched immediately into what I knew to be the opening chords of "Montana," one of the few songs played both as group numbers and by Mona at her solo gigs. Our table was mere feet from the stage, but with more and more dancers on the floor, my view was becoming blocked.

"Come on, Hev!" Jules reached across the table and grabbed my hand. "Let's go down by the stage!" she yelled to me.

I nodded and she released me. I stood up and left Flaco behind looking flummoxed at my sudden departure. I followed Jules into the crowd as we blazed a trail to a good spot in front of stage left, where Petey loomed above us and we had a great side view of Mona. "Montana" kept them dancing, with LeClaire taking over the rollicking piano part Mona had played at the coffeehouse.

LeClaire's talents were also highlighted on the next song, a haunting electronic melody I particularly liked although the dark lyrics spoke of isolation and emotional detachment. I noticed the Jamaican/Irish/French keyboardist had painted over the "M" on the back of one of her synthesizers—a Yamaha—to make it an "H." Yahaha! Petey had a weird, dissonant solo on this song that somehow fit it perfectly. Mona and Handsome Pete the drummer were rock solid underneath with the driving bass line that kept the whole thing moving. The best part was the chorus, a wailing, "We're not in Kaaansaaaaaaas…anymore."

After three up-tempo numbers, the crowd was ready for a ballad and a break from their manic dancing. I was surprised, however, to hear the band segue into a slow and sexy blues riff—it was another new song to me.

Mona spoke to the crowd over the introduction as applause for the previous song died down. "Thank you, thank you," she said authoritatively, her husky voice coming through loud and clear. "We are Bertha's Attic. How's everybody doing tonight?"

A happy roar answered her, with a rebel yell thrown in at the end by somebody.

Mona said, "Yeah, me too!" with a big grin, then began to sing in her best throaty contralto. The lighting guy shone a pink spot on her for this mellower bluesy mood.

What can I say?
What can I do?
Since you went away
I'm totally blue
You left me alone
All on my own
Well, all I can say is
Fuck you.

She spoke the last two words instead of singing them, which emphasized the punch line. A ripple of laughter ran around the crowd from those who were actually listening to the words. Most of the dancers were intent on their hip-grinding clinches, though, and focusing on the sultry blues music, not the lyrics.

Jules was now standing close behind me—very close—as we both faced the stage. She reached forward to encircle my waist with her arms, but I gently shrugged out of her embrace and turned to face her for a moment, giving her a quick and discreet, I hoped, head shake.

I read her lips as she said "What?"

"Not here," I said in her ear.

As much as I loved the way she touched me, I was definitely not comfortable with her touching me in a very public place. For crying out loud, it was probably only moments before Flaco would track us down. Not to mention Jackson, whom I hadn't thought about in at least five minutes. So much for vigilance. I scanned the crowd around us, but saw only dancers. Jules looked dolefully at me and shook her head. I leaned in again.

"Later," I breathed into her ear, not sure exactly what I was promising.

She brightened at that and settled for incidental contact, of which there was plenty in the jostling crowd.

When the slow song ended, LeClaire brought the dancers out of their blues-induced torpor with a spicy Latin riff on her piano. Bass, guitar and drums coordinated to punctuate the rhythmic lick and launch another catchy pop rocker which had the crowd dancing exuberantly. I hoped everyone was too busy dancing to pay attention to the lyrics on this one, since I knew from Mona that it was about sexually transmitted disease. Yuck. "Burning Love" was the not-so-subtle title. Hell of catchy tune, though. Mona dreamed of recording it in a studio with a full horn section. Some day.

She exchanged semi-witty banter with the crowd during the pause before the next song. She had an innate sense of when they needed a break and how to keep them in the palm of her hand. I checked my watch—not quite the midpoint of their forty-five minute set. Things were going great, I thought.

Mona peered down at the crowd directly in front of the stage at one point with her hand shading her eyes from the lights. I didn't know if she could see me, but gave her a double thumbs-up in case she could. The band went on to play several more of Mona's Greatest Hits, with more and more people swelling the crowd on the dance floor.

Flaco finally tracked us down halfway through the eighth tune, which was the only reggae song Bertha's Attic performed. I could tell Jules was dying to dance, but I quelled her with my eyes, hoping she wouldn't abandon me to boogie with some other girl. Speaking of which, where was Ashley? Not that I really cared, but Jules had said she was around somewhere. Margo was MIA too. Probably still stuck at the Bowl.

Flaco asked me to dance, but I told him I wanted to watch the band. Period. He looked disappointed and started to put his arm around my shoulders. I told him it was too hot for that and I just wanted to watch the band. He finally got the point and moved back six whole inches, where I could see him giving me puzzled looks from time to time in my peripheral vision. Clearly, the night was not going the way he had planned.

Jules, standing on the other side of me, brushed up against me "accidentally" to avoid the cocktail waitress, who was making her way through the crowd with her tray over her head like a native guide beating her way through the jungle. Flaco bought the three of us some fresh drinks, which, if I'd had any conscience, I would have turned down, but thirst won out over scruples. Again.

Maybe I should have been thrilled to be standing there between two people who wanted me. I almost wished I was alone instead. The tension was making me feel a little sick, to tell the truth. I really wished Flaco would just magically disappear. I knew what he wanted and it wasn't really me. It was just some of my body parts.

It was different with Jules, though. No one had ever made me feel the way she made me feel. There was a connection between us that was missing in my previous relationships. I always got the feeling that guys saw me as a collection of the aforementioned body parts (four, by my calculations, if you count "boobs" as one) rather than a desirable whole. Somehow, Jules made me feel like she wanted me, Heavenly, the entire package, not just the orifices and squeezy things.

The band started up what was often their final song—ironically (for me) called "All the Wrong Men." Mona fervently thanked the crowd over the low-key intro the rest of the band was playing, reminding us to tip our waitresses. This song started quietly, then built to an awe-inspiring climax, with a brilliant extended solo from Petey, making it perfect for the last song of the set. And the way things were going, they were sure to get an encore tonight, I thought.

Five minutes later, I was screaming myself hoarse as the concluding chord rang out. The crowd was enthusiastic in its applause, yelling, clapping, whistling.

Mona cried out one last, "Thank you!" as the band headed backstage, but the crowd would have none of it.

The clapping and yelling progressed to foot stomping and chanting, even, of what I think was "Bertha, Bertha." I wondered if they thought Mona was Bertha. It didn't matter. All that mattered was the love in the air and the band coming back for an encore.

The applause ratcheted up for a second when they reappeared on stage to take their places, then died down to a breathless silence. The lights were dimmed to a single white spot, this time trained directly on Petey, who struck a Rock God pose with his guitar. There was some movement on the stage behind him, but I couldn't see what was happening in the shadows.

I couldn't restrain myself from screaming, "Go, Petey!"

I saw him smile, then his face got serious again as he readied himself to play. With a flourish, he rattled off an oddly familiar riff with lots of distortion. Seven notes sounded, the last one drawn out and lingering. He paused, as if listening for a reply—we all strained to hear it along with him—then played the same seven notes again, but more urgently as if demanding an answer.

A second spot came on with a thud, blinding in its brilliance.

A dark figure stood alone in the center of the stage, dressed all in black, its back to the audience. It wasn't Mona, obviously, since she was about a foot shorter than whoever this was. The figure slowly turned to reveal—Ashley! With her trombone! She tootled out the same seven notes Petey had played and he immediately responded in kind. They began to play the line together, faster and faster, with Handsome Pete adding sonorous booms on his floor tom until it suddenly dawned on me and the rest of the crowd what we were hearing—the introduction to "Crazy Train!" Ozzy Osbourne! With a trombone! Oh, my God!

The crowd went nuts when Petey did one of those screaming slides down the fret board to launch into the verse. The rest of the band leaped in as one as Mona reclaimed her microphone from Ashley to sing.

Jules was practically jumping for joy, grabbing my arm and shouting in my ear, "It's Ash, it's Ash!" as if I couldn't see with my own two eyes.

Ashley cut an imposing figure in a man's suit (black with a charcoal pinstripe), a black T-shirt underneath, her black and white checkerboard Vans and a black commando beret perched jauntily on her mightily spiked hair. She continued playing along as the band tore through "Crazy Train," even stepping up to Mona's mike to take a brief solo at one point. It was insane, but somehow it worked.

The applause was near hysterical when they finished—I'd never heard such a ruckus on a Dollar Night before. Despite calls for a second encore, they really were done then and walked off the stage waving and blowing kisses to the crowd, triumphant in their glory. The sound guy turned the lights on for the pre-headliner break. .38 Special came up anticlimactically on the PA.

Jules and I fought our way through the buzzing crowd over to stage right with Flaco trailing behind us. On the far side of the stage there, a brief flight of stairs led to the back doors of the club where the bands loaded in and out. In point of fact, Bertha's Attic was now back on the stage, hurriedly packing up their equipment since they had to get it out of there so the Think System could play.

A bouncer guarded the stairs—a simple length of rope at waist height kept the customers from that part of the club which was for band members and employees only. He stared us down as we approached, but I wasn't trying to invade the holy of holies. I simply wanted to get Mona's attention for a second. "Mona! Hey, Mon!"

She looked up and saw me, grinned, then gave me a "just a sec" gesture.

In the meantime, Ashley came down the stairs behind the bouncer. "Jules, did you see?" She looked flushed and happy. I'd never seen her so animated before.

The bouncer held up the rope for her so she could join us. As she did, a group of squealing young women descended upon her and Jules and began to spirit them away. Jules broke free long enough to tell me these were their friends and they were off to party at her and Ash's apartment.

"You'll come join us, right? Bring the band too!" she said.

Her sideways flick of a glance at Flaco made it clear he was not included in that invitation, which was fine with me. He gaped at the congratulatory group surrounding Ashley—lots of cropped hair, tattoos and piercings in that group.

"Um, let me check with Mona, okay?" I told her. "I think we're gonna stick around for the headliner."

And for Jackson Miller to finally show and be dragged off by the police, I hoped. I was bummed Jules was leaving, but at least that would give me a chance to talk to Flaco. And by "talk to," I meant dump.

"Okay, but I will see you later," Jules said, with emphasis on the "will."

I nodded. She hugged me goodbye, her hand lingering on my forearm as she pulled away, trailing down to my wrist and then my hand. She pointed at me portentously, walking slowly backward to her friends, mouthing "later" once more.

What with people heading toward the bar and the restrooms during the break, the front of the dance floor was suddenly rather open. Flaco and I looked at each other in the relative calm.

He said, "So you wanted to talk?"

Uh…I did and I didn't. Fortunately, I was saved by Mona, who was now crouching at the corner of the stage and signaling for me to come over.

"Oh, my God, Mona, that was so killer!" I gushed to her, meaning every word of it. I'd known her all my life, but she still impressed the shit out of me. When she wasn't driving me crazy. "You guys were totally amazing tonight! The crowd was loving it, could you tell?"

"Did Mars make it?" she asked me.

"I don't think so. I haven't seen her yet. Sorry."

She shrugged philosophically. Not even her sister's absence could dim her joy and deep satisfaction in her accomplishment that night. "Well, maybe she'll make the next one if they ask us to play again," she said, trying to be cool about it.

"Oh, they have to," I told her seriously. "There's no way they won't ask you."

"Maybe so," she said modestly. "Hey, look, we gotta pack it up here, but I want to hear the headliner, so I'll meet you back at the table in a few, okay?"

"Okay."

"We really were good tonight, weren't we?" she said with satisfaction.

"You were spectacular, Mona. Congratulations, woman."

She smiled shyly (for her) and then stood up to finish clearing the band's stuff from the stage. I saw Petey staggering out the back door with her amp on his shoulder. At least her boyfriend was useful. I turned back to mine, who was still waiting patiently. He wasn't a bad guy, I guess. I just didn't want to waste any more time on him.

"Come on, Flaco," I said. "Let's go to the front bar where it's a little quieter, okay?"

I finally felt ready to deal with him with no further delay. As we passed the restrooms, though, he asked me to wait at the coat check while he visited the men's room. With a sigh, I headed toward the coat check, a popular landmark at which to meet someone. The doorway which was the sole entrance to this part of the club was close at hand, so you had a good view of who was coming in. I picked a spot out of the way of foot traffic where I could see the men's room exit. Hurry up, Flaco, I thought. Let's just get this over with. Someone stepped into my line of vision, cutting off my view of the doorway. I took a step back because the person was right in front of me, then belatedly focused on his face.

Jackson Miller.

Startled, I put my hand on my chest to keep my heart from jumping out of it and took another hurried step backward only to find that I was up against the exterior wall of the coat check stand. "Jesus, Jackson, you scared the crap out of me!"

The words just flew out of my mouth. I had never actually spoken to him in person before, of course, but I felt I knew him nonetheless. He looked terrible. Unshaven, gaunt, with a frantic look in his eye. He stepped up to me and put his hand on the wall at the level of my head so he was right over me. I hate it when guys do that. I could smell the stress sweat on him. Trying not to be too obvious about it, I glanced around to see if any cop-like people were in the vicinity. No such luck.

"Who are you looking for?" he demanded, turning his head to see.

"Nobody, just my friend. He's in the restroom," I told him, hoping I sounded convincing. I tried to get his attention back. "Look, you wanted to see me?"

"Yeah," he said, looking at me. "Yeah."

I didn't much like the way he was looking at me. His eyes were bloodshot, his hair was messy. His nostrils flared as he exhaled. His breath smelled medicinal, like some kind of chemical.

"Well, uh, about that clipping…" I started hesitantly.

"Don't give it to me here," he said sharply, looking around again in his paranoid fashion. "There's too many people here," he muttered to himself.

His manner suddenly made a perceptible switch. He gave me a smile that was more ghastly than friendly and said persuasively, "I need your help, Heavenly. You know that, right? You're the only one who can help me now. I can explain everything, I promise, if you'll just listen to me. But there's too many people here and it's too loud. Can we go talk in your car?"

He was creeping me out. Where the hell were the cops? "I didn't bring my car," I told him. "Why don't we go to the front bar? We can get a table and talk there."

"Too crowded," he said automatically. He thought for a second. "There's a place up the street that's quiet—you know the old ice factory?"

The ice factory? He had to be out of his mind if he thought I was going there with him. I was about to tell him that when both of us had our attention diverted by the appearance of a uniformed police officer in the doorway. It was my old friend, Rich Pacheco. I'd never been so glad to see someone in my whole life.

Jackson hissed something unintelligible under his breath, grabbed both my arms and whirled me behind a knot of people standing nearby. I watched as Pacheco shook hands with the bouncer and walked the length of the bar, scrutinizing the crowd and yet missing us back in our dark corner. He disappeared down the steps onto the dance floor. Before I could think to scream or kick him in the shins or pitch a hissy fit, Jackson released me and backed away rapidly.

"Wait!" I yelled at him.

He yelled back over the crowd noise, "Meet me there, Heavenly! Alone. And if you're not there in fifteen minutes, I'm gone."

"No, wait—" I cried despairingly, garnering some odd looks from the people around me.

"Fifteen minutes," he yelled ominously, then he was out the doorway and out of my sight.

I was torn—should I chase after him (and what exactly would I do if I caught him?) or find Pacheco? I ran to the top of the stairs overlooking the dance floor and scanned desperately for the latter. There were hundreds of people in the club now, milling about on the dance floor, going up and down the stairs, seated at the tables on the sides. I didn't see him anywhere. In a big place like that, with all those people on the move, I could have searched for an hour and not found him.

"Pacheco!" I yelled out, just in case he was somewhere close. Nope. I looked at my watch—quarter after eleven. If Jackson meant what he'd said, I had a fifteen-minute window of opportunity to get the cops to the ice factory to apprehend him. I needed a phone. Fortunately, there was a pay phone right outside by the box office.

I spun on my heel and ran that way, darting through the crowd. A hand snaked out and grabbed my arm, stopping me in my tracks. I struggled to break free. "Lemme go!"

"Heavenly, what are you doing?" Flaco said, bewildered.

"Look, I don't have time to explain, but it's an emergency, so either let me go or come with me!" I managed to yank my arm out of his grasp and resumed my sprint toward the entrance.

Racing past the surprised bouncers at both the inner and outer doorways, I was outside in the semifresh air a few seconds later, with Flaco hot on my heels until the outer bouncer stopped him. I don't know if he thought Flaco was chasing me, or if it was just a general "don't run in the club" speech, but the two of them started arguing.

While Flaco dealt with that, I ran to the pay phone, not noticing at first the piece of paper taped to the wall above it. I threw some change in the slot, which I probably didn't need to call 911, but it didn't matter—I couldn't get a dial tone. I flipped the thingamajigger, but still no tone. The sign finally registered— "out of order." Damn. It was seventeen minutes after eleven now.

I ran back over to the entrance, but the bouncer forestalled me. He had just let Flaco out and wasn't about to let either one of us back in. "No reentry after eleven, miss."

"But—"

The look on his face and the beefy arms folded across his broad chest told me he was in no mood to argue the point. I cast about wildly for another option. If I couldn't get back in the club…and I couldn't call the cops…and the clock was ticking…well, maybe if I could get to the ice factory and keep Jackson there for a little bit, someone else could contact the cops and get them there in time to catch him. Someone else…but Flaco couldn't get back in the club either to find Pacheco. And how could I get to the factory? It wasn't far, but I wasn't about to walk there in the dark. Flaco was looking at me questioningly, to say the least. God only knows what look was on my face.

I grabbed his hand. "Come on!"

"Where are we going now?" he asked, but allowed himself to be pulled along as I raced around the side of the building.

"The back parking lot," I panted. "Got to find Mona."

I was glad to have him with me for the first time that night. I wouldn't have wanted to venture down that dark side street by myself. I found the band congregated near the Monamobile which was parked under a bright light. Providentially, Flaco had parked his white van back there too. He went over to get something out of it while I talked with Mona. Impelled by the urgency of the situation, I imparted the facts to her in less than thirty seconds, ending with, "So, come on, you gotta give me a ride over there!"

She, however, was squinting up at me as if I'd lost my marbles. "You want us to go to the old, abandoned ice factory in the middle of the night to meet the crazy guy? What is this, a fuckin' *Scooby-Doo* episode?"

I was practically dancing in my frustration. "Come on, Mona, we gotta go! It's almost eleven thirty and if he leaves, God knows when we'll have another opportunity to catch him!"

She still wasn't moving. "Well, we can't take the Monamobile because the guys are loading it," she said.

"Well, in case you forgot, my Camaro's at your apartment!"

"Plus," she said as if I hadn't spoken, "I think we ought to take at least one guy with us, just to be on the safe side."

"Well, fine, let's bring Petey, then, but we gotta go now!"

"He's loading the stuff. We can't leave Handsome Pete and LeClaire alone with the equipment like that."

I looked over at the drummer and keyboardist—they were off to the side, giggling and sharing yet another joint. While I watched, LeClaire pulled a hip flask out of the back pocket of her jumpsuit, took a long pull, then handed it to the drummer. Flaco walked up to them, shook hands with Handsome Pete and started talking with him. Mona was right. Damn it. But she wasn't finished.

"Look, Hev, this is a bad idea. Let's just find another phone somewhere, call the cops and let them deal with him."

"Mona, he'll be gone by the time they get there if I'm not there to stall him. And if he gets away—this guy knows what I look like, where I live, where I work. We've got to stop him now, here, tonight!"

Something in my tone finally seemed to get through to her. "All right, fine," she said. "But we still need a ride. Hey, Flaco can drive us, right, Flaco?"

Flaco and Handsome Pete seemed to be concluding some transaction and were shaking hands again. He looked up when he heard his name and walked over to us.

"Drive you where, ladies?" he asked.

"The ice factory," I said shortly, then held up a hand to stop any more questions. "I'll explain everything later, okay, but we need to go right now. I have to meet someone there."

I grabbed Mona and dragged her over to the white van, with Flaco scrambling to catch up. She had to sit on my lap since the van had bucket seats. She rolled down the window as Petey came out the back door of the club with another load of equipment.

"Petey!" she called to him as Flaco started up the van.

Petey jogged over to us obediently and deftly caught the car keys she tossed him.

"Find a phone, call nine-one-one and tell the cops to meet us at the ice factory ASAP, okay? They need to come catch that Jackson Miller guy, you know, the guy from Hev's apartment."

I added, "Tell them to send Grausteiner, okay? Grau-stein-er. And Pacheco's in the club somewhere, if you can find him too."

Petey looked startled, but he was used to following orders from Mona, so like the good soldier he was, he simply nodded and sped off on his mission.

Flaco had started to pull the van out of the parking place, but now paused to say, "Whoa! Cops?"

"Yes, cops," I said impatiently. "Let's go!"

When he didn't immediately floor it, I said, "Please, Flaco— we've got to go right now. Please—for me?"

I touched his arm and gave him the big puppy dog eyes. What a shit I am. He looked doubtful, but I guess it worked since he put it in gear and off we went. Less than two minutes later, we were pulling off the street into the rutted dirt parking lot of the old factory, out of use and abandoned for decades. The only light was from the van's headlights and a single streetlight back on the corner. The tail end of a freight train rumbled past, not twenty feet away on the tracks.

"Where is he?" Mona demanded.

"I don't know," I said, peering into the darkness.

Surely not inside? There was no way we were going inside, I thought. I had no idea how we would even get in there short of breaking a window. Flaco had slowed the van to a crawl as we drove through the parking lot, then onto a service road that led to the back. He carefully steered down the dark passageway.

"So we're meeting that guy who used to live in your apartment?" he asked me, sounding dumbfounded.

I had almost forgotten about Flaco videotaping Werner's apartment the weekend before when we'd all discussed the Jackson situation. Last Saturday seemed so long ago now. "Yeah," I told him. "Make a left here, will you?"

We were coming around the back to where a loading dock ran the length of the building. I saw no other vehicles. No lights either, but I could see the tiny red glow of a cigarette by the dock. I pointed without speaking and the other two mutely nodded. We all seemed infected by the eerie, deserted feeling that suffused the place.

As Flaco eased the van to a stop, Jackson moved out of the shadows into the edge of the headlights' beam to show himself. Standing on the ground in front of the head-high loading dock, he held up a hand in greeting or warning—I wasn't sure which. Flaco turned the engine off, but left the lights on to provide some illumination.

"This is a bad idea," Mona sang under her breath to me as the three of us got out.

"Well, what's he going to do?" I countered in a low tone with some fake bravado thrown in that I wasn't really feeling. "There's three of us and only one of him, right?"

She made a noncommittal noise in her throat. We crunched over the gravel and dirt surface until we were about ten feet from him.

"You brought people," he said to me accusingly. He seemed perturbed.

"Just a couple of friends," I said in what I hoped was a calming manner.

It was quiet back there. Deathly quiet, as a matter of fact. Even though downtown was just a few blocks away, it felt almost like we were out in the country. I listened in vain for an approaching siren, but all I heard was the wind in the trees that lined the perimeter of the property and the mournful cry of the now distant freight train.

"I didn't expect so many," he mumbled, more to himself than to me. He seemed taken aback, like he didn't know what to do with three of us. He hadn't really thought I would come on my own, had he? A sudden chill ran through me as I imagined what might be happening if I had.

Surely Petey must have called the cops by now. If nothing else, he could have run across the street to Rocco's—they'd let him use the phone in their office. The police must be on their way, I told myself. All I needed to do was keep him talking until they got there. But how was I supposed to do that? Oddly, what popped into my mind was yet another piece of Murdocks' Advice For The Romantically Challenged: Guys love to talk about themselves.

"So, Jackson," I said. "You said you wanted to explain?"

His head snapped up. His mood seemed to shift again. In a curiously wheedling tone, he said, "You've got the clipping, right? You didn't really give it to the cops, did you?"

Some instinct told me to lie and to tell him what he so obviously wanted to hear. "Yeah, I got it. It's in the van."

I hoped Mona and Flaco, who were standing on either side of me, would know to play along. Thankfully, neither of them said a word.

"Well, give it to me then." He started forward, but stopped when I held up my hand.

"Hang on, hang on," I said. "I will, but I got a couple questions for you first. You know, just to satisfy my curiosity." I have to admit, I actually was curious. Scared too, but I really wanted to know the whole story. Killed the cat...

Jackson said, "Well, you saw the clipping, so you probably figured it out. A smart girl like you."

Did I detect a hint of sarcasm there? "Well," I said. "I figured out your name's not Jackson Miller—it's William Sikes, right?"

He neither confirmed nor denied this, just stared at me, beady-eyed. I tried again, hoping to get him talking. "You went to prison..." I said in an encouraging tone, although that wasn't a very encouraging phrase, come to think of it.

But he angrily took the bait. "For an accident!" he snarled. "Four and a half years out of my life for a fuckin' accident."

His complaining sounded familiar to me—just like the arrogant grievances voiced by the Public Defender's clients every day, I thought. Just like a criminal. I realized with a jolt that I hadn't been thinking of him as a criminal, exactly, before. As someone who had made a terrible, irresponsible, stupid mistake with tragic consequences and gone to prison for it, but not a criminal. Not a villain with that insane vanity. Maybe I was wrong about that. Maybe Werner had been wrong about that too.

Mona surprised me by jumping in. "But then you won the lottery, right?" she said. "So everything was A-okay again."

He snorted derisively. "Yeah, that's what I thought at first too. See, when I got out of the joint, I couldn't even get a job. People I'd known all my life wouldn't speak to me. They'd cross the street if they saw me coming. Treated me like dirt, the bastards. But then I won the lotto. Jesus—more money than I'd ever dreamed of. After all I'd been through. You have no idea what that's like, bunch of preppy college kids like you…" He trailed off as he thought of it.

We were none of us college kids or preppies, but it wasn't the moment to argue those points. I tried to pull him back on topic. "So what happened?"

"I'll tell you what happened—they treated me worse than ever after that. Threatened to burn down the house I bought. Threatened my ma. Calling and hanging up at all hours of the day and night. No one can live like that. No one."

"So what'd you do?" Mona asked.

"I fucking left, that's what I did. Came out here, changed my name all legal-like in the courts and started over. I saw this place in a magazine once and it looked just about perfect. It was perfect too, just the way it was supposed to be, until that…that…" He sputtered in rage, apparently lost for a word that would be bad enough to describe Werner.

"Uh, Werner?" I supplied.

"Right, that bastard cop, Werner!"

Mona, with her usual knack of getting straight to the point, said, "How did Werner even know who you were?"

"He went back east last winter when his mother died. Turned out she lived one town over from where I grew up. He was packing up some of her stuff, wrapping it in old newspapers when he saw my face in the article. How unlucky is that, huh?" His face twisted with fury as he recalled the chain of events. He was working himself into a real tizzy.

Where were the cops? Why didn't they come? "Did Werner tell you this?" I asked. Just keep him talking, Hev.

"Yeah, the rat bastard loved telling me every little detail and putting the screws to me."

"So he was blackmailing you?" I said.

"Hell, yeah, he was blackmailing me!" he shouted, taking another step forward. "The fucker was trying to ruin my life! I tried to get away from him, to start another new life, a fresh start this time, clean and sober, but he wouldn't let go. He kept coming after me. And all I wanted was to be left alone…" The last sentence was almost a howl, certainly a plea for our sympathy. I wasn't sure he deserved it.

Mona said, "So you killed him." A statement, not a question. The stark words hung there in the darkness while we waited for his answer.

"No, no," he exclaimed, throwing his hands up to deny her words and taking one more step toward us. "That was another accident. I didn't mean to—we were just talking, but he wouldn't listen to reason. He wouldn't listen to me…and the door came down on his head…" His tone was pleading.

I felt sick. What was he saying? Had he killed Werner?

"It was an accident," he said, looking desperately from Mona to me to Flaco. "But the cops are never going to believe me. An ex-con? And a dead cop? They'll never believe me. They'll send me away for life this time, I know it. And I'm not going back. I'm never going back to prison, you hear me?"

He'd grown more and more agitated as he recounted his sorry tale. Mona was right—we shouldn't have come. What was I thinking, putting the other two at risk? I silently berated myself for my poor decision-making.

Jackson took a big, shuddering breath and underwent yet another of his mood swings. He stared directly at me. His words menacing and cold, he said, "So I need that clipping, Heavenly."

"Why?" Mona said argumentatively. I wasn't sure that was the best approach, but it probably didn't matter. "Why do you need it?" she went on. "You've still got lots of money, right? Just take it and go—sail your boat to Mexico or wherever."

He looked at her with his eyes narrowed, as if deciding whether to answer. I answered her myself. "Because that newspaper clipping is the only thing linking him to Werner that provides a motive," I said. "If he takes the clipping and then goes, no one will ever know the connection."

"But, Hev," she said. "With or without the clipping, we all know what it says…" Her voice trailed off as she realized the implication of these words.

Flaco, who had been amazingly quiet throughout the conversation, apparently decided it was time for him to step up. I don't know who was more startled when he spoke, me or Jackson.

"Hey, come on, buddy," he said to Jackson, palms out in entreaty. He took a few steps toward him. "We can work this out, man to man, right?"

"Stop," Jackson said, fumbling with the back of his shirt. "Stop." That last word was hardly more than a whisper. He looked scared. Which seemed odd—shouldn't we be the ones looking scared?

"Flaco, wait," I said urgently.

Mona grabbed my arm to prevent me from going after him. He turned to say something to me just as Jackson produced a gun from under his shirt and hit Flaco on the back of the head with it as hard as he could. Flaco went down without a sound, his mouth making a silent "O" of astonishment as he fell.

"Oh, God, now you've done it," Jackson said, his voice high-pitched as he shakily aimed the gun at me and Mona, frozen in the harsh glare of the headlights with Flaco prostrate at our feet. "Move him over there," he told us, pointing toward the foot of some stairs that led to the top of the loading dock.

He was too heavy for us to carry, so we had to drag him. I prayed he was still breathing and that we weren't hurting him further. In the lights from the van, I saw a trickle of blood had run down the back of his head into his shirt collar. Mona and I exchanged a single wordless glance over Flaco's still form, then slowly turned to face Jackson, who had followed us. We were less than ten feet apart. He was pointing the gun at first me, then Mona, with trembling hands.

"You made me do this. You're making me do this," he said. He took one of his hands off the gun to feel behind him for the loading dock's wall, almost as if he needed the support. He sounded frantic and despairing. I knew how he felt.

I wondered if I would feel the bullet rip into my flesh when I threw myself at him. There was no way I was going to let him shoot Mona. Not on her Dollar Night. I tensed my muscles for the leap.

There was a roaring in my ears that I thought was entirely internal, but then realized was automotive as the Monamobile tore around the corner, practically on two wheels. It fishtailed in the gravel as the driver fought for and reclaimed control, then headed straight for us, the noise from its big engine an overpowering din. I caught just a flash in profile of the car's occupant as it sped by— Margo, coolly behind the wheel.

The Monamobile's headlamps vividly lit up Jackson with his back to the concrete wall. His eyes were wide in horror, the gun forgotten as he held up his hands to ward off the oncoming car. "Noooooo!" he wailed as the Monamobile slammed into first him, then the solid wall behind, crumpling the front of the car in an almighty crash of steel and glass meeting concrete at high speed.

"Margo!" Mona screamed.

I grabbed her arm. The deafening collision rang in my ears, but was almost immediately followed by an unnerving silence. The only sounds were the ticking of hot metal and a loose hubcap rolling away, as if to distance itself from the grisly scene.

What was left of the top half of Jackson Miller was now a sickening mess facedown on the crumpled hood of the Monamobile. The shattered wall behind him bore testament to the violence of the impact. The windshield was smashed, the front third of the car mangled beyond repair, but the passenger compartment was still more or less intact. That car was a tank—they just don't make 'em like that anymore.

As we watched, a slender figure slowly raised itself behind the steering wheel and weakly flopped a pale arm out the open window.

"Hey, Mona," the driver said to her sister. "There's your boyfriend."

EPILOGUE

Thirty seconds later, two cop cars came careening around the corner, sirens wailing, lights a-flashing. Grausteiner was in one, Pacheco in the other. Petey—such a sensible boy—had first run across the street to Rocco's to call 911. Back inside the Mongol (via the back door) and looking for Pacheco on the dance floor, he'd found Margo, who had finally arrived. When Petey told her what was going on, she grabbed Mona's car keys out of his hand without a word and sprinted out the back of the club, knocking the bouncer guarding that way flat on his butt. Since Handsome Pete and LeClaire had failed to load a single piece of equipment, at least none of that was damaged.

Margo had some scratches and bruises from her final ride in the Monamobile, but suffered no permanent ill effects. All hail the Monamobile. Which was totaled, of course. I could hardly believe Mona had bothered to insure it, but she had. Unfortunately, a check for scrap metal was all she had to look forward to.

On a brighter note, Bertha's Attic was offered a Saturday night gig at the Mongol in August opening for Geographic Tongue, so things were looking up in that department.

I never did manage to break up with Flaco. Turned out to be a moot point. He too was fine despite the bump on the noggin, but unfortunately, when Pacheco was tending to him at the scene, a joint fell out of his pocket. One thing led to another—Flaco and Mrs. Romanoff were arrested a few days later for growing hydroponic pot in her apartment. Possession with intent to sell was just one of a long list of charges I heard they faced. Oh, well. Margo was then offered the job of on-site property manager for the apartment building. She was happy about that, as it paid better than her Bowl-O-Rama job and enabled her to quit the bartending.

Last, but not least, we found a good home for Chopper. Jules's parents offered to take him in at their property up in the redwoods that he so loved. Jules and I planned to take him there soon, then she and I were going camping on the beach up the coast for a few days. And nights.

I'm still having a hard time deciding who was the villain between Jackson and Werner. One was responsible for the deaths of at least four people. The other was a blackmailer who, in the end, started a chain of events that led to his victim's death. I know I played a part in Jackson's death too and I'm not sure how I feel about that. The cops had lots of questions for me and the Murdock sisters, but when all was said and done, they let us go. I don't know if they thought we were innocent, exactly, but no charges were filed.

I'm left with my own unanswered questions. Can I atone for Jackson's death? Should I? Maybe there are some things for which you cannot atone. All I can say is, let she who is without sin cast the first stone.

I'll tell you one thing, though—I saw a lot of villains come through the Public Defender and you know what? They looked just like you and me. Maybe that seed is buried deep in all of us, just waiting for the right combination of events to bring it out. Maybe it's only luck that keeps it from germinating.

I hoped I wasn't a villain. I was a liar, though, even if only by omission. I still hadn't told anybody about me and Jules. Not even Mona. But everybody has their secrets, I guess.

Someday, I thought. Someday I would tell them the truth. Someday, I might be free. But for then, if I knew and Jules knew— well, maybe that was enough truth for then. For the summer of 1982.